D1079173

DONATIONS This book is to be returned on or before
the last date stamped below

DONATIONS			DOV
01/19			

LYNN BRITTNEY

C158024440

Published by Mirror Books,
an imprint of Trinity Mirror plc,
1 Canada Square,
London E14 5AP, England

www.mirrorbooks.co.uk

© Lynn Brittney 2017

The rights of Lynn Brittney
to be identified as the author of this book have been asserted,
in accordance with the Copyright, Designs and Patents Act 1988.

ISBN 978-1-907324-82-6

All rights reserved. No part of this publication may be reproduced, stored in a
retrieval system, or transmitted, in any form or by any means without the prior
written permission of the publisher, nor be otherwise circulated in any form of
binding or cover other than that in which it is published and without a similar
condition being imposed on the subsequent purchaser.

First paperback edition

Printed and bound in Great Britain
by CPI Group (UK) Ltd, Croydon, CR0 4YY

Every effort has been made to fulfil requirements with regard to
reproducing copyright material. The author and publisher will be
glad to rectify any omissions at the earliest opportunity.

Front cover images: Topfoto ArenaPAL, Superstock, Mirrorpix, iStockphoto

CONTENTS

To Nellie and Arthur Skinner,
my grandparents, who met and
married during the First World War.
Their daily experiences in London,
during that period, have formed the
core of the *Mayfair 100* books.

CHAPTER ONE

LONDON. MAY, 1915
"I Refuse to Speak to a Man"

Lady Harriet sat before him – composed and pale. Chief Inspector Beech detected a slight trembling in her hands. She was so young, in her early twenties, and yet possessed of an impressive gravity. He spoke softly and tried to be reassuring.

"Lady Harriet, you must know that this is a very serious situation. I only want to help you."

She pressed her lips together, whether in obstinacy or pain he could not tell, but she did finally speak.

"I have told you, Mr Beech, I can only speak to a woman – preferably one of my own class and married. I will not… cannot…discuss my husband's death with a man, no matter how courteous and refined he may be."

Beech sighed. "Lady Harriet, you have confessed to your husband's murder and you refuse to enlighten us as to the circumstances. I do not want to have to place you in custody…"

"No! You can't!" Beech's words were interrupted by the maid, who had been hovering nearby, anxiously. "My lady is ill! She cannot be put in prison!"

Lady Harriet stirred and raised a hand to silence her maid. Beech thought he caught a small flicker of pain pass across her face.

"Esme, that will do!" she admonished her maid.

Beech noted the maid's eyes fill with tears – not, he thought, from the admonition but from genuine concern about her mistress.

He changed tack. "Lady Harriet, do you have a physician that might attend upon you?"

Lady Harriet shook her pale face.

"There is only my husband's doctor and I should not care to be examined by him."

There was a small trace of venom in her voice, which Beech mentally added to the sparse information he had so far gathered.

"Perhaps a female physician might be sought?" he tentatively suggested.

Lady Harriet's eyes widened in surprise.

"Is there such a thing?"

Beech looked at her in astonishment.

"There is an entire hospital full of female doctors in Euston Road…and there is also a London Medical School for Women."

"What sort of women become doctors?" she replied. "Are they of good reputation?

Beech realised that he was dealing with an aristocratic young woman whose view of the world was severely limited.

"Lady Harriet, for a woman to become a doctor requires a great deal of skill and intellect, not to mention the money to allow them to train for such a long time. So, yes, I would hazard a guess that most female doctors come from wealthy families and would be, what you would call, of 'good reputation'."

Lady Harriet dropped her head and a small flush came into her pale cheeks as she understood Beech's gentle criticism of her attitude.

"You must forgive me," she said softly, "I have little understanding of the world and…this…has all been such a shock." She raised her eyes to look at him again. Her iron discipline was beginning to fail her and a tear rolled slowly down one cheek. "Esme," she whispered hoarsely, "I think I need some medicine…"

Esme ran swiftly to her side with a bottle and a spoon. Beech watched for Lady Harriet's response to the medication and, judging by her shallow breathing and relaxation of her tensed hands, he deduced that it was some form of opioid and that he needed to take immediate action to have her examined.

"Lady Harriet, I shall arrange for a female doctor to attend upon you as soon as possible. Perhaps Esme could show me out?"

Lady Harriet nodded briefly and motioned Esme away. Beech stood and bowed to the dazed young woman and followed the maid into the hallway.

"Esme, may I look at that bottle, please?

Esme looked concerned but handed the bottle over.

"It was the master's medication," she hastily explained, "but I've been giving it to my lady ever since this morning when…*it* …happened. I had to give my lady something! I think she's in terrible pain, sir." She looked miserable.

"You probably did the right thing, Esme." Beech tried to be reassuring. "The name on this bottle…this is the doctor who was looking after your master?"

Esme nodded. "Doctor McKinley. He has his practice in Harley Street, number forty two…may he rot in hell!" she added with feeling.

"Why do you say that, Esme?"

The maid bit her lip.

Beech could see that she was reluctant to talk, so he reassured her.

"Your mistress is in grave danger. Murder is a serious business. You must tell me what you know."

"I don't know anything, sir," she said sullenly. "I only know that when the master came back from the war and started being treated by Doctor McKinley, he turned into a monster. If he had been a dog, someone would have shot him and that's all I'm going to say on the matter."

"Very well. I'm going to organise a lady doctor to come and see your mistress. It might be better if you put her to bed, ready for the doctor's arrival."

Esme looked at him piteously. "She won't move, sir. I don't know what's wrong with her but she has been sitting in that chair in the library since the master died, and she refuses to move. I think she's in terrible pain." She lowered her voice. "You saw the spots of blood that go from the bedroom to the library. That blood is hers. God help her." She began to cry softly.

Beech felt a sense of alarm.

"Then I must hurry. Go back to your mistress, and help will be sent as soon as possible."

Out on the street, after a cursory word to the constable guarding the front entrance, Beech hailed a motor taxi and instructed the driver to take him straight to the Women's Hospital. As the taxi pulled away, Beech saw the mortuary wagon arriving to remove the husband's corpse. His mind kept going back to the face of the young aristocratic woman he had just left. He knew so many young women like her. Brought up in the cloistered world of the rural aristocracy, home tutored in "ladylike" subjects, brought to the cattle market of the London Season to be found a husband, and then married off to a suitably noble and moneyed young man. At the age of eighteen they were thrust into a physical adult relationship with a virtual stranger, which often made them miserable for the rest of their lives. In Lady Harriet's case it had ended in tragedy. The husband, turned by his war

4

injuries and opioid drugs into a savage, which, whatever he had done to his young wife, had resulted in him lying dead in their bedroom with a pair of scissors through his heart. And the young wife, trained from birth to be self-contained and never discuss private matters with anyone, was now in God-knows what state, physically and mentally, but refusing to ask for help or explain her act of probable self-defence.

His anger and frustration mounted. The Metropolitan Police was simply not capable of dealing with such cases. Beech knew that, in the last year, since the outbreak of war, the young male population being largely absent, many of the crimes now involved women, and the Criminal Investigation Department was not trained to deal with them adequately.

The Commissioner and the Home Office flatly refused to set up a women's police force – the best they would do was allow the militant suffragette groups, and other women, to organise volunteer women's police forces to supervise and control the influx of women seeking war work into the large cities. But these volunteer groups had no powers to investigate or arrest. They merely dealt with security and reported any problems. Perhaps, he reflected, the Lady Harriet case could alter matters. This was the first aristocratic criminal case he had encountered and it could tip the balance in favour of a plan he had been contemplating for the last few months.

The taxi arrived at the Women's Hospital and Beech instructed the driver to wait, then ran into the lobby.

"Where is Doctor Allardyce?" he shouted at the woman on the reception desk, whilst waving his warrant card.

The startled woman called back, "Ward Four, but you can't go up there!"

Beech halted in his tracks.

"No men allowed!" the woman said firmly, pointing to a

sign which said "NO MEN ALLOWED BEYOND THIS POINT."

"Of course, I understand," Beech spluttered, momentarily flustered. "It is a matter of grave urgency. Is it possible you could fetch her for me? I'd be awfully grateful."

Struck by his politeness, the woman smiled and called across to a passing female orderly.

"Annie, can you fetch Doctor Allardyce, please? This gentleman needs to speak with her urgently."

"Who shall I say wants her?" said the orderly, who looked to Beech as though she had been bred to haul heavy weights and would stand no nonsense, even from the most aggressive of men.

"Chief Inspector Beech, if you would be so kind." He flashed the orderly a respectful smile and she grunted her appreciation.

Beech looked around and found an empty seat amongst the other men who were, presumably, waiting for permission to visit female patients, and watched the orderly plod up the stairs. He fidgeted as he waited for what seemed like an eternity but was rewarded by the sight of a familiar face coming down the stairs, flanked by the orderly and an equally formidable Matron. He was instantly struck by how different she looked to the last time he saw her.

"Peter! What a pleasant surprise!" Caroline Allardyce beamed at Beech, who stood expectantly. "Just bear with me a moment whilst I give Matron some instructions." She turned to her companion to write something in a book. The business done, she advanced upon Beech and planted a kiss on his cheek. The other waiting men grinned and Beech felt himself flushing.

"Good Lord, what have you done to your hair!" he asked

without thinking, and Caroline smiled.

"I've cropped it, you goose! All the professional women are doing it now! Saves ages in the morning not having to fiddle around and put it up in a ladylike bun." She seemed amused at Beech's apparent dismay. "To what do I owe the pleasure of this visit?"

"I need you to come with me, at once. Can you do that?"

Beech's sense of urgency startled her.

"Er...yes. Just let me get rid of this white coat..." She gave him a quizzical look and started to unbutton her coat and hand it to the woman at the reception desk. "Could you please dispose of this for me, Mary? Thank you. Now——" she turned back to Beech "——I'm intrigued. What is so urgent that you have come all the way from Scotland Yard to get me?"

Beech grabbed her arm and propelled her towards the door. "I have an urgent case for you to examine and there is no time to waste."

Caroline pulled away. "Wait a minute, if I am to examine a patient...it is a live patient we are talking about, isn't it?" Beech nodded. "Then I need to get my bag."

"Of course...sorry...what was I thinking? Can you run and get it and I'll meet you in the taxi? It's just outside."

"I'll be two shakes of a lamb's tail." Caroline disappeared and Beech made his way to the taxi, and saluted a thank you to the driver for waiting. As he climbed inside, he felt himself relax a little. Caroline always had that effect on him. Solid and reliable. Good old Caro. He'd known her since they were children in Berkshire and she had always been a positive, friendly influence. Always someone he could talk to.

There was a waft of perfume as Caroline climbed into the taxi with her bulky black bag. "Now, Peter Beech, tell me all about this emergency case of yours."

Beech moved forward in his seat, pulled down the partition that separated the driver from the passengers, and instructed the driver to return to the address in Belgravia, then he made sure the partition was closed firmly.

Speaking in a hushed voice he told Caroline of the events of the day. His department had received a message from the local beat bobby that Lord Murcheson had been murdered during the night. Beech had arrived at the address to find that Lady Murcheson had confessed to the murder but would say nothing further.

"I think her husband attacked her and she killed him in self-defence and I also think that he damaged her internally. She left a trail of blood from the bedroom to the library and she will not or cannot move from the chair in which she is sitting. She is in a great deal of pain and her maid is giving her opiates. I fear she may die before we learn the whole truth but she will not allow a male physician to examine her and she will not elaborate on the events to a male police officer."

Caroline drew a deep breath. "Poor woman. But she won't be the first upper-class victim of sexual violence I have tended to."

Beech was astonished. "Good God! Surely not!"

Caroline gave him a rueful smile. "Sadly, it is true. Only doctors know what goes on behind closed doors – at all levels of society. If you knew how many top-drawer ladies I have repaired after botched abortions, you would never sleep at night."

Beech shook his head sadly. "I fear I'm somewhat naïve when it comes to women. And that is not a good attribute for a policeman."

Caroline laughed and squeezed his hand gently. "Dear Peter, I don't think anyone in your social circle understood why you chose to become a policeman, any more than they understood why I chose to become a doctor. I can still hear my mother saying, 'Why, in God's name, do you want to delve into the unsavoury side of life, Caroline? No one will want to marry you now!'"

Beech laughed. "Sounds like my mother! She actually said to me, 'Peter, your father would turn in his grave! No one of *our* class goes into the police force. That is a job for the *lower orders* who can better deal with the criminal element of society!' I guess we are just two misfits, Caro."

"Nonsense!" Caroline's briskness jerked Beech out of his momentary self-pity. "If there is one good thing that has come out of this dreadful war, it is the breaking down of the barriers between the classes. By the time this war has finished we shall be living in a meritocracy and the upper class will be finished. Besides…who will inherit their estates? There will be no men left in another couple of years. Thank God you're out of it. How's the leg, by the way?"

Beech grinned. "Still gives me hell – especially at night – but thank you for asking. Ah! We're here!"

The taxi stopped and the passengers bundled out. The constable opened the front door of the house for them and they found Esme standing, trembling and tearful, in the hallway. She flung herself at Beech.

"Thank God you've come back sir! My lady is in a stupor and I can't rouse her! Please God, I hope the doctor can save her!"

"Show Doctor Allardyce into the library," Beech urged. "I'll wait here." He gave a grateful nod to Caroline as he sat in the nearest armchair.

Caroline and her black bag disappeared with Esme, and he waited. After a few minutes he heard a scream and leapt

9

to his feet, uncertain whether he should violate the privacy of the library; just then the maid came staggering out of the door in a state of shock.

"Oh my God!" she screamed, before she dropped to the ground in a dead faint.

Beech hammered on the closed door. "Caroline! In God's name, what has happened?!!"

The door was opened a fraction by a bloody hand and Caroline's drawn face appeared behind it.

"If they have a telephone here, call the Women's Hospital and tell them to send an ambulance," she said quickly. "Lady Harriet is haemorrhaging. I'm going to try and do what I can here to stem the bleeding but she needs to be hospitalized immediately."

Beech nodded, leapt over the prone body of the maid and ran down to the servants' quarters. He found the butler, cook and several staff huddled around the kitchen table. They looked frightened and miserable.

"Where's the telephone?!" he shouted urgently.

The butler stood up.

"It's in my quarters through here, sir." He motioned Beech to follow him.

They went down a corridor and into a small room where a telephone was standing on a table by a single bed. Beech grabbed it and jabbed at the cradle several times.

"Exchange, how may I help you?" a woman's voice answered.

"This is Chief Inspector Beech of the Metropolitan Police. I need to be connected to the Women's Hospital immediately. It is an emergency."

"Connecting you, sir."

There was a click and silence. Beech felt his heart pounding, then he remembered the maid.

"Your mistress's maid is in a dead faint in the hallway. You'd better minister to her."

The butler looked grave. "At once, sir," he said, grabbing a bottle of brandy from a shelf and departing in haste.

"Women's Hospital," a voice said, as the line crackled into life.

"This is Chief Inspector Beech calling on behalf of Doctor Allardyce. She requests that you send an ambulance as a matter of some urgency."

"Of course, sir. May I have the address please?"

Beech gave them the information and, once again, stressed the urgency. The man on the end of the line assured him that the ambulance would be there as soon as possible. Beech noticed that his hands were trembling as he replaced the ear piece.

As he made his way back through the kitchen, a tearful cook barred his way.

"Is Lady Harriet dead, sir?" she asked fearfully.

"Not yet," was Beech's grim reply. "I shall be wanting to question all of you, once Lady Harriet is on her way to hospital. Do you understand?"

"Anything we can do to help, sir," came a voice from over the cook's shoulder. It was the butler, who was supporting a revived Esme and guiding her towards a chair.

"Good. Is all the staff here? I take it that no one is missing?"

Beech noted that looks were exchanged between the assembled staff.

"Well?" he asked impatiently.

"My skivvy," the cook said in a quiet voice. "She didn't appear this morning to light the oven and her bed's not been slept in."

"I see," Beech replied, nodding to them all grimly. "Does she have a family home that she may have returned to?"

"No, sir. Lady Harriet took her in, a year ago, from Dr Barnardo's Homes. She's an orphan. She's got no one." The cook became more distressed. "I can't believe that Polly has anything to do with this terrible business! She's a good girl. A hard worker and she worshipped Lady Harriet."

"Hm. Well, good girl or not, we need to find her and ask her some questions. I will deal with this later."

Upstairs, Beech could hear faint moaning coming from the library, which signalled that, for the moment, Lady Harriet was clinging on to life. He sent a small prayer of thanks heavenwards that Caroline had been able to drop everything and assist him.

The events of today had strengthened his resolve to pursue his plan with his superiors. He needed the assistance of women if he were to successfully deal with crime in London. Caroline was one woman he would want on his team and the other was someone he was reluctant to ask, because of their personal history. But he knew that she would be perfect for the job.

The clanging bell of the ambulance could be heard in the distance and it brought him back to the matter in hand. He knocked softly on the library door.

"Caro, the ambulance is about to arrive; prepare your patient."

"Nearly done!" came the muffled reply. "I'll be damned if I'm going to let this woman die."

Yes, thought Beech, *Caroline would be an essential part of the team.*

CHAPTER TWO

"Women? In the Police Force? It Will Never Do"

By the time Beech had supervised the removal of Lady Harriet and Caroline to the Women's Hospital, it was almost two in the afternoon. Beech instructed the butler that the bedroom in which the crime took place was to be kept locked and undisturbed until he returned. Then he realised that he was hungry. He decided to kill two birds with one stone by tracking down the Commissioner of the Metropolitan Police in his club and begging some lunch from him.

Another taxi was hailed and Beech rehearsed in his mind the conversation he hoped he would have with Sir Edward Henry. He admired the man, who had transformed the Metropolitan Police with the latest scientific developments by introducing police dogs, fingerprinting, typewriters and the telegraph to Scotland Yard. And he knew that the man was compassionate – he had even spoken in the defence of a London cab driver who had shot him three years earlier and taken some interest in the rehabilitation of the man – but, somehow, like all those men in senior positions in the services and government, he had a blind spot about the employment of women.

Even when war was declared, Sir Edward had declared publicly that only men were suitable to be police officers, and he had been mightily disgruntled when the suffragette organisations had ignored him and volunteered to set up patrols. Beech knew that what had annoyed Sir Edward the most was the fact that many of the suffragettes were "well connected" and had used their influence in government circles to override his opinion. Sir Edward Henry, despite his knighthood – given for meritorious work in the administration of police forces throughout the Empire – was from middle-class origins. His father had been an Irish doctor, and he was sensitive that, in some circles, he was regarded with disdain as someone who had risen to his position from his humble start as a clerk for Lloyd's of London.

Beech cursed the strictures of the class system, which, so often, kept him from doing his job effectively. He actually found that being the son of a baronet was more of a hindrance than anything else. Still, he felt that, despite this, his relationship with Sir Edward was good and, as the taxi arrived at Pall Mall, he prayed that it would stand him in good stead in the forthcoming discussion.

Beech savoured the cool marble interior of the foyer of the Athenaeum Club and he asked the nearest steward if Sir Edward was within.

"Sir Edward is about to start a late lunch, alone, sir"

"Then could you possibly give Sir Edward my apologies for disturbing him and request whether Chief Inspector Beech might join him for lunch?"

The steward inclined his head and set off up the long staircase to the dining room. Beech hoped that his imposition would not be viewed with annoyance – but he was rewarded by the steward returning and indicating permission.

Sir Edward, fortunately, seemed in good spirits. When Beech apologised for the intrusion, explaining that he needed to discuss a matter of some delicacy but that he was also starving, Sir Edward grinned and motioned him to sit.

"Food first, Beech. Then we can adjourn to the library for this 'matter of delicacy'."

Lunch passed pleasantly, with much discussion about the

merits of police dogs, a subject close to the Commissioner's heart, whilst Beech devoured steak pie and claret.

Once in the library, ensconced in comfortable armchairs, Beech nervously began his explanation of the day's events whilst Sir Edward alternated between looking grave and tutting.

Having finished outlining the crime involving Lady Harriet and the problems it had presented, Beech cleared his throat, lowered his voice and hoped for the best.

"I know, Sir Edward, your views on women police officers…" he began.

"Not just my views, Beech," Sir Edward said gruffly, "but those of successive Home Secretaries. I have no doubt that the right sort of woman might make an excellent police officer but the politically motivated suffragettes have done more harm than good in that direction. No one on the police force or in the Home Office wants to work with them. You can't have a decade of women knocking the hats off policemen and worse, and then expect male officers to welcome them into the fold, as it were."

"I understand that, sir. I really do. But you know, as well as I do, that London is now teeming with women, working in all sorts of jobs previously held by men. The face of the capital's crime is changing and we are poorly equipped to deal with female crime."

Sir Edward shook his head. "I agree with you but it won't alter the attitude of the police force and the Home Office."

Beech nodded but persisted. "What if I were to suggest an unofficial solution…an experiment, if you like…something that would operate outside of Scotland Yard and not affect the day-to-day running of the police force?"

"Go on," Sir Edward replied, seemingly amenable.

Beech then outlined his proposal. To create a small team of two women – a detective and a doctor – and two men – one to safeguard the women and another to do complementary detective work. "I would find a private office for them and pass them cases which require their special talents."

"Mm." Sir Edward appeared to consider the possibility. "What sort of women?" he enquired.

"Women of good education and from good families. I know the two women I have in mind…I know their people. Whilst they are independent women, they are not suffragettes – possibly a bit bluestocking but nothing radical."

Sir Edward smiled. "And the men for your proposed team?"

Beech began to feel confident. Sir Edward was asking all the right questions. "I would like to have a young policeman called Billy Rigsby. He's over six feet, strong and lively. He was wounded at Mons last year and invalided out with a head injury and a shattered left hand. He is fit and well now, but frustrated by the injury to his hand. I think he would welcome being in a special unit. The other is one of the retired detectives that have been brought back into service, Arthur Tollman. He used to work for Special Branch, so he is skilled in intelligence gathering, and he is a widower with three daughters, so is used to the company of women."

"We would not be able to put any women on the payroll," warned Sir Edward.

It was Beech's turn to smile. "Neither of the women in question have any need of money, and I think – well, I hope – that they would welcome a chance to assist us."

Sir Edward looked hard at Beech. "If I were to sanction such an enterprise, it would be on the understanding that this is a private arrangement between you and I. You would be able to divert some funds to the 'team' only on the understanding that the women are never mentioned and that their names never appear on any paperwork. Am I clear on that point?"

Beech's face broke into a wide grin. "Absolutely, Sir Edward. You have my word that discretion will be paramount."

"And," continued Sir Edward, "this special team must not take you away from your essential duties at Scotland Yard."

"Absolutely not. Again, you have my word."

"Then we shall shake hands on our agreement on the understanding that you will keep me informed, privately, of all progress."

Beech stood and extended his hand, which Sir Edward grasped and shook.

"Now," said the Commissioner, with a tone of finality, "you can go about your business of handling this Lady Harriet tragedy and bringing it to a speedy conclusion."

"Of course, Sir Edward. And thank you for your support."

"Let's hope I don't regret it, Beech," was the Commissioner's parting shot.

Out in the fresh spring breeze, Beech felt heady with success. He decided to go to the Women's Hospital first and check on the progress of Lady Harriet. He hoped that Caroline had been able to summon her skills to keep the lady alive; it would be horrible for her to have so tragic an end. Also were she to have pulled through then she could be questioned in due course. This time he decided to take an omnibus and sprinted across the road, dodging horses and mechanised transport as fast as his injured leg would allow him. Leaping on to the platform of a passing omnibus finally caused a piercing pain in his thigh and he was grateful to find a seat and rest.

The bus was filled with women but both the conductor and driver were older men. Thank God, he reflected, that he had managed to persuade the Commissioner to support his plan! He looked around and noted that the passengers were all "working" women, dressed smartly for office and shop work – the Civil Service in Whitehall had been forced to take on large numbers of women once war started – even the bootmakers in Pall Mall were employing women, much to the distaste of their elderly gentlemen customers. Yes, times had changed with a vengeance and the police force had a long way to go to catch up.

He listened to the idle chatter of his fellow travellers as the bus made its way around Trafalgar Square and along the Strand. He became aware of several women casting disapproving glances at him and he began to feel uncomfortable. He knew that a man of his age, not in uniform, was liable to attract criticism and he cursed his decision to forgo taking a taxi. He decided that when he left the bus he would noticeably limp, so that these women would understand that he was war-wounded and not war-shirking – and then he felt embarrassed that he was being tyrannised into caring about their opinions. So, it was a grateful Beech who limped off the omnibus at the Euston Road and was rewarded by several smiles and waves from the women who had now revised their view of him.

In fact, as he walked the remaining few yards to the Women's Hospital, he found that he was, actually, unable to walk without limping, and the pain in his thigh had developed into a dull ache that would not lessen. The limp became so pronounced that Caroline Allardyce expressed her concern when she saw him.

"Peter, I want to have a look at that leg right now!" she said firmly when she realised he was limping beside her to her office.

"Don't be silly, Caro," he said, feeling himself getting flustered.

She turned to him with an amused look on her face. "Don't tell me you are embarrassed about taking off your trousers in front of me!"

"Well…yes…I am, actually. And I'd rather not have this conversation in the corridor." He had noted the female orderly who had sniggered as she passed by.

Caroline opened the door. "Inside please, Mr Beech, and we'll have no more nonsense about being examined by a woman doctor."

Beech looked at her determined face and felt it was useless to protest. He realised that he was so easily intimidated by women and found it difficult, as a police officer, to assert his authority, when necessary. He was sure that many men in the police force felt the same and, to Beech, that was another reason for setting up his "special team". He reluctantly went behind the screen and stripped off his trousers, noting that the scar on his thigh was a livid red.

He gingerly laid on the examination couch and winced as Caroline's fingers probed his scar.

"I think you have an infection, Peter. I can see a small amount of oozing from the top of the scar. I shall paint it with iodine and hope that it settles everything down. You've been overdoing it again, haven't you?"

Beech sighed. "I suppose I have. But it's hard to treat oneself like an invalid when there is so much to be done."

"Perhaps you should delegate more," Caroline answered, as she painted his thigh bright orange.

"Funny you should say that…" he began to explain to Caroline his plan to set up a team to investigate crimes involving women.

She looked up at him with interest as he finished explaining.

"Two women, you said?"

19

Beech nodded.

"So, obviously, you will be asking Victoria?" There was something in her voice that made Beech raise his eyebrows.

"You don't think that would be a good idea?"

"For you, personally – no," Caroline answered firmly. "For this team you want to put together, you have no option. No one has a deductive brain quite like Victoria. She would be perfect for the job."

Beech felt embarrassed. "Really, Caro…Victoria rejected my marriage proposal several years ago. I think I can safely say that we have all put that behind us."

Caroline snorted. "Don't be silly, Peter! You have carried a torch for Victoria ever since you reached the age of sixteen and, now that she is a widow, I wonder if you don't fancy your chances with her again."

Beech flushed. "You're the one being silly! Can I get dressed now?"

Caroline shook her head. "Not unless you want your expensive trousers stained with iodine. Anyway, I think I should bandage your thigh to keep the scar clean and give it some support."

"If you must." Beech was beginning to feel awkward and trapped, lying on a couch in his underwear with Caroline discussing his private life.

"Don't sulk. I'll be as quick as I can," and she started to deftly wind a bandage around his thigh.

Beech cleared his throat. "Ahem…I was wondering how Lady Harriet is?"

Caroline sighed. "Gravely ill. I had to remove her womb and the foetus it was carrying."

"Oh God." Beech closed his eyes in despair.

Caroline continued. "How in God's name that woman

managed to dress herself and walk down the stairs to where we found her, I don't know. By the time I came to perform surgery there was a very large bruise forming on her abdomen – in the perfect shape of a boot."

"You mean…?"

"Yes. Her husband had stamped on her – hard – probably with the deliberate intent of killing her unborn child."

Beech felt nauseous. "How old was the unborn child?"

"A couple of months – barely the size of my hand. And Peter," she continued, "the pain would have been so intense that she would not have been able to get herself upright to stab her husband in the chest. I'm convinced of that. Someone else must have stabbed him. And probably dressed her and helped her downstairs. She was in agony. Her injuries were severe. Not only to her womb but to her bladder and bowel as well. I managed to repair those but we are in the hands of the nursing staff now. She may succumb to infection so you had better interview her as soon as she is able to respond."

"She won't talk to me. I've tried." Beech sat up and Caroline helped him into his trousers. "She will only talk to a woman. She said, 'one who is of her own class and preferably married.' So I must go now and fetch Victoria as quickly as possible. In the meantime, if we don't get back in time, Caroline, you must talk to her. Get as much out of her as you can."

"I'll try." Caroline flashed him a smile. "Give Victoria my love – and please stay off that leg as much as you can. Do you want some pain relief?"

Beech shook his head. "No, thank you. That way lies madness, as evidenced by Lady Harriet's husband. I've seen too many war wounded become addicted to opiates."

"Well, good luck, Peter, and hurry back. I'm anxious to be part of this team of yours!"

Beech smiled and brushed her cheek with a perfunctory kiss. "Thanks old thing. I can always rely on you."

"Yes, you can always rely on me," she murmured quietly and gave him a small smile.

Beech looked at her quizzically for a moment, sensing her change of mood but not sure why. "Is everything alright?"

"Yes, of course," she replied with forced brightness. "Now off you go and fetch Victoria!"

Beech nodded and limped away. He had a disconcerting feeling that he had said something wrong but, of course, it would never have occurred to Peter Beech that Caroline longed to be more to him than "a reliable old thing".

Caroline watched him limp down the corridor.

"Yes, you can always rely on me," she murmured quietly, her heart heavy with jealousy.

CHAPTER THREE

Reopening Old Wounds

The concourse at Waterloo was heaving with people, mostly soldiers, some returning home, some wounded or on leave, and other new fresh recruits leaving for France. Beech felt his chest tighten at the memory of returning on an ambulance train, and he cursed the fact that there was no other way to get to Berkshire. He noted the faces of the new recruits change swiftly from casual grins to barely disguised discomfort when the trains disgorged their maimed cargoes in front of their eyes.

Damn the War Office, he thought. Surely someone could organise things so that the young men going to France left at a different time from the wounded coming back!

Irritated by the lack of tact displayed by the military, he pushed his way through the throng to find his platform, praying that his train would be relatively free of people. He was in no mood to engage in conversation and his leg hurt considerably. Caroline's application of iodine had stung like the blazes and had set up a throbbing ache that would not diminish.

There had been a second battle in Ypres, in April, and Beech assumed that the wounded were now coming through – hence the scrum in the concourse. Victoria's husband had been killed in the first battle of Ypres, six months before, and he wondered if this was really a tactful time to approach her.

Caroline had been right, of course. Beech had secretly renewed his hope that Victoria Ellingham would, now that she was widowed, reconsider their once-close relationship. He had been shattered when she gently turned down his marriage proposal in 1910, and explained to him that she was in love with the feckless son of an Irish Earl. He had watched, with mounting disquiet, the first year of their marriage, while her husband drank and gambled his way through his personal fortune, and Victoria turned from an elegant socialite into a pale recluse. He was able to do nothing other than offer his silent support whenever she needed him. And, he confessed to himself, he had felt guilt at his relief when he heard, from his hospital bed, that Victoria's husband had fallen at Ypres. This would be the first time that they had met since her husband's death. They had exchanged strange, passive letters in the last six months but nothing more.

In the blessed seclusion of a first-class carriage, Beech folded up his overcoat and placed it on the seat opposite, so that he could raise up his aching leg without getting the dust from his shoes on the seat. Thankfully, no other person entered the compartment as the train pulled away and Beech leant his head to one side and dozed fitfully.

The gentle prodding of a ticket inspector awoke him and he realised, with a start, that Bracknell Station was just two more stops away. He had obviously needed the rest. He eased his leg down from the seat and stood up to dispel the stiffness. He opened the small window of the carriage to draw some cold air into his lungs and he hoped that Victoria's mother, Lady Maud, would have a large supper set for his arrival as, once again, he felt extremely hungry.

It was almost dark as Beech alighted from the train but he was able to make out the familiar figure of William, Lady Maud's elderly coachman, standing by a pony and trap in the lane.

"Good to see you again, Mr Beech," said William affably as Beech nodded with pleasure. As they bobbed along the lanes to the big house, Beech felt a sense of joy at revisiting his youth. Riding in a trap in the countryside took him back to a time before war, mechanisation and responsibilities. He smiled broadly at fond memories of long summers, parties and laughter and he pushed away the thought that life would never be like that again. *One has to hope,* he reasoned, *that once this madness is over we can all find some pleasure in our lives once more.*

Lady Maud was waiting on the steps as the trap slowed to a halt. Beech was momentarily disappointed that Victoria was not by her side to greet him but he swiftly brushed that aside, mentally telling himself to stop behaving like a besotted youth.

"Peter!" Maud's arms were flung wide and she took him into her ample embrace. "I was astonished but very, very pleased that you telephoned. We haven't seen you for such a long time."

Beech mumbled something about being incredibly busy and Maud gave him a knowing look.

"Of course you were, my boy. But it was for the best. Victoria needed a long spell of recovery anyway. Come into the house, at once. There is a distinct chill in the air."

Beech gratefully followed Maud up the steps but she stopped in concern.

"Peter, you're limping!"

"Yes, the war wound has flared up a bit. But I'll be alright. Caroline patched me up this afternoon."

Maud beamed. "Caroline Allardyce? She's such a lovely and clever girl. How is she doing?"

"Pretty well, I think," said Peter, as he finished ascending the steps and entered the warmth of the great house. "Is that food I smell?"

"Of course, my dear. I hope you don't mind rabbit pie. It's Cook's wartime speciality."

"Maud, I'm so hungry, I could eat a horse!"

"Bless us! We haven't quite come to that yet! Come in, come in and have a brandy first. You look a little pale to me."

Sitting by the fire, brandy in hand, Beech began to relax. He ventured a few tentative questions about Victoria.

"How is she? Is she well?"

"Peter – I do believe she is on the mend. In the last couple of months she has been working with the VAD at the local officer's hospital and, at last, I have begun to see some roses in her cheeks. It's not enough for her agile mind, of course, but it has been instrumental in reviving her spirits." Maud looked gravely at Beech. "I can't tell you what a state she was in when she came back to us after Edwin left for the front."

"It must be harrowing for lots of women to say goodbye to their husbands and send them off to war."

Maud pursed her lips. "No, it wasn't that, dear boy. The marriage was, frankly, dreadful – well, you know that. Victoria, being a serious-minded girl, was unfortunately attracted to a lively wastrel – there is no other way of describing him. In the three years after their marriage, I watched the self-esteem shrivel away inside her. The person who came back to live with me was not the daughter I had raised. She was a shell, Peter, a shell."

Beech felt uncomfortable stirrings of guilt. "I wish I could have done more."

Maud dismissed his guilt with a shrug. "What could you have done? What could *anyone* have done? As her mother, I was distraught that I could do nothing. She had made her choice and she had to either live with it or undo it. I tell you, dear boy, I was more than willing to accept the fact that we might suffer the shame of divorce but, frankly, anything would have been better than the existence they were living. I mean, they were two steps away from destitution when Edwin left. Tradesmen had not been paid, staff had left for better employment, and the house was falling apart. And, of course, after Edwin was killed, Victoria became unhinged..."

"She still loved him then?"

Maud gave a hollow laugh. "Oh my dear, no, emphatically not. All her grief was guilt. Pure guilt. I do believe that, deep down, she actually felt she had been released and she found it very difficult to cope with that emotion. But, thankfully, she has pulled herself through it and I think, once you see her, you will find some of the old spark has returned."

Beech felt some guilt himself. He realised that, just at that moment, he was elated that Victoria had fallen out of love with her husband. He managed to express regret to Maud that he had been unable to support Victoria at her husband's funeral.

Maud shrugged again. "You were in hospital, my dear! In any event, your presence would have only made Victoria worse. I think she always felt regret that she turned you down, you know."

Beech flushed. "Perhaps it was for the best."

"Oh, I don't know. But, Peter, if you are thinking of proposing again, I should leave it for a few more months if I were you."

"Good God! I wasn't thinking any such thing!" he lied. "I've come here with a business proposal, that's all!"

Maud looked askance at him. "If you say so, my dear. I'm intrigued, I must say. But I shall stifle my natural nosiness and let you tell us both at supper. Victoria should be home soon. Her shift finished half an hour ago and they should be back any moment."

"They?"

"Victoria and Jenkins, the butler. I always send him to

escort Victoria home. I can't have her walking back in the dark alone!"

As if on cue, the front door opened and closed, and voices were heard in the hallway. Victoria burst into the room, in full nurse's uniform, beaming.

"Peter? I couldn't believe when Jenkins told me that you were coming to visit! Oh, it's been such a long time!"

Victoria flew across the room and enveloped the standing Beech in a hug. He felt her thin arms around his neck and, when he clasped her body, his hands brushed her razor-sharp shoulder blades. *Too thin! Too thin!* he thought anxiously, but he forced his mouth to smile.

She pulled away, laughing. "I'm so sorry – I probably smell of carbolic soap! I've been scrubbing equipment all afternoon." She took his hands and looked fondly at him. "It's so good to see you, Peter. Really." She turned to her mother. "I'm just going to get changed, Ma, but you start dinner, both of you. I won't be long." She flashed Beech another smile and left, in a flurry of stiff, white cotton.

Beech turned a stricken face to Maud. "She's skin and bone," he said concerned.

Maud patted his arm. "Don't worry, Peter. We're shovelling food into her as fast as Cook can make it. She'll be back to her old self soon."

Dinner was a delight. Beech and Victoria reminisced over old times – each careful not to mention either her marriage or his war experiences – and they laughed together as Maud watched over them with pleasure.

Finally, after an extravagant dessert, "Especially designed to fatten me up," pronounced Victoria airily, all three retired to the drawing room for coffee and a warm by the fire.

"Coffee?!" Beech was incredulous. "Where on earth did

you get coffee? It's practically disappeared in London!"

"Ah. Well, Ma hoarded like mad during the first days of the war," said Victoria mischievously. "Didn't you, Ma?"

"I did, I'm afraid, and I'm not proud of it," said Maud, winking at Beech, "but I could see the writing on the wall. All this guff about 'It'll be over by Christmas!' I could see it dragging on for a long time, and I was right. And no one was going to deprive me of my after-dinner cup of coffee! Mind you, we have to use that dreadful tinned milk stuff in it – but I refuse to use those ghastly saccharin tablets for sweetening. We are fortunate to have stores of honey in the cellar."

Beech savoured the taste of the first cup of coffee he had drunk in almost a year.

"Now," Maud continued firmly, "I cannot wait any longer, Peter. You must tell us about this business proposition of yours."

"Oh?" Victoria looked at them both. "Is it something exciting?"

Beech took a deep breath and explained, for the third time that day, the case of Lord Murcheson's murder and his tragic wife. Maud and Victoria were, at once, both suitably shocked and sympathetic. Then Beech told them about his proposal to Sir Edward and the acceptance of the "secret" team. Then, he took the plunge and told them his idea for the members of the team. There was a silence and Beech held his breath.

Victoria and Maud looked at each other but Beech could not tell their emotions.

Finally, Victoria spoke.

"Do you think I should do this, Ma?"

"Victoria, if you think you are strong enough, I think you should," her mother replied.

Beech allowed himself to breathe again.

"In fact," Maud continued, "ever since I paid for you to study law at London University, I have been wondering when all that money and hours of study would be put to good use. Frankly, darling, a mind like yours is wasted washing bedpans. The Law Society may not, yet, allow women to practise as solicitors but I think that keeping your hand in by working with the police would be no bad idea."

Victoria looked at her cup of coffee, thinking hard. Then she slowly smiled and looked at Beech. "I think it would be a good idea too."

Beech exhaled in triumph.

"Of course, I should have to make two conditions," Maud said firmly, raising her voice so that they would be in no doubt that she meant business. Beech and Victoria looked at her anxiously. "Firstly, I will have to accompany Victoria to London," she stated and seeing Beech move to protest, she swiftly added, "but only to look after her, not to be involved in her work." Beech relaxed again. "And, secondly, I propose that we use our London house as the base for your team. We have lots of empty rooms and that would mean that Victoria could 'live above the shop' as it were."

Beech looked at Victoria, she nodded in encouragement, and he beamed his acceptance. "Brilliant! Maud, you are a genius!"

"Of course I am," she murmured. "Where do you think Victoria gets her brains from? Perhaps Caroline would like to move in with us, too?" she suggested. "I'm sure she has some poky little room at the hospital but I'm equally sure she would like a nice warm bed and decent food when she is not on call."

"Another brilliant idea, Ma," said Victoria happily. "What about *this* house and the staff?"

"Well, I have another plan..."

Beech marvelled at how Maud had obviously worked out everything in detail in such a short time. "I have been feeling guilty about not contributing more to the war effort," she continued, "so I propose to offer the house as another military hospital for the duration of the war. Jenkins and our coachman, William, can stay here and make sure that the War Office don't ruin the place, and we will take Cook and Mary with us. I am bored out of my mind in the country anyway. I shall look forward to being a silent but supportive part of your new team, Peter."

Beech gave a wry smile. "Supportive you shall be, without a doubt, but silent, I fear, may prove a challenge for you, Maud."

"Cheeky pup!" she chortled. "Now we should all get some sleep because that poor Lady Harriet is waiting to talk to my daughter, and you need to get the milk train in the morning. Cook, Mary and I will follow on the last train because we shall have a lot of work to do tomorrow. Come along, children!"

A few minutes later, as he sank into a warm bed, Beech felt nothing but satisfaction at the day's accomplishments. The team was beginning to form, they now had a place from which to work, and he had seen Victoria smiling for the first time in a long while.

CHAPTER FOUR

"Billy Will Be Your Strong Right Hand"

P.C. Billy Rigsby stood in the relative quiet of the early morning at Waterloo Station. He was absolutely still, like a statue – six feet seven inches from toe to top of his helmet – and he waited patiently with eager anticipation. The Clerk Sergeant had come to him late last night and told him that he was being seconded to a special unit – orders of Chief Inspector Beech.

"Why me?" Billy had asked, secretly delighted that he was going to get out from behind a desk.

"I dunno, perhaps he wants someone thumped?" the Sergeant had replied sarcastically, and Billy had grinned. "Orders are for you to report to Waterloo Station at eight tomorrow morning and meet the Chief Inspector off a train."

The reference to "thumping" someone was because everyone at Scotland Yard knew that, prior to the war, Billy Rigsby, a.k.a 'The Greek', had been the youngest ever light heavyweight boxing champion of The Grenadier Guards. His nickname had come from the fact that his Sergeant Major, who ran the boxing team, once said of him, "Stripped down, he looks like a bleedin' Greek God but he's got the most vicious right hand I've ever seen." From then on, he had been referred to by the rest of the Regiment as "The Greek." Glory days – all wiped out on the battlefield at Mons, when he ended up in a field hospital with a shattered left hand, a head wound and a severe case of shell shock. The Guards didn't want him anymore. "You can't fire a rifle properly with a gammy hand, son," they told him while he was still in the hospital. But they found him a place in the police force – although the Met wasn't entirely sure what to do with him either and, for the last five months, Billy Rigsby had languished in the clerical department at Scotland Yard, while his pent-up energy nearly drove him insane. He prayed fervently that this new job would give him more physical work. Something suited to his talents.

"Constable," a female voice said and Billy looked down at a small Red Cross nurse holding a mug of tea. "The girls thought you could do with a brew," she said, nodding towards a gaggle of nurses manning a tea wagon who waved and giggled.

Billy flashed them a disarming smile and a wink as he took off his helmet and accepted the mug of tea. The small nurse in front of him gasped as the removal of his helmet revealed a scar, which went from his hairline, across his right cheekbone, finishing almost at the corner of his mouth.

"Does your helmet strap make that scar hurt?" she enquired anxiously.

"Nah," said Billy nonchalantly. "I'm used to it now. Thanks for the tea, miss. I'll bring the mug back when I'm finished."

Flustered, she hurried off to impart the news to her colleagues that the tall, handsome policeman would be coming over to return his mug. Billy grinned. He liked women – too much, his mother said – and they definitely liked him. The scar, he had found, had added to his appeal, rather than diminished it. *Shame about the bloody hand though*, he thought to himself as he awkwardly tried to hold the mug with his black-gloved left hand, which he was unable to clench.

Billy looked up from his mug to see that the arrivals board was being changed and he noted, with a start, that the Chief Inspector's train was due any minute. He raced over to the

Red Cross wagon, dumped his mug, and shouted "Thanks girls! Most welcome!", and ran full-pelt over to the platform, leaving a clutch of nurses disappointed at being deprived of the hoped-for conversation.

He put his helmet back on and stood, ramrod straight, at the ticket barrier. He knew the Chief Inspector quite well. Beech had always taken an interest in him, as they had both been invalided out of the army at the same time and they had both been in the Guards – Billy in the Grenadiers and Beech in the Coldstream. Both regiments were taught to despise each other because of some dispute in the seventeenth century, but Billy found the whole thing a nonsense. "A soldier is a soldier," he used to say. "We all bleed the same."

Beech alighted from the train and Billy noted that he was accompanied by an ethereally beautiful woman. *Wife?* He wondered. Whoever she was, she was a bit on the thin side for Billy's liking.

On reaching the ticket barrier, Beech extended his hand and, for a moment, Billy was confused as he realised he was expected to shake it. Embarrassed at this break from protocol, he nevertheless co-operated with the handshake and said gruffly, "Good train journey, sir?"

"Yes, yes!" Beech seemed enthusiastic. "P.C. Rigsby – Billy – I am glad you are to be a part of my special team. May I introduce another member of that team – Victoria Ellingham."

Momentarily, Billy was stunned and he managed a cursory nod and a croaked "Ma-am" by way of acknowledgement.

Beech smiled. "I can see you are somewhat taken aback, P.C. Rigsby. All will be revealed shortly. Ah! Here's the porter with Mrs Ellingham's luggage!" A small mountain of suitcases was wheeled past and Billy recognised expensive luggage when he saw it. "We shall take a taxi to the Women's Hospital and I will explain everything on the way," Beech commanded everyone to follow and a bemused Billy took up the rear. It had been a long time since he had been in a taxi – not something a Constable's pay would stretch to – and he was unsure how to deal with this unusual situation.

It took a while to carefully load the luggage into the front of the taxi cab beside the driver, then Beech and Victoria sat inside. Billy took off his helmet and hunched down to peer into the cab. "Um…there's really not enough room for me, sir. I'll find other transport and meet you there."

"Nonsense!" said Beech, as breezily he could. "Victoria, sit on my lap, then you can squeeze in beside me, Rigsby. I really must talk to you."

Victoria obligingly moved onto Beech's lap, and Billy reluctantly manoeuvred himself into the vacant space and, once seated, he stared fixedly ahead, clutching his helmet in embarrassment.

Then Beech began to talk about the need for women to be involved in the policing of women's crimes. He explained, without too much of the horrific detail, the case of Lady Harriet, who refused to speak to anyone other than a woman. Then, finally, he detailed his conversation with the Commissioner and the team he was being allowed to set up. By the end of all that, Billy Rigsby was looking squarely at Beech and seemed to have overcome his discomfort at the lady perched on the Chief Inspector's lap. When Beech explained that Victoria was a trained lawyer, Billy exclaimed, "Get away!", and flashed her an admiring smile.

"So what, exactly, would be my role in this team, sir?" Billy asked hopefully.

"Well, firstly as a bodyguard for the two ladies," Beech explained and Billy nodded. 'Strong arm' he could do. He began to feel more relaxed about everything. "And, secondly," Beech continued, "if the ladies uncover a crime, you, of course, as a serving policeman, will be the only one with the actual power of arrest."

"P.C. Rigsby seems to be happy now," murmured Victoria to Beech, noting the smile that was slowly spreading across Billy's face.

Yes, Billy was happy. The whole set-up was unconventional but that suited his rebellious nature. It had to be kept a secret and he rather liked that too. But, most of all, he understood the role he was to play. Being a bodyguard and making arrests appealed to his strong sense of masculinity. Billy was a very happy young man indeed.

On arrival at the Women's Hospital, the taxi disgorged its occupants and was told to wait. Billy, still clutching his helmet, followed the others obediently.

A woman in a white coat was being embraced enthusiastically by Victoria Ellingham and Billy hung back a little, awaiting instructions.

"Rigsby," said Beech, "Meet another member of our team, Doctor Caroline Allardyce." This time Billy was prepared and he extended his hand to the female doctor with relish. "Caroline," Beech added, "Billy will be your strong right hand."

"How very obliging of you, Peter, to provide us with our own personal Adonis," Caroline said dryly as she shook Billy's hand.

Billy laughed. He didn't understand what she had called him but it sounded Greek and he figured it was complimentary. He liked this one. She had curves in all the right places and a look of fun in her eyes.

"Now behave yourself, Caro," admonished Beech. "Let's

not frighten the poor lad before we've started work. How is Lady Harriet?"

Caroline became businesslike. "She's awake but heavily drugged. It will be touch and go, Peter. She won't talk to me. I have tried but she doesn't regard me as her equal. I think, whatever the sex, she regards doctors as higher servants, I'm afraid. You know – one step above butlers. I do believe that this woman was raised in the Georgian era. I've never met any young woman with such entrenched and enclosed views of Society. Let's hope that Victoria has more luck."

"You must introduce Victoria as the Honourable Mrs Ellingham," counselled Beech. Victoria made a small protest but Beech insisted. "No, no. Caroline is not exaggerating. Lady Harriet has the most developed sense of snobbery. You must go in with all titles on display or we shall never get anything out of her. Now——" he turned to Billy "——you and I, Rigsby, shall leave the ladies to their task and we shall visit our new headquarters and then the crime scene."

"Yes, sir." Billy stood to attention and then made a little bow to the women. "Ladies, pleased to make your acquaintance." And with that the men left.

Caroline watched them lope back to the taxi with a look of wonderment on her face. "Wherever did Peter find such a specimen?" she murmured. "I shall ask P.C Rigsby to donate his body to medical science when he dies. I've never seen anything like it."

"Caroline, you're incorrigible!" Victoria was greatly amused. "Stop salivating and show me to Lady Harriet's room!"

Caroline interrupted her reverie to say, "Do you know, I've just noticed how terribly thin you are, Victoria! Are you quite well?"

"I'm fine and I'm eating for England! I have truly missed you, Caroline. And, by the way, I loathe your hair."

The two friends linked arms, laughing, and made their way up the stairs.

✳

Beech and Billy arrived at Lady Maud's house in Hanover Square and it took the two of them to unload and transport Victoria's luggage to the front door.

"Why *do* women own so many clothes?" sighed an exasperated Beech, after he had unlocked the door and Billy had piled the suitcases up in the hallway. Billy grinned and then whistled in appreciation at the grandeur of the interior of the house.

"Is this to be our HQ, sir?" he said in a disbelieving voice.

"Ha! Yes! Courtesy of Mrs Ellingham's mother, Lady Maud. Who will be joining us later, by the way, along with her cook and maid. So, you shall have good grub, lively conversation and a decent bed to sleep in."

"What, sir? *I* get to sleep here?" Billy could hardly believe his luck.

"Well, we can't have you dossing down at the station house, can we?" Beech was quite emphatic. "It's your job to look after the ladies, Rigsby, and I'm afraid that may be a twenty-four hour job. I should have warned you, I'm sorry."

"No, no apology needed, sir! Believe me, I'm only too happy to oblige." Billy felt like the cat that got the cream.

Beech patted him on the shoulder. "Good man. Chose you for your Guards' discipline and all that."

"Yes, sir. Won't let you down, sir."

Beech was restless. "Look, Rigsby, we'll sort out your actual room and stuff later. Right now, I really want to go back to the crime scene. Oblige me by hailing another taxi cab, would you?"

"Right away, sir." Billy stepped swiftly out on to the pavement, put on his helmet, spotted a passing taxi and blew a piercing blast on his police whistle. The taxi obligingly swerved into the kerb and Billy opened the door for his new Chief and then followed him into the cab.

On the way to Belgravia, Beech filled the young policeman in on the more intimate details of Lady Harriet's injuries.

Billy sucked in a breath through his teeth. "Sounds like the bastard husband got his dues, sir, if you don't mind me saying."

"Mm. My sentiments exactly, Rigsby. But the problem is that Doctor Allardyce believes that Lady Harriet would have been so badly injured that she would not have been able to inflict the fatal blow on her husband, so I think we are looking for someone else who stabbed Lord Murcheson to save the wife from further attack."

"The butler, sir?"

Beech laughed. "That would be nice and pat! But I think not. Another man would possibly have struck Lord Murcheson a blow and knocked him out, or shot him or, at the very least, restrained him. Stabbing him through the heart with a pair of scissors strikes me...and I may be wrong in my assumption... as a woman's action. What do you think?"

Billy was flattered to be asked his opinion. He felt that the Chief Inspector was right and told him so.

"Which brings me to my next point." Beech looked at Billy with some embarrassment. "I have noted that you seem to have a way with the fairer sex, Rigsby. Would I be wrong in that observation?"

Billy laughed and flushed a little. "I must admit, I like to chat to the ladies and they seem to like to chat back, if you know what I mean."

Beech smiled. "Quite. You have an ability that I entirely lack. Oh, I mean I can talk to ladies, if I've known them for a very long time – but not with any great ease. So, I think it might be best if you have a little chat with the female servants in the Murcheson household. Not question them…just go down in the kitchen and make yourself at home. Get the cook to give you a cup of tea and a sticky bun. Let the women chat around you, as it were. Do you get my drift?"

"Perfectly, sir. Don't you worry; it'll be like visiting my womenfolk at home. Before you know it, they'll be telling me all their aches and pains and all the neighbourhood gossip. Leave it to me."

"Good man." Beech heaved a sigh of relief. "Knew I could count on you."

Once in the house in Belgravia, Beech told the butler that he would need to undertake a detailed examination of the bedroom in which the murder had taken place.

"Of course, sir," the butler nodded in deference. "Will there be anything else that you require?"

"Er, yes." Beech adopted an air of authority. "I shall require you to attend upon me in the bedroom please, as I have some further questions for you. But first, could you take my constable downstairs to your cook? He's been on his feet since the early hours and is in desperate need of a cup of tea and some food."

"At once, sir." The butler inclined his head towards Beech and motioned with his hand for Billy to follow him.

"Thank you, Chief Inspector. Most kind of you." Billy winked at Beech as he passed by.

The butler opened the kitchen door at the bottom of the

stairs. "I'm sure you can fend for yourself, constable. Just ask Cook for what you want." Then the butler turned back up the stairs.

Billy stepped through the half-opened door and grinned.

"So," he said cheerily, "which one of you lovely ladies is going to make a starving policeman a cup of tea and a sandwich?"

Four women's mouths opened as they gazed upon Billy Rigsby and, suddenly, the kitchen burst into a frenzy of activity as they sat him down and began catering to this unexpected gift of the day.

CHAPTER FIVE

Lady Harriet's Confession

Victoria sat patiently beside Lady Harriet's bed. Caroline had introduced her, in the manner ordered by Beech, and the sick woman had indicated that Victoria was acceptable. After a brief exchange regarding Victoria's background, resulting in a thin smile and a nod from the patient, the woman had closed her eyes and lapsed into unconsciousness. Caroline had warned Victoria, before they entered the room, that Lady Harriet would lapse in and out of consciousness as her condition was grave and required powerful drugs. All Victoria could do was wait.

She looked around the room. Caroline said that the maid, Esme, had arrived last night to bring Lady Harriet's personal items. All Victoria could see on the side table was a Bible, a Book of Common Prayer and some handkerchiefs. She opened the Bible and read the inscription:

To Harriet, Faithful Daughter in Christ, from Sr. Mary Francis

She replaced the Bible and then looked at the Book of Common Prayer. It too had an inscription:

To Lady Harriet Montcrieff on her wedding day
from your Sisters in Christ

"It was given to me when I left the convent," said a soft voice from the bed, which made Victoria start.

"You were a nun before you married?"

Lady Harriet smiled. "No. I was placed in the care of the convent when both my parents died in an accident in India. It was an Anglican convent in London."

"Was it a school? Were there other children there, Lady Harriet?"

"No. Just me. And one novice of my age. I was eleven when I went there. They were very kind."

Victoria understood immediately why this woman lying in the bed was so unworldly and could not bring herself to speak to a male police officer. *My God,* she thought, *couldn't they have sent her to a boarding school with girls of her own age?*

"How did you meet your husband then?"

The smile faded from Lady Harriet's face and she turned her head away, staring fixedly at the door, rather than into Victoria's face.

"My husband came from a good aristocratic family, who were patrons of the church. The Archbishop arranged for us to meet – chaperoned, of course. He… seemed…was…very kind, in our courtship days."

"And *after* you married?" As soon as she said the words, Victoria saw a small flush creep across the woman's otherwise deathly pale face.

"He…was…very patient with me. I had no understanding of the physical side of marriage. At first it revolted me…" She looked at Victoria and one small tear trickled from the outside corner of her eye on to the pillow. "I don't suppose you can understand that."

"Of course I can," Victoria answered gently. "Especially for someone as innocent as you must have been."

"Is your husband a good man?" Lady Harriet turned her face back.

Victoria hesitated, then drew in a long breath. "My husband died last year, at the battle of Ypres. Ours was not a happy marriage but he was not a *bad* man – just..." she struggled to find the right word "...lost, I think would best describe his personality."

"Lost. Yes. A good word." Lady Harriet's hand moved a few inches and covered Victoria's hand momentarily. "My husband was lost, when he came back from France. He... he...was not patient anymore. His personality changed and the medicines his doctor prescribed made him worse. He would fly into rages and...and...force himself upon me..." Her head turned away again in embarrassment "...sometimes brutally." She shuddered at the memory and Victoria clasped her hand firmly in reassurance. "Then, come the morning, he would no longer remember that he had...violated me...and would accuse me of lying. In these last few weeks, as he became more and more reliant on the medicines he...couldn't...he was..."

"Impotent," Victoria said, knowing the word that Lady Harriet was struggling to find.

"Yes. So...when I told him that I was expecting a child... he flew into a rage and accused me of having a lover." She laughed hollowly and then she cried out in physical pain.

Victoria sped to the door and called for a nurse.

"Lady Harriet appears to be in tremendous pain," she said, as both a nurse and the Matron appeared in the corridor.

The Matron looked at her watch. "I can give her half a dose of morphine but no more. Nurse, fetch Dr Allardyce." The nurse marched briskly away, whilst the Matron propelled a trolley into Lady Harriet's room.

"Lady Harriet," she said whilst arming a syringe, "I shall give you some pain relief but the doctor will need to examine you."

Victoria felt it wise to step outside the room whilst the Matron gave the injection and she briefly nodded to Caroline as she sped past to enter the room as well. She heard Lady Harriet cry out in pain several times and deduced that the situation was serious. Matron came out of the room and then returned with a large brown bottle of fluid. Finally, both Matron and Caroline appeared, looking grave and, after a brief discussion, Matron left. Caroline approached Victoria.

"It's not good," she said quietly, "her abdomen is swollen and painful, and an infection has certainly developed. There is little we can do for her, other than apply topical antiseptics. I fear she does not have the strength for me to open her up again and irrigate the wound. Damn!"

Caroline seemed close to tears, and Victoria grasped her arm in sympathy.

"You did your best, Caro – no one could have done more."

Caroline was fighting back the tears. "If only I had been called soon after she received her injuries! Any damage to the bowel will only spread infection the longer it is left and the poor woman sat there, in agony, for almost sixteen hours, refusing any kind of assistance..." she trailed off, knowing any further discussion was useless. She wiped her eyes and turned to Victoria. "She is asking to speak to you again but, I warn you, she is heavily drugged, and I don't know how much longer she will last. If there are any problems, just call us."

Victoria nodded and gave Caroline's arm one last squeeze before re-entering the room and sitting once more beside Lady Harriet.

Lady Harriet stirred, her glazed eyes struggling to focus on Victoria.

"Mrs Ellingham?" she asked weakly.

"Yes, Lady Harriet, I am here." She took the young

woman's hand again.

"I want to make a full confession and sign it. Will you write it down for me?"

Victoria nodded and reached inside her handbag to produce a notepad and pen.

"May I have some water first, please?"

Victoria poured some water into an invalid cup and gently raised Lady Harriet's head, so that she could drink.

"Thank you." She sank back on to the pillows and began to dictate, slowly.

"I, Lady Harriet Anne Cecilia Murcheson nee Montcrieff, aged twenty-two years, do hereby state, being of sound mind and fully aware of my actions, that I did, in the early morning of Wednesday the twenty-eighth of May, 1915, stab my husband, Lord Murcheson, fatally, in self-defence, after he brutally attacked and injured me." She paused to allow Victoria time to catch up, then she resumed. "I wish to state, for the record, that no other person was involved in this tragic event – that I alone was responsible." Then she whispered, "May God have mercy on my soul."

Victoria finished writing and said, "Is that all you wish to say, Lady Harriet?"

"Yes."

Victoria placed the fountain pen in Lady Harriet's right hand and held the pad up, so that she could sign her name without raising her body in any way.

That done, Victoria signed her own name below, as a witness, and dated the document.

"You will make sure that Chief Inspector Beech receives it?"

"Yes, Lady Harriet." Victoria took the fountain pen out of her hand and sat down again. "Is there anything further that

I can do for you?"

"Could you possibly contact my solicitor and ask him to come and see me, with the utmost urgency? I wish to amend my will. His name is Sir Arnold Chester and his practice is at twenty-seven Lincoln's Inn Fields. I'm afraid I don't know the telephone number."

"I shall go and see him right away, Lady Harriet."

"You have been most kind, Mrs Ellingham. I wonder, could I ask one more thing of you?"

"Of course."

"Could you ask my maid, Esme, to fetch the Reverend Mitchell? I should like some spiritual comfort before I die."

Victoria took her hand again. "Lady Harriet, it is to be hoped that you will not die. The staff here is doing everything possible to help you recover. You must summon your will. Often it is the power of the mind that determines whether illness conquers us or not. Believe me, I know."

Lady Harriet smiled and she squeezed Victoria's hand. "I do believe you. But I have reconciled myself to dying – and perhaps it is for the best. I can only hope that God will forgive me my sins and receive me into Heaven."

Victoria felt like weeping. *She is nothing more than a child! And has had such a miserable existence.* "Lady Harriet, I do believe that you, of all people, will be received into Heaven with great blessings." She gently kissed her on her forehead and watched her as she lapsed into a quiet slumber.

On her way out, Victoria sought out Caroline and showed her the signed confession. Caroline shook her head in dismay.

"I don't believe she did it, you know. I don't believe she would have been capable."

Victoria agreed. "But this confession proves that she is protecting someone that she really cares about – and I believe it is another woman. Anyway, I must go – I have several errands to run. I shall see you at our house later?"

Caroline nodded. "My shift finishes in two hours. I'll see you then. I'll instruct Matron to telephone me if Lady Harriet…takes a turn for the worse. What's your number again?"

"Mayfair one hundred," called Victoria over her shoulder, as she left in a hurry.

It took Victoria the best part of an hour to find Sir Arnold Chester, as he was not in his chambers, nor was he in the Law Courts in the Strand, as she had been told, but an usher at the Courts took her across to a public house opposite the Law Courts, and pointed Sir Arnold out. He appeared to be celebrating with several barristers. He sounded annoyed when she interrupted his conversation but when she explained that Lady Harriet Murcheson was at death's door, he was immediately apologetic and assured her that he would collect Lady Harriet's papers and go immediately to the Women's Hospital.

Victoria then hailed a taxi cab and made her way to the Murcheson house. Beech and Billy were just leaving as she arrived.

"Peter! Thank goodness I've caught you. I can kill two birds with one stone." She produced her notepad with Lady Harriet's signed confession.

Beech looked grave. "Is there any chance she will recover?" he asked.

Victoria shook her head. "The poor thing is in the grip of a bad infection and I doubt she will last until tonight. And she will say nothing more. That confession is her final word."

Billy kicked a stone across the pavement in frustration. "She didn't do it, ma'am," he said vehemently. "I'm pretty sure I know who did."

"P.C Rigsby has uncovered some pretty interesting information," added Beech, "and—" he raised a gentlemen's hatbox in his right hand " —I have a collection of the husband's medications here that may shed some light on the proceedings. Rigsby and I are going to the mortuary now to see if the pathologist has finished the forensic examination of the body."

"Right, well, I have to instruct Lady Harriet's maid to fetch a vicar and then I think I'll go home."

"Good." It was obvious that Beech wanted to press on. "We'll all meet at your house and compare notes. Oh, by the way, Victoria," Beech added, "Arthur Tollman, the last member of the team, may arrive before I get there. Would you mind awfully telling him what's going on? Tell him I'll fill him in on his exact job description when I get there."

"Will do."

Beech and Billy hurried off and Victoria rang the bell of the Murcheson house. The butler answered and Victoria told him that she had a message for Esme, from Lady Harriet.

"How is my lady?" the butler enquired gravely.

"Very, very ill, I'm afraid. It's unlikely she will live much longer."

The butler seemed genuinely distressed. "I am sorry to hear that. The staff will find her loss hard to bear." Then he became businesslike. "I will fetch Esme, madam, if you would kindly wait in the drawing room," and he ushered her into the first room off the hallway.

Esme swiftly appeared, curtsied and stood, trembling in front of Victoria.

"I am Mrs Ellingham, Esme," Victoria to the girl, kindly. "Try not to be distressed, but Her Ladyship is gravely ill in hospital and has asked if you would take Reverend Mitchell to the Women's Hospital. She needs spiritual comfort."

Esme at once burst into tears and began wailing. "It's all my fault, madam! It's all my fault!"

Victoria sat the girl down beside her on the sofa and tried to calm her. "What is your fault, Esme? Can you tell me?"

Eventually, through her tears, Esme told Victoria about refusing to take turns with Polly, the scullery maid, outside Lady Harriet's door at night.

"She asked me…Polly did…if I would take turns with her, at night…to sit in a chair outside my lady's room…and I said no, I was too tired…" There was a fresh burst of weeping from Esme, where she could hardly get the words out and Victoria tried to be patient. Esme's sobs subsided once again and she resumed, "Polly used to sit in a chair outside Lady Harriet's room and if His Lordship started prowling, she would say that the mistress was ill and couldn't be disturbed. I don't know how she did it. She must have been so tired and he…he was so frightening. I was so scared of him. That was why I wouldn't take turns with her. But I tried to make up for it by covering for her in the day so she could go and have a nap." She looked at Victoria with misery on her face. "I was a coward, Madam, and I'm so, so sorry."

"Where is this Polly?"

Esme shrugged. "Dunno, madam. She was nowhere to be seen yesterday morning, after…it happened. I think she ran away. She probably saw it all and ran off frightened. I dunno."

Just then Victoria heard the front door open and close. She went to the window and caught a glimpse of the butler hurrying down the street in a heavy overcoat. She returned to Esme.

"Esme, I perfectly understand that you were frightened by Lord Murcheson. From the sound of it, anyone would. It's all been a horrid business. Have you told anyone else about what Polly was doing?"

Esme shook her head. "No, madam, but I think Mr Dodds knew."

"Mr Dodds?"

"The butler, madam." Esme looked at the door and lowered her voice. "I never understood, madam, why Mr Dodds didn't protect Lady Harriet properly. I mean he was the only man in the house. It shouldn't have fallen to a young scullery maid to look after my lady."

"No indeed." Victoria was still thinking about the butler leaving so suddenly, and she wondered if he had heard some of Esme's confession through the door.

"Now," she said briskly, "you must dry your eyes, and go and fetch the Reverend Mitchell. Your poor mistress may not survive the night and she urgently wants to speak to her parish priest."

The girl looked in danger of crying again and Victoria became stern. "Esme! If you are truly sorry for not helping your mistress before this tragedy, then you must make every effort to help her now!"

"Yes, madam. I shall." Esme leapt to her feet, produced a handkerchief and blew her nose. "I'll see you out, madam, and then I'll get my coat and hat and go and get the Reverend."

"Good girl." Victoria paused as they made their way to the drawing room door. "Oh, and Esme," she counselled, "please keep our little conversation to yourself. Please don't discuss the matter with any of the other staff."

"No madam. I promise."

Once out in the street, Victoria realised that it was long past lunchtime; her feet were aching and she desperately needed a cup of tea.

I shall find a café and gather my thoughts before I go home, she thought, as she walked towards Hyde Park Corner, and I know just the place.

Her pace quickened at the thought of tea and pastries at Fortnum and Mason.

I shall show Ma the receipt, she thought, smiling to herself. She'll be so pleased that I'm eating fattening pastries again!

For a moment her spirits sank, as memories of the past flashed in her mind, but then she shook herself, lifted her head high, and strode on determinedly.

CHAPTER SIX

More Arrivals

"You must be Mr Tollman!" said Victoria brightly, as she opened the door. "I'm afraid I'm the only one here, at the moment, but Peter told me to fill you in on what's happening."

"Peter?" enquired Arthur, as he stepped into the house.

"Oh sorry!" Victoria smiled. "I mean Chief Inspector Beech, of course."

"Ah," replied Arthur, "And *you* are, Miss?"

"Oh, sorry again!" Victoria extended her hand. "Victoria Ellingham, part of your new team. Would you like a cup of tea, Mr Tollman?"

"That would be most welcome, Miss Ellingham," replied Arthur affably, "then perhaps you would tell me a little bit more about this 'team' I'm supposed to be part of?"

"Yes, of course." Victoria led the way down to the kitchen. "I'm afraid we don't have any staff at the moment – not until my mother arrives. She's due this evening sometime and she's bringing Cook and Mary with her."

Arthur looked bemused. "Would you like me to make the tea, Miss?"

"Good Lord, no! I'm perfectly capable of making a pot of tea, Mr Tollman and, by the way, it's Mrs. I'm *Mrs* Ellingham. But, in fact, I'd much rather you called me Victoria."

Arthur sucked air through his teeth. "Oh, I couldn't do that, Mrs Ellingham. I'd prefer to keep it professional."

Victoria smiled at such old-fashioned propriety, while she lit the stove and filled the kettle.

"So…about the team…"

Arthur Tollman sat patiently, occasionally raising an eyebrow, as Victoria explained Beech's vision for the dealing of crime cases in the female population. When she had finished, he smiled and shook his head in disbelief.

"Well, Mrs Ellingham, I think I've heard it all now. In my whole, very long career as a policeman, I don't believe I have heard anything like it – and that includes a spell in Special Branch, where all kinds of strange things happen!" He seemed to find the whole thing amusing.

"You don't dislike the idea, Mr Tollman?" Victoria felt a little anxious.

"No, no, madam. Far from it. As the father of three grown-up unmarried daughters, I know only too well how the fairer sex can run rings around the menfolk! And a policeman is not immune from female trickery, I can assure you. Dear me. So, this team is to be the Chief Inspector, yourself, a lady doctor, me and The Greek?"

"The Greek?" Victoria was confused.

"Yes, Billy Rigsby – aka The Greek," and he explained to her about Billy's past life as a young boxing champion.

"Good Lord! Well, that explains the physique then!" Victoria was greatly amused. "Caroline will love to hear all about Billy the Greek's boxing prowess!"

"So, I understand that the lady doctor will have her uses but may I ask, without wishing to cause offence, Mrs Ellingham, what equips you for this job?"

"No offence taken, Mr Tollman. My speciality is the law – I studied it for three years at London University – and your Chief Inspector is fond of saying that I have a deductive brain. Tit for tat now, Mr Tollman, tell me why Mr Beech chose you."

"Well, Mrs Ellingham, I suppose you might say that I have

an unusual brain, a bit like yours, except that my speciality is that I never forget anything. I store it up here—" he tapped his temple with his fingers "—like a squirrel storing away nuts and, in almost forty years of policing, that represents a lot of nuts! Also, I'm a bit of a ferret too. I like delving into records and the like, doing research."

"A squirrel *and* a ferret! Goodness! You *are* going to be useful! I don't suppose you play cribbage as well?"

"As a matter of fact I play exceedingly well. Why do you ask?"

Victoria laughed as she poured the boiling water into the teapot. "My mother is going to find you a delightful companion! Just don't ever play her for money. She's a fiend!"

"I shall store that piece of information away for future use, Mrs Ellingham," Arthur replied with pleasure.

"I have some biscuits too. Would you care for one, Mr Tollman?"

"I never say no to a biscuit with a cup of tea, Mrs Ellingham."

So they sat on either side of the kitchen table, with their tea and biscuits, while Victoria explained the details, so far, of the Murcheson case.

Beech and Billy stood silently over the eviscerated body of Lord Murcheson whilst the pathologist, Bernard Spilsbury, explained his findings.

"The murder victim died after being pierced through the heart with a pair of scissors, obviously, but I doubt he would have been long for this world anyway. His liver and kidneys were shot to pieces by whatever drugs he was taking. His brain had started to deteriorate. The white matter of the brain was degraded and there were other signs of damage – the sort I would expect in the brain of an eighty-year old man who had had several small strokes. There are various lacerations on the body consistent with someone constantly scratching at severe skin irritation and yet there is no sign of any dermatological reason for the itching which obviously plagued him. The lungs showed signs of early pneumonia, which I have seen before in opiate addicts because the drug persistently makes the breathing shallow and therefore allows bacteria to sit in the lungs. The septum of his nose is beginning to decay, which leads me to believe that he was sniffing some drug. Oh, and he also had syphilis."

"Good God!" Beech was appalled. "He was only twenty-five years old!"

"Yes," Spilsbury continued, "like most of the other young men fighting in the war. Here," he said, unceremoniously turning the body on to its side, displaying a puckered scar of about eight inches, running alongside the spine, "is the reason for this young man's deterioration. There are pieces of metal in there – I cannot tell whether they are bullets or shrapnel – that are dangerously close to the spine. I assume that the field surgeons decided it was too risky to remove them and no one in London had the courage to do so either. He must have been in tremendous pain – hence the drug regime. The presence of a canker on his male member, a sore near his mouth and swollen lymph glands, is what makes me assume that he was in the primary stage of syphilis. Probably contracted it sometime within the last three months."

"Poor bugger," said Billy with feeling.

Spilsbury gave a wry smile. "Yes. Well, it's possible, though I have not found any physical evidence of sodomy. He was a maimed and dying, syphilitic drug addict – that I know for sure."

"Thank you, Mr Spilsbury," said Beech, staring at the terrible body on the slab and feeling the dull ache in his leg start up again.

"I'll send you my written report during the week, but now, if you'll excuse me, I must wash up and go home for dinner. I won't shake your hands – for your sake."

Beech smiled briefly and nodded. When they got outside, he stood for a moment and took several deep breaths of air.

"How does that bloke go home and eat dinner every night?" wondered Billy, still in a state of shock. "I mean I've seen my share of shattered bodies on the battlefield but to look at a body laid out like that and tell us what a pitiful and awful existence he had – well, it beggars belief!"

"It does indeed, Rigsby," agreed Beech, "it does indeed. Just goes to show that being a member of the British aristocracy means nothing when you come back from France in an ambulance train."

"So who gave him all the drugs, sir?" Billy sounded angry. "Was it his doctor?"

"I don't know," said Beech, looking at the leather hatbox in his hand. "Some of the bottles I've got in here appear to be patent medicines one would buy at any chemist shop. We need to go to the house and show the contents of this bag to Doctor Allardyce. She may be able to give us an opinion."

Lady Maud had arrived, with so many suitcases, wicker baskets and boxes that it took two taxi cabs to ferry her and her servants from the station. Arthur Tollman and the two cab drivers unloaded everything into the hallway, and the drivers were paid handsomely.

"What a journey!" Maud announced. "We all need a stiff

brandy! Victoria, find the decanter and give Cook and Mary a good glassful!"

"Mother," Victoria said, shaking her head in disbelief, "why on earth did you bring all this stuff?"

"Cook and I were not going to leave behind all her preserves and all the other delights she's been preparing over the winter months," Maud replied with gusto. "There's a large ham in that basket by the way. Isn't that right, Mrs Beddowes?"

"Oh yes, Your Ladyship," said Mrs Beddowes, unbuttoning her coat and fanning herself with her hand. "There's a big jar of pickled eggs, some pickled cucumbers, relishes, jams, cured ham, sausages, bacon – oh, and there will be a basket of vegetables coming down on the train every week."

"We do have food shops in London, you know," murmured Victoria, by way of protest.

"Yes, but at what price, Miss Victoria?! At what price?"

Victoria could think of no riposte to Mrs Beddowes' observation and she suddenly noticed Arthur Tollman grinning broadly.

"Ah, Mother, Mrs Beddowes, Mary, this is Detective Sergeant Arthur Tollman, he's going to be staying here with us."

"Er…begging your pardon, Mrs Ellingham," Arthur interrupted, "I shan't be sleeping over. I've got my daughters to get home to. Don't like to leave them alone at night. Besides, I only live in Clapham. The omnibus comes right to Park Lane. It's no bother." He suddenly realised that he had interrupted the introductions. "Begging your pardon, ladies, I am very pleased to meet you all."

"Ma," Victoria said mischievously, "Mr Tollman plays a mean game of cribbage."

Lady Maud's eyes lit up and she offered her hand immediately. "I'm exceedingly pleased to meet you, Mr Tollman! We shall get along famously."

"I have no doubt we will, Your Ladyship," said Arthur, winking at Victoria.

"But first, brandy!" pronounced Maud. "To revive the spirits and then we shall get this house organised and shipshape!"

＊

Lady Harriet was exhausted. Despite her pain and the tightening grip of the infection, she had summoned her iron will and dealt with her solicitor and said prayers with her vicar. Now she could sleep and Caroline could tell that the fragile young woman did not care whether she woke again or not.

"You must rest, Lady Harriet," she said firmly to her patient. "We shall give you some more pain relief and nurse will feed you some nourishing soup. Your body needs to fight this infection."

Lady Harriet nodded. "You have all been most kind. But I needed to get my affairs in order. If it is God's will to take me, he will, and it will be no reflection on the care you have given me."

Caroline left her and issued instructions for the patient to be fed before the morphine was administered. It was all she could do. Earlier, she and another female doctor had been called into Lady Harriet's room to witness her signing the amendments to her will. Sir Arnold had been careful to fold the paper so that none of the contents of the new will were visible to those signing it. Caroline had lingered outside the door so that she could speak to Arnold as he left.

"Sir, are you aware that your client has given a written confession to the police stating that she murdered her husband in self-defence?"

Sir Arnold had looked grave. "I am aware of this, doctor,

and I shall be contesting the matter. I do not believe that Lady Harriet, even severely provoked, would be capable of such a thing. I have known her since she became a ward of the court at the age of eleven. Besides, I am somewhat dismayed that such a confession was taken from her without her legal representation being present."

"The confession was not taken under duress," Caroline had assured him, "Lady Harriet insisted upon it. However, I am in accord with your feelings on this matter. As a physician, I do not believe that her injuries would have allowed her to perform the act of killing her husband and I would be prepared to state that fact in the courts, should it come to it."

Sir Arnold had nodded in satisfaction.

"One more thing," Caroline continued, "because of the nature of the case, I should warn you that the police will probably want to know about the changes that Lady Harriet has made to her will."

Sir Arnold had looked grim. "The police must do what they see fit. I shall protect my client's private wishes by whatever means possible. Good day, young lady."

Now Caroline could do nothing further. Lady Harriet would be fed and given pain relief. A nurse would sponge her down with cold water every two hours, in an attempt to bring down her fever, and they would continue to apply antiseptic to her surgical wound, in the hope that it would filter through to the infection beneath. Caroline left instructions with Matron to be called if Lady Harriet deteriorated, then signed off from her shift.

When she arrived at the house, Billy opened the door, which lifted her spirits, and he protectively cupped her elbow in his good hand to guide her through the maze of opened boxes and baskets in the hallway.

"It's like Christmas here, miss!" he said gleefully as they arrived at the drawing room. "I've been unpacking a feast, I have!"

Caroline laughed as he opened a box and showed her some beautifully labelled jars of honey. He picked up the box as though it were filled with feathers and said, "Everyone's down in the kitchen helping out. Cook's giving us all instructions and even Lady Maud is putting stuff on shelves in the larder. It's a right do!"

"That I *have* to see!" Caroline felt the cares of the hospital drop away as she followed Billy down the stairs.

"Caroline, my darling!" called Lady Maud from the larder doorway. "Come and give me a big hug!"

Caroline duly obliged and Maud surveyed her at arm's length.

"Mm. A little thin, I think. All you modern girls are the same! I think we shall have to put you on the same feeding regime as Victoria! Lots of steamed puddings, Cook!" she called over her shoulder to the beaming Mrs Beddowes who was busily unpacking what looked like green beans in glass jars.

"Well, you've certainly come prepared to feed an army, Maud! Look at all these provisions!"

"Well, of course I have, Caroline! We may not be quite an army but we have three hungry policemen – I mean look at this young man!" She pointed to Billy, who grinned. "He looks as though he eats his own weight every day! And then we have two working young ladies, who are far too thin and need to be fattened up and, finally, myself, Cook and Mary and our ample girths signify that we are rather fond of our food."

Mary giggled and Cook tutted with mock disapproval.

Arthur Tollman appeared from the butler's quarters with

an armful of dust sheets. "Where shall I put these, milady?" he enquired.

Maud thought for a moment. "I think that all the dust sheets can be put in the servants' quarters at the top of the house, because we shan't be using those. Mary and Cook are sleeping down here. We're going to turn my husband's old study into a bedroom for PC Rigsby here, and Victoria, Caroline and myself will sleep in the bedrooms on the first floor."

"Very well, milady." Arthur walked over to Billy and dumped the dust-sheets into his arms. "*You* can run up the stairs with those, lad. I'm a bit long in the tooth to be doing that."

"Righto," said Billy obligingly and bounded off up the kitchen stairs, two at a time.

Arthur extended his hand to Caroline. "You must be Doctor Allardyce, Miss; I'm Detective Sergeant Arthur Tollman. I've heard a lot about you from Mrs E."

"Mrs E? Oh, you mean Mrs Ellingham! Pleased to meet you, Mr Tollman."

Caroline shook hands and smiled. "Well, isn't this jolly?" she said, to no one in particular. "Where's the rest of 'the team'?"

"Ah," said Lady Maud, "Peter is rearranging the study so that PC Rigsby can bring down two of the camp beds to sleep on. There is a sofa in there but when he laid down on it, it was a good two feet too small! He's such a giant, bless him! And Victoria is removing all the dust sheets in the bedrooms and airing the beds before Mary goes round and lays fires for everyone. Would you like to go and give them both a hand, Caroline? The sooner we all get sorted out, the sooner we can have supper. It will only be cold ham and pickles, I'm afraid. We can't expect Mrs Beddowes to start cooking tonight."

"No, ma-am," said Cook, "this range will need cleaning out and a fire laid. I shall let it burn all night, then it will be nice and warm for bread baking in the morning."

"This is all such fun!" Lady Maud said conspiratorially to Caroline. "It reminds me of my youth, camping on Lady Marchmont's lawn in the summer with my cousins!" She turned back to the larder with a satisfied chortle and resumed her shelf stacking.

CHAPTER SEVEN

The Serious Work Begins

Supper was an egalitarian affair; everyone sat together at the huge dining table upstairs. Cook was flustered by this notion but Lady Maud insisted.

"Just this once, Mrs Beddowes," she stated. "It won't signal a complete breakdown of society."

Nevertheless, everyone unconsciously seated themselves in their own social group – Lady Maud, Mr Beech, Caroline and Victoria together – Arthur, Billy, Mrs Beddowes and Mary in their own foursome. Mary had laid the table and Mrs Beddowes carved the giant ham. Any awkwardness was dispelled by everyone watching in awe as Billy ate as fast as Mrs Beddowes could carve successive slices of ham.

"Somewhat like a combine harvester," murmured Lady Maud.

Billy suddenly became aware that everyone was watching him and paused, ham on fork, raised towards his mouth, embarrassed.

"Sorry," he mumbled awkwardly, "got used to eating fast in the army."

"Gracious, my dear! It is *we* who should apologise," offered Lady Maud, "for being so rude as to stare at such a healthy appetite in progress!"

"He's a growing lad," said Mrs Beddowes fondly, as she carved him another slice of ham. Mary, meanwhile, unable to take her eyes off Billy, ladled him another spoonful of chutney.

"I certainly hope not!" spluttered Lady Maud, "we have no

more camp beds to put together!"

Following the ripple of laughter around the table, all awkwardness was dissipated and the company settled down to an agreeable supper full of conversation about Lady Maud's "horrendous" journey into London.

"I shall be more than happy to wrap a little something up for you to take home to your daughters, Mr Tollman," whispered Mrs Beddowes into Arthur's ear.

"That's most kind of you, Mrs Beddowes," Arthur whispered back, "but young Billy, over there, may not leave much to wrap up."

"Bless him," she said, watching Billy resume his feast, albeit a little slower than before.

After supper, Mary and Mrs Beddowes cleared away and Lady Maud pronounced that she would go to bed, as it had been a long and tiring day.

"That will leave you and your team, Peter, to discuss your special work in private, in the library. Mary will bring you up a pot of coffee and you can beaver away."

And so the team retired to their allotted work room and proceeded to inform each other of what nuggets of information had been picked up during the day.

Beech started.

"Rigsby and I went to see the forensic pathologist but I will spare you the details, for the sake of the ladies present…"

"Oh for goodness sake, Peter! I *am* a doctor!" protested Caroline.

"And I have spent the last few months working as a voluntary nurse!" added Victoria. "I'm sure that neither of us will be shocked by what you have to say."

Beech shrugged. "Very well then." He spoke matter-of-factly, looking directly at the two women, as if to challenge them. Billy, meanwhile, looked at the floor in embarrassment, as he knew what was coming. "Lord Murcheson was in extreme pain from either bullets or shrapnel that were located near to his spine, which the surgeons felt unable to remove. He was also, according to the pathologist, dying anyway from drug addiction, pneumonia and…er…syphilis."

Neither woman flinched but there was a small silence.

Caroline spoke first. "What did the pathologist note about the body, with regard to drug addiction?"

"Um…Rigsby took detailed notes. Rigsby?"

Billy stood up and retrieved a small notepad from his jacket pocket and read "Liver and kidneys were shot…White matter of the brain was degraded…signs of small strokes…signs of perpetual scratching himself…pneumonia caused by shallow breathing…inside of his nose was decayed…"

"Heroin," both Caroline and Arthur spoke together and startled each other.

"How did you know that, Mr Tollman?"

"Oh, I've seen it before, doctor," explained Arthur, "only in the last ten years, mind. This heroin stuff is fairly new. Some of the East London gangs sniff the powder and when they croak, the post mortem always describes this kind of damage to the body."

"Yes, you're right," said Caroline, "I think heroin is going to become a grave problem in the coming years. It's highly addictive but some doctors still, would you believe, give it to patients addicted to morphine as an *alternative!* And, of course, there are some patent medicines and 'tonics' on the shelves of pharmacies that contain the drug as well. Madness."

"I am a little concerned about the syphilis…" Victoria said suddenly, and Billy looked at the floor again in embarrassment. "Could he have passed it on to Lady Harriet?"

"Oh God! I hadn't even picked up on that!" Caroline exclaimed. "As if that poor woman doesn't have enough problems right now."

"Although," Victoria continued, "she did confess to me that her husband was impotent in the last couple of months."

Billy was biting his lower lip by now, unsure of how to react to this clinical discussion between two ladies.

"Well, that's another side effect of heroin, of course. Let us hope that it has proved her salvation. We have no way of knowing whether she is in the primary stage of syphilis until she displays the usual symptoms."

Fearful that Caroline was about to list the symptoms, Billy suddenly blurted out, "I found out some useful information from the staff at the house!"

All eyes turned towards him.

"Yes, Rigsby," said Beech, realizing Billy's discomfiture, "time to move on to our other evidence I think. Tell us what you found out."

"Right—" Billy relaxed a little "—well, there were four women present: the cook, Esme the lady's maid, a parlourmaid called Anne, and a laundry woman called Betsy, who comes in three times a week. The footman valet had gone off to war and the only man left was the butler, Mr Dodds. He, apparently, had also been acting as the master's valet, so, if anyone knew what the state of Lord Murcheson was, it was Dodds. The women told me that there was usually a scullery maid called Polly, aged fifteen. She is an orphan, taken in a year ago by Lady Harriet from Barnardo's Girls' Village at Ilford in Essex. Polly was…is…, apparently, very close to Her Ladyship, who would give her regular Bible lessons every day, after afternoon tea. The cook was a bit huffy about that, 'cos she wanted the girl to wash the tea things, but she said she wouldn't hear a word said against Polly, who was a good and kind girl. Esme said the same but I got the feeling that she was keeping something back. The laundry woman didn't really know Polly that well and the parlourmaid was two bob short of a pound, if you don't mind me saying, and I couldn't get much out of her except giggling. The cook said Polly had disappeared without a trace, the night of the murder, and Esme said her bed hadn't been slept in. None of them had much time for the butler. The cook even called him 'a weasel'. All of them were very fond of Lady Harriet, saying she was 'a poor slip of a girl' really, had led a very sheltered life, shouldn't have been married off to Lord Murcheson, who was a bit of a lad before his marriage, and that Lady Harriet was very religious. That's it."

"Extraordinary—" Beech looked in admiration at Rigsby "—and you found all that out in half an hour?"

Billy grinned. "It wasn't any hardship, sir."

Arthur laughed. "I can see, Chief Inspector, that you have no experience of how a gaggle of women relish a good gossip – er, present company excepted, of course."

Victoria chimed in. "Well, that pretty much squares with what I found out." She decided to ignore Arthur's misogynist comment. "Lady Harriet told me that she, too, was an orphan and was sent to live in an Anglican convent at the age of eleven until – and pardon my description but I can find no other way of putting it – the Church sold her into marriage with the son of one of their rich patrons."

A collective utterance of dismay went around the room.

"Poor woman!" said Caroline with feeling. "That, I may say, explains a great deal."

"Doesn't it just?" said Tollman.

"Anyway," Victoria continued, "she describes her husband as violating her, brutally, in the first couple of months after his return from France, but then not being able to remember anything about such acts the day after they occurred."

"The heroin again," muttered Caroline.

"And when she found herself pregnant and told him, he became violent, refusing to believe the child was his, and accusing her of having a lover."

"So he obviously stamped on her abdomen in a deliberate attempt to kill the child," stated Caroline. "It's a pity he's not still alive otherwise we could have him hung!"

"Then," said Victoria firmly, overriding Caroline, "when I went to the house to carry out Lady Harriet's request to have Esme send the vicar to the hospital, Esme burst into tears and said it was all her fault."

"Eh?" Beech was startled.

"What she meant was that she hadn't played her part in keeping His Lordship away from his wife. Apparently, the little scullery maid, Polly, used to sit on a chair outside her mistress's door every night and, if His Lordship came a-knocking, would tell him that her mistress was ill and could not be disturbed."

"That must have taken some courage on her part," observed Arthur.

"Exactly, Mr Tollman. Courage that Esme lacked. Polly had asked her to take turns but she wouldn't; she was too frightened. But she said that she used to cover for Polly, so that she could take naps during the day. She also expressed some scorn for the butler whom she felt should have protected Lady Harriet and the other females from the deranged husband."

"So it looks more and more as though the vanished Polly may have been the one who stabbed His Lordship, to protect her mistress," said Beech.

"It would seem so, Peter," Victoria agreed, "but there is one more thing. While I was dealing with Esme, the butler put on his overcoat and rushed off down the street. I don't know if that is relevant."

"I think that butler's a wrong 'un," chimed in Billy with a look of disgust on his face. "Man like that. He was probably pandering to his master. Maybe he was the one who got him the drugs and fixed him up with prossies."

"Hold on, son, hold on," counselled the wise Arthur. "Let's let the evidence speak for us. Let's not jump to conclusions just because we don't like someone."

"Right. Sorry. Got carried away," Billy nodded apologetically.

"However," said Beech, giving Billy a reassuring pat on the back, "it's a theory worth bearing in mind when we question this Mr Dodds further."

Arthur took a deep breath and said thoughtfully, "Here's another theory we might contemplate, sir: whether this Polly did do the deed, to help her mistress, which seems to make sense. After all, Mrs E here told me that Doctor Allardyce is convinced that someone must have helped Her Ladyship dress and get down the stairs because she was so injured she would not have been able to do it herself…"

"That's right," said Caroline, "I remain convinced of that."

"So," continued Arthur, "what with these two, Polly and Her Ladyship being so close, might Her Ladyship not have sent Polly to her old convent − a place where she knew she would be safe?"

"I think you have something there, Tollman," agreed Beech. He turned to Victoria. "Did she mention the name of the convent?"

Victoria shook her head. "And it wasn't written in her bible, either. All I know is that it is an Anglican convent in London and a Sister Mary Francis lives there − or did, when Lady

Harriet was there."

"Tollman?" Beech looked hopefully at the Detective Sergeant.

"Yes, sir. First thing in the morning I shall take myself off to Lambeth Palace to review the records of the Anglican convents in London and their inhabitants. If a Sister Mary Francis is, or ever was, on the registers, I will find her."

"Good man!" Beech then put the leather hatbox on the table and opened it up. "Now, Caroline, if you would like to cast your eye over this lot and tell me what they are, please." He revealed at least twenty bottles, packets and small boxes of various sizes and shapes.

"Good God!" Caroline came over to the table and began rifling through them and opening the various packets and boxes. "Well, these two are Forced March tablets, issued by the British Army and they contain a drug called cocaine..."

"Oh, I remember those!" exclaimed Billy. "They used to issue them before a battle and they'd fire you up so much you couldn't go to sleep!"

"Exactly," said Caroline firmly, "they suppress any hunger and give a man greater endurance – or so the manufacturers would have you believe. They are a mixture of stimulant with some pain relief but, ultimately they addle the brain and make reflexes slow, and I do wonder how many men have been killed or injured in battle due to these pills."

She caught the look that passed between Beech and Billy and inwardly cursed herself for being so tactless, but the damage was done and she decided to press on. "These two brown bottles here, the ones issued by a doctor, are for Luminal, which is a sedative and hypnotic made from a relatively new drug called phenobarbitone. It has been used in my hospital to successfully control seizures in epileptics, and I'm not sure why

71

our victim would have been prescribed this, unless the doctor mistook the muscle spasms caused by withdrawal from other drugs, as being some form of epilepsy. In which case he must be a very bad doctor and should be struck off!"

She looked at some of the other bottles and sighed. "These three here, as you can see, are clearly labelled 'Heroin' and are a German patent medicine for coughs, which was freely available, in this form, over the counter. I thought it had gone out of circulation in 1910, after the German company stopped making it, but, obviously, some pharmacist had some old supplies or knew a way to obtain it from somewhere. That other bottle, over there, is an opium-based patent medicine, usually given to infants with colic, and very often kills them, but you can buy it over any chemist's counter."

She opened a few of the packets, which contained powders. "These powders could be either heroin or cocaine but, given the personality traits of the husband, described by several of the household staff and by Lady Harriet, I suspect it's probably heroin. That, I think you can buy from any chemist, again for coughs or blocked sinuses, and I think they recommend that you sniff it off the back of the hand like snuff."

She opened the last two boxes. "These, I think, are opium pellets. Mr Tollman, what do you think?"

Arthur looked at them, picked one up in his hand and rolled it between his fingers. "Yes, miss, I think you're right. They're waxy, like the sort of pellets pharmacists make by hand. 'Mother's Little Helpers', we used to call these back in the days when I was a beat bobby. Half the women in the East End were taking them just to get a decent night's sleep."

"So," concluded Caroline, "we have a veritable chemist's shop here of dangerous drugs that our victim was probably taking in great quantities, and I'm not surprised that he continually attacked his wife and then could remember nothing about it afterwards. The Government really should do something about this uncontrolled trade. I have one wealthy woman in my hospital who was severely addicted to Vin Mariani – a red Bordeaux wine which included cocaine and was endorsed by many famous people, including the Pope, as a tonic which overcame fatigue. She stockpiled it in her wine cellar, then the Mariani company ceased to exist last year, and her stockpile ran out. Since January of this year she has been hospitalised with agonising body pains, sweats, chills and periodic vomiting. We don't know how long it will take her to recover from the effects of this drug. She drank three glasses a day for five years." Caroline threw the packet of opium pellets down on the table in disgust.

There was a momentary silence when no one could think of anything to say; then Beech spoke.

"Right. Well. Plan of action for tomorrow. Tollman, you will research the convent. Victoria, you will wait here for Mr Tollman to return with the necessary information and he will then accompany you to the convent, where you will ascertain if Polly the scullery maid is present and, if so, you will summon Mr Tollman to bring her in for questioning. Caroline, since you feel so strongly about the matter, you may, in any spare time you have tomorrow, scout around the pharmacies in Belgravia to see whether any of them sold these products and, if so, to whom. Was it Lord Murcheson who purchased them, which I doubt, or was it the butler? And, Caroline," he warned, "I know you feel passionately about this but please, on this occasion employ some tact."

"Yes of course," she replied, suitably chastened.

"And while you are all employed with those tasks," he said by way of conclusion, "Rigsby and I will interview the butler, formally. Perhaps with a little menace, eh, Rigsby? But nothing too drastic."

Billy smiled. "Trust me, sir. I can put the frighteners on, without laying a finger on him."

"Quite. Now Tollman, you and I must get off to our homes and the rest of the team must go to bed."

As Billy lay in his makeshift bed at last, he congratulated himself on getting probably the best job he'd ever had in his life.

Good grub, he thought, nice surroundings, interesting work and, if the butler should happen to try and make a run for it tomorrow, I can give him a good thumping as well. Champion.

CHAPTER EIGHT

Heroin and Holiness

Caroline made an early start of her round of the chemist shops as she was not due to start her shift at the hospital until two in the afternoon. She decided to simply be a customer with an 'anxious mother' who had difficulty sleeping, and see what products the various chemist's offered by way of medication.

There were five shops within walking distance of the Murcheson house, according to Arthur Tollman, fount of all knowledge, who had imparted the information before he left the previous night.

As she stepped into the first chemist's, she was relieved to see that both of the assistants were engaged with customers, which gave her the opportunity to browse the displays and see what was being offered. There were various 'nerve tonics', all containing high levels of alcohol and either laudanum, cocaine or heroin; there were three types of 'infant colic' remedies, Street's Infants' Quietness, Atkinson's Infants' Preservative, and Mrs Winslow's Soothing Syrup – all containing opium. There were various diarrhoea remedies containing laudanum or opium/belladonna tinctures or morphine. There were bottles of 'vapour oil' for inhaling to clear the chest, which contained alcohol and opium. There were Cocaine Toothache Drops and cocaine and quinine throat lozenges. She then spotted some bottles of Glyco Heroin, a pneumonia remedy. The array of products was bewildering and Caroline began to feel increasingly frustrated.

An assistant appeared at her elbow.

"May I help you, madam?" he enquired.

Caroline took a deep breath and adopted a confidential air. "My mother is suffering from acute anxiety – my brother is away in France, you understand – and she worries so for his safety. She is quite unable to sleep at night and my uncle recommended heroin powders as an effective remedy for the problem – but I don't see them here on the shelves."

"Oh yes, madam," the young man said affably, "we sell them all the time. They usually go there." He pointed to an empty spot on the shelves.

"Oh dear!" Caroline exclaimed. "Have you run out?"

"No, no, madam," the young man assured her hastily. "We have simply been too busy this morning to restock the shelves. If you would like to take a seat, I will fetch some from the stock room."

He indicated a row of wooden chairs in the corner of the shop, and Caroline took a seat. After a few moments he returned with a cardboard box, labelled "Heroin Powders" in blue writing, with the shop name and address below. Caroline took the box and opened it, all the folded paper sachets containing the powders were similarly printed with the name and address of the chemist's shop. This was not what she was looking for – Lord Murcheson's packets of powders were in her handbag and she knew that they were all plain, devoid of any printing whatsoever, with a particular type of envelope fold that did not match the chemist's packets. Nevertheless, she felt an obligation to buy the product and left the shop dissatisfied.

The story was the same in every shop she entered. Heroin powders would be produced and each shop had prepared its own product and labelled each packet clearly with its own trademark and dosage details. There was nothing for it. She would have to go into the Women's Hospital and speak to the pharmacist on duty. Perhaps she had been mistaken in thinking that the murder victim's powders were heroin. Caroline waited for the next omnibus and considered her options.

✳

Arthur Tollman had returned from Lambeth Palace armed with the knowledge that Sister Mary Francis was still very much alive and was now the Reverend Mother of an enclosed order of Anglican nuns near Newgate, in the City of London.

"Enclosed is not good, Mrs E," he explained to Victoria. "They may refuse to see you. Enclosed orders don't like to speak to anyone from the outside world."

"Ye Gods! And this is where Lady Harriet was brought up! What an environment for a child!" Victoria was disgusted. "Well, enclosed or not, we must give it a try. Perhaps the mention of Lady Harriet's name might open the door. We'll try that tactic."

"Well, you will, Mrs E," counselled Arthur. "I doubt if they'll allow me within the walls – let alone speak to me – even if I tell them I'm from the police force."

"Alright, Mr Tollman," Victoria said, putting on her coat. "Let's give it our best shot."

Victoria insisted they take a taxi cab as to take an omnibus would require two changes. Inside the taxi, Arthur advised her on how she should proceed, if she were able to get inside the convent.

"I suggest, Mrs E, that you adopt the 'Lady Harriet is gravely ill and she wanted the Reverend Mother to know' ploy, in order to get an interview. Then, after discussing Lady Harriet's situation just say that milady wanted Polly to be at her bedside and see what reaction you get."

"Righto," said Victoria breezily, "I appreciate the advice, Mr Tollman. But what do I do if they produce Polly and then either they or she refuses to come with me?"

"Then you must call me to come in and arrest the girl on suspicion of murder," he said firmly. "There can be no beating about the bush. The convent can protest all it wants but a policeman has the right of entry to arrest a suspect."

"Can't she claim sanctuary or something – it being a holy place?" Victoria asked naïvely.

Arthur chuckled. "No, Mrs E. They abolished that privilege in the seventeenth century. I thought you studied law?" he chided her gently.

"So I did, Mr Tollman, but there wasn't any reference whatsoever in my studies about the rights of religious organisations. I must plug that gap in my knowledge, at once!"

Arthur liked Victoria tremendously. He recognized in her the same thirst for knowledge that he possessed. He reflected that perhaps women like Victoria would be an asset to the police force, once the prejudice set up by the suffragettes had all blown over.

In fact, he thought, I shouldn't be surprised if this war turns everything on its head. Who knows? Women might get the vote after all.

He shook his head in amused disbelief.

Victoria noticed his amusement and said, "Sorry, Mr Tollman, I must seem such a novice to you. No pun intended."

It took him a moment to understand the nun analogy and he smiled broadly.

"Far from it, Mrs E. I was just thinking to myself how much the police force might actually appreciate a lively brain like yours, if only they could take the blinkers off and bring themselves to employ women. Believe me, you would run rings around some of the young men recruits I've had to take in hand! Take our young Billy, for example. Good lad – very good lad – but he doesn't have a deductive bone in his body."

"Ah—" Victoria smiled "—but I'm sure he has other talents!"

Arthur nodded. "He does, he does. He's honest, which is sometimes hard to find in the London police force where the temptation to be corrupt often overwhelms common sense; he's willing, which is a pleasure when I can honestly say I've had my fill of young coppers who don't want to get their hands dirty or do the boring clerical work; and he's disciplined because of his Guards training. Billy Rigsby will always follow orders to the letter. He'll be a bloody good policeman one day but probably not a detective…oops, pardon my French, Madam." Arthur realised he'd got a bit carried away.

Victoria laughed. "Mr Tollman, please don't ever apologise for swearing in my presence. I come from a long line of army wives and daughters. I've heard far worse, I can assure you."

"Daughter of the Regiment, eh?" Arthur was impressed. "What regiment, may I ask?"

"My father was a Colonel in the Royal Fusiliers, as was my grandfather and my great grandfather. My father died in the Boer War and my grandfather died in the Crimean War. I don't remember where my great grandfather died – somewhere in India, I think. We're a family of very self-sufficient widows," she added briskly, then she smiled, "Well, you've met my mother, so you know that."

Arthur returned her smile. "I am a fervent admirer of your mother. A clever and resourceful woman."

Victoria laughed. "Ha! You wait until she thrashes you at cribbage! You may not admire her quite so much then! Oh, look! We're here."

They bundled out of the taxi and Victoria insisted on paying, much to Arthur's embarrassment. The taxi driver gave him a sardonic look, which prompted Arthur to assert his masculinity, produce his warrant card and demand a receipt. The taxi driver wiped the smile off his face and wrote out a note.

As he drove off, Arthur said to Victoria, "Always get a receipt, Mrs E. We give them to the Chief Inspector and he reimburses us. It comes out of the budget." He added, by way of a lecture, "We can't have wealthy young ladies subsidising the London police force, you know."

Suitably chastened, Victoria agreed that she would remember the instruction and they approached the convent building. It was indistinguishable from the commercial buildings around it save for its lack of any kind of nameplate. All the other buildings had big shiny brass plates beside their doors pronouncing them to be banks or investment houses. The convent had a small plaque on its black door, beneath a large, closed grille and barely noticeable to the casual passer-by. It read "The Community of St Martha – please ring the bell".

They looked to the side of the door and there was a large brass button bell. Victoria pressed it and Arthur deliberately stood to one side of the door so that he could not be seen by whoever might open the grille.

"Introduce yourself as 'The Honourable'," he hissed, and when a questioning look crossed Victoria's face he said, "Trust me!", with a sense of urgency.

The grille slid to one side. Victoria could see nothing through the thin slats of metal.

"This is an enclosed religious order. We do not receive visitors," said a woman's voice from the blackness.

"Forgive me," Victoria said loudly, "this is a matter of some urgency. My name is The Honourable Victoria Ellingham and I have been sent by Lady Harriet Murcheson to speak with the Reverend Mother."

"One moment, please." The grille slid shut and Victoria raised her eyebrows and shrugged at Arthur. He motioned to her to stay there and wait.

After a few moments, the grille opened again and the voice said, "Reverend Mother will receive you. I will open the door and you may enter."

"Thank you," she replied and gave Arthur a "thumbs-up" as various bolts were slid to one side on the heavy door. She stepped inside to the cool and dark interior. The receiving nun inclined her head, bolted the door firmly shut and motioned Victoria to follow her. Not a word was spoken by either of them until the nun opened the door to an office and announced, "Reverend Mother, this is The Honourable Victoria Ellingham."

"Thank you, Sister Agnes," said the Reverend Mother softly as the nun inclined her head and left. "Miss – Mrs? Ellingham, please take a seat," and she indicated the guest chair by the desk.

"It's Mrs Ellingham, Reverend Mother. And thank you for seeing me," Victoria said as she sat and removed her gloves.

"May I offer you some tea?"

"Most kind, but no thank you."

"Now, Mrs Ellingham, I believe you have been sent by Lady Harriet Murcheson? How is Lady Harriet? We understand she is ill?"

The revelation that the Reverend Mother knew about Lady Harriet's illness was startling to Victoria but she was careful not to give any indication of surprise.

"She is gravely ill, Reverend Mother, and, at present, is

fighting for her life in the Women's Hospital."

"Oh!" Tears sprang to the elderly nun's eyes. "I had no idea! I was told merely that she was ill, there were no details given. We shall pray for her, of course. What has caused her illness?"

Victoria was perplexed by the fact that, if Polly was within the convent and she had told the Reverend Mother that Lady Harriet was ill, why had she not told them about the murder?

"Reverend Mother, this will come as a shock to you, but Lady Harriet's husband has been murdered..."

The Reverend Mother gasped in horror and made the sign of the cross.

"Before he was murdered," Victoria continued, "he brutally attacked Lady Harriet. He injured her so badly that she had to be operated upon and she now hovers between life and death in the hospital."

By now, the tears were freely trickling down the Reverend Mother's face and she murmured "My poor Harriet..." as though she were her mother. It was obvious that she cared deeply about the woman who had once been in her charge.

"Before she lapsed into unconsciousness, Lady Harriet asked if I could fetch the young girl, Polly, to her bedside," Victoria lied.

"But Polly has gone!" said the Reverend Mother in surprise. "Her uncle came for her yesterday afternoon!"

"Her uncle?" Victoria was alarmed.

"Yes. Mr Dodds. He brought her here – let me see – three nights ago – in the early hours of the morning. It was about an hour before Lauds – our three a.m. observation of prayer. It was most disconcerting! He rang the bell at the back of the convent, the tradesman's entrance, and Sister Augusta, who was in the kitchen at the time, answered. She thought it might have been an early milk delivery, which we have sometimes received at that hour. Mr Dodds was standing there with the poor little girl, who was, Sister Augusta said, shivering and in some distress. He said that Lady Harriet had sent the girl to us for safekeeping as there was an emergency at home and she was ill."

"What an odd thing to do!" Victoria interrupted.

"Well, yes," Reverend Mother continued. "But Sister Augusta was also one of those sisters who took a great part in the raising of Lady Harriet and she immediately took the girl in and her uncle left."

"What did the girl, Polly, say during her time here, Reverend Mother?"

"Absolutely nothing, apart from 'thank you' every time she was given food, a bed or clothing. She was totally mute and obviously in some distress. I myself tried to talk to her – to ascertain what exactly had happened in Lady Harriet's house – but she just looked miserable and shook her head. But she never once cried. None of us ever saw her cry. And when her uncle came to take her away yesterday..."

"Sorry to interrupt, Reverend Mother, but when was this?"

"Between None and Vespers – I would say about five o'clock in the afternoon. This time, I was summoned and I spoke to the man at the rear entrance while Sister Martha went to fetch Polly. He seemed quite calm and said that the emergency was over and Lady Harriet was better. He would not be drawn on the exact nature of the 'emergency' and when Polly saw him and he repeated what he had said to me, it was the first time I saw the girl smile and she seemed to go with him willingly. He said, before leaving, that Lady Harriet would visit us to explain everything, so I was surprised when you arrived instead."

Victoria stood and said with some urgency, "Reverend Mother, I thank you for all your help today but I must leave now, as the girl Polly may be in great danger. The man who brought her here and retrieved her is not her uncle and, as I have told you, Lady Harriet lies gravely ill in the hospital. I must seek the help of the police immediately."

"Of course, of course!" Reverend Mother was agitated. "I do hope that we have not contributed to this dreadful situation…if we had known…we never would have let the girl leave. We are too trusting, I suppose…" her voice trailed off in despair.

"You were not to know," said Victoria, by way of reassurance. "Rest assured the police will find Polly and let us hope that Lady Harriet will recover and come to see you in due course."

"We shall pray for you, Mrs Ellingham, Pray for your success."

Victoria was shown out into the street and she grabbed the patiently waiting Arthur.

"Polly has been taken somewhere by the butler, Dodds. He brought her here in the early hours after the murder and he collected her yesterday evening. Said he was her uncle."

Arthur looked grim-faced. "We need to telephone the Chief Inspector," he said. "Follow me. We'll go up Petticoat Lane to get to Bishopsgate Police Station. It's the City Police mob and they don't like the Met poaching on their territory but I'll think of something."

Victoria nodded and followed Arthur at breakneck speed through the street-market maze known as Petticoat Lane. There were indeed a large number of petticoats hanging up on the market stalls. The market traders, mostly Jewish, judging by their clothing and hairstyles, were shouting out their wares. Rack after rack of women's clothing was on view. Adjacent streets were selling fruit and vegetables and the main thoroughfare was teeming with the working classes of the East End, browsing and shopping. Arthur grabbed her hand and began ducking and diving in and out of the crowd, pulling her after him. Victoria found it fascinating and vowed to return with Caroline but, for now, all she could do was concentrate on keeping her footing and keeping up with Arthur.

Eventually, they reached the main street of Bishopsgate and Arthur stopped. "There's the station," he said, pointing across the road, "Now I'm going to go over there and flash my warrant card and ask to use the telephone. I think you'd better wait outside, Mrs Ellingham, if you wouldn't mind. I may be some time. I need to telephone the Murcheson house because that's where Mr Beech said he was going today, and then, if he's not there I need to telephone your home and, finally, Scotland Yard. Let's hope I can track him down."

Victoria nodded and decided to pretend to look in the nearest shop, which turned out to be a tobacconist's with a rather interesting display of pipes and other smoking paraphernalia.

Surprisingly, Arthur appeared rather sooner than she thought he would.

"No luck?" she asked.

"On the contrary, I got Mr Beech first time. He's still at the Murcheson house. The butler hasn't been seen since yesterday and the cook discovered two bloodstained items of clothing in the dustbins. He says he'll meet us back in Mayfair."

CHAPTER NINE

Dodds is on the Run

Billy placed the pot of tea in front of the distressed women and reassured them that everything would be fine. Cook was not convinced.

"I shan't be able to sleep a wink tonight, knowing that Mr Dodds was probably the one who murdered His Lordship and he could come back at any time…" she stifled a sob.

"We don't know that, as yet," said Beech firmly, entering from the butler's quarters after taking Arthur's phone call. "What we do know is this…" and he sat down and helped himself to a cup of tea "…our colleague has just informed us that Mr Dodds took the girl Polly to the Community of St Martha – an Anglican convent in the City of London – in the early hours of the morning of Lord Murcheson's murder. He left her there, she spoke very little to the nuns, giving no indication whatsoever of what had taken place in this house, and Mr Dodds collected her from the convent yesterday in the late afternoon, early evening."

"That was the last time we saw him," said Esme, "he went out while I was talking to that nice lady who came from visiting Lady Harriet in hospital."

"And he hasn't been back since, nor has his bed been slept in," contributed the parlourmaid, Anne, her eyes wide with fear.

"It sounds to me like he did the evil deed," said Cook, refusing to be swayed from her opinion, "and he's taken poor Polly captive because she saw him do it!"

All three of the women began to sob quietly and Beech looked at Billy in exasperation.

Billy patted the Cook's hand. "Don't take on so, missus," he said. "Let me have a quiet word with the Chief Inspector and see what we can do."

Beech and Billy went to Dodds' room for a talk.

"I could stay here for a few nights, sir," he offered. "Give the women some peace of mind."

Beech shook his head. "I appreciate the gesture, Rigsby, but you are too valuable to the team to act as a protector for these women. We need to find another constable to do this job. Any suggestions?"

Billy thought for a moment. "Well, there are blokes I know through the Sports Association, sir. Hopkins – he's handy with his fists if there's a problem. Or there's Eastman – he's a tall bloke, like me, and he's a fast runner."

"I think we'll go for the fast runner. If Dodds turns up in the middle of the night, it's likely he would run from a policeman rather than fight him. I'll call the Yard. Eastman, you say?"

"Yes, sir. Harold Eastman. Usually works a beat on St James Division, sir. Around Piccadilly."

"Right. I'll telephone the division and get him seconded to this job. He need know nothing more than he is here to protect the females and apprehend a fugitive, should Dodds come back. You go back and tell the staff in the kitchen."

Billy went back to the fearful women and told them the good news, for which he was rewarded with kisses and hugs from all concerned. Cook decided to fetch some cake and they were all seated around the table when Betsy, the laundry woman, arrived. Beech took her into the butler's quarters to show her the bloodstained clothing that the cook had found in the dustbin. Betsy examined them carefully.

"Well, that's definitely Lady Harriet's nightdress. I wash that every week. But the apron – well, I'm not sure. It could be Polly's – but it looks a bit on the large side to me. It's possible that she might have been wearing the only clean and ironed apron available. Perhaps she dirtied her own and came down here and got a replacement." Betsy pointed to the shelves in a room opposite, where white linen was folded on shelves. "I can soon tell you," she said, marching across the corridor. She rummaged in the dirty linen bin, casting aprons aside on to the floor, as she spoke. "All the staff have four aprons, except Polly. She rarely gets asked to serve up-stairs, so she only has one white serving apron. Well, those two are Esme's – see the face powder on the skirts? She wears it, although she shouldn't, and she sits down on her bed to put the powder on her face and there's always some on the apron skirts after a couple of days. She's wearing a clean one and there's one on the shelf. These two grey aprons here are Anne's. She wears them when she lays the fires and she always ends up getting black leading off the grate and soot from the chimney on her aprons. Of course, she's wearing her serving apron at the moment and—" she looked on the shelves "—there's her spare one. Anne is much bigger than Polly around the bust, sir. I know her aprons. And here—" she lifted two blue cotton aprons off the shelf "—are Polly's kitchen aprons and her one, white serving apron. Cook's aprons are in her room. So, all the aprons are accounted for, sir, and I don't know where that bloodstained apron has come from."

Caroline checked in on Lady Harriet. Matron had reported no change. Temperature still high, abdomen swollen and painful, patient sleeping most of the time, except when the nurses woke her to feed her soup and deal with necessities. One of the nurses was applying a cold compress to the forehead, in an attempt to bring down the fever, when Caroline came into the room. She motioned her to continue whilst she checked Lady Harriet's heart and examined her abdomen. Matron was right. There was no change.

Frustrated by her day so far, she made a detour to the hospital pharmacy. She wanted to ask Mabel Summersby, the pharmacist, about the packet of suspected heroin she had in her pocket.

Mabel was avidly reading a scientific journal when Caroline entered and was utterly oblivious to anyone else being in the room. Caroline smiled.

Mabel really is the most terrible swot, she thought, in amusement.

Every time she saw the middle-aged pharmacist, she had her nose in some book or journal – eager to learn more.

"Trying to get ahead of the men, eh?" observed Caroline wryly, and Mabel looked up, vaguely, and then smiled.

"Ah, Caroline…I'm actually reading the Journal of the British Roentgen Society. The Society has finally produced a set of safety guidelines for dealing with X-rays – and not before time, I might add. Animal studies proved ten years ago that overexposure to X-rays causes cancer and degrades many of the internal organs."

Caroline raised her eyebrows at this particular piece of knowledge and resolved to consult Mabel before pressing for the hospital to acquire a mobile Roentgen machine after the war. She produced the neatly folded packet from her pocket and put it in front of Mabel.

"I suspect that this is heroin but I can't be sure and, also, I don't know where it has come from, since it is not labelled as coming from a pharmacy."

"Why do you suspect it is heroin?" asked Mabel, curiously.

"Because it came from the possessions of a patient's husband, who took a great many drugs. I've identified all the rest – they were patented drugs and clearly identified as so – oh, apart from some hand-rolled pills, which I suspect are opium. But this powder eludes me. It could be cocaine, I suppose. I wondered if you could test it for me?"

"Of course, but there are a couple of tests we can do here and now." Mabel switched an electric lamp on, opened the packet of powder and held it under the lamp. "It's not cocaine," she said firmly. "Cocaine is more crystalline and it sort of sparkles under harsh light, no matter how finely it is ground." Next, she licked her finger and dabbed it into the powder and tasted it. She pulled a face. "Ugh, that's bitter! Exceptionally so! It is probably heroin but mixed with quinine, which makes it extra bitter but gives an extra excitement to the brain." She took a tiny spoon and added some of the powder to a test tube of water. The water turned slightly cloudy but most of the powder remained on top. Mabel took down from the shelves a large brown bottle labelled "Citric Acid" and added a small amount to the test tube. Immediately the water began to produce small bubbles and the powder began to sink from the top and dissolve. "My feeling is that this is heroin, which will only dissolve in water in the presence of some acid. It has quinine added but—" she peered at the test tube "—I suspect something else as well. There is a powdery residue there which could be anything – chalk, sodium bicarbonate – I won't know until I do further tests. I'll tell you one thing though," she added, "this is not pharmaceutical-grade heroin. This is the sort of stuff sold by criminal gangs."

"How do you know that, Mabel?" asked Caroline, in admiration of Mabel's encyclopaedic knowledge.

"Because when I worked at the London Hospital, it's the sort of stuff we would confiscate from the gang members when they came into the hospital with knife wounds. They sell it and by mixing the pure heroin with other substances, they could make a little go a long way, and make more money, I suppose."

"Thank you, that's most helpful. There is something else you might be able to help me with."

Mabel perked up in interest.

"I have a patient with severe abdominal injuries," Caroline continued, "and, despite all my precautions during surgery, she has developed an infection, and I fear she is not strong enough for me to open her up again to irrigate the wound. Is there anything I could apply externally that might help? We have applied topical antiseptics as per standard procedure, but time is running out and I'm wondering if there is anything else I may have not thought of. Anything is worth a shot at this point as it's looking terribly serious."

Mabel's eyes lit up. "Wintergreen," she said emphatically. "Try a wintergreen poultice. It contains methyl salicylate, which metabolises into salicylic acid, the stuff in Aspirin tablets. Aspirin is proving to be a good anti-inflammatory and it also thins the blood, so it may filter through the wound and cut down inflammation and also, hopefully, stop her getting any blood clots. Give it a try."

Caroline smiled. "Mabel, you're a genius! Let me know if you find out any more about the heroin powder. Here's my telephone number if I'm off duty." She wrote "Mayfair 100" on a piece of paper. "Out of curiosity, why did you leave the London?"

Mabel snorted derisively. "They had five pharmacists and I was the only woman. The only thing they would let me do was hand-roll pills and suppositories. At least here I'm my own boss and I can do experiments."

"Of course, silly of me to ask." Caroline flashed her a grateful smile and set off to find Matron and order a winter-green poultice for Lady Harriet.

The team had assembled back at Lady Maud's house and were being fortified by some of Mrs Beddowes' scones and a large pot of tea.

"So," said Beech, after hearing the full account of Victoria's conversation with the Reverend Mother, "we have a missing girl, abducted by the butler, who also appears to be on the run, and we have a bloodstained apron that does not appear to have been worn by the missing girl. What are we to make of that?"

"The butler did it, like I said all along," said Billy, through a mouthful of scone.

"Wearing a woman's apron, I suppose?" commented Arthur drily.

Billy paused, digesting this observation, and finding no answer, decided to butter another scone while he thought about it.

"I'm fearful for Polly's life, Peter," said Victoria, "as it seems she probably witnessed something which has put her in danger. If only we had a photograph of her that we could circulate amongst the police force."

Arthur stirred and the assembled company could almost hear the cogs whirring around in his brain. "Did the staff say that Polly came from Doctor Barnardo's?" he asked slowly.

"Yes," said Beech, hopefully.

"Then Barnardo's will have a photograph of her. They take a picture of all the orphans when they arrive and when they leave. Part of their policy. Sadly, not all their children go on to lead respectable lives in paid work. I have had occasion, in my career, to use Doctor Barnardo's photographs to find some right little tearaways in the East End."

Victoria patted Arthur on the back. "Your experience and memory have come to the rescue again, Mr Tollman," she said admiringly.

Ingesting a second scone seemed to wake up Billy's desire to contribute to the team and he said suddenly, "The cook said that the butler had only come to work at the Murcheson house when His Lordship came back from the front. And she didn't rate him much as a butler either. Said he didn't seem to know what a butler should do half the time."

Beech nodded. "That's a useful nugget of information, Rigsby, very useful."

Billy grinned with pleasure.

Arthur took in a deep breath and everyone looked at him expectantly. "I might be taking a bit of a leap in the dark here, sir, but is it possible that the butler has a criminal record? He seems an untrustworthy sort of chap. We may have his photograph in the files at the Yard."

"Brilliant, Tollman!" exclaimed Beech. "Then I suggest, if everyone is suitably refreshed, you and I go to the Yard and start looking at photographs whilst Mrs Ellingham and Rigsby go to Doctor Barnardo's and seek a photograph of Polly. Rigsby, once you have the photograph of the girl, escort Mrs Ellingham back here and then bring it over to the Yard. We'll get their printing presses working on any photographs we can dig up and then, tomorrow, we should be able to circulate them."

＊

Billy and Victoria took a taxi cab to Liverpool Street and caught the Great Eastern train to Ilford. Billy was not as comfortable in her presence as he was with the doctor but he soon found himself responding with ease to Victoria's gentle questioning. He found himself telling her all about his childhood in Hoxton, his family – largely female – and his absentee father, who was in the army.

"Didn't really know him, Miss," he answered cheerfully in response to Victoria's question about his father. "He was away in the army for most of my young life and then he got killed in South Africa when I was about eight or nine. All I remember was a really big, cheerful bloke who always brought me home nice presents. My mum worshipped him. She never said a bad word about him. That's why I joined the Grenadier Guards, Miss. Same regiment as him."

Victoria smiled. "Was he a boxer too?"

Billy grinned and nodded. "I suppose I'm more like him than I thought," he conceded.

"How did you start in boxing, Mr Rigsby?" She found everything about the young policemen extremely fascinating.

"Please, Miss, just call me Billy."

Victoria nodded happily. "Of course."

Billy told her all about life in Hoxton, which caused the smile to fade a little from her lips. "Violent place is Hoxton, Miss. Lots of street gangs. Vicious. Petty criminals most of them. Like the Silver Hatchet gang – they operate out of Highbury way, just up the road from where I lived. Then there was the Hoxton Boys, the Canonbury Boys…" Billy detailed gang after gang who roamed the streets, mostly fighting turf wars with each other and making the locals' lives a misery.

Victoria murmured her distaste and Billy shrugged.

"Anyway," Billy continued, "my mum and her sisters decided that they weren't going to see me go the way of the other boys in the neighbourhood but they knew that if I was going to stay out of the gangs I would have to be able to look after myself. So they packed me off, every evening after school, to the boxing school at Hoxton Baths when I was about ten. By the time I was fifteen I was boxing in amateur bouts in the ring at the Baths – and winning too." He grinned again. "Then I went in the Grenadier Guards at eighteen and I started boxing for the regiment. Army Light Heavyweight Champion two years running." Then the grin dropped from his face as he looked at his damaged hand. "Won't be doing that no more," he said dully.

Victoria felt a stab of pity but decided, sensibly, to be positive.

"But now you have a new life!" she said breezily, "And I don't know about you but I'm enjoying the challenge immensely!"

Billy snapped out of his moment of self-pity and rewarded her with another grin. "You're dead right there, Miss. This looks like it's going to be a rum do. I feel like I'm a proper policeman now and no mistake!"

Victoria laughed and decided to tell Billy all about her spell at London University training in law. "There were only three women studying amongst all these irritating men and every time the professors covered a point of law that involved anything to do with prostitution, homosexuality or divorce, they would bar us from the lectures and we would have to go and look up the legislation in the library." She looked at Billy with amusement because, although she found it ridiculous, she could tell that the young policeman wasn't sure.

"I expect they thought they were protecting you, Miss," he offered helpfully.

"I suppose you're right," she conceded. "But the world is changing and, as this war has shown, women have to become involved in the unpleasant side of life. And when they allow women to become practising lawyers and to have the vote, perhaps we will also be able to change things for the better."

Billy looked uncertain and was about to comment when he suddenly realised that they were at Ilford Station.

"Sorry, Miss, but here's our stop!"

Outside the station, Victoria was astonished to find that the only form of transport available was horse-drawn.

"Good Lord! We're barely outside of London and we seem to have gone back in time!" she murmured to Billy as he helped her into the hansom cab. The small town that huddled around Ilford Station soon gave way to lush countryside, causing Victoria to revise her hitherto unreasonable prejudice of anywhere east of London. "It's really rather beautiful," she commented.

Billy nodded. "I'd like my old mum to move out here," he said wistfully. "Out of Hoxton, Bit of fresh air. But she won't leave the smoke. She says all her family are there and then she says, 'And I won't see you so much, Billy, and then what would I do? It would break my heart!'"

Victoria was even more astonished when the hansom turned into what appeared to be the grounds of a stately home but the plaque on the pillars of the driveway proclaimed "Barnardo's Girls' Village".

"*This* is an *orphanage*?" She looked at Billy in astonishment. "I had no idea! I thought they were all grim places, like workhouses—" she fumbled for the right description "—like in *Oliver Twist*."

The cab trotted past rolling, manicured lawns and landscaped groves of trees and she began to see clusters of large

Mock Tudor houses ahead. "Quite amazing," she murmured.

When they drew to a halt, several girls in starched white aprons walked past the hansom and went into the main building. Victoria continued to be impressed.

Billy asked the cab to wait and they went into the building themselves. Almost immediately, a woman came out of a door near to the entrance, looking concerned.

"Oh dear," she said at once. "The girls said there was a policeman outside, I do hope it is not bad news!" She recovered her composure and extended her hand. "I'm Mrs Mitchell, the Senior Superintendent here. How can I help?"

Victoria shook her hand and explained the situation about Lord Murcheson's murder and Polly having gone missing.

Mrs Mitchell's face betrayed her horror. "Not Polly Sutton! Oh dear me! No, Polly can't possibly be involved in anything nefarious! She is one of our sweetest pupils!"

Victoria assured Mrs Mitchell that they were not accusing Polly of anything, they were merely concerned that she could be in danger because she may have witnessed the crime. "We have come to you in the hope that you can provide a photograph of Polly so that we can make a thorough search for her."

"Yes, yes, of course. Anything we can do to help. Please, come in the office and I shall find a photograph." Mrs Mitchell recovered her composure and offered them tea, which they accepted gratefully. The Superintendent went off to find the necessary photograph whilst a young girl brought in a tray of tea.

Billy removed his helmet and the young girl winced slightly at the sight of his facial scar.

"War wound," said Billy, with a smile, by way of explanation, and the girl blushed.

Victoria looked at the girl with interest. Her hair was

beautifully brushed and braided. Her clothes were spotless and the fact that she was wearing the starched white apron seemed to suggest that she was a resident of the establishment.

"Thank you, dear," said Victoria gently. Then she asked the girl's name.

"Emily, Miss," came the soft reply.

"And do you live here, Emily?"

The girl nodded.

"How long have you lived here, if you don't mind me asking?"

"All my life, Miss. I was a foundling, Miss."

Victoria thought her heart would explode for the girl but she continued the conversation.

"Do you like it here, Emily?"

The girl smiled. "Oh yes, Miss!"

Victoria persisted. "How old are you?"

"Twelve, Miss. When I'm fourteen, I'm going to go into service," she volunteered cheerfully.

Mrs Mitchell appeared, clutching a photograph. "That will be all, Emily, thank you," she said in a firm but kind voice and Emily gave a little curtsey and left. "I do hope the girl hasn't been bothering you with her chatter. We try to teach our girls to be seen and not heard."

"No, no!" Victoria protested. "She was charming. It was I who initiated a conversation. She told me that she will go into service when she is fourteen."

Mrs Mitchell gave a small smile. "Yes, well that is what we train them for. The girls learn housekeeping skills and we prepare the boys for the armed forces. We try to do the best that we can for them. All the households our girls are placed with are thoroughly vetted. Which makes Polly Sutton's predicament so inexplicable."

"Presumably, you vetted the Murcheson household and Polly was placed there *before* Lord Murcheson came back from the war?" Victoria asked.

"Yes. That is correct. Lady Harriet herself was extremely kind and we thought there would be no problem. Whatever happened?"

Victoria paused for a moment, unsure how to proceed, but then decided that the Superintendent should be informed. "Lord Murcheson came back from the war very damaged, I'm afraid. Physically as well as mentally. The police do not yet know who murdered him but they do know that he was violent and abusive in the months leading up to his murder."

Mrs Mitchell looked anguished. "Oh dear. Poor Polly and poor Lady Harriet. Who could have foreseen such a thing?"

Victoria felt she had to give some advice. "Mrs Mitchell, there is a strong possibility that many men may come back in a similar condition to Lord Murcheson. This war does seem to be taking a terrible toll on our menfolk. You may want to give some thought to that when you place your charges in service in the future. Or perhaps you might give your girls some...support...which of course, I'm sure you do..." she added hastily, not wishing to appear critical. "I'm sure that they can contact you if their placement should become... difficult."

Mrs Mitchell looked flustered. Victoria was obviously raising questions that had not been fully addressed before.

"Yes," she responded. "Yes. Of course the girls can always contact us if there are problems but perhaps I should raise it with the Board of Governors, in the light of Polly Sutton's case. Perhaps we should make provisions for the unusual war situation...as you say. We really don't know what is going to happen in the future, do we?"

Victoria smiled, satisfied that she had made her point. Mrs Mitchell handed over the photograph and they made their exit.

Victoria didn't really look at the photograph until she and Billy were back on the train headed for London.

"Look, Billy." She held the photograph out for him to see. "That's what bravery and loyalty looks like."

Billy nodded. "That poor girl's not had it easy in life, has she? Mind you—" he gazed out of the window at the retreating countryside "—if I was a foundling, I can honestly say I'd be very happy to be in a place like that Girls' Village. Good for Doctor Barnardo, that's what I say."

Arthur and Beech had spent the morning in the Criminal Investigation Department, leafing through large leather-bound books of photographs. Arthur reflected that this had only been possible due to Chief Inspector Beech's seniority. If he had tried to access the files by himself – a lowly Detective Sergeant who had been pensioned off and then re-commissioned – he would have faced a barrage of questions about why he wanted access to the files, what case he was working on and what authority he had. Beech had been able to walk in and demand unrestricted access without question.

The boys in the CID didn't like being kept out of the picture when there was an investigation going on. They had heard, through the grapevine, that Beech had set up a special task force and they were none too happy about it.

If they knew about the ladies involved in our little team, thought Arthur, they'd be lodging a formal complaint with the Commissioner.

As it was, he could see that they kept giving the two men

sideways glances. They were definitely not happy being kept at arm's length.

After two hours of non-stop searching, punctuated only by mugs of tea, Beech stretched and look frustrated. "This is getting us nowhere," he muttered, and Arthur looked at the pile of books still to be done.

"I can search on my own, sir. There's no need for you to waste valuable time," he suggested.

"God no!" Beech was adamant that he would continue. "I just need to stretch my leg, otherwise it stiffens up and gives me hell. I'll just take a turn around the building and get a bit of exercise."

As he got up and left, Arthur waited for the detectives to start coming over. He smiled to himself as the first one appeared in Beech's vacated seat.

"What's all this new task force about then, Tollman?" he asked, with no preamble.

Arthur looked up into the face of one Detective Sergeant Carter. A very ambitious man and the one detective that Arthur would have laid money on being the first to try and glean some information.

"Nothing for you to get your hands dirty with, Carter," replied Arthur dismissively. "Just something for old blokes like me to while away their time on."

"Oh yes?" Carter persisted. "You don't know what I might like to get involved in. I might fancy a promotion."

Arthur laughed hollowly. "Well, you won't get honours doing what I'm doing, Carter. It's just old cases...tying up loose ends...that sort of thing."

"Oh? Old cases, you say." An edge came into Carter's voice. "That wouldn't be an implied criticism of this department would it, Tollman? I mean you wouldn't be trying to prove that we haven't been doing our job properly, would you?"

Out of the corner of his eye, Arthur caught a description on the page in front of him. It said: "George Sumpter, aka George Dodds, aka George Egan. Arrested for petty theft 23rd March 1913. Prosecuted at Clerkenwell. Sentenced to 1 year in Pentonville". Arthur realised that he didn't know what Dodds looked like, so he would have to await the return of the Chief Inspector. He laid his hand firmly on the page and looked up at Carter.

"Are you *worried* that you haven't been doing your job properly, Carter?" asked Arthur, looking steadily at the man opposite. "It sounds to me, son, as though you are worried."

Carter looked hard at Arthur, trying to read any implications in his face but failing. His mouth curled into a sneer and he was about to say something when Beech loped into view.

"Perhaps you'd like to raise your concerns with the Chief Inspector?" Arthur nodded in the direction of the advancing Beech and smiled, with a hint of sarcasm.

Beech had arrived. "Keeping my seat warm for me, Detective Sergeant?" he asked breezily. He had caught the looks exchanged between Carter and Arthur, and had decided to defuse the situation.

"Yes, sir!" Carter leapt to his feet, blustering. "Just passing the time of day with DS Tollman here. We haven't seen each other in a while."

"Well, that's good but I'm sure you have work to do," murmured Beech, seemingly engrossed in the book in front of him.

"Yes sir!" Carter moved off, but not before flashing Arthur a look of distrust which signalled that their conversation was not over.

"The jackals are circling, I see," said Beech quietly. "Any

problems?"

"No, sir," answered Arthur. "They've heard about the team…"

"Good God! Not the…" Beech looked alarmed.

"No, sir." Arthur interrupted firmly. "Just me and Rigsby being pulled off normal duties. I told them it's all about investigating old cases. Just boring administration work."

"Good man!" Beech was relieved.

"That one—" Arthur nodded towards the retreating Carter "—is worried that we're going to sully the reputation of the CID, but he's also sniffing around to see if he might get his feet under the table. We'll have to watch him."

Beech nodded.

"I've found something, sir," Arthur continued, "but I need you to identify the man." He slid the heavy book over to Beech.

"That's him," Beech said with certainty. "He's put on a bit of weight since then but it's definitely him."

At that point, Billy Rigsby appeared, which caused the CID men to pause whatever they were doing and watch him, stonily, as he made his way across the room.

"Bit of a chill in here," observed Billy under his breath to Arthur.

"Ignore them, lad."

"I've got the picture of Polly, sir," Billy said quietly.

"And we have what we were looking for," replied Beech, removing the photograph from the file. "Let's take them down to the printing department."

As the trio left, Arthur noted that Carter made a move on the identification books and began to leaf through to find out what they had removed. He sighed.

So unrelentingly territorial, he thought. We're going to have to watch Carter. He's too bloody nosy.

CHAPTER TEN

Bearding the Lionesses in Their Den

The team sat patiently in the library, after breakfast, waiting for the delivery of Polly's photographs. The printing press at the Yard had worked all night and Beech had already distributed hundreds of photographs of Dodds through the transport network to all London police stations. If he was in London, the beat bobbies would find him. Caroline and Victoria, posing as doctor and nurse, with Victoria dressed in her VAD uniform, would distribute the pictures of Polly to all the volunteer policewomen who were working out of two offices – both in Westminster. Beech had decided that the women police volunteers would be told that Polly was suspected of having a communicable disease and that, on no account, should any of the volunteers approach her, but just telephone in her whereabouts to the team.

"After all," commented Beech, "these volunteer women have no powers of detention or arrest and we do not want them to engage with Dodds, if Polly is still in his company. He could be dangerous."

It had also been decided, after Caroline had reported her conversation with the hospital pharmacist about the heroin and its likely source, that Arthur and Billy would investigate the London gangs.

"Dodds, or Sumpter, whatever his real name is, was arrested and tried in the Clerkenwell area," Arthur observed, "so, I suggest we start with the Sabini gang in Little Italy."

"Do you want to be armed?" Beech asked.

Arthur declined with a shake of the head. "In my experience, sir, the gangs rarely use guns. They prefer to settle their differences with their fists, belt buckles, knives and razors. But they won't touch us if we are just making enquiries."

Caroline was alarmed. "It all sounds very dangerous, Mr Tollman!"

Arthur smiled. "Begging your pardon, Doctor Allardyce, but I would rather stick my head in a gang hideout than negotiate with the suffragette harridans that are running the volunteer policewoman patrols."

"Don't you approve of women getting the vote, Arthur?" asked Victoria with amusement.

"I can't say as I approve or disapprove, Mrs E," replied Arthur in a measured tone. "What I *don't* approve of is the violence that some of these women have resorted to in order to further their cause. We've had policemen and members of the public injured and even killed by suffragettes. In 1913, just before I retired, we had three buildings in London bombed and two burnt down by the WSPU. That sort of thing is just not necessary, in my opinion. And it certainly hasn't furthered the cause of women being employed in the police. As far as the average policeman is concerned, it would be like us employing criminals to do policing."

"Yes, I can see your point, Arthur," agreed Victoria.

"However," Arthur conceded, "I will say that the other group of women police volunteers, the WSPP, organised by the National Union for Women Workers, are altogether a different kettle of fish. They make it a policy of not using suffragettes and they are more concerned with women's safety. *Those* women I can deal with. The WSPU lot scare me to death."

Caroline was transfixed by Billy, who was binding his rigid left hand with tape. "Can I do that for you, Constable

Rigsby?" she asked.

"That would be helpful, Miss," said Billy, who was finding himself increasingly frustrated by trying to do it himself.

Caroline removed the mess of tape that was round his scarred hand and began the process again.

"Make it tight, Miss," he said, "around the knuckles – but leave the thumb free."

"How did you get this injury?" she asked, noting the scar that went across the back of his hand from between the thumb and forefinger.

"Shrapnel," he said diffidently, "nearly cut my thumb off. Gave me this as well," he added, pointing to the scar on his face. "But it doesn't matter." He seemed quite cheerful. "*This* is the hand that I punch with." He raised up his right hand and it was sporting a gleaming brass knuckle duster.

"Well, that's going to do some damage," murmured Beech, somewhat in awe.

"Most definitely, sir," said Billy with relish.

"Don't worry, sir," Arthur reassured Beech, "I'll keep young Billy here in check. We won't have any unnecessary brawling."

The doorbell rang and there was some exchange of conversation in the hall. Mrs Beddowes knocked and put her head around the library door.

"Chief Inspector Beech, there is a delivery for you and the man wants a signature."

"At once, Mrs Beddowes," said Beech, following her out into the hallway. A police van was busy unloading two boxes into the hallway. Beech signed the chit and the van left. "These boxes are far too heavy for the ladies to carry," he muttered, to no one in particular.

"They could use the old perambulator," said Lady Maud in his ear, making him jump.

"Beg your pardon, Maud?"

"The old perambulator. The one Nanny used to use when Victoria was small. It's up in the attic. I kept it for when I have grandchildren. Might as well put it to use. I expect we can send young Constable Rigsby up to get it."

Billy was duly despatched and the perambulator was brought down and dusted off. He then lifted the two boxes into the contraption.

"Perfect fit," he pronounced, as everyone gathered around.

"Victoria," said Beech, "see if you can push the thing."

Victoria pushed it around the hallway with ease. "No problem. And it will get lighter, of course, as we proceed."

Caroline laughed. "In your VAD uniform, you look just like a nanny anyway!"

"Would it be unseemly if I came with you?" enquired Lady Maud. "Only I should rather like to see these women volunteers. One has heard so much about them."

The women looked at Beech for permission.

"Well, as long as you keep up the pretence, Maud, and don't breathe a word about what we're doing here, I don't see why not."

"Cross my heart!" said Lady Maud sincerely and added, "What fun!", to Caroline and Victoria.

"I think we should pretend that Polly is Lady Maud's servant," Caroline added, "and she has gone missing after being exposed to a tropical disease."

Lady Maud took up the story with gusto. "We can say that my brother was visiting from China and he went down with yellow fever."

Beech raised his eyes heavenwards. "Just don't make it too fanciful, ladies. We don't want it to cause a panic amongst the women patrols."

"Oh, quite." Lady Maud was suitably chastened. "I shall just get my coat and hat and we can be on our way."

Beech turned to Arthur. "Would I be of any use if I came with you, Tollman?" he enquired.

Arthur shook his head firmly. "No, sir, with all due respect. I know these villains and they know me – and Billy, well he's a bit of muscle, for show, if you like, sir. If you come with us – a Chief Inspector, and all – word will spread like wildfire around the rookeries that this enquiry is something more important, and Dodds will go to ground for sure."

"Of course, I understand," agreed Beech, feeling a little surplus to requirements. "Then I think the best thing I can do is go back to the Yard so that any of the bobbies who spot Dodds know where to find me."

"That would be sensible, sir." Arthur was relieved. He was going to have his hands full keeping Billy in check. Having to watch the Chief Inspector's back would be too much for him to handle.

So they all went their separate ways. The ladies set off for the offices of the women's patrols, Arthur and Billy went about their grim business and Beech decided to take a leisurely stroll back to the Yard.

When Victoria, Caroline and Lady Maud arrived at the Westminster offices of the newly named Women's Police Service, the relaxed jollity of their journey by foot was instantly dispelled when they were confronted by the WPS 'Commandant' Margaret Damer Dawson and her assistant Mary Allen. For once, Lady Maud was lost for words as she shook hands with the two women in uniform with severely cropped hair. Damer Dawson was also wearing a monocle.

Caroline – sensing with some amusement that Lady Maud had never encountered such masculine women before, and was unsure how to proceed – smoothly took charge.

"Thank you for seeing us this morning, Commandant," she began, "I'm Doctor Allardyce from The Women's Hospital, this is my nurse, Mrs Ellingham, and Lady Maud has already introduced herself. We have come here in the hope that you might be able to give us some assistance."

"Take a seat, ladies," Damer Dawson said gruffly. "Please explain how the WPS can help you."

"A young servant girl of Lady Maud's has disappeared," Caroline continued, "and we fear that she may have contracted a contagious disease…"

"My brother has become ill with yellow fever…" Maud had found her voice, albeit a weak one.

"The police have been kind enough to reproduce the girl's photograph and we wondered if it could be circulated amongst your volunteers and if they could telephone us if they spot her."

"Seems simple enough," agreed the Commandant.

"You understand that, on no account, must they personally engage with the girl? We would not wish any of your ladies to contract the disease." Caroline handed over a sample photograph. "You will see that, on the back of the photograph, is printed the warning 'Do not approach this girl. Please telephone Mayfair one hundred and report her whereabouts'."

"How many of these photographs do you have?" enquired the Commandant.

"We have two boxes in a perambulator outside. One box for your group of volunteers, and one box for the Women's Special Police Patrols." She tried to ignore the scowl that this produced on the face of Damer Dawson.

As expected, the Commandant wasted no time in belittling the organisation that, in her eyes, were the 'competition'.

"The WSPP is a largely ineffective body of well-meaning but disorganised middle-class women. However, I understand that you wish to employ every possible resource to find this girl. Allen," she barked to her assistant, "go and get one of these boxes and start the distribution to our officers."

"Yes, sir," replied Allen, and Caroline spotted a small flicker of disapproval on Lady Maud's face.

"Most kind, Commandant," Caroline murmured. "Nurse Ellingham, could you please show the Assistant Commandant where we have left the boxes."

"Yes, Doctor Allardyce," Victoria said with a perfectly straight face, and stood up. Miss Allen opened the door for her and they left.

Lady Maud could not resist being nosy. "Miss Damer Dawson – I believe your mother is Lady Walsingham?"

"Yes," the answer was brief and unrevealing.

"Oh. I met her several times during The Season. How is she?"

"I presume she is well, Lady Maud. We haven't really spoken in a while."

Caroline sensed that they had outstayed their welcome, so she thanked the Commandant once more for her assistance and ushered Lady Maud out of the office to the waiting Victoria.

"The box was lifted out of the perambulator without any effort and has gone off to work its magic," she informed the other two.

Maud looked flustered. "I do believe, "she whispered conspiratorially," that is the first time I have had a conversation with a Sapphist."

Caroline laughed. "It probably isn't, Maud," she whispered back. "They don't all look like army majors, you know."

Maud looked alarmed. "Do you mean one can't always tell? Dear me! I feel my education has been sadly lacking."

Then they all looked at each other and laughed.

"Right," said Victoria briskly, turning the perambulator around, "off to the next lot!"

The office of the WSPP was in busy disarray and a cheerful woman called Miss Gardiner announced that she was the Secretary and would be happy to see them. Once again Caroline went through the story of Polly and Miss Gardiner seemed most concerned.

"We shall, of course, distribute the photographs immediately," said Miss Gardiner, without hesitation. "Can I offer you ladies a cup of tea?"

Lady Maud smiled broadly. "How civilised!" she exclaimed cheerily. "More civilised than your colleagues down the road," she added without any attempt at tact.

"Ah," replied Miss Gardiner, with a satisfied smile, "I was wondering if you had visited the WPS, Lady Maud. Quite formidable, aren't they?"

"Yes. Thank you, Miss Gardiner. Formidable is the word I was looking for."

Tea was ordered and the ladies sat around a desk quizzing Miss Gardiner on the work that her own organisation was undertaking.

"I'm afraid we have evolved into a sort of 'moral guardianship', which some of the women feel a little unhappy about," she explained as she poured tea briskly.

"How so?" asked Caroline, puzzled.

"Sadly, the war has brought to light some of the less refined behaviour amongst women in London," Miss Gardiner continued. "Many seem to have taken the presence of soldiers in the city as a licence to set themselves up as amateur prostitutes. Our ladies seem to spend most of their time stopping women from soliciting in the public houses and other areas frequented by soldiers. Not to mention separating couples in public places where young girls seem to be happy to part with their favours for no money at all."

"Good Lord!" exclaimed Lady Maud. "Society seems to have gone to hell in a handbasket!"

"Mm." Miss Gardiner agreed. "Obviously, ladies, we are talking about a minority who engage in this kind of behaviour. The majority of women in London are hard-working, decent individuals who are doing their bit. But it is the minority that we find ourselves in the WSPP having to deal with. The male police force has no idea how to deal with it. Obviously it's not an offence to give sexual favours to a man, if you are not charging for it. All we can do is take the girls to one side and caution them. Fortunately, many of the armies, particularly the overseas regiments, seemed to have issued their men with prophylactics and stern warnings about disease. The New Zealanders appear to be particularly well provided for," she added and then regaled them with a story about one of their volunteer policewomen being shown a bag full of "rubbers" by an obliging squaddie from New Zealand.

"Gracious!" Lady Maud almost choked on her biscuit. "I can see I've led a very sheltered life! But how on earth do your ladies cope with all this immorality?"

"We only send married women out on such patrols," answered Miss Gardiner, as though it was nothing more than picking up litter. "We send the single girls into the workplaces to police matters there."

"And what do your ladies do in the workplaces?" asked Victoria, fascinated by this glimpse into gritty police work.

"Well," Miss Gardiner warmed to her subject and helped herself to another biscuit, "they break up fights – very common in the factories, where the women work in difficult and stressful environments – and they watch for any theft. Again, this can arise quite often in offices, where women bring handbags containing money and personal items. And, we often have to deal with medical emergencies, mostly in the munitions factories, where the women can be struck down due to exposure to TNT, fumes from lead and other metals. All our ladies have comprehensive first aid training," she added, "but most of it is common sense."

"Do they not have proper medics in the munitions factories?" asked Caroline anxiously.

"Oh no, Doctor Allardyce!" Miss Gardiner seemed astonished that Caroline would assume such a thing. "Sometimes they have a doctor who goes in once a month and does some basic inspections. But we have been petitioning the Government for some time to introduce safety measures and permanent medical supervision but we just keep being fobbed off and told that we mustn't disrupt the war effort. Perhaps *you* could do something?"

"Perhaps I could," said Caroline, grimly.

"How splendid!" Miss Gardiner could sense another convert to the women's cause. "I'll just get the reports we have done. Feel free to take them away with you and have a good read. You can return them when you're finished. There's no rush."

Miss Gardiner bustled out to find the necessary documents

and the three women looked at each other in disbelief.

"Well, I don't know about you girls but I shall feel in need of a good bath when I get home," declared Lady Maud. "All this exposure to the seamier side of life has left me feeling distinctly grubby."

"I had no idea," murmured Victoria. "I feel I must have a look at the Factories Act when I get home and see what can be done about the legislation."

"And I must have a word with the Board of the Women's Hospital and see if we can't get together a team to visit these factories. I've read about the cases of TNT poisoning that are springing up."

"And what does *that* do to one, Caroline?" asked Lady Maud, with a look that made it clear she knew that the answer was going to be unpleasant.

"The nitric acid in TNT powder turns the skin yellow and, if the exposure is prolonged, it can cause anaemia, liver and spleen enlargement, and I shouldn't be surprised if it caused infertility or birth defects."

"I do wish I hadn't asked," Lady Maud murmured, setting down her tea and looking rather queasy.

Miss Gardiner returned with a sheaf of papers and asked Caroline if she would sign a book before taking them.

"Has your research noted any incidence of birth defects amongst women in the munitions industry?" Caroline asked.

"Not yet," Miss Gardiner responded. "Because most of the men are away, we haven't had much incidence of pregnancy amongst the workers. But we do have concern, obviously, over the number of women who are allowed to breastfeed their infants during their lunch break. The grandmothers bring the babies to the factory gates," she added by way of explanation. "Sometimes, my ladies have reported as many as fifty babies being fed outside. Obviously, the breast milk must be tainted, wouldn't you think?"

Caroline nodded in resigned agreement, her resolve hardening.

Lady Maud rose abruptly and thanked Miss Gardiner for her hospitality. "We must be on our way now," she said firmly. "We have much work to do."

"Of course." Miss Gardiner opened the door. "We shall distribute your photographs as quickly as we can, ladies, and, rest assured, we shall scour the city for your young servant."

Lady Maud drew a deep breath, once they were all out in the fresh air. "I'm sorry," she said, "I can only take so much human misery in one day. I felt the need for some air and now I feel the need for a brandy. We must head for the nearest hotel." With that, she marched briskly towards Victoria Station and the comfort of the salon in the Grosvenor Hotel. A bemused porter was left in charge of the empty perambulator, as Lady Maud led the party towards some deep armchairs and called over a waiter.

Once the drinks had been delivered, Lady Maud took a large mouthful of brandy and fanned herself with the dining menu. "Thank goodness it is no longer considered bad form for women to order a drink in a hotel! Mind you," she added, "I do feel as though I am, at this very moment, contributing to the decline of polite society."

Caroline and Victoria laughed.

Lady Maud, however, was not amused. "Seriously, girls—" she looked at them both with a worried expression on her face "—where will this all end? This war appears to have opened a chasm in the moral fabric of the country! Young girls engaged in amateur—" she looked around and lowered her voice "—prostitution…or worse, not even being paid for their services!

One can only hope that the German Navy doesn't cut off our supply of rubber from Malaysia, otherwise we shall have an horrific population explosion!"

Realising what she had just said, she then burst into laughter herself. "Good Lord! Victoria, your father would turn in his grave if he could see me now – ordering strong drink in a hotel and discussing sex! And what about the Commandant and her Assistant? Poor Lady Walsingham... to have a daughter who shaves her head and wears a monocle. How awkward."

"Well, mother, you have certainly experienced a vignette of modern life today, haven't you? Victoria smiled sympathetically.

"I should think I have! And I'm very worried about you two girls having to deal with it all the time. Especially you, Caroline. All these awful medical conditions caused by immorality and war. Not something I would care to have to cope with."

"Well..." Caroline clutched the sheaf of WSPP reports to her chest "...I suppose the scientist in me finds it all rather fascinating but I do agree that this war may throw more health problems at the medical profession than was ever dreamed of twenty years ago. The trouble is that doctors are just not prepared for modern warfare and all its brutality. We are just beginning to get the wounded back from the second battle at Ypres with gas poisoning. The Germans are beginning to use it on a wholesale basis and the effects are horrific. I hear that we still haven't issued our army with proper anti-gas masks..."

"No...no more!" Lady Maud interrupted emphatically. "I can't take any more horror today! We shall now repair to the dining room and have some lunch, and I forbid any conversation about anything other than fashion, the Royal Family and babies. Are we quite clear?"

"Absolutely!" Caroline and Victoria said in unison as Lady Maud rose and imperiously summoned the Head Waiter to show them to a table.

CHAPTER ELEVEN

Awash With Drugs

No sooner had Beech arrived at his desk than a constable appeared with an urgent message from the Murcheson house. "Please come at once. Your constable is gravely ill," the message read, and Beech noted that the time on the message was just five minutes ago. He lost no time in summoning a police car to drive him with all possible speed to Belgravia. There he was met by a distraught cook who informed him, between sobs, that she had been unable to rouse Constable Eastman all morning and he was still, seemingly, unconscious, "if not worse!" she wailed. "We let him sleep in this morning because he said he would stay awake during the night, in case Dodds came back. But Esme took him a cup of tea at lunchtime and she couldn't rouse him. Lordy, haven't we had enough death in this house, sir?" she continued in some distress as Beech made his way down to Dodds' room, off the kitchen.

Eastman was lying on the bed, still in his trousers, shirt and braces. Whatever had overcome him was swift and happened before he had time to undress. Beech was able to discern some faint, shallow breathing and an odour. *Of what? Pears?* Unhesitatingly, he grabbed the telephone and dialled the exchange, requesting an ambulance with the utmost urgency.

By now, there was a little huddle of tearful female staff in the doorway. "Will he live, sir?" asked a tremulous Esme.

"It may be touch and go," answered Beech, as he replaced the receiver. "The constable appears to have been poisoned."

The cook shrieked her distress. "It weren't nothing I gave

him, sir! We all ate the same mutton pie with treacle pudding for afters and we're all alright."

Beech looked stern. "You're quite sure about that? There was nothing that Constable Eastman ate or drank that was different from all of you?"

"Well, he did have five mugs of cocoa, sir," said the parlourmaid, Anne, in a timid voice.

"But we all had a mug, too," Esme pointed out. "It was just that the constable said he loved cocoa and he always drank lots of it."

"Where is this cocoa?" asked Beech. Esme pointed to a shelf behind him.

"It's Mr Dodds' special blend, sir," she said. "He said he gave it to the master, God rest his soul. He said that a good mug of cocoa always helped people sleep."

"And it does, too, sir," added the cook, drying her eyes on her apron. "I never used to sleep well at all until Mr Dodds shared his special cocoa with us."

Beech opened the tin and sniffed the cocoa powder gingerly. "Well, it smells like cocoa but I suspect it has something in it that has caused the constable to be taken ill. That would probably explain, too, why you all slept through the night of the murder and did not hear Lady Harriet or her husband screaming."

Cook looked horrified. "Do you mean to say that that awful Mr Dodds has been *drugging* us every night?"

"Well, yes. It would seem so."

The ambulance bell could suddenly be heard in the distance and Beech screwed up the lid of the cocoa jar and motioned the women to make way.

"I can't lift Eastman up; he's a dead weight. He'll have to be stretchered. Ladies, I suggest you make yourself scarce, so that the ambulance men can have ready access."

"But, sir, what about our protection? We shall be even more afraid of Dodds coming back…now that we know he's capable of anything." Cook looked as though she was about to start crying again.

"Well, Constable Rigsby will have to stay here tonight, until I can find a replacement. Will that suit you, ladies?" There were general smiles and murmurs of relief all round as Beech left to instruct the ambulance crew.

*

Caroline arrived at the Women's Hospital feeling sluggish and bloated after the large lunch forced upon her in the Grosvenor Hotel by Lady Maud.

At least I won't have to worry about eating this evening, she thought gratefully, as she unlocked her consulting room and started her preparations for ward rounds.

She was just buttoning up her white coat when a flustered Beech arrived.

"Hello, old thing," he said distractedly and brandished a tin of cocoa at her.

"It's a little early for cocoa, isn't it, Peter?" she said dryly. "It's only two-thirty in the afternoon."

"Ah, yes. The cocoa. Look, the constable I installed at the Murcheson house appears to have been poisoned…"

"Good Lord!"

"…yes. And the cocoa would appear to be the culprit. I was wondering if your pharmacist lady might be able to do some tests?"

Caroline smiled. "Mabel would love to do that. Come with me."

She walked briskly down the corridor, Beech trailing

behind her, and informed the receptionist that she was taking the Chief Inspector through to the pharmacy. It was down in the bowels of the building and, as usual, the ever-busy Mabel was peering down a microscope and making some notes.

"Mabel! I've brought Chief Inspector Beech to see you," Caroline announced and Mabel looked up expectantly.

"Pleased to meet you, Chief Inspector," she said breezily. "I won't shake your hand at the moment, though. I'm just dealing with some tuberculosis bacterium."

"Er…I quite understand," said Beech, suddenly feeling outnumbered by very intelligent women who made him feel rather inadequate.

"Mabel," Caroline said cheerily, "Peter has a suspected poisoning case he needs some help with."

Mabel looked as though someone had brought her a box of chocolates. "Splendid!" she exclaimed. "Let me just wash and disinfect my hands and I'll be right with you."

Whilst she was preparing herself, Beech explained the situation.

"I've just had to hospitalise one of my constables who was found in a stupor having consumed five mugs of cocoa last night. The cocoa was a special concoction of a man, who is now on the run, and he was giving it to the staff of the house where he worked, so that they would sleep soundly at night. I was hoping you might be able to tell me what's in this tin."

He placed the tin of cocoa on Mabel's workbench, and she opened it carefully and sniffed.

"Definitely cocoa," she said with a grin, "but I do detect a slightly acrid undertone," she added, as though appraising fine wine. "Let's have a proper look." Taking a long-handled spoon, she carefully scooped a little of the powder on to a glass slide and deftly slid it under her microscope. "Did you notice any odours from the body?" she asked.

"Yes!" Beech remembered swiftly. "Like pears, or some sort of fruit?"

"Chloral hydrate!" said Caroline and Mabel together.

Mabel peered into her microscope. "Yes, it looks as though it's chloral hydrate mixed in with the cocoa. I can see some colourless globules. Is your constable a big man?"

"Yes," said Beech, "about six feet two but not stocky. I'm told he's a fast runner, so he's on the thin side, if you understand me. Will he live?" Beech asked anxiously.

"I would think so," answered Mabel, "but I can't be certain. It depends on the state of his liver and kidneys. He must have ingested – let's see…" she looked at the instructions on the tin "…three heaped teaspoons per cup, so that's fifteen heaped teaspoons…my guess is around 10 grams of chloral hydrate, which can be a fatal dose but probably not enough to kill a big man. How long had he been unconscious?"

"At least fourteen hours, I understand."

"Ah, well, he should be fine. Deaths from overdose usually occur within eight hours or less." She peered in the microscope again. "Plus the fact that the man who mixed the chloral hydrate with the cocoa used Dutch processed cocoa, where it has been washed with potassium carbonate, which makes the cocoa darker and almost alkaline, as opposed to unprocessed cocoa, which is very acidic. Chloral hydrate can begin to degrade in potency when it comes into contact with alkalines, so it may actually have lost a little of its strength lying in the tin with the processed cocoa." She looked satisfied and smiled at Beech. "Your man should live providing, as I said, he has a healthy liver and kidneys, but he could have prolonged vomiting or diarrhoea when he comes round, so I should warn the hospital to turn him on his side whilst he's still unconscious.

Oh, and tell them not to bother with a stomach pump. He will have metabolized the chloral hydrate hours ago."

"I'll phone them," volunteered Caroline. "Where is he? Charing Cross?"

Beech nodded and turned to Mabel. "Thank you…er…"

"Mabel…" she gently reminded him.

"Thank you, Mabel. I really appreciate your assistance. That was very impressive." Beech offered his hand.

"Anytime," said Mabel. "I mean that. I enjoy analysis. Feel free to contact me anytime."

"I may just hold you to that," Beech answered, shaking Mabel's hand with sincere appreciation.

"Oh, by the way, Caroline," Mabel added, "I did some more tests on your sample of heroin. It was mixed with hydrated magnesium silicate and cornstarch…in other words, talcum powder. Which means it is definitely adulterated by criminals, not a pharmacy."

"Why do you say, that, Mabel? asked Beech, curiously.

"A pharmacist would never use talc in one of their powders. Not for any moral reason, I hasten to add – some of the disreputable chemists use far worse adulterants – but just because talc is not soluble in water and leaves a greasy film of powder on a glass. Most chemists produce powders that are supposed to be dissolved in a glass of liquid. No, the heroin I tested was meant to be sniffed and that is the favourite method of application on the streets."

"Thank you, Mabel." Caroline flashed her a grateful smile.

"Yes, thank you indeed, Mabel. Most helpful." Beech was truly impressed.

As Caroline and Beech made their way back to the front door, he said quietly, "That lady could be a very useful addition to our team."

Caroline laughed softly. "Mabel would love that. Really she would. Shall I invite her round for tea one day and we can offer her membership?"

Beech smiled. "Once we have this case done and dusted, and we have the tacit approval from the Commissioner to continue, I think that would be a very good idea." He pecked Caroline on the cheek. "I shall see you later."

"Much later," she answered. "I'm working the night shift."

"Ah. Much later then." And off he went, clutching his tin of cocoa.

Billy and Tollman were seated on an omnibus on their way to Holborn. From there, they would walk through to Clerkenwell and the Anglo-Italian Club, where they hoped to find the leader of the Sabini Gang.

Billy realised he didn't know much about Arthur Tollman, who had been in a separate department from him at the Yard, so he asked Tollman a few questions about his family.

"How old are your daughters then, Mr Tollman?"

Arthur gave a wry smile. "Eighteen, nineteen and twenty. A widower's nightmare, lad, I can tell you."

Billy's interest was piqued. "Oh. How's that then?"

Arthur looked at him sideways and laughed. "Use your imagination, lad! Three females, all of marriageable age, all with plenty to say for themselves. I tell you, lad, I find chasing villains a rest from home life!"

Billy laughed. "Garn! It can't be that bad."

Arthur sighed. "Billy, I know you are fond of the ladies and have a way with them but try and imagine being my age, sitting down of an evening, just wanting a bit of peace and quiet and a read of the evening paper - but I don't get the chance. All I get is an earache from the constant chatter of three spirited females – and that's on a good day; on a bad day it can be constant squabbling!"

Billy found it impossible to put himself in Arthur's shoes and replied, "I dunno, they sound like fun, your daughters. Are they courting?"

Arthur made a face. "Now and then," was the enigmatic reply. He decided to enlarge upon that point. "What I mean is that the oldest one gets a gentleman friend, who comes a-calling on a Sunday – which means I can't relax and lounge around in my shirtsleeves and slippers. No, I have to put a jacket on and make polite conversation with some gormless youth whilst having some artificial meal called "high tea". Then, the two younger daughters take a fancy to said gormless youth and start making eyes at him, thus causing the oldest one to take umbrage, and said youth is sent packing so that the three daughters can have a barney that lasts until Sunday bedtime. It's purgatory, lad. A never-ending purgatory."

Billy laughed. "You should invite me round for this high tea, Mr Tollman."

"Never in a million years, lad. Never in a million years."

Billy's face fell. "Why? Wouldn't you want me as a prospective son-in-law, then?" He seemed genuinely affronted as Tollman shook his head.

"Billy, lad, I would like nothing more than if a strapping, reliable lad like you took one of my daughters off my hands but someone as handsome as you would be torn limb from limb before you raised that first salmon sandwich to your lips. Once my daughters got an eyeful of you, you'd be mincemeat. Trust me. I wouldn't want that on my conscience."

Billy took this as a compliment and was just about to respond when a middle-aged woman in front turned round and said cheekily, "I've got two lovely daughters, darlin'. You can come round to my house for tea any time!"

"Thank you, missus!" Billy laughed. "But my boss here thinks I'm a danger to women, so I'd better not!"

Tollman nudged Billy. "Sorry to interrupt, lad, but this is our stop."

Billy gave the woman in front a wink as they got up and left. Several women waved and blushed from the omnibus as Billy and Tollman walked away.

"See what I mean, lad," said Tollman. "You're like catnip to a bunch of cats. You ain't setting foot in my house, that's for sure."

They walked up Gray's Inn Road in companionable silence, then Tollman's tone changed. He wanted to talk about the seriousness of the task ahead.

"When we walk in this club, Billy, you say nothing. Do you hear me? You're there to be seen and not heard. Silent intimidation unless provoked. Understand?"

"Gotcha," said Billy firmly. "Nasty crew are they, these Eyeties?"

"All these gangs are the same, lad; you should know that."

Billy nodded.

"Darby Sabini can be a reasonable bloke," Tollman continued. "Depends what sort of mood he's in. But be warned. If he gets riled he's got a helluva punch. Broke a man's jaw with just one right hook last year. Boxes under the name of Fred Handley."

Billy stopped in his tracks. "Handley?! Blimey, I know Fred Handley! Trains at Hoxton Baths like I used to. I didn't know he was Italian! He don't have an accent or anything."

Tollman smiled. "Doesn't speak Italian either, even though his father's from Italy. Darby Sabini and his brothers – there are four – work the racetracks, intimidating the bookies with various levels of nasty violence. But, of course, their business may go down the tubes if the Government decides to close down horse racing for the duration of the war, as has been rumoured. I wouldn't normally suspect the Sabinis of selling drugs but who knows what these gangs have decided to try in order to supplement their usual incomes."

Tollman led the way round the corner into Theobald's Road. "You must know this area well, Billy, seeing as you come from Hoxton."

Billy shrugged. "I know it but it wasn't actually a place any sensible bloke would enter. Little Italy is worse than Chinatown in some ways. They don't like English blokes much. Especially coppers."

"Mm. Although, I've had my suspicions for some time, that the Sabinis have got certain coppers on their payroll. They seem to be unusually fireproof sometimes. Whenever they have a fight with another gang, the Sabinis always seem to get ignored when the police turn up to make arrests."

Billy's face set hard at this information. "I'd like to get my hands on any of those bent coppers, Mr Tollman. I think they are the worst kind of scum. I mean I didn't set out in life to make the police my career but now I'm in the force, I don't see the point in not doing an honest job. It's worse than being a criminal."

"It's not always black and white, lad. Let's hope you stay honest, Billy. But just make sure that when you *do* marry, your private life is lived far away from the reach of these gangs. I have known a few coppers who have co-operated with them because their wives and families have been threatened. There's bent coppers and there's desperate coppers."

They turned down a side street to see a stocky man

standing guard outside a basement well. At the sight of Billy and Tollman, the man turned and swiftly went down the stairs – presumably to report the approach of the police.

"That's the place," Tollman nodded to Billy. "Remember, lad, don't be provoked into anything rash."

"Yes, sir."

Tollman went down the steps and entered first. Billy had to remove his helmet before he could duck down through the doorway.

There was a movement of chairs, as Billy's frame filled the doorway, and several men, heads down to avoid recognition, slipped out of the door at the back of the bar. Tollman made a mental note of this as he flashed his warrant card at the barman. *Always note all the exits when you enter the presence of criminals,* his old sergeant had told him when he was a young copper. *You always want to know how to get out of a place in a hurry.*

"I'm looking for Darby Sabini," he said in a firm voice, to no one in particular, and was rewarded with a reply from the back of the smoke-filled room.

"Detective Sergeant Tollman," said the voice, with an element of jovial surprise. "I thought they'd put you out to pasture." A barrel-chested young man walked forward with an icy smile on his face.

"Ah well," replied Tollman, "they had to bring the experienced coppers back on account of all the young ones going off to war, didn't they? By the way, Darby, when are you going to do your bit?"

Sabini flushed slightly and the smile on his face slipped a little. "I would love to do my bit for King and Country, Mr Tollman, but I got turned down on account of a medical condition, didn't I?"

"And what medical condition would that be then? A severe

case of malingering? Or would it be idle bones?"

Sabini's mouth drew up into a sneer. "I see you haven't lost that famous sense of humour, Mr Tollman—" he paused and then said menacingly "—despite you being widowed an' all. My condolences on the loss of your lady wife."

Tollman didn't rise to the bait. He merely replied, "I'm surprised that your—" he paused for emphasis "—'medical condition' allows you to still box."

"Nah. I don't do much of that anymore, Mr Tollman. I'm more of a fight promoter. Speaking of fights—" Sabini eyed Billy curiously "—your copper there looks familiar. I feel I should know him."

"Billy Rigsby," answered Tollman. Billy stared straight ahead, his back ramrod straight, but he could feel Sabini's eyes boring into him.

"Billy Rigsby!" It was almost a yelp of recognition. "Hoxton boy? Fought light heavyweight afore you went in the army?"

Billy nodded.

"Well, well. What's a Hoxton boy doing joining the filth, eh?"

"Keep a civil tongue in your head, Darby," Tollman warned.

Sabini began to circle Billy with a predatory look on his face. "I heard you was invalided out of the Guards and can't box no more. Crippled hand, they say. Ain't that a shame, boys?" he addressed the men in the room and they laughed.

Billy twitched. He had a powerful urge to punch Sabini and was desperately trying to control himself.

Sabini crouched and started shadow boxing around Billy, goading him.

"So you can't do the old one-two anymore, eh, Billy Rigsby?" He demonstrated a quick right-left combination jab at Billy, coming within inches of Billy's stomach. Billy felt his heartbeat quicken and clenched his good hand around the knuckleduster he was wearing under his glove.

Sabini continued to dance around Billy and goad him. "What are the police doing employing a cripple, eh? I bet you're no use to man nor beast, with that hand? Is it your old punching hand, Billy?

"No," said Billy suddenly, causing Sabini to stop in his tracks and Tollman to say "Rigsby!" in a warning bark.

"It's this one," said Billy, ignoring Tollman and raising his rigid left hand. Quick as a flash, before Tollman could stop him, Billy extended his arm and caught Darby Sabini square in the throat, hitting his Adam's apple with the hard scarred cartilage between his bound finger knuckles and the base of his thumb. Before Darby could react and even catch his breath, Billy had pushed him back, by the throat, until he had him pinned against the wall. "*This* is the hand that I punch with!" and he raised his right hand, as though he was going to smash it into Sabini's face.

There was a sound of chairs scraping and falling as Sabini's men stood up to take Billy on, but then Tollman's hand closed firmly over Billy's clenched fist and he said, "Enough! That's enough, lad! Take your hand away from Mr Sabini's throat and let me talk to him."

Billy, shocked out of his blind rage, obediently dropped his right arm and reluctantly let Sabini out of the vice-like grip of his left hand. Sabini gasped for breath and had a coughing fit, motioning to his men to stand down.

"I always knowed you were a useful fighter, Billy," he said hoarsely. "And you ain't lost that killer instinct, I see."

"Barman," said Tollman matter-of-factly, tossing some coins on the table, "get Mr Sabini a brandy."

The barman duly obliged and Tollman sat Sabini down at the nearest table and drew up a chair next to him. Billy stood stiffly to attention and feared that he had disgraced himself until Tollman, his back to Sabini, gave him a wink and a nod. Billy relaxed.

"What is it that you want, Mr Tollman?" Sabini croaked.

Tollman slapped the picture of Dodds on the table. "Dodds aka Sumpter aka Egan. Know him?"

Sabini curled his lip. "I know him. Right toerag. Don't come from these parts."

Tollman raised an eyebrow. "Oh? So how come he's been before the beak at Clerkenwell, then? Seems like this might be his home patch to me."

Sabini shook his head. "I dunno," he said, then he added in exasperation, "look, he used to run with the Titanics – that's probably when he got done over at Clerkenwell. Then he joined up. Then I heard he got invalided out of the army for whatever reason, and then he got some fancy job over Belgravia way. Last I heard he was a part-time ponce and was mixing it with a gang up West. I don't know and I don't care. He's a small-time piece of dirt and I wouldn't have him in my manor if you paid me."

"So you wouldn't know anything about where he might have got a load of drugs, then, Darby?" Tollman looked hard at Sabini.

Sabini looked genuinely affronted. "Drugs! Leave it out, Sergeant Tollman! I don't touch drugs, you know that! Strictly the turf and the ring. I'm a sporting man. I leave the drugs to the foreign scum."

Arthur snorted at this Italian calling other immigrants foreign scum.

"So which 'foreign scum' would we be talking about,

Darby?" he asked quietly.

"Look—" Sabini lowered his voice and leaned forward "—I don't want no trouble from the West End gangs. I'm happy at the moment to let them Irish boys slug it out with the King's Cross boys. They leave me alone and I leave them alone."

"Oh, so we're talking Irish scum, are we? Exactly who? The McAusland brothers?"

Sabini looked at the floor and said quietly, "I ain't saying no more."

"That'll do," replied Tollman and he picked up the picture of Dodds. "If Mr Dodds or Sumpter or whatever he's called, should turn up on your doorstep, you would tell me, wouldn't you, Darby?"

Sabini looked at Tollman and said sarcastically, "Of course, Mr Tollman, I'll send my valet with the news!"

Tollman pulled Sabini towards him and spoke very softly in his ear. "If I were you, I'd think very carefully about protecting a man who is wanted for murder…" Sabini stiffened and shot Tollman an anxious look. "…after all, you wouldn't want me to write you up as an accessory, would you?"

"I thought you said it was drugs!" hissed Sabini.

"Did I? Oh no, lad. Dodds is wanted for a hanging offence and anyone involved will be taken down with him, mark my words."

With a satisfied look, Tollman stood up, tipped his hat at Sabini and said, "Come along PC Rigsby."

As they turned to go out of the door, Sabini called to Billy. Expecting a threat of retribution, Billy turned, with a menacing look on his face, only to be surprised by Sabini saying, "Billy, if you get fed up of working for the filth, come and see me. I could use some muscle like you."

Billy said nothing and turned on his heel.

Outside, Tollman slapped Billy on the back and said, "Well, we got some sort of a result! How about I buy you a plate of pie and mash before we head up West?"

CHAPTER TWELVE

The World Has Changed Beyond Recognition

Over plates of steaming pie and mash, liberally strewn with salt, pepper and vinegar, Tollman took it upon himself to educate Billy Rigsby in the ways of policing.

"I'm aware, lad, that you have been somewhat thrust into this job," he said, watching, with some awe, Billy eating at his usual frantic pace. "So I feel it is my job to give you some instruction." He could stand it no longer and put his hand up to stop Billy's shovelling hand in mid-journey up to his mouth.

"Number one," he said firmly, "learn to eat slower. A copper with indigestion is no good to anyone."

"I never get indigestion, Mr Tollman," said a puzzled Billy.

"Not you, lad. *Me.* It's giving me indigestion just watching you. You're not in the army now. No one is going to swipe your food or set a time limit on how long you have to eat. Just…slow…down."

"Yes, Mr Tollman," Billy said meekly and began to eat in an exaggerated form of slow motion. Tollman raised his eyebrows and shook his head. He had a feeling that this was going to be hard work.

"Right," Tollman continued, "now this morning, you were unable to control yourself and obey my order to be seen and not heard."

Billy looked ashamed. "Yes, sir. I'm sorry about that."

Tollman gave a wry smile. "Don't be, lad. I was betting on you doing something of the sort. Hoping you would, in fact."

"You were?" Billy looked confused. "So why did you tell me not to?"

Tollman looked at him steadily. "It's a copper's job to understand human nature, lad. If you understand people, then you know what to expect from them. You can anticipate what they are going to do. I have known Darby Sabini for a long time. Since he was a nipper, in fact. He's always been a cocky little bugger. Likes to be king of the hill. Likes to show he's boss. But he's careful around the police. Especially ones that he can't intimidate – like me. But, he always has to flex his muscles. I knew he would probably have a go at you because you are young and he knew you had a crippled hand. I also knew that you wouldn't be able to stop yourself retaliating and I had every faith that you would be able to best him in front of his men. That then puts him in a position of weakness and that makes him easier for me to question. It's like tenderising meat, son. Don't get me wrong," he added, "I'm not advocating slapping every criminal around to get the information that we want but it works with these violent gangs. It's all about who's top dog, especially when you're on their turf, surrounded by their men. Understand?"

Billy nodded. "It's like that in the army," he observed with a flash of intuition. "Survival in the barrack room is all about your reputation and whether you can be intimidated or not."

Tollman smiled. "Exactly."

They ate for a little while in silence, while the canny Tollman waited for Billy to digest this information and come to the next conclusion.

"So how do you want to play this West End gang, then, Mr Tollman?"

Tollman looked satisfied. Billy was shaping up nicely.

"Ah, now the Irish boys in the West End are a different

kettle of fish. They're not your jumped-up little hooligans who terrorise the racetracks and slit bookmakers' throats if they don't pay protection money. Sure, the West End boys run their own form of protection rackets but they are more like your businessmen. They run establishments – nightclubs, pubs, strip joints – they control the girls, the liquor and the drugs. They resort to violence when someone tries to muscle in on their turf but we, the police, can't threaten them. They've got too many powerful connections…"

"How d'you mean?" asked Billy, so fascinated by this glimpse of the underworld that he had temporarily ceased eating.

Tollman snorted with grim humour. "Oh, lad, you'd be amazed at how many titled people, judges and top-ranking policemen patronise their establishments, use their girls, drink their liquor and take their drugs. Makes them fireproof, see? You can't raid their clubs. You're just as likely to find yourself face-to-face with one of your bosses if you storm in flashing your warrant cards. No, you have to *negotiate*. You have to offer them something in order to get them to give you information."

"But we haven't got nothing to offer them!" exclaimed Billy.

"Oh yes we have, lad. Immunity from prosecution in a murder trial. Everyone backs off when a hanging offence is on the table. They know that even their top-drawer clientele won't protect them if it's a case of murder. Especially if the victim is a Lord. That's front-page news, Billy. These men don't like being in the newspapers. If they kill one of their own, no one cares. If they kill a member of the Establishment then it's no holds barred and the press has a field day."

Billy was confused. "But they weren't involved in Lord Murcheson's death, were they?"

"We don't know that. *They* don't know that." Tollman

answered patiently. "If Dodds is one of their men, then they are involved. If they supplied the drugs to Dodds or directly to His Lordship, then they are involved. Offences to the Person Act 1861, lad, states than any person who aids, abets, counsels or procures in the business of a murder is known as an accessory and may be punished in the same way as the murderer himself. Course it's up to the courts what punishment they hand down to an accessory. They could commute the sentence to life imprisonment – but I think not in the case of the murder of a peer of the realm." Tollman sucked air in through his teeth and shook his head. "No, I think it would be the rope, no mistake."

Tollman took a large mouthful of pie and ate in silence for a moment. "So" he resumed, "that is how we shall proceed. Politely and firmly putting our cards on the table and see what deal we can come up with. I think you need to be in plain clothes for this one, Billy," he added, "so we shall have to go back to Mayfair."

"No," Billy answered, "I haven't moved all my stuff there yet. I've still got my civvies back at the station house in Pimlico."

"Then that is where we shall go," Tollman announced, clearing the last morsel from his plate.

"Tube train would be quicker, Mr Tollman."

"Oh no, lad!" he said firmly. "You won't get me going down the Tube, no way."

"Claustrophobic?" volunteered Billy sympathetically.

"No lad," chuckled Tollman. "I never go down the Tube because it's infested with pickpockets and if I see one in the act, I feel obliged to arrest him, which puts the noses of the Transport Division out, because they think it's an implied criticism that they are not doing their job properly – which it is, of course – and then I get given the runaround as far as the paperwork is concerned and that puts me out of action for the rest of the day." He slapped Billy on the arm. "Stick with me, son, and I will teach you more about policing than they ever could at some fancy police college!"

And off they went to get Billy out of uniform before they went "up West" for some little "negotiations".

Beech returned to the base in Mayfair, after he had lodged the firmly sealed tin of cocoa in the Evidence Department and filled in the necessary paperwork. Victoria was on her own, as Lady Maud, feeling the effects of the Grosvenor Hotel luncheon, had retired to have an afternoon nap. Beech found Victoria poring over legislation pertaining to factories and making copious notes.

"What's all this then?" he asked curiously and she explained to him their conversation with Miss Gardiner at the WSPP about the plight of the girls in the munitions factories.

"You couldn't resist a bit of campaigning I suppose?" he said with a slight tone of concern in his voice.

"Caroline too!" she said defensively. "She's hoping to persuade the Board of the Women's Hospital to do something about regular health inspections."

"Mm. Just exactly when are you and Caroline going to find the time to do all these things?" he commented.

"Oh, Peter, don't fuss! I like being busy." Victoria's face set into a stubborn look that Beech knew only too well.

"I'm only concerned about your health, Victoria," he said. Momentarily covering her hand with his and giving it a squeeze. "You are still fragile."

Victoria pulled her hand away and said briskly, "Rubbish! I've never felt better in my life! You were absolutely right,

Peter, to involve me in this work. I've never felt so useful and I haven't had so much energy since…gosh! Has it really only been three days since we started?"

Beech realised that she had been embarrassed by the touch of his hand and it depressed him somewhat. He rationalised that too much water had passed under the bridge for his relationship with Victoria to resume its previous closeness.

She noticed his downcast look and said softly, "Be patient, Peter." And she put her hand over his, where it still lay on the table. He looked at her hopefully but she continued, "Let's just enjoy being friends and colleagues for the moment. Don't let us spoil this splendid enterprise by letting confused emotions get in the way."

He squeezed her hand again and gave her a regretful smile. "You're absolutely right, old thing," he said sadly. "Friends and colleagues." Then he took his hand away and walked over to the window to compose himself.

"Of course, you don't know about the drama we had at lunchtime," he said breezily over his shoulder.

"Oh?"

"Yes. The policeman guarding the Murcheson house got poisoned…which reminds me—" he broke off hastily and strode for the door "—I must ring the hospital and get a progress report. I'll be back in a tick and will fill you in on the details then."

As the door closed, Victoria sat quite still for a moment, thinking about what had just happened between them. She had just seen in Beech's face a diluted version of the look he gave her when she rejected his marriage proposal all those years ago. She sighed. It seemed as though she was always rebuffing him, when she knew, deep down, that she cared very deeply about him.

It's just that poor Peter always seems to choose the wrong time to approach me, she thought with frustration. I don't know how we are ever going to be able to get beyond this.

Just then, Beech came back into the room with a relaxed smile on his face. "Constable Eastman is recovering, Hallelujah! He's awake and feeling very nauseous but he is able to keep down some water and he looks to be on the mend. Thank God!" He flopped down in a chair.

"I'm so pleased," said Victoria enthusiastically, "but perhaps you could fill me in now on what transpired between him being poisoned and then recovering?"

"Of course!" Beech then proceeded to tell her all about Eastman, the cocoa, Caroline and the redoubtable pharmacist, Mabel. Victoria listened happily, watching and admiring Beech's expressive face as he described the events of the day.

Just be patient, my darling, she thought. *Just be patient.*

Billy Rigsby looked a swell in his "civvies" – brown trousers and jacket, shirt, waistcoat, cravat and brown Derby hat.

"Well, ain't you the picture?" commented Tollman as Billy appeared. "I suppose these are the togs you wear out on the town, are they? Very smart. Right ladykiller you look."

Billy flushed a little. "Too posh?" he enquired anxiously. "Only I haven't got nothing else."

"Well, you make me look a bit underdressed, lad—" Tollman looked down at his own dull grey overcoat, black trousers and waistcoat "—but, I don't mind. Nah, you'll be fine. As long as you show off those muscles of yours, I don't care what you're wearing."

Out in the street, Tollman hailed a taxi and directed the driver to take them to Soho Square.

"We'll see if the McAusland boys are at their club." He looked at his fob watch. "Four o'clock. Hmm. Might be a bit early but we'll see."

When the taxi pulled up outside the Club Tango, everything seemed locked up. It was one of the more salubrious establishments on the street, in that it had a proper sign above the door, there were lights – not lit at the moment – around the frontage and pictures of tango dancers displayed in front of curtains in the windows. It was not, as Tollman observed, one of the usual disreputable basement or back alley clubs that had sprung up all over Soho, whose sole purpose was cheap liquor and prostitution. No, this was a pukka establishment. A fitting headquarters for a criminal gang with pretensions towards legitimate business.

Before he rang the bell, Tollman turned to Billy and said, "This time, son, I really do want you to keep your mouth shut and your fists by your side. Understood?"

Billy nodded.

"These people are far more dangerous than the Sabinis," Tollman continued. "We shall show them some unnatural respect when we get in here. So, whatever you see or hear inside this place – you don't react, you don't say or do anything. Just save it for my ears only, when we are back outside and away from here. Got it?"

"I hear you, Mr Tollman. I won't let you down."

"Good lad." Tollman took a deep breath and rang the front bell. After a few minutes, a scowling, heavyset man opened the door.

"We ain't open yet," he said gruffly.

Tollman flashed his warrant card. "Just need a quick word with your bosses," he said, with a casual air.

The man glared, nodded and opened the door wider,

motioning Tollman and Billy inside.

It was plush. Very plush. There were statues on tables in the foyer, mirrors and red flock wallpaper. Tollman was impressed. The corridor opened on to a large club area, with a bar, tables, a dance area and a small stage for the band. The barman gave them a glance but then continued to wipe and lay out trays of champagne glasses. A waiter was cleaning tables and a lone saxophonist was on the stage, cleaning and assembling his instrument.

"Wait here," the heavy said, as he shuffled off to a door beside the stage. Tollman looked around and muttered to Billy, "This is how the other half live, son. Who'd have thought there was a war on, eh?"

Billy nodded, too overawed to even raise a smile.

Just then, some girls came through the door. They were wearing scanty satin evening dresses and a great deal of make-up. One of them caught sight of Tollman and Billy, and sashayed across, expectantly.

"Sorry, love," said Tollman firmly, as the girl approached. "Here on business, not pleasure."

"Pity," she said, flashing a smile at Billy. "Let me know if you change your mind," and she winked as she moved off to the bar area.

"Don't even think about it, lad," Tollman warned, under his breath. "Just to buy her one drink would cost you a week's wages."

"I know," Billy murmured in response, "I'm not stupid."

The door opened again and two suited men appeared. They were so similar that they could almost be twins. Both had the same curly ginger hair and the same freckled faces that only a mother could love.

"We're in business," muttered Tollman. "Meet the

McAusland brothers."

The brothers looked affable and the first brother extended a hand for Tollman and Billy to shake. The second brother did likewise.

"Detective Sergeant Tollman, and this is Constable Rigsby," Tollman affected introductions.

"I'm Matt and this is my brother Mike," the first brother said genially. His voice was a curious hybrid accent of London and Ireland. "Take a seat, gentlemen," he added, motioning to the nearest table and they all sat. Matt McAusland raised his arm and clicked his fingers and the barman came over. "Aidan, bring a pot of coffee and four cups, there's a good lad." The barman nodded and disappeared. Matt looked at Tollman and raised his eyebrows. "What can we do for you, gentlemen?" he enquired.

Tollman produced two pictures from his pocket and laid the first on the table. "Would you happen to know this man, sir?" he enquired casually.

Both brothers made a great play of scrutinising the photograph carefully. Tollman caught a brief look that passed between them.

"Why are the police interested in him?" asked Matt, looking directly at Tollman.

Tollman stirred and took his time to answer. "He's wanted in connection with the abduction of a young girl and, possibly, a murder."

Matt tutted. "Murdering a young girl, is it?" Tollman sensed McAusland was fishing for more information and decided to give it to him.

"No. Just abduction as regards the girl. The murder is of…" he paused and leant forward, lowering his voice confidentially "…a titled gentleman who could possibly be one of your customers."

Tollman watched as the two brothers digested this piece of information, looked at each other uneasily, and looked back at the policemen.

"I would need the name of this titled gentleman, if I were to verify that he was one of our customers," replied Matt, warily.

Tollman shook his head. "I'm sorry, sir, I can't give you that because it is a matter of national security. He felt Billy stir at this piece of fiction and pressed the toe of his boot over Billy's by way of warning. "You see, the titled gentleman was involved in work for the Government. There may or may not be state secrets involved. Either way, the murder, and anyone remotely involved in it, will be looking at a capital offence for both murder and treason. Of course, all of this is confidential, gentlemen, you understand."

The two brothers nodded. Tollman could see that they were weighing up their options and he decided to give them some more information to digest. "There was also a large – very large – quantity of drugs involved in this case. It's possible that someone was supplying either this man—" he pointed at the photograph "—or the titled gentleman himself with this large quantity of drugs, which may have been instrumental in his death." Tollman fancied that he saw some of the colour drain from Matt McAusland's face and Mike McAusland looked down at his hands intently.

Just then, the barman appeared with a tray of coffee, set it down and began to pour out four cups. There was silence whilst this was done, which suited Tollman, watching, as he did, the brothers silently communicate a concerned look.

I'll be getting some co-operation in a minute, he thought, nothing puts the frighteners up a couple of villains more than the thought of being involved with a hanging offence.

The barman left and, finally, the second brother, with a nod of encouragement from the other, spoke.

"We know this man," Mike said, tapping the photograph, "and we don't like him. He doesn't work for us. He's a small-time pimp who makes it his business to recruit amateurs into prostitution. He's tried to muscle in on some of our girls but they just tell him to get lost. He's even offered them drugs but our girls are not into that sort of thing. We make it clear to our girls that they have to stay clean if they want to work with high-class punters. We don't deal in drugs. Why would we, DS Tollman? We make more money with booze and the girls. We don't need the trouble that drugs bring."

"Besides," added Matt, in the spirit of further co-operation, "our customers tend to bring their own drugs into this establishment. We don't like it, do we, Mike?" His brother shook his head. "But what can you do? You'd be surprised how many lords and ladies are partial to their cocaine. Even judges," he added mischievously.

Tollman gave a thin smile. "I have no doubt, sir. I don't suppose you would know the popular source of these drugs for the upper classes, would you?" he asked hopefully.

The McAusland brothers laughed. "Doctors and chemists, Mr Tollman! There's no deception about it!" Matt McAusland clearly found it amusing that Tollman should be so naïve.

Tollman allowed him his little moment of superiority. "You know you can buy all sorts of potions from any chemist shop. The purer stuff is given freely by the doctors up and down Harley Street for ladies' headaches, m'lords' wheezy chest – you name it. We don't compete with that. What's the point?"

Tollman nodded in appreciation, then said, "The trouble is, we have in our possession some quantities of heroin that we know is the sort of stuff supplied by gangs..."

145

Matt McAusland knitted his eyebrows together in concern. "How would you know that then, Detective Sergeant?"

"The quality of it and the way it's packaged. We've had it examined and it's definitely street stuff. Very dangerous in our opinion."

Mike McAusland looked angry. "If that weasel Sumpter has been giving our customers dodgy stuff, then I'll…"

"You'll what, sir?" Tollman prompted.

"I'll have to have a word with him…" Mike replied, subsiding into an angry mutter "…when I see him…"

Tollman put the photograph of Polly on the table. "This is the girl that Dodds aka Sumpter has abducted. Well, she's more of a child, really…" he decided to throw that into the mix. "So I suppose we're talking about trafficking a minor, white slavery etc."

The McAusland brothers looked at the photograph cursorily. Tollman could see that Matt McAusland was losing his patience now, clearly uneasy that the possible charges against Dodds were mounting up and that they were being associated with them.

"Mr Tollman, we haven't seen Sumpter, or whatever his name is, in a very long time. We don't traffic drugs or children and we don't approve of murdering titled gentlemen…even if they owed us money or made us very angry. It's bad for business. But…" he paused for effect "…we will now make it our business to look for this piece of rubbish and we will hand him over to you."

"Thank you, Mr McAusland," Tollman replied.

"Course – we might give him a good kicking first, for causing us so much grief, but I don't suppose you would care about that, would you, Detective Sergeant?"

"I'll take him in any condition, Mr McAusland, as long as

he's capable of talking."

"Right, well, if you'll excuse us, gentlemen, we have business to conduct."

The brothers stood and extended their hands.

Mike McAusland caught sight of the girl at the bar, who was still eyeing up Billy, and grinned. "What did you say your name was, Constable?" he asked.

"Er…Rigsby…sir," answered Billy uncertainly.

"Well, Rigsby, judging by the looks that one of our girls over there is giving you, I would bet that you are very popular with the ladies, yes?"

Billy was flustered. "I couldn't say, sir," he mumbled.

Mike McAusland nodded and said conspiratorially, "Well, if you get tired of being a policeman any time soon, I know a few titled ladies that you could amuse, if you get my drift."

Billy flushed and the McAusland brothers laughed.

"Let's be going, son," said Tollman, steering Billy towards the exit.

When they were out in the street, Tollman turned to him and said, with some amazement, "That's two jobs you've been offered in one day – and both of them crooked!"

Billy looked embarrassed. "It's not my fault, Mr Tollman."

Tollman shook his head in disbelief. "I revise my lesson of earlier in the day. When it comes to bent coppers – there's the criminal bent copper who's in it for the take, there's the desperate bent copper, who's involved 'cos his nearest and dearest have been threatened, and there's the enticed bent copper, who's offered a better-paying opportunity!"

Billy was annoyed. "Well, I'm not any of those, Mr Tollman!"

"No, lad, and see you keep it that way, an' all."

✳

Back at Mayfair, Beech, Victoria, Tollman and Billy gathered over dinner to share their news of the day. Billy and Tollman were shocked to learn that PC Eastman had been poisoned and that it was with the "special" cocoa powder Dodds had been feeding the staff at the Murcheson house.

"So I'm sorry, Rigsby," said Beech apologetically, "but I promised the Murcheson staff that you would spend the night there while I sort out a replacement for Eastman."

Billy shrugged. "That's alright, sir." He didn't mind, as long as he had a decent bed.

"So, how did your talk with the Sabini gang go, Tollman? Any joy?" Beech was hopeful but Tollman explained that they had reached a dead end.

"Darby Sabini knows Dodds, and dislikes him. He was adamant that his gang weren't involved with drugs, in any shape or form, and I believed him. He said Dodds had been running around with the West End gangs, so Billy and I went to see the McAusland brothers."

"Did you? By God!" Beech knew of their reputation and was impressed. "How did that go?"

"It was interesting, sir, but not really productive. They also knew Dodds, said he was a small-time pimp who recruited amateur women into prostitution. They said he'd tried to lure their girls away from the club by offering them drugs but the girls told him to push off. The McAuslands said that their girls were clean and had to be to work in the club with all the top-drawer clients that patronised the place. They've got themselves a proper cut-glass establishment there. They also said that there was no point in them peddling drugs as all their customers brought their own, which they obtained from their own doctors or pharmacists. They have, however, offered to try and find Dodds for us, because they are annoyed and concerned that they might be tarred with the same brush and don't want their business reputation damaged." Tollman gave a small mirthless laugh. "Quite something, sir, when you have to do deals with villains like they are the managing director of Harrods."

"Indeed," agreed Beech. "So, we are now in the hands of all the people – police, volunteers and criminals – who are on the lookout for Polly and Dodds. I feel as though we are not progressing as swiftly as we should."

"Perhaps you and I, Peter, should go and see Lady Harriet's lawyer and find out what she has put in her will," volunteered Victoria.

"Yes," said Beech, "although I suspect that he will be quite resistant to allowing us to see the information. I should also like to go and visit this doctor of the late Lord Murcheson, but I would prefer Caroline to be present for that interview. I don't want to be blinded by medical science."

Tollman stood up from the table and announced that he needed to be getting back home. Rigsby offered to accompany him part of the way, as he needed to get over to the Murcheson house. So the two men left.

There was a moment of awkward silence between Victoria and Beech when, thankfully, Lady Maud swept in and announced that she would only be having a sandwich, due to her overindulgence at luncheon, and asked if anyone would care for a game of cards?

Victoria and Beech smiled and both agreed.

"As long as we don't play for money, Ma, or matchsticks, or any other form of wager," Victoria said firmly.

"I don't know what you could possibly mean!" replied Lady Maud in mock annoyance, and the three of them settled down happily to a game of Knock Out Whist.

✳

Beech slept fitfully on Billy Rigsby's camp beds. He was in that state of half-awake, half-dreaming and he was distressed. He was dreaming that Victoria was standing in No Man's Land and he was calling to her, desperately, to make her move to safety. Shells were exploding above her head but she was ignoring everything. He felt as though he couldn't move. He was waiting for the whistle to go over the top and then it came…except it wasn't a whistle, it was a shrill and insistent bell. Beech awoke with a jolt, his head thick with images and his underwear soaked in sweat. The ringing persisted and he realised that it was coming from the telephone in the hallway and he struggled to make his legs work and get him off the low camp beds. He staggered to the door. He could still hear explosions in his befuddled brain and he couldn't understand why they wouldn't stop. As he reached the telephone and a cool breeze hit his face from an opened window in the front hall, it brought a moment of clarity. But he thought he heard another explosion as he lifted the trumpet from the cradle and put it to his ear.

"Mayfair one hundred," he said in a befuddled voice.

"Peter?!" It was Caroline and she sounded surprised. "Peter, why are you there? I was expecting to speak to Billy."

"Er…Rigsby had to spend the night at the Murcheson house. What's wrong?" He could tell that Caroline had an anxious edge to her voice.

"Good God, man! London is being bombed! Peter, look out of the window! Towards the East!"

"What?! Hold on while I look." Beech dropped the telephone receiver and raced out into the street. Above the buildings he could see the red glow of fire and high – so high that it was almost just a whisper of a shape in the dark night sky – was a huge Zeppelin, pointing south. He then became aware of some women screaming in the distance and the sound of multiple fire engine bells coming from all directions and heading away from Mayfair. Then he saw a few flashes of heavy gunfire in the distance, presumably from some gun battery along the Thames. Suddenly realising that he was standing in the street in his vest and long johns, he darted back inside and back to the telephone.

"Caroline! Caro! Are you still there?" He joggled the cradle frantically.

"Yes! Yes! I'm still here! But I must go very soon. We have been told that some wounded will be coming into the hospital. I just telephoned to tell Billy that Hoxton has been hit. That is where his family lives, isn't it?"

"Yes," replied Beech, "I think so. I'll ring him immediately. Caroline, are you going to be alright? Has the hospital been hit?"

"No, thankfully," she replied with relief, "and the police have told us that the Zeppelin is moving eastwards now. It has dropped bombs on Stoke Newington, Dalston, Hoxton, Hackney and now Shoreditch. The rest of the East End will suffer too, I've no doubt, until the monsters run out of bombs. Peter, I must go now! I'll ring later!" Then there was silence at the other end of the telephone.

By now, Lady Maud, the servants and Victoria were all standing either in the hallway or on the stairs. Mrs Beddowes and Mary looked tearful.

Beech looked at them helplessly. "A Zeppelin bombing raid on East London," he announced, as yet another faint explosion was heard in the distance.

"Oh my God!" Lady Maud was appalled. "How could

the Germans do this? Innocent women and children! I never thought I would live to see such monstrous behaviour in all my life!" She swayed a little and sat down on the stairs, her nightgown billowing around her.

Beech darted back into the study and grabbed his overcoat, hastily covering up his state of undress, and reappeared.

"Caroline rang from the hospital," he explained to everyone, "to say that large parts of north and east London have been bombed and that the Zeppelin is moving away eastwards. But I think that everyone should go down into the kitchen in case the Kaiser has thought to send us a companion Zeppelin to target other parts of London."

"He wouldn't dare bomb his own cousins in Buckingham Palace!" an outraged Lady Maud ventured.

"Is the King at the Palace?" wondered Victoria. "German spies could quite easily find out if the Royal Family are absent and the Kaiser could choose to bomb us while they're away."

Beech reassured them all that the King had announced that he would stay in Buckingham Palace for the duration of the war. "Now, ladies, please, down into the basement. Have yourselves a hot cup of tea and calm down. I must go over to the Murcheson house and tell Constable Rigsby what has happened. I shall bring the Murcheson staff back here for the night, if that is suitable, Lady Maud." She nodded and murmured her approval. "Good. Then I can keep an eye on all of you. But, please remember…our work here is secret, so not a word to the Murcheson servants, please."

"The world has changed beyond recognition tonight," said Lady Maud disconsolately. "Completely beyond recognition."

"Peter, how will you get to Belgravia?" asked Victoria anxiously.

"I shall walk, Victoria," he said firmly. "I think that taxis and police cars will have better things to do than ferry me a mile or so," and he went to get dressed.

The women huddled in the kitchen around the table whilst Mrs Beddowes put a kettle of water on the hob.

"If you ask me, the Germans are all vile criminals!" she said with feeling, as she banged the kettle down on the stove. "First it's gassing our men at the front, then it's bombing women and children in their beds. It's…"she struggled to find the word "…inhuman. That's what it is. Inhuman."

Everyone agreed.

"My husband would have been beside himself with anger," reflected Lady Maud. "Any decent soldier would. To take the battlefield to the home and hearth is deplorable. I hope the Kaiser is proud of himself."

"To think he's related to our own Royal Family. The King must be so ashamed tonight."

Beech stuck his head around the door. "I'm off, ladies," he announced. "Please stay indoors and keep safe. I shall be back as soon as I can. I really don't feel that the Germans will do any more bombing of London tonight," he added, "but, sadly, I don't believe it will be the last sortie they make. I think tonight was a test and, having been successful, they will be back for more."

As he strode through the streets, Beech could see that lights were on in all the houses in Mayfair when they should have been quiet and dark.

Yes, he thought, reflecting on Maud's words from earlier, the world has changed, and pretty soon the Government is going to have to issue a blackout order to stop the Germans finding their targets so easily.

In the distance, as he walked across Hyde Park Corner and looked to his left, he could just make out the shape, very high up, of the silently retreating Zeppelin, making its ponderous way towards the mouth of the River Thames.

And we have to find a way to stop them, he thought, his mind racing. More than just one-pound guns. We have to get up there in the sky and blow them up.

But he knew that the fragile aeroplanes of the Royal Flying Corps could never get up as high as a Zeppelin and he wondered what on earth could be used instead. There was also the question of *knowing* that they were coming. Zeppelins were silent-running and so high up that it was almost impossible to spot them approaching. Beech reflected that he had heard that Paris was surrounded by barrage balloons which were tethered to the ground and filled with helium, like the Zeppelins. The balloons and their lines prevented the airships from getting low enough to drop their bombs. London would have to think about such measures now. Passing behind Buckingham Palace, he caught a glimmer of light through the trees. *I expect the King is having a sleepless night, like the rest of us,* he thought, as he quickened his stride towards Belgravia and the unpleasant task of telling Billy Rigsby his family may have been wiped out by German bombs.

CHAPTER THIRTEEN

"It's the Poor What Always Cops It"

Billy was in a state of panic. When Beech had turned up at the Murcheson house, banging on the basement door, fit to wake the dead, Billy had lurched from his bed, wondering what had happened. He'd been expecting to be told that Dodds or the girl had been found – or something to do with the case – but when Beech had told him gravely that Hoxton had been bombed by a Zeppelin, his world had fallen apart. He couldn't breathe and Beech, recognising a case of shock from his months in the trenches, had forced a brandy down Billy's throat and helped him dress, talking to him all the while – reassuring him that he would manage, he would cope.

"We'll go to the nearest fire station and see if they have a tender going out and can give you a lift," Beech had said. "If necessary, I'll call the Yard and see if they can get a vehicle out. We'll get you there, Billy. By hook or by crook."

Beech had propelled Billy towards the door and called back to the trembling Cook, "I'll be back as soon as I can! Get your ladies dressed and ready. I shall be taking you to Mayfair as soon as I get back." Then he had gripped the stumbling Billy firmly under the elbow and supported him towards the fire station near Victoria Station. All the way there he had kept up his constant reassuring, morale-boosting talk until it gradually began to seep into Billy's brain and he began to respond.

Billy had turned a tear-stained face towards Beech and finally said, "I want to kill a German with my bare hands, sir. I want to kill someone…" then he had trailed off, realising how stupid and ineffectual he had sounded.

Beech had been encouraged. Anger was good. Anger was motivating. "We all want to kill a German tonight, Rigsby. But you find your mother and her sisters and sort them out first, alright?"

Billy had nodded and wiped his tears from his face.

Beech's instincts had been right. When they got to the fire station, the firemen were just loading up more hoses for another run to the East End.

Beech had flashed his warrant card. "I've got an officer here who has family in Hoxton. Can you give him a lift?"

A fireman had jumped down and shouted, "No problem! Can he get up on the top of the tender with my men?"

Beech had helped Billy up on to the raised area behind the driving seat.

"Mind your head on the ladder, son," the fireman had shouted above the din of the ladder being winched into its travelling position in between the firemen and just above their heads. The fireman behind Billy, sensing that he was a bit insecure, had grasped him firmly on the shoulder and had said, "I'll keep hold of you, lad! We don't want to have to stop and pick you up off the road!"

Beech had shouted, "Let me know how you get on!" as the fire engine growled into life and started clanging its bell.

So now Billy was speeding towards Hoxton, grateful that the noise of the bell was preventing him from focusing his thoughts into something terrible and unable to cry because his face was bearing the full brunt of the wind caused by the speed at which they were travelling.

His chest grew tighter as he could now smell the smoke of countless fires and it brought back the terrors of Mons and the choking smoke of the battlefield. He could feel his body trembling and, obviously, so could the sympathetic fireman behind who simply placed his other hand firmly on Billy's other shoulder and patted it.

As the fire engine turned into the Goswell Road, Billy could see the fires burning and he couldn't swallow. All he could think about was his mother and her little dog, her beloved Timmy, and how he would cope if he had to drag her body out of the rubble. He could see that the fire engine was going to go past the end of his road and he yelled, "Can you let me off here!", to the driver. The engine slowed and Billy scrabbled off, falling over as he hit the road. He stood upright and waved a grateful thanks to the crew as the fire engine gathered speed again, then he began to run, faster than he had ever run in his life.

Number twenty five…number twenty seven…number twenty nine…the house was still there! Tears began to run down his face. "Mum! Mum!" he started screaming and he kicked down the front door with such force that it splintered one of the hinges. "Mum!" he yelled again and suddenly, like a bolt of lightning, a little brown-and-white terrier hurtled down the hallway at him, yapping manically, and threw himself into his arms. The familiar figure of his mother, in her dressing gown, her hair in rags, appeared in the kitchen doorway,

"Look what you've done to my front door, Billy!" she said in annoyance as her son flung himself to his knees and sobbed with relief. "There, there, son," she said cradling his head to her stomach, "don't take on so. Me and Timmy's alright. Your old mum's too tough for the Germans and no mistake."

Billy laughed through his tears and stood up. "You gave me a fright, ma," he said, holding back yet more tears. "I thought I was going to have to dig your lifeless body out of the rubble."

"Gawd, you've got some imagination, you have," she said softly, stroking his hair. "Come and sit down, son, and have a tot of gin. I can't offer you no cup of tea, 'cos they've turned the gas off."

"What about Sissy and Ada?" Billy said, wiping his face with his hands and enquiring after his aunts.

"Both fine. Ada's missed it all, on account of her visiting her sister-in-law in Brighton this week, and Sissy's just gone up the road to get a jug of tea from them ladies running a tea stall, bless 'em. You got to hand it to the British, Billy. Whenever there's an emergency, there'll always be some kindly souls out there running a tea stall. They come over from Liverpool Street Station, Sissy said, where they were serving tea to returning sailors. Good job they come over here too, 'cos we hear that bloody Zeppelin is heading over that way now. God! You'd think it would have run out of bombs by this time, wouldn't you?"

A small, wet nose nuzzled Billy's hand and he leant down and picked up Timmy.

"Poor little soul," said Billy's mum. "He didn't know what was happening when the bombs dropped. I thought he was going to have a heart attack. I couldn't bear it if my little Timmy died," and for the first time that night, she allowed herself a little spell of crying. Billy, his mum and the dog, huddled together in a grateful embrace, which was only broken by a raucous voice calling, "Bloody hell! What happened to your door, Elsie?!"

"Oh, here we go, Sissy's back. Man the lifeboats." Billy's mum laughed.

Sissy appeared, carrying a large metal jug filled with steaming hot tea. Her face was a picture of astonishment. "The Kaiser been round and personally smashed your front door in, Elsie?" she asked.

Elsie chuckled. "Don't be daft. It was Billy. He thought his old mum was a gonner and he kicked the door in!'"

Sissy put down the jug and gave Billy a big hug and a large wet kiss on his cheek. "Soppy sod," she said, brushing away a stray tear. "You look like you've been dragged through a hedge backwards," she said, producing a handkerchief, spitting on it and proceeding to clean Billy's face. He felt like he was five years old again and screwed up his face.

"Leave it out, Aunty!" he protested, trying to stand up, but she pushed him back onto the chair and continued to wipe the tear stains from his cheeks. "There!" she pronounced herself finished. "Time for a cup of tea, I think. I'm that parched, I feel as though I've just walked through a desert." She busied herself finding cups and pouring tea.

They all sat and drank, in silence, listening to the shouting and general mayhem in the street, punctuated by a not-so-distant explosion.

"Half of the next street's gone," said Sissy quietly. She tried hard not to cry, and added brokenly, "Those six Bradshaw kids at number sixty-two and old Arthur at number ninety." She set her face hard and said bitterly, "It's always the poor what cops it. I don't suppose they've had any bombs fall on the fancy mansions up West."

Everyone bowed their heads and stared into their cups of tea, unable to think of anything to say.

Finally Elsie said, "We've been lucky tonight. I shall say a prayer for those who were lost."

Billy stirred. "Maybe I should go outside and help." He stood up and buttoned up his greatcoat.

Elsie grabbed his arm. "It's too dangerous, Billy, I don't want to be mourning you as well!"

"Ma," he said reassuringly, patting her hand, "the Zeppelin has moved away. It's not dangerous anymore. I'm a policeman and there's people out there who need help. You two stay here with the dog and try and get some rest. I'll be back before morning and we'll sort something out. Alright, Mum?"

Elsie nodded.

"You be careful out there!" called Sissy, as Billy walked down the hallway,

"And put that bloody door up straight!" she bawled, as a parting shot. Billy grinned and lifted the door on its one remaining hinge and propped it up in its frame. Then he turned, put his helmet on, and braced himself for action.

Sissy was right. Their street was untouched, save for a few windows blown in and the odd crumbled chimney. It was the next street that had borne the brunt of the bombs and, as he looked towards the horizon, it seemed as though north of Hoxton was in flames.

Billy strode towards the collapsed houses and saw that there was a fire crew and three policemen shifting rubble. He tapped the nearest policeman on the shoulder. "Want some help?" he said briskly.

The policeman nodded. "Start shifting rubble as fast as you can, mate. We're hoping for some live ones."

Billy took off his greatcoat and helmet, laid them at the side of the road and started work.

By five o'clock in the morning, Billy, and all the other men, were exhausted. A pale dawn had managed to filter through the pall of smoke and dust that hung over the north and east of London. The Zeppelin had long disappeared out over the horizon and fires were now burning in Shoreditch and Whitechapel. The night had been punctuated by constant ringing bells from fire engines and ambulances, ferrying backwards and forwards with firemen, doctors and nurses. The wounded had gradually come out of their houses – people who had been blown across their front room by the force of the blast but had been too frightened to come out until they were sure that the Zeppelin had passed. Nurses were dealing with cuts and bruises at the side of the road, while those with broken bones were loaded into ambulances.

Clearing the rubble had been a fruitless task. Three dead bodies had been removed but, so far, no living beings except for one cat that had survived in a pocket of air underneath what had once been a staircase. One of the men gave it some water and, after a few hesitant steps, it had curled up on Billy's greatcoat and fallen asleep. The Liverpool Street tea wagon had drawn up close by and men were pausing to gratefully take mouthfuls of tea. One of the recently arrived firemen said to Billy, "You look like hell, lad. Take a break and let the new blokes take over."

Billy sank to the ground gratefully by his greatcoat and looked at the sleeping cat. He was wondering what to do about it, when a young girl with a bandaged arm came up and asked, "Is that your cat, mister?"

Billy shook his head. "Pulled it out of the ruins over there." He pointed at the furthest pile of rubble, which now seemed much smaller.

"It's my grandma's then," she said dully and she picked up the cat, stroking it and murmuring, "Come on, Samson," as she walked away.

Poor little beggar's lost her grandma but she's not crying, thought Billy, and, despite his tiredness, he felt a small surge of anger once more and decided to go back to his mother's house.

He found Sissy and his mother asleep, slumped over the

kitchen table with the dog at their feet. He gently picked up the metal jug and tiptoed out to get a refill for them. "Don't put too much milk in it," whispered Sissy, without raising her head and Billy smiled.

After Billy had left for Hoxton, Beech had walked back to the Murcheson house to find a small rebellion on his hands. The three women were dressed and had hastily packed bags at their feet but Cook had announced that she and Anne were leaving London and the Murcheson house for good.

"Lady Harriet's likely to die, sir. There's no one here to cook for and now the Germans are dropping bombs on us. I'm off to my brother's house in Surrey and Anne here has got family in Wales. Sorry, sir, but we see no point in staying." The woman had been adamant and Beech had been powerless to persuade her otherwise. Esme had been tearful and didn't want to stay in the house on her own, so Beech had managed to persuade her to come back to Mayfair with him. The house had been locked up and they had all gone their separate ways – Cook to Victoria Station, Anne to wait for a night bus to Paddington Station, Beech and Esme departing on foot to Mayfair.

By the time they had reached Mayfair, Beech was worrying about the Belgravia house being empty and the possibility of losing the opportunity to apprehend Dodds, should he return. So, with a cursory explanation to Victoria regarding the situation, he had turned on his heel and had walked back, yet again, to Belgravia.

Unable to sleep, he had lain awake on Dodds' bed, fully clothed, until the light began to creep into the basement and he had decided to make some tea and find something to eat.

Looking at the kitchen clock, he had realised that it was now almost seven in the morning. It was whilst he was investigating the multitude of cupboards in the kitchen that he was startled by banging on the basement door and he opened it to find a dirty and dishevelled Billy Rigsby in front of him, carrying two bags and flanked by two women and a dog.

"I didn't know where else to take them, sir," said Billy, apologetically.

A relieved Beech suddenly found himself in the midst of a whirlwind of activity. Billy's mother and aunt, who had apparently both been in service in their youth, settled in, and it wasn't long before they were producing food from all quarters of the kitchen, whilst Billy was making up the sluggish fire that Cook had left to burn itself out in the stove.

"Oh thank you for being so kind, sir," chattered Elsie, as she took a large cast-iron frying pan down from a hook on the wall. "We was beside ourselves in Hoxton, what with no gas and running water. Billy said you wouldn't mind if we stopped here for a bit. We won't be no trouble – will we, Sissy?"

"No," Sissy added, "we'll keep the place spick and span and we don't mind sleeping in a cupboard, if that's all there is. And Timmy here is no trouble."

"I think he wants to go out, Ma," said Billy, nodding at the dog, who was whining by the back door.

Elsie unlocked the door and let the little terrier out. "Sissy!" she shrieked, making Beech jump. "Look at this garden!"

Sissy rushed over to admire the view. "That dog of yours will think he's died and gone to heaven," she said in wonder.

Billy sat down opposite Beech and looked apologetic again. "Sorry, sir. The ladies in my family are a bit loud."

Beech grinned. "Don't apologise, Rigsby. It's delightful. I am so relieved that they are alive and well. How was it in Hoxton?"

"Grim, sir," and Billy explained all about the damage, the dead bodies, the smoke, fire, explosions and general horror that he had experienced. "The East End was lucky last night, if you can call it that, sir," he added. "One of the ambulance drivers said that he had heard at the London Hospital that there were only a couple of dozen killed. It could have been much more."

Beech nodded soberly. "I fear that they will come back," he said. Then he looked around at Elsie, who was beginning to fry bacon. "That smells good!" he exclaimed.

"I'm going to do us all a big fry-up, Mr Beech," she said cheerfully. "Ooh, that dog can smell bacon a mile off!" she added as Timmy came skittering in through the open back door, tail wagging. Sissy appeared with some eggs and mushrooms and the two of them began some serious work, frying up, slicing and buttering bread.

"I expect we'll have a furious cook descend on us from upstairs in a minute," warned Sissy.

"Er...no, you won't," answered Beech and then gave a detailed explanation of the staff mutiny. "So you will have the house to yourselves for the foreseeable future," he added.

When they were all tucking into the feast laid before them and Timmy had been given his own saucer of chopped up bacon, Beech decided to explain the whole case of the Murcheson murder and the subsequent events of the last three days. Elsie and Sissy tutted between mouthfuls.

"So how is this poor Lady Harriet?" asked Elsie.

"Suspended between life and death, the last I heard, and no news either way since," replied Beech, helping himself to another slice of bread to mop up his egg yolk. "I hope it won't bother you – being in a house where a murder has taken place?" Beech was suddenly concerned.

Billy grinned. "My aunt Sissy used to work for the local undertaker, sir. Dead bodies don't bother her none."

"Good Lord!"

Sissy nodded. "I used to lay them out – you know, wash the bodies, brush their hair, put a bit of make-up on the ladies – that sort of thing," she said nonchalantly. "Besides, I don't believe in ghosts. If such a thing existed, London would be full of them, Mr Beech," she said with an air of finality. "You wouldn't be able to move for the spirits of the dead."

"Quite." Beech was fascinated by these two strong and capable women. "It strikes me, ladies," he ventured, "that you would be doing Lady Harriet a favour by keeping this place in reasonable shape whilst she's ill. A bit of light dusting, that sort of thing. If you wouldn't mind?"

Elsie beamed. "In return for a safe place to sleep, Mr Beech! I should think we'd be more than happy to do that!"

Beech felt duty-bound, however, to warn them about the possibility of Dodds returning.

Sissy was scornful. "He won't get far past the threshold whilst we're here, sir! Don't you worry."

Beech seemed unsure until Billy said, laughing, "Who do you think taught me to throw a punch, sir? My aunt Sissy's the best boxing coach I ever had!"

Sissy clenched her fist in mock anger and growled. They all subsided in laughter.

Beech stood and patted his stomach in satisfaction. "Well, ladies, I must go to Scotland Yard now and deal with the over-night reports. Doubtless I shall have a mountain of paperwork to deal with, given last night's activity. Thank you for that splendid meal, which will set me up for the rest of the day." He turned to Billy. "Rigsby, you must get some sleep, you must be done in. Perhaps we could gather at Lady Maud's house around lunchtime? Tollman will hold the fort until then."

"Yes, sir."

Beech let himself out and the Rigsby clan gathered for a hug of congratulation.

"I told you he was a good man, didn't I?" Billy chided them.

"He's a proper gentleman," agreed Elsie.

"Fancy him just letting us take over this place!" Sissy marvelled. "And not a word about Timmy, either!" She turned to Elsie in triumph. "This is going to put Ada's nose out of joint, Else! She's always banging on about her sister-in-law's cottage in Brighton, like it was some palace or something. Well, now we can write to her and tell her that we're living up the road from the King and Queen. She'll have a right fit!"

Tollman arrived at Mayfair, with the early edition of the newspaper under his arm, to find a clutch of women, still in their nightdresses, eating breakfast in the kitchen.

Lady Maud looked up from her toast and exclaimed, "Mr Tollman! Do excuse our attire but Mr Beech insisted we spend the night in the basement. I'm glad you managed to find us."

"I just followed the sound of voices, Your Ladyship," he said bemused, as Mrs Beddowes pressed a cup of tea into his hand. "Is everyone alright?" he enquired, "only it was a rum do in London last night."

"It was indeed, Mr Tollman, a rum do," Lady Maud agreed soberly.

Victoria explained the sequence of events – Caroline's phone call, Beech's mission over to the Murcheson house to tell Billy that Hoxton had been bombed and Beech's return with Esme.

"Did Billy find his family?" Tollman asked anxiously.

"We don't know, as yet," Victoria answered, "but I'm hoping that Peter will ring us as soon as he knows anything."

Right on cue, the telephone in the hallway began to ring and Tollman went up the back stairs to answer it.

"Tollman?" Beech said.

"Yes, sir, I've just arrived. What's the news?"

"All good, thankfully. Billy's mother and aunt are alive and well and billeted at the Murcheson house…"

"Are they, sir?!" Tollman was startled at the development.

"Yes, I thought it killed two birds with one stone, so to speak. They have a place to stay and in return they undertake to keep everything in good order. Better than having the place empty."

"Yes, sir. A good idea."

"So, Tollman…Rigsby is getting some much-needed rest, I am at the Yard dealing with the reports from last night and I suggest that we all convene at lunchtime. I don't know what time Doctor Allardyce will be back, as she was hard at work last night dealing with the consequences of the bombing. So you will have to hold the fort, as it were."

"No problem, sir. I suspect it will be quiet, as I shall suggest that all the ladies here go and have a nap."

"Good man. I shall see you at lunchtime." The receiver went dead and Tollman replaced it on the cradle. He smiled to himself as he went back down to the kitchen to impart the good news.

If I can get them all to have a nap, he thought, then I can have a read of the paper and maybe forty winks myself.

After all, he'd been up half the night with three hysterical daughters thinking they were all going to be bombed into oblivion. He deserved to put his feet up.

CHAPTER FOURTEEN

London on the Rampage

Scotland Yard was on high alert when an exhausted Beech arrived. Not only were there men to be despatched to continue with the clear-up in the East End but reports were coming in from the beat bobbies that hordes of "day-trippers" were turning up to see the damage and, in a distasteful manner, they were picking over the ruins for "souvenirs". Then, there came an alert that there were people gathering in outraged protest outside Buckingham Palace, somehow feeling that the King could do something about the Kaiser's war crimes, and, finally – worst of all – crowds were attacking any premises with German-sounding names, smashing windows and threatening grievous bodily harm. London's police force was stretched to the limit.

Beech joined the Commissioner, the other Divisional Detective Inspectors and Chief Constables in a strategy meeting. He was so tired that he felt almost distant from the proceedings but, nonetheless, realised that he would have to push through his tiredness and contribute some sensible options. Eventually, it was decided that the King's Household Police would have to deal with the crowd outside the Palace. Then it was suggested that they would have to request that the River Police, based at the Port of London, temporarily assist in dealing with the attacks on the shops and businesses in the East End of London. The rest would be dealt with by the foot patrols and some extra help.

"Perhaps we could bus in some of the women's patrols to

help with crowd control at the sites of the bombings?" Beech ventured and was rewarded with several disdainful looks.

The Commissioner gave a small smile and said, "Actually, Beech, that's not a bad idea. The WPS scare the hell out of me, so perhaps they can do the same with these unsavoury day-trippers!" The men around the table laughed and Beech felt a flush of pleasure. "When we've finished here, perhaps you could get one of your men to organise some charabancs so we can get Margaret Damer Dawson's women over there?" Sir Edward added, looking at Beech, who nodded in agreement.

"I have a meeting this morning with the Home Secretary and various representatives of the War Office," Sir Edward continued. "I don't know if anything will come out of it. We failed to agree on sensible measures to be taken earlier this month when the Lusitania was sunk and we had to deal with the riots afterwards. I think that this time, however, we shall have to insist on a full blackout of London." There was a general murmur of despair around the table. "I know, I know," Sir Edward continued, "it only makes our job of policing the capital harder but we cannot give the Zeppelins targets to aim at, can we, gentlemen?" Everyone reluctantly agreed. "However, we may still encounter resistance from those Members of Parliament who have vested interests in the entertainment establishments of the West End. Who knows? But they surely cannot defend their interests in the light of last night's tragedy. What is also needed," he continued, "is a more stringent defence system around London. We all know that. The Admiralty are just not producing the goods. Their warning system to us last night was both inadequate and late. We could have done with a lot more notice of the approaching Zeppelin and then we could have, possibly, evacuated people. I'm afraid that this is just the start of these raids and Military

Intelligence informs me that the Kaiser has issued orders that his people may not bomb Central and West London, for fear of killing his relatives. So it looks as though the East End may be the target again. They are trying to put the docks along the river out of action and demoralise the population at the same time. The difficulty, as we all know, is that we simply do not have enough men to deal with this added problem. The War Office may have to look at volunteer patrols and that, I'm afraid gentlemen, brings us back to the women again."

There was a collective murmur of dissatisfaction and one or two of the Chief Constables expressed their concern that their men did not want to work alongside the women's groups.

"These are difficult times, gentlemen," said Sir Edward with no small amount of impatience. "You must counsel your men to put aside their prejudices. I am not suggesting that these women become fully fledged police officers – far from it – but we must use every resource we have available for these non-criminal activities. I can't have us using trained police officers for crowd control, rescue operations and guarding foreign businesses. If we are facing a complete blackout of night-time London, the criminal population are going to see it as an opportunity to commit crimes with impunity. We have to concentrate all our efforts in that direction. For example," he added, "*if* – and I stress – *if* we can get the Admiralty to give us better warning of Zeppelins crossing the coastline at any point, we can use the women's patrols to rouse people from their beds and get them down into the Underground train stations. That, at least, might cut down on the level of casualties. We must speak to the Transport Division about implementing an orderly and safe system of accepting an influx of people into the stations after dark. It will require them to undertake all kinds of supervisory measures, which they won't like, I'm sure, but nevertheless it must be done."

The meeting dragged on for another hour, during which they pored over maps of gas supplies and electricity conduits and generally talked about defence measures. There was a discussion about providing police protection at the hospitals, which was dismissed due to the sheer number of hospitals that had sprung up in the capital over the last year, while the number of available police officers had dwindled.

"I am told by the War Office," Sir Edward relayed to the assembly, "that, despite the number of large houses in London that have been given over to be temporary army hospitals, the hospital system is at breaking point. There are currently fifteen thousand wounded men being held in France because we have no beds for them in London. The Germans' use of poison gas at Ypres last month has created an unprecedented number of wounded. I hope that the Home Secretary will decide to relocate many of these hospitals out into the countryside as we cannot be responsible for the mass evacuation of patients into underground locations in the event of more Zeppelin raids. We simply don't have the manpower to cope."

The meeting eventually broke up in an atmosphere of despondency. Never had London's police force been so hard-pressed and yet the public continued to urge young men to enlist and fight in France. None of the senior police officers present could see how the situation could be improved. One by one the men drifted out, back to their units, but Sir Edward signalled silently to Beech to remain. When just the two of them were left, the Commissioner quietly asked Beech how the Murcheson case was progressing.

Beech shook his head. "Slowly, sir, I'm afraid. We have circulated photographs of the missing butler and the scullery maid amongst the regular force and the women's patrols. Nothing as yet but we are hopeful."

"Mm. And how is your new team shaping up?"

Beech brightened. "Better than expected, sir. We have also enlisted the help of a female pharmacist who has been jolly helpful in the analysis of various substances."

Sir Edward smiled. "So, your females all have special talents, then?"

Beech laughed. "Yes sir! A doctor, a lawyer and, now, a pharmacist. Oh and I think I may have acquired two re-doubtable East End women as general factotums – you know, nurses, caretakers and bodyguards."

"Bodyguards! Good Lord! Are they that fearsome, then?"

"Well, one, apparently, has a pretty good right hook."

Sir Edward laughed and patted Beech on the back. "Well done, man," he said jovially. "I can see that you are making good use of what meagre resources are to hand. Keep me posted."

"Will do, sir."

Sir Edward then left for his undoubtedly gruelling meeting with the government bodies that would decide the fate of London in the foreseeable future.

Billy had gone off to Mayfair and Sissy and Elsie were ex-ploring the Murcheson house. Elsie had decided that they should take their boots off in case they made any marks on the floors.

"We don't want to give ourselves any more work than is necessary, do we?" commented Elsie, as Sissy begrudgingly took off her boots and left them in the kitchen.

They climbed up to the top of the house, Timmy scampering

behind them, and began to investigate. Timmy took a fancy to a servant's bed in the attic, and no amount of cajoling would make him relinquish his snug place on the blanket.

"Oh, leave him," said Sissy, in the end. "He'll come down again when he's hungry." So they left him, curled up in a ball and faintly snoring.

Each room was inspected for dust and pronounced in need of a good "going over". Lady Harriet's room was locked, of course, as Beech had requested.

"The murder room," said Sissy, when she realised the door wouldn't open and Elsie remarked that she wouldn't want to go in there anyway.

"I reckon they must have some dust sheets somewhere," Sissy observed, as they examined more bedrooms "We should cover some of the big pieces of furniture up. Save it getting dusty while it's not being used."

They pronounced the first-floor dining room as "beautiful" but didn't care much for the wallpaper. Elsie thought it looked too cheap for a Lord's house and Sissy agreed. They were just about to go into the drawing room and give that the benefit of their discriminating taste when Sissy grabbed Elsie's arm and mouthed, "I heard a door close." They stood like statues and strained to listen. They had left the door between the main house and the basement open and they clearly heard another door open and close again.

"Follow me," Sissy whispered, as she tiptoed in her stockinged feet down the grand staircase towards the open basement door, followed by an anxious and reluctant Elsie. They heard a man's voice, gruff and common. It appeared he was talking to someone. Elsie tugged at Sissy's sleeve and mouthed, "Telephone," and Sissy nodded. They edged closer towards the open door and Sissy soundlessly extricated a brass-handled walking stick from the stand in the hall and then brandished it like a club, ready to attack should the unknown man come up the stairs.

They listened, barely breathing, and they heard the man say, "I need the money tonight, I'm going away," then there was a pause and he said menacingly, "You'd better, or I'll have to tell the police everything." Sissy and Elsie looked at each other in alarm. "Dodds," Sissy mouthed and Elsie nodded. Then the man said, "Eight o'clock at the Queen's Head. Don't be late or it'll be the worse for you."

The women heard drawers opening and closing, the clatter of items being knocked to the floor and footsteps back and forth as the man appeared to be searching for something. They heard the scraping of a chair and grunting as he seemed to be making an effort to move or retrieve objects. Then he exclaimed "Bloody woman!" and something was thrown, which smashed into pieces. Sissy tightened her grip on the walking stick and poised herself for action but then they heard the basement door slam. Quick as a flash, Sissy grabbed Elsie and they darted over to the front window, dropped down and peered over the sill. They both saw an angry man ascending the basement steps carrying a large carpet bag and he walked swiftly past the front of the house and down the road. The women turned round and sank to the floor, exhaling in relief.

"I thought we was gonners there, Sissy," said Elsie, trembling from the ordeal.

"Nah," replied her sister, scornfully, "I would have laid him out with this." She waved the walking stick feebly in the air and they both giggled.

At that point, a curious Timmy appeared at the top of the stairs and cocked his head to one side.

"Oh, *now* you decide to make an appearance!" Elsie exclaimed sarcastically. "Can't rely on *you* to defend us, can we?"

Timmy barked half-heartedly and they giggled again.

"'Old up!" said Sissy suddenly, "we'd better ring Billy and tell him what's gone on. What did he say that number was again?"

"Mayfair one hundred," Elsie replied as they heaved themselves up and went downstairs to survey the damage.

The kitchen looked as though it had been torn apart and Dodds' room had been stripped of items that were previously on shelves. The small wardrobe in the corner had been left open and was bare.

"He's been and got his stuff...looks like he's going on the run," Sissy observed. "He won't be back – but put the bolt on the door anyway – and I'll phone Billy. Don't touch nothing!" she warned. "Billy's boss will want to have a look at everything."

Elsie looked at her, frustrated. "How can I put the bolt across if I can't touch nothing?"

"I didn't mean don't touch the bolt, flannel-head!" was Sissy scornful response, as she made for the telephone.

A disgruntled Elsie shot the bolt and glared at her sister's retreating back. "Well, people should say what they mean!" she said loudly.

Beech had just arrived at the Mayfair house when Sissy rang. Then he was just about to organise Billy's return to the house, when Caroline arrived, fresh from the hospital. No sooner had she dropped her bag on the hall table when the telephone rang again and Mrs Beddowes announced that Polly had been sighted at an address in Pimlico.

The team were galvanised into action.

Beech issued orders. "Billy, take Lady Harriet's parlourmaid with you. If Dodds has broken items in the kitchen or taken things, Esme might be able to tell you what is missing. Make sure you take detailed notes!"

Billy nodded and sped down to the kitchen to grab Esme.

Tollman, meanwhile, was looking at the address Mrs Beddowes had written down on a piece of paper. "I know this place," he volunteered. "It's a brothel run by a woman called Maisie Perkins."

Beech was momentarily halted by this piece of information. "Let's hope we are not too late for Polly's sake," he commented grimly. "Who phoned it in?"

"One of the WSPP volunteers. It says here she saw Polly's face at the downstairs window."

Beech turned to Caroline. "Caro, I know you must be dead on your feet, but could you go with Tollman on this one? The girl may need medical attention and, in any event, she may prefer to speak to a woman, rather than a man."

Caroline nodded. "Not a problem, Peter. I'm perfectly fine. I'm used to doing all-nighters. I find I usually don't feel tired until about four in the afternoon."

Beech nodded gratefully. He turned to Victoria. "I think it might be time for you to pay a visit to Lady Harriet's solicitor, if you don't mind?"

Victoria beamed. "Thank goodness! I thought you were going to leave me out of the team this morning!"

"As if I would," murmured Beech, as she sped past him to fetch her coat.

"By the way," announced Caroline loudly, to everyone, "Lady Harriet's temperature went down overnight and she was awake for a whole hour and able to eat some solid food."

A small cheer rippled around the hallway as they all digested this piece of news.

"Well, that's a result!" said Billy, as he put his helmet on and was joined by Esme.

"It certainly is, Billy," said Caroline cheerfully, "I don't like losing patients!"

Everyone went their separate ways, buoyed by the knowledge that, at last, they seemed to be making some progress with the case. Dodds had surfaced, Polly had been sighted and Lady Harriet was pulling through.

✳

Billy surveyed the mess in the kitchen and then carefully picked his way through the broken crockery to look at the butler's room off to the side. He took his notebook out.

"Well, he's definitely scarpered," he observed. "Lucky you weren't in the kitchen when he arrived." Both women nodded their agreement.

"He obviously had a key," said Sissy, "'cos that door was locked from the inside after you left and the key was up on the wall there." She pointed to the key hanging on the hook nearby.

"Well, he would have," piped up Esme. "Thank God I wasn't here on my own! I should have fainted dead away, I should!"

"Just to make sure," said Billy, retrieving a picture of Dodds from his pocket. "Is this the man you saw?"

Sissy and Elsie both murmured assent.

"Just look at him!" Sissy commented. "Don't he look the master criminal?"

Billy grinned. "Well, it's an offenders' photograph. Taken when he was charged with a crime. These pictures make everyone look evil."

"Can I put the kettle on, Billy?" asked Elsie, clutching Timmy in her arms for fear of him cutting his paws on the broken china on the floor. "Only I feel in need of a brew, my nerves are that frayed."

"Course you can, Ma," said Billy. He motioned to the parlourmaid. "Now, Esme, look at the floor and tell me what Dodds has smashed and why."

Esme looked carefully at the various pieces of china and pottery on the floor, then she said triumphantly, "They're all Cook's tradesman pots! He must have been after the money that she puts aside to pay the butcher, the fishmonger and so on. She keeps it all in separate pots and bowls up on the shelf there. Only, he must have been disappointed," she added, "'cos she took all the money with her. Said Lady Harriet could at least pay for her and Annie's train fares. I reckon there was probably ten pounds all told!"

"No wonder that man was so angry!" observed Sissy. "He shouted 'bloody woman!' afore he smashed things."

"Right," said Billy, writing in his book, "Esme, be a good girl and sweep this lot up, then we'll sit down and have a cup of tea, and you two can tell me, in detail, what you saw and heard."

In the cab, on the way to Pimlico, Tollman filled Caroline in on his knowledge of the premises they were about to visit.

"It's what I would call a medium-grade establishment, Doctor," he said. "Pimlico houses are large and not cheap to rent. Maisie Perkins runs a knocking shop that's a cut above the low-grade places you usually find around the main railway stations. But, I suspect, that that is because it is within brisk walking distance of the Houses of Parliament, if you get my drift, Doctor," and he winked, knowingly.

Caroline nodded but did not smile. "I do indeed, Mr Tollman," she replied. "Only last week I had to tell a refined lady – wife of a Member of Parliament – that she had contracted a venereal disease from her husband. He probably caught it from an establishment like the one we are about to visit."

"Actually, Doctor," Tollman responded thoughtfully, "I'm not sure that he did. Maisie Perkins runs a clean shop. All clients have to be clean, suited and booted, if you get my drift and, I believe, she has a doctor on call for all her girls."

"Really?" Caroline's interest was piqued. "I shall take notes. Perhaps I can teach some of the poorer prostitutes some of her practices. We spend too much time at the Women's Hospital and the London treating syphilis and repairing botched abortions."

Tollman shook his head in wonder. *What a strange and sordid profession for an upper-class woman to be engaged in!* He looked at Caroline with renewed respect.

Madame Perkins, for that is what she insisted on being called, was strangely welcoming when Tollman rang the front doorbell.

"I suppose you've come looking for that girl!" she announced, as soon as she opened the door and Tollman flashed his warrant card. "Well, she's gone! I told her to go and now I need protection from George Sumpter!"

She motioned Caroline and Tollman to follow her into the back parlour and bawled down to the kitchen "Evelyne! Bring me a pot of tea and three cups, at once!"

Once inside the parlour, all three of them sat on expensively upholstered chairs and Madame began her tale. As she spoke, an astonished Caroline realised that this plump, middle-aged woman before them was middle class, with good taste in décor and furniture, judging by the surroundings, and behaved, for all the world, as though she was running a hat shop not a brothel.

"George Sumpter brought that young girl, Polly, here the night before last. Now you understand, Detective Sergeant, that I don't usually have many dealings with a man like George Sumpter, but he has brought me young ladies in the past who wished to work in the…er…profession."

"I understand," said Tollman, making notes.

The tea arrived, delivered by a respectable-looking maid, and there was a pause whilst Madame poured everyone a cup of tea and observed the niceties of sugar and milk.

Cup in hand and fortified by a mouthful of tea, Madame resumed. "I say that, in the past, George Sumpter had brought girls to me. However, I do not mean to imply that I employed them. Oh no! Hardly any of them were suitable for my establishment, which, as you know, Detective Sergeant, prides itself on its discerning taste, refined young ladies and utter discretion. I think, that out of fifteen girls he may have brought to my door, only two were suitable."

"And Sumpter would get a fee from you, for every girl he supplied?" asked Tollman.

"Yes," Madame continued, "after one month had passed and the girl had proved satisfactory. You must understand—" her voice had a note of urgency and she leaned forward to emphasise her point "—I am not a white slaver! I do not take girls into my establishment that do not wish to be here. It is all voluntary. No one is kept here against their will and they are all properly instructed before they start work. No one is under any illusion about the nature of the work. George Sumpter, I have heard, runs a small business using amateurs. Overpainted doxies who are not properly trained."

"But what about, Polly?" Caroline was becoming impatient.

Madame shot her a troubled glance. "Well, this is my point, dear. He turned up with this young girl – virtually a child, for goodness sake! I must stress that all my ladies are over the age of twenty-one. Any gentleman looking for unsavoury services, involving underage girls, must go elsewhere. I will not tolerate it!"

"Polly?" Tollman reminded her gently, which brought Madame back from her flurry of indignation.

"Yes, well, the poor child was obviously distressed and Sumpter was up to no good. He did not offer her to me as an employee – which I would have refused anyway – but said that she needed to be hidden here for a while and then he threatened me. He said that if I told anyone about the girl, he would 'do for me', whatever that means. I have no doubt that it meant some sort of violence."

"What did Polly say?" asked Caroline, aching for Madame to get to the point.

"She said that something bad had happened where she worked but she wouldn't enlarge on that. She was upset about Sumpter – kept calling him Mr Dodds – and she said that he had promised to take her home and that he had said that everything was alright now. But it obviously wasn't." Madame's carefully controlled façade was beginning to crumble. "I asked her if she had any family and she said no, she was an orphan from Barnardo's, so I suggested that she went back there, for protection. I gave her some money for the railway train and she left. I was just about to contact Scotland Yard, in the vain hope that I might be offered some protection, when *you* arrived, Detective Sergeant." Madame looked flustered again and addressed Caroline. "I'm sorry, Miss, but I'm not quite sure who *you* are."

"I'm a doctor," Caroline answered simply. "The police thought that Polly might be in need of medical attention and they asked me to attend."

"Ah, I see. Well, apart from being upset, she seemed in perfect health to me," Madame volunteered. "If there had been any problem, I would have called my own doctor in to examine her."

"And who *is* your doctor, Madame?" Caroline enquired.

Madame looked affronted. "Discretion is my byword, Miss…"

"*Doctor* Allardyce," Caroline said firmly. "And I can assure you that neither DS Tollman nor I will divulge the name of your doctor to anyone else."

Madame shook her head. "My doctor is of the top rank. From Harley Street. He has many titled patients. If it were known that he also administered to my girls – if even a whisper were to get out – it would ruin his business! You must understand."

Caroline reluctantly agreed with Madame but, nonetheless, she remained curious as to the identity of this egalitarian doctor.

"So, am I to get some protection, Detective Sergeant?" Madame persisted.

"Yes, Madame," Tollman nodded. "Do you have a telephone here?"

"Of course."

"Then if I might use it to organise a protective detail?"

"You must understand, Detective Sergeant—" Madame was most insistent "—I cannot have a uniformed policeman outside my front door. In fact I cannot have a uniformed policeman in the house. It must be discreet. What would my clients think?"

Tollman sighed. "I shall organise some plain-clothed muscle, Madame, just until we have George Sumpter under arrest. Now, the telephone?"

"Ah, yes. In the hallway, there is a booth set in an alcove."

Tollman left to make a call, leaving Caroline and Madame in uneasy silence.

"Madame," Caroline said, deciding to be as respectful as possible, "when I was enquiring about your doctor earlier, I was merely concerned that you and your ladies were getting the best possible attention and help with disease prevention."

Madame relaxed a little and smiled. "You need not worry, Doctor Allardyce," she replied, her tone reassuring, "my ladies are regularly inspected, our clients must disinfect themselves before partaking and they must always wear protection. It is the amateur trollops on the streets – brought here by the fascination of soldiers in uniform – these are the ones who spread disease."

"Do you see the clients yourself?"

Madame raised her eyebrows. "Do you mean…?"

"Oh, no, no!" Caroline apologised hastily. "I meant, do you physically see them, when they arrive? Before they avail themselves of the services?"

"Oh yes!" replied Madame. "I receive all the clients in the front parlour and I make small talk with them, offer them stimulants and so on, whilst they are waiting for the girl of their choice."

"I see. So has your doctor taught you and your ladies to be aware of signs on the face or lips that could be an indication of venereal disease?" Caroline found it amusing that Madame visibly bristled at the word "venereal".

I do believe, Caroline thought to herself, that she has convinced herself she is running a bridge club or some other refined gathering!

"Of course!" was Madame's curt reply. "Really, Doctor, I have been running this business for nearly twenty-five years and I have never lost a girl to *any* kind of disease."

Caroline was nothing if not dogged in her pursuit of information. "And may I ask what stimulants you offer your clients?"

"Oh, some powders that my doctor provides and, of course, we have all the spirits – whisky, brandy, port, and we have fine cigars – whatever a gentleman may fancy. Although these may become more difficult to obtain if this wretched war continues."

"May I see?"

Madame smiled. "Of course. Follow me." She led the way into a large room at the front of the house, which, to Caroline, was much more of her idea of how a brothel should be decorated. There were red plush sofas, walnut tables littered with postcards of nude and semi-nude women, there was erotic art on the wall and, along one side of the room was a sideboard displaying several full decanters of spirits, a large cigar box, bowls of prophylactics and some silver bowls containing the exact same packets of heroin that had been in the possession of Lord Murcheson. Caroline picked one up. The fold of the paper was the same.

She waved one in the air as she enquired, "And you said that your doctor provides these packets of stimulants?"

Madame nodded. "We get a fresh supply every month. In fact, George Sumpter delivers them."

"Oh?" Caroline was surprised. "You didn't mention that before!"

"Didn't I?" Madame looked flustered again. "Well, I suppose it didn't seem to be very important in the light of this other matter with the girl."

Tollman stuck his head around the door and was momentarily lost for words at the sight of the décor.

"Er…Madame," he said, "I have arranged for one of our finest policemen, in plain clothes, to take up residence here until we apprehend Sumpter. He will be here within the hour. So I suggest you lock your doors and sit tight until he arrives."

"Of course, Detective Sergeant. We have no clients until seven o'clock this evening anyway." Madame seemed satisfied and led the way to the front door.

Outside in the street, Tollman and Caroline looked at each and laughed.

"Well, Mr Tollman, that was the greatest exercise in self-delusion I've ever witnessed," said Caroline, shaking her head in disbelief. "I do believe the woman thinks she's running some sort of finishing school!"

"You couldn't make it up, could you, Doctor?" agreed Tollman.

Beech and Victoria decided to take the omnibus to Fleet Street. It was a crisp May afternoon that seemed to lift people's spirits, despite the horrors of the night before. The sun was shining weakly on London, as if to soothe its soul. The crowds had obviously decided to cheer themselves up and make the most of the daytime safety. The flower sellers, who usually struggled to sell their wares all along the Strand, had almost empty baskets. Men were sporting flowers in their lapels and there seemed to be a mood of defiant jollity. The newspaper sellers had replaced their early morning posters pronouncing the horror of the Zeppelin attack with messages of bravado. "The King says we shall prevail!" read one. "Killer Kaiser will be shot!" read another.

Victoria wondered how brave Londoners would be if the Zeppelin attacks became a regular occurrence.

It's hard to maintain an air of defiance in the face of continuous terror, she thought but then she remembered her months at the army hospital in Berkshire, where the men, some terribly wounded and maimed for life, seemed to summon resources of cheerfulness and courage despite everything. *Part of the British character, I suppose,* she reasoned. Just like the women in her family. Always marrying soldiers, always being widowed, but always resourceful.

"Penny for them?" said Beech suddenly, making her start.

"Sorry?"

"Penny for your thoughts," repeated Beech. "You seemed miles away."

"Oh." She smiled in embarrassment. "Sorry. I was just thinking how London seems to have sprung back to its old self – despite last night's horrors."

"Yes," said Beech, but he was thinking about the meeting at the Yard and Sir Edward's grim prediction of how London's authorities would cope in the event of more Zeppelin attacks. "We're here," he said, as the omnibus drew up outside the Law Courts, and they scrabbled quickly to get off.

The walk through Lincoln's Inn Fields was pleasant. Some ladies were playing tennis. Soldiers, presumably on leave, were laying on the grass with their jackets undone. Birds chattered and hopped about in the trees. An elderly man was walking two dogs. All seemed tranquil and yet, Beech reasoned, barely three miles away, people's homes had been reduced to rubble.

As Victoria and Beech approached number twenty-seven,

Victoria pointed out that Sir Arnold was approaching his chambers from the opposite direction. They met outside the front door. Beech flashed his warrant card and a slightly irritated Sir Arnold bade them enter. He knew what they were here for and he was not of a mind to play ball – a frame of mind he made perfectly clear as soon as they sat down in his rooms.

"I am quite sure that you are here to ask me about the contents of Lady Harriet's will," Sir Arnold said briskly, "but I am equally sure that I will not breach a client's expectation of confidentiality."

Beech sighed but summoned a small, determined smile.

"Sir Arnold," he began, "I know that many solicitors have a poor opinion of the police force…"

Sir Arnold drew his brows together as if to prepare himself for a lecture.

"…but," Beech continued, "in this case, we are valiantly trying to prove your client's innocence. I, myself, was the first person to interview her after the murder occurred and I can testify that she was in tremendous pain and unable to move. Doctor Allardyce, whom I believe you met in the Women's Hospital, attended Lady Harriet in her home, where she began to haemorrhage internally and it was only the presence of Doctor Allardyce that saved her life. She also is willing to testify that Lady Harriet would have been unable to physically commit the murder of her husband. Mrs Ellingham here—" Victoria flashed Sir Arnold a brief smile "—took down Lady Harriet's confession." Beech noticed the disapproving look that crossed Sir Arnold's face and he hastily added, "at Lady Harriet's insistence, I may add, as she thought she was about to die, and she is also of the opinion that Lady Harriet's confession is an attempt to protect someone. So," Beech concluded, "all in all, we will do our utmost to prevent your client from ever being accused of a murder that she did not commit but we need to see the will and ascertain whether she may have said anything that may give us a clue and enable us to put the real perpetrator behind bars."

Beech sat back and prayed that Sir Arnold would see sense. There was a moment of silence, then Sir Arnold stirred. He rose and opened a wooden cabinet, retrieved some documents and sat down again, placing the documents on the desk. He then looked at Victoria and said pointedly, "I wonder if I might have your opinion on a painting in my clerk's office, Mrs Ellingham? A lady of your refinement might be able to pronounce upon its origins, don't you think?"

Victoria looked confused, but then Beech said firmly, "I think you should have a look, Mrs Ellingham. I believe you may be able to help Sir Arnold."

She realised that she was being asked to leave the room with Sir Arnold on a pretext, so that Beech could look at the documents on the desk.

"Of course, Sir Arnold," she said affably, "it would be a pleasure." So the elderly solicitor, with a nod of understanding to Beech, led the way into the next room, closing the door firmly behind them, leaving Beech to glean what information he could from the last Will and Testament of Lady Harriet Murcheson.

CHAPTER FIFTEEN

The Stake Out

It was time for snacks and comparing notes back at the house in Mayfair. Mrs Beddowes set to work cutting bread, ham, tongue, cheese, and everyone in the library fell on the resulting sandwiches as though they had not eaten for many days. Caroline and Beech were tipping over into extreme fatigue but Billy and Tollman were raring to go.

"My aunt said that they overheard Dodds on the telephone, asking someone to bring money at eight o'clock tonight to the Queen's Head," confirmed Billy, helping himself to more pickles. "And it must be the Queen's Head on Piccadilly, because Esme said Dodds was always talking about going up Piccadilly on his days off."

"I know it well," said Tollman, to no one's surprise. "Since the war started it has been the haunt of servicemen from all over the world. Usually packed by eight o'clock in the evening."

Beech decided that Billy and Tollman should spend the evening at the public house, in order to intercept Dodds.

"I have telephoned Barnardo's," Caroline said wearily, her half-eaten sandwich on a plate signalling to everyone that she was too tired to eat. "Polly hasn't turned up there yet but they have assured me that they will keep her there and telephone us the moment she arrives."

Beech nodded. "Good. Caroline, you must go to bed at once. You look completely done in."

For once, Caroline offered no resistance, mumbled her

apologies to the assembly and left to catch some much-needed sleep.

"That is one very hard-working lady," said Tollman quietly, after Caroline had left. Then he proceeded to recount the full details of their visit to Madame Perkins' establishment in Pimlico. "Doctor Allardyce discovered that Madame offers her clients the same packages of heroin as we found amongst Lord Murcheson's effects. Folded in the same way, and apparently delivered by Dodds, in quantity, once a month."

"Supplied to him by whom?" asked Beech.

Tollman shook his head. "Madame wouldn't say but I'm willing to bet it's the doctor who 'looks after' her girls. She says that he is a top-notch doctor in Harley Street with an elite client list. Mind you," he added scornfully, "Maisie Perkins is away with the fairies, so it wouldn't surprise me if she has persuaded herself that that is the case and her doctor is really some grubby little back-street abortionist."

"Or," suggested Victoria, "he could be the doctor who was looking after Lord Murcheson?"

"That's a possibility," Beech replied. "We haven't interviewed him yet and I would prefer Caroline to be present when we do, so it will have to wait until tomorrow now."

"Did you find out anything at the solicitors, sir?" asked Tollman.

"Not really," said Beech despondently. "Lady Harriet had left a whopping amount in trust for Polly, to be paid to her in sums each year of two hundred pounds."

Billy whistled appreciatively. "That's more than I earn a year! A sum like that could set a young girl up for life!"

"Quite," said Beech. "So I think one could take that as an expression of Lady Harriet's gratitude. There was one other thing," he added, "Lady Harriet had left a sum of two hundred and fifty pounds to George Dodds." Everyone looked surprised as Beech consulted his notes and read them out loud. "On the understanding that he must never speak of the events of the night of my husband's death and must sign a contract to that effect."

"It strikes me, sir," Tollman observed, "that Her Ladyship believes that Dodds knows that Polly killed Lord Murcheson and she wishes him to keep his secret in return for the money."

"I am of the same opinion," Beech agreed. "And we cannot move any further along with this case until we speak to either Dodds or Polly."

"Hopefully, we shall have Dodds before the end of the day," said Tollman, then he asked, "Billy? Have you still got your army uniform? Your khakis, I mean, not your dress uniform?"

Billy nodded. "I have, Mr Tollman. My original uniform got cut off me in hospital, but they gave me a new one to travel home in. It's at the station house."

"Then you must go and get kitted up, lad! And I must go back to Clapham and put on my Sunday clothes. Tonight we shall be a soldier and his old dad, out for a drink before you get shipped off." Tollman seemed to be relishing the thought of an undercover operation.

"Do you want some backup, Tollman?" offered Beech. "This Dodds seems to be a nasty piece of work."

Tollman shook his head. "No, sir. I might sign out a handgun from the Yard, if you would authorise it. Otherwise, I'm sure that Billy can bring Mr Dodds under control."

"I shall telephone straight away."

"Thank you, sir."

Tollman and Billy departed, arranging to meet up at a public house in Panton Street and from there they would move on to the Queen's Head at Piccadilly.

After they left, Lady Maud stuck her head around the door and said, "I've just passed Caroline's room and the poor girl has fallen asleep, fully clothed, half off and half on the bed. She must have been exhausted!"

"As am I," murmured Beech, beginning to feel very light-headed.

"Why don't you stay here tonight, my boy?" said Lady Maud. "You've been on your feet for nearly twenty-four hours, without sleep. At least take a nap on Billy's camp beds before you set off for your home."

Beech agreed that a nap would be a sensible idea but added that, before he did so, he wanted to talk to both of them about something.

"The events of last night, and the subsequent meeting I had at Scotland Yard, made me feel very guilty about having enticed you both to come to London," he said gravely. "There is every possibility that these Zeppelin attacks could continue. There is even a possibility that the Germans, having started on their foul course of total war against combatants and civilians, could resort to dropping poison gas on London. I should never forgive myself if I had been the cause of you being injured, or worse. I wonder if you shouldn't go back to Berkshire and sit out the war in relative safety." He flopped down in an armchair despairingly.

Both Lady Maud and Victoria loudly protested and then began to compete with each other to give reasons why it was important for them all to stay in London.

"…such valuable work…"

"…can't sit out the war in the countryside…"

"…one needs to contribute…"

"…and feel needed…"

"…can't run away from things…"

The reasons to stay came thick and fast as mother and daughter looked at each other for support and agreement.

A faint snore broke into the babble of protestations and they both stopped speaking as they realised that Beech was sound asleep.

Victoria covered him over with a knitted blanket, while Lady Maud placed a cushion behind his head and they tiptoed out, turning the light off as they left.

Tollman was nursing half a pint of shandy as he waited for Billy Rigsby to arrive. He could feel the weight of the revolver in his jacket pocket but he doubted that he would need to use it. He disliked using firearms on the streets of London. Too many innocent people could accidentally get shot. Besides, there were very few crooks who chose to use guns. Only a madman courted the death penalty.

Billy and Tollman had finally decided to meet at the Union Arms in Panton Street – a boxing pub, which had once been owned by the famous 19th-century bare-knuckle fighter, Tom Cribb. Tollman was examining some of the engravings of old-time boxers hanging behind the bar, when Billy arrived, looking every inch the squaddie he was supposed to be for tonight's operation.

"Very smart, lad," said Tollman appreciatively.

"Could have made me an officer – seeing as we're pretending," said Billy cheekily.

"And what would an officer be doing, drinking in a low tavern in Piccadilly with all the squaddies and trollops?" Tollman grinned. "Nah, lad, if you were an officer, you'd be having a night out at your club in Pall Mall, not slumming it with the hoi polloi."

"True," agreed Billy. "Are you going to buy me a drink, then, Mr Tollman?"

Begrudgingly, Tollman put two pennies on the bar and ordered half a pint of beer. Billy looked distinctly unimpressed but Tollman reminded him that they were working and he would be no use if he tried to apprehend a villain when he was three sheets to the wind.

They downed their halves in companionable silence and then made their way to the Queen's Head. Compared to the quiet of the Union, this pub was loud and bursting at the seams with men in khaki and women in flounces and frills.

"Busy, ain't it?" Billy bellowed to Tollman as he pushed his way through to the bar. Tollman nodded grimly. Not only was it busy but it seemed as though an entire regiment of guardsmen were in tonight. Everyone stood at least six inches taller than Tollman and he was having difficulty seeing anything useful. Suddenly, Billy unceremoniously grabbed Tollman's collar and almost lifted him from the ground, dragging him through the press of bodies until he deposited him on a bar stool at the very corner of the bar, with a clear view of the door.

"Better...*Dad*?" Billy winked at the flustered Tollman, who was straightening his flat cap and trying to maintain a sense of dignity.

"Thank you, *son*," he said gruffly. "Your round, I think."

Billy ordered another two half pints and turned round to survey the crowd.

"Blimey!" he yelled cheerfully at Tollman, "There's a rum crowd in tonight!"

A piano struck up, over beyond the mass of bodies, and a boozy cheer went up. Discordant voices began singing

"For Belgium put the kibosh on the Kaiser;
Europe took the stick and made him sore;

On his throne it hurts to sit,
And when John Bull starts to hit,
He will never sit upon it any more..."

Tollman winced at this wholesale murder of the music and took a swig of beer. It was warm and flat and he glared at the barman, who was pulling pints of the same dreadful brew as fast as his hands would allow it.

Billy stood with his back to the bar and scanned the crowd, then looked at Tollman and shook his head, indicating that he could see no sign of Dodds as yet. Tollman reflected on the sorry state of the world as he looked at the young women hanging around the necks of the soldiers.

So young, he thought, overpainted and powdered like stage actresses. All on the make. Just out to part young men from their money as fast as possible.

He suddenly felt very old. Forty years of police work still hadn't prepared him for how quickly society was changing.

"Want to buy a nice girl a drink?" said a loud female voice in his ear and he turned to see a smiling female with rouged cheeks and scarlet lips.

"No," he said curtly. "Be off with you."

Her smile faded and she scowled. "Please yourself, grandad," she said rudely and pushed her way through the crowd to find another victim. Tollman noted that she had not spoken in the grating tones of the East End but in the softer accent of South London.

Could be one of my own daughters, he thought with a shudder and resolved to give them a moral lecture when he got back home.

Suddenly, Billy's head jerked to an alert position and he turned to Tollman. "Behind the bar!" he said in a harsh whisper, barely audible in the din. Tollman casually looked in the direction of the barman and, beyond him, Dodds was visible, having just entered from a door at the back. Dodds appeared to scan the crowd and then he signalled to someone – Billy and Tollman craned to see who that person might be but it was impossible to tell, in the melee. Then Dodds disappeared back through the door and closed it behind him. Billy looked at Tollman for orders. Tollman signalled to wait, just for a moment. He was watching to see if anyone was trying to get behind the bar and follow Dodds.

They waited for a few seconds, then Tollman turned to Billy and shouted, "Whoever it is must have gone out the front way and round the side alley! You go after Dodds – I'll try and get out the front!"

Billy nodded and scrambled over the bar, much to the indignation of the barman, who produced a cosh from his pocket and began to threaten Billy.

"Police!" shouted Billy, fumbling for his warrant card and dodging the well-aimed blow from the cosh. "Police, you bloody fool!" Warrant card held high, Billy edged towards the back door as the barman froze in confusion.

Meanwhile, Tollman, with every bit of strength he could muster, was pushing through the mostly drunk and unyielding press of bodies. It was a frustrating exercise. Tollman realised he was not powerful enough to make them move, so he pulled out a police whistle from his pocket and gave one loud and insistent blast which stunned the revellers into silence.

"Police!" he shouted. "Make a path!" The people tried to edge out of the way but barely made an inch of space, so Tollman roughly pushed people, without ceremony, in order to make his way to the entrance.

Billy, finding the door locked, was attempting to kick it in, much to the annoyance of the barman, who was shouting loudly in protest and threatening to use the cosh again. Billy turned and laid him out with a powerful right hook and the barman staggered back and slumped down beneath the bar. "Obstructing the police!" Billy yelled to the women on the other side of the bar who had started screaming, then the door finally splintered from its lock and gave way.

Tollman, now out in the fresh air, took in a couple of lungfuls and darted to the left and the side alley that he knew led to the back of the pub. Running as fast as his legs would allow him, he cursed his age and hoped that Billy could cope until he got there. Rounding the corner, he could just make out, in the dim light hanging above the back door of the pub, Billy was crouching over a man's figure.

"You've got him!" he panted happily as he drew close.

Billy stood upright, his face set in grim defeat. "Not before someone else did for him," and he pointed to the prone figure of George Dodds, who lay dead on the cobbles with a knife through his chest.

It was going to be a long night. Billy and Tollman had to corral all the customers of the public house into groups for interview, knowing that it would be a fruitless task. Most of the soldiers were too drunk to understand what was going on – none of them, of course, had seen anything. The women were fearful that they were going to be locked up for soliciting and none of them were talking either. Both policemen realised that whoever Dodds had arranged to meet had killed him and was long gone.

Their only hope was the barman, who eventually came round from Billy's knockout blow and was nursing a swelling, and probably cracked, cheekbone and a great deal of grievance.

Billy roughly slapped a cold, wet cloth on the barman's

face and told him to "act like a man". The barman realised that there was no sympathy coming from the older policeman either.

"I don't know nothing," he sullenly replied and flinched as Billy ostentatiously clenched his fist and moved it slightly forward, as though to punch him once more. "I only know that Sumpter was going to meet someone here. He comes here a lot. Half the girls in the pub work for him. I let him – or used to let him – work his trade here and he would bung me a few quid. Then he asked to use the back room to meet someone and I said fine. I don't know no more than that. He didn't say who it was and I didn't ask. What about my smashed door? Who's gonna pay for that?" he added aggressively.

Tollman smiled, without any humour in his face, and said sarcastically, "Well, you can ask the station sergeant about that when we charge you with running a knocking shop, can't you, son?"

The colour drained from the barman's face, making his red and purple cheekbone and eye look all the more garish. "Look! I wasn't running the racket! Sumpter was! Take him down for it! I just turned a blind eye!"

"Well, of course we would arrest Sumpter, if we could – but you see, he's lying dead in your back alley with a knife through him. So you could be facing an accessory-to-murder charge as well, son," said Tollman simply. The barman looked as though he was going to be sick. "Billy, find a bucket," warned Tollman. Billy produced a slop bucket from under the bar and they stood patiently whilst the barman retched repeatedly into the dregs of ale.

"Look," said the barman, breathing heavily and wiping his mouth. "I'll tell you anything you want to know. I don't know much – I swear to God – but I'll tell you what I do know."

Tollman nodded. "Billy," he said, "clear the patrons out and lock up, then we'll get down to business."

Billy nodded and began to unceremoniously haul drunken squaddies up by their collars and throw them out into the street. Weeping and flustered women pushed past him, anxious to be lost in the night. The bar room was soon cleared and then Billy checked the toilets, found two soldiers passed out in the urinals and hauled them, semi-conscious, out into the alley, leaving them to recover in the cold night air. Once that was all done, he locked and bolted the main door and they sat down to cross-examine the barman.

They learnt that Sumpter/Dodds had been running a low-grade prostitution racket out of the Queen's Head for the past year. He had also been selling drugs to soldiers.

"Where did he get his supply?" asked Tollman.

The barman shrugged. "Some doctor, I think he said." Then he added that he had been on the verge of ending his arrangement with Sumpter because he'd had a few visits from a representative of the McAusland brothers. They said that Sumpter was messing up their business around Piccadilly and they didn't like it. "The McAuslands own three clubs and a couple of pubs in this area," he said, "they were threatening to smash up the Queen's Head, me and Sumpter, if it carried on. I was gonna tell him it was over – I didn't want the aggravation – when he comes to me and tells me he's leaving the country and that someone was coming with some money for him tonight. He didn't say who," he added hastily.

"Did he tell you what he got up to, when he wasn't in this pub running his racket? asked Tollman.

The barman shook his head. "He didn't say and I didn't ask."

"He must have given you a way of contacting him, when he

wasn't here," Tollman persisted.

"He gave me a telephone number. Belgravia exchange. He said that if anyone answered the telephone other than him, I should ring off. He was most insistent on that."

Tollman nodded. He was satisfied that he had obtained all the information he was going to get from the man.

"Write the number down for me," Tollman said, handing the man a piece of paper and a pencil. "Then I guess that will be all." He stood up and looked at the barman, who was looking fearful. "Count yourself lucky that we have better things to do than arrest a little toerag like you—" the barman exhaled in relief "—but I'm putting you on warning," Tollman continued. "If I find out that this amateur prostitution racket is continuing in your establishment, I'll be down on you like a ton of bricks, do you hear me?"

The barman nodded furiously.

"Now, I shall make a telephone call to the local police station and they will be down here with a body wagon. They may ask you a few questions and I'm sure I can rely on you to tell them that you know nothing and that you didn't see anything. Alright?"

The barman nodded furiously again.

"You can tell them that we were here, looking for Sumpter and they can contact me at Scotland Yard for more information. Got that? I'll tell them who I am and they can take it from there."

Tollman made the telephone call and then motioned to Billy that they were leaving. Outside, Billy asked, "What do we do now, Mr Tollman?"

"We need to speak to the McAuslands now," said Tollman grimly. "I need to know if they were responsible for this night's work."

Piccadilly was packed with soldiers and sailors, anxious to have a good time and part with their money before shipping back to hell on the high seas or the Western Front. For the most part, they were jovial or drunk. Progress was slow because they kept collaring the uniformed Billy, figuring that he was knowledgeable about the best places to get more drink or find girls. Billy brushed them off with a smile and a pat on the back but Tollman was getting irritable.

"I've always hated the West End," he muttered to Billy, after the fourth such encounter. "And now I hate it even more. Immorality and futility. Most of these men have got families back home and their mothers are just about able to put food on the table. Yet, here they are, throwing their money at publicans and good-time girls, when they should be thinking of their families. I'm getting old, lad," he added, by way of an apology.

"No, I know what you mean, Mr Tollman," Billy answered sympathetically. "This war doesn't seem like any other war. Too many amateur servicemen," he explained. "They don't think like regular army men. To us, and men like my dad, fighting in the army is just a job, and you did it so as you could take care of your family, and you knew what you were expected to do. Most of these men are just farm labourers and servants in uniform. They have no idea what's waiting for them. They think it's all a lark with better pay than they were used to. Those of them who have been through some months in the trenches, come up West to get as drunk as possible to blot it all out. At least, that's what I think."

Tollman looked impressed by Billy's little speech. "I think you have hit the nail on the head, Billy, lad," he said, patting him on the back. "Never figured you for a deep thinker but I was obviously wrong."

"I have my moments, Mr Tollman," said Billy, grinning.

✳

Club Tango in Soho was in full swing, lights ablaze, and a succession of well-dressed and well-heeled patrons were drifting through the open door in obvious merriment. The thickset bruiser who had admitted them before was standing by the doorway, looking uncomfortable in his evening suit.

"We can't go in the front door," counselled Tollman, "that would not go down well with the owners. There must be a back entrance."

They walked to the intersection of the streets and turned right to find an alley where the club obviously took its deliveries. As they passed the row of dustbins, Billy spied a door that announced "Club Tango. Tradesman's Entrance".

They knocked and another well-dressed bruiser opened the door and was about to tell them to clear off, when Tollman flashed his warrant card.

"Be a good chap and tell your bosses that Detective Sergeant Tollman wants an urgent word. Tell them it can't wait."

The bruiser scowled and shut the door on them whilst he went to relay the message.

"Told you I should have been dressed as an officer," said Billy light-heartedly. "Then we could have gone in the front way."

Tollman was amused. "And who would I be, then? Your batman?"

The door opened and the bruiser motioned them in and up a small staircase near the door. "Office is there," he growled, pointing to a door and he went back to his post. Tollman knocked and a voice said "Enter!"

The McAusland brothers were waiting expectantly.

Tollman noted that they seemed bemused as to the reason for the visit, not prepared, as he thought they might be.

"So soon, Detective Sergeant?" asked Matt, "and I note that you are hardly dressed for a night on the town." There was some amusement in his voice but Tollman let that pass.

"The lad looks good in uniform," commented Mike, giving Billy the once-over. "Sure you won't reconsider that job offer?" He grinned but Billy ignored him.

"I'll keep this brief," said Tollman matter-of-factly. "Sumpter is dead. Knifed in a back alley about an hour ago."

"Is he? By God!" Matt McAusland seemed genuinely surprised at the news.

"Well, that's one piece of scum no one will miss," Mike added.

"Except us, of course," said Tollman tersely. "We were very anxious to interview the man and that opportunity has now been denied to us."

"And you think it was our doing?" asked Matt scornfully.

"Was it?" Tollman was not in the mood to beat about the bush.

Matt McAusland stirred in his chair and motioned Tollman to sit opposite him. "Let's get this straight, Detective Sergeant," he said evenly, eager to impress upon Tollman his desire to be honest. "My brother and I don't do murder – even if it is a weasel like Sumpter. We have our businesses and our reputations to protect. We are not stupid. Neither of us has any desire for the hangman's noose. *If* we had found Sumpter – and I will admit that we were looking for him – we would have roughed him up and dumped him on the doorstep of the nearest police station, as we promised. He was an irritation to us, but a very minor one. We would have been very happy to see him locked up for life. But murder?" He shook his head.

"Nah. Not our style, Detective Sergeant, not our style."

Matt McAusland rose from behind his desk and went over to a curtain in the middle of the wall. He drew the curtain to one side and invited Tollman to come and look.

Tollman obliged and found himself looking down into the belly of the nightclub and the throng of people dancing to the band, which could only be heard faintly from the room in which they were standing.

"Look," said McAusland, inclining his head towards the scene below. "I don't know how familiar you are with the top echelon of society, but from where we are standing I can point out three High Court judges, two Lords, a Baronet, and several Society ladies who appear regularly in the pages of the *Tatler*."

Tollman nodded appreciatively and his quick brain also registered the identity of another person amongst the crowd – a piece of information he would keep to himself for the moment.

"So," McAusland continued, "do you really think that we would put all of that in jeopardy for a piece of no-account rubbish like Sumpter?"

Tollman shook his head. "No, I don't," he said firmly. "Sorry to have disturbed you, gentlemen," and he offered his hand.

McAusland shook it, followed by his brother.

"You're a good copper, Detective Sergeant," said Matt McAusland, as Tollman and Billy turned to go. "Pleasure to make your acquaintance."

Tollman nodded and they left.

Out in the back alley, once the door had been closed on them again, Billy asked, "Do you believe them, Mr Tollman?"

"Yes, lad," said Tollman quietly. "It's like I said to you

before, it all comes down to motivation. What I saw in that club was a powerful motivation for those two men to keep on the right side of the law." They walked for a while and then Tollman said, "I'll tell you who else I saw in that club." He paused and looked at Billy. "Detective Sergeant Carter."

Billy's eyes widened. "Bent?" he offered.

Tollman shrugged. "Maybe. I've always had my doubts about Carter. Too pushy and aggressive. It wouldn't surprise me if he was bent. But we have to give him the benefit of the doubt. He may have been working undercover...you never know. But I shall keep my eye on him from now on, that's for sure."

It was decided, before they parted, that Tollman would catch the bus home, because he was anxious to lecture his daughters on the evils of going up to the West End of London in search of amusement. Billy would walk back to Mayfair and impart the frustrating news to Beech that Dodds was dead and that they had been cheated of speaking to the one person who could have progressed the investigation of the murder of Lord Murcheson.

CHAPTER SIXTEEN

"Who the Hell Killed Dodds?"

It was a glum gathering at breakfast the next morning. Billy, finding Beech fast asleep when he had returned from the West End, had decided not to wake him, but had then been rewarded by the full force of Beech's irritation in the morning. Billy accepted the dressing-down meekly, suspecting that Beech was more annoyed with himself for falling deeply asleep, fully clothed, in a chair, than he was with Billy for not waking him up with the news about Dodds.

Once the news had been relayed to everyone at the breakfast table, a general air of frustration prevailed.

"We have to go and see this doctor, Caroline," said Beech. "Are you free this morning?"

Caroline said that she was and would gladly accompany Beech on the visit. "I should like to see for myself what kind of doctor turns a young man back from the war into a raging drug addict," she added sourly.

Beech shot her an anxious look but decided he would wait until they were en route to Harley Street before he gave her a lecture about how she must conduct herself in the interview.

Tollman arrived, with his usual morning newspaper tucked under his arm, and he smiled briefly at Victoria, as she poured him a cup of tea.

"So, Tollman," said Beech, buttering another slice of toast, "last night was somewhat of a disaster?"

Tollman, sensing criticism in Beech's voice, raised an eyebrow at Billy, who just shrugged.

"The place was packed, sir." Tollman explained. "Dodds came out from the back room, signalled to someone in the crowd and then disappeared again. Billy broke the back-room door down, whilst I tried to push through the crowds to the front door. By the time Billy got to Dodds, he'd been knifed. We questioned the customers – most of whom were drunk – and questioned the barman at length. Dodds had been paying him to allow an amateur prostitution racket to be run in the pub but he didn't know who Dodds was meeting. He said that Dodds announced that someone was bringing him some money so that he could leave the country. I handed Dodds' body over to St James' station. They said they would process the evidence, such as it was, and let us know if they found anything further."

Beech grunted. "So who do we think killed him? Polly?"

Tollman sighed with dissatisfaction at this theory. "I saw no one in that pub that wasn't dressed up to the nines, looking like a Drury Lane Fairy," he said. "Now I grant you, sir, young Polly could have got herself tarted up specifically to meet him and kill him but we have to remember that whoever Dodds was meeting was going to bring him some money. Polly had no money except what Maisie Perkins gave her for her train fare. If Dodds was expecting to leave the country, then we must assume he was expecting a large amount of money."

"Could it have been Maisie Perkins?" ventured Caroline. "I mean she could just have been telling us a complete pack of lies and, all along, she was Dodds' accomplice and intended to kill him rather than give him money."

Tollman screwed his face into an expression of indecision. Caroline's theory wasn't going to satisfy him either. "I've known Maisie Perkins for a great number of years – not per-sonally, you understand – but she has cropped up in a lot of cases that have involved top-ranking Society gentlemen. She's convinced herself that she is providing a genteel public service and recoils in horror from anything to do with violence and I just can't persuade myself that she would perform this act. Besides, we didn't see her at the pub – although I admit she could have been in disguise – but let's not forget that Madame Perkins is not young and certainly not agile. Whoever legged it round the back of that pub, knifed Dodds, and then disappeared, was someone strong and fit."

"Yes, of course," agreed Beech. "And you didn't see anyone running away at all?" he asked Billy.

"No, sir," said Billy firmly. "Mind you, it was dark in that alley. But I didn't hear any footsteps either."

"I think you should go back and have a look in daylight, Tollman," Beech's tone implied that he meant immediately and Tollman took a last mouthful of his tea, before saying, "Yes, sir. Come on Billy. Get your coat, lad."

"Perhaps I could go too?" asked Victoria, "I'm quite good at spotting things?"

Everyone looked at Beech for permission and smiled when he nodded.

"I'll just get my coat and hat, and I'll be right with you, Mr Tollman," said Victoria, as she sped out and up the stairs.

Once the trio had departed, Beech decided that probably now would be a good time to tell Caroline how to behave when they went to see the doctor. He decided to have one more slice of bacon first, before he plunged into, what would undoubtedly become, a lively argument.

＊

"I'm not sure that this was a good idea, Mrs E," said Tollman with distaste, as he guided Victoria past the pools of vomit in the side alley of the pub.

"Oh really, Mr Tollman," she tried to be light-hearted and positive, "I have seen far worse when I was working in a hospital!" Privately, though, she found the alleyway disgusting. It smelt like a urinal, or worse, and began to make her feel a little queasy. Turning into the back alley, which could be accessed through a tall metal gate, provided a little respite. It seemed as though not many of the customers had progressed beyond the gate and the cobbles were relatively clear of human detritus.

"Billy," ordered Tollman, "knock up the landlord and ask him if he's washed anything down in the alley since last night."

Billy duly hammered on the door, for some time, until the face of the man appeared at the door, his cheekbone hugely swollen and various shades of red, blue and purple.

"You again!" he said, with some difficulty, given the swelling of his cheek and lip. "What do you want now?" He was clearly not happy to be roused from his bed.

"Have you cleaned out the back here since last night?"

The reply was scornful. "Do I look as though I felt like cleaning the back alley last night?!" And he slammed the door.

"He says no," said Billy, grinning.

"Was that your handiwork, Constable Rigsby?" asked Victoria, not quite sure whether to approve or disapprove.

"It was self-defence, Miss. Bloke came at me with a cosh. Obstructed me in the course of my duties." Then he winked.

Victoria allowed herself a small smile but, deep down, felt she should be disapproving.

"So," said Tollman in a business-like manner, "Dodds' body was lying here," and he indicated the area, "facing this way," and he pointed back towards the gate.

"Obviously, he was expecting someone to come down the side alley to meet him," observed Victoria. "They stabbed him and he fell backwards, still facing in the direction he was expecting his visitor to come from. I take it he was stabbed in the front, not the back of the chest? Only you didn't say," she added by way of clarification.

"Yes, Mrs E," Tollman confirmed, "stabbed, I imagine, right through the heart, I'd guess, as it seemed that he must have died almost instantly."

"And you passed no one in the side alley as you came around the back?"

"No."

"Then," said Victoria, turning away from Tollman, "the perpetrator must have made his escape this way—" she pointed down the alley "—and that is where we should look for clues."

They instinctively formed a line across the alley – Victoria on the left, Billy in the middle and Tollman on the right – and began to slowly walk the escape route, inch by inch,. The alley ran between two streets, so there were back doors on either side and, occasionally, Tollman or Victoria would stop and examine the contents of those doorways very closely.

"Look at this," said Victoria, stopping suddenly and she pointed to a small line of rubbish – pieces of paper and ends of cigarette roll-ups.

"What are we looking at, Miss?" asked Billy, bemused.

"That rubbish is in a perfect diagonal line from the corner. That means that the door was opened and it pushed that rubbish into a perfect line. It's possible that the murderer escaped through this door."

Tollman respected her view but introduced a note of caution. "Mm, but that door could have been opened at any time – either before or after the murder. But it's worth investigating. Billy, go round the front and see what this building is."

Billy nodded and set off back to the side alley. Victoria and Tollman continued their laborious search. They had progressed about ten feet when Billy opened the door behind them.

"Mr Tollman!" he announced, "I think you might find this place of interest!"

As Victoria and Tollman turned back, Billy looked alarmed. "Um…not sure it's suitable for Mrs Ellingham to enter…"

Victoria looked puzzled as Billy whispered in Tollman's ear and Tollman nodded. He turned to Victoria and said, as diplomatically as he could, "I'm sorry, Mrs E, but I think it would be best if you went and had a nice cup of tea somewhere and we will join you afterwards." Victoria opened her mouth to protest but Tollman shook his head, "Sorry, Mrs E, I won't be budged on this one. There are some things I'm prepared to expose a lady to and some I'm not. So I will escort you round to the front and point you in the direction of Lyons' Corner House, shall I?" Tollman firmly took Victoria's arm and propelled her towards the side alley, calling over his shoulder, "I'll meet you round the front, Billy!"

Once they had negotiated the unpleasant side alley and were on the main street, Victoria stopped dead in her tracks and said stubbornly, "I refuse to take another step until you tell me what it is that you are not prepared to 'expose' me to. Really, Mr Tollman, this high-handedness is quite unacceptable…"

"It's a molly shop…" he said flatly, to interrupt her.

"A what?"

"Molly shop is a police term for a male brothel that caters to the tastes of certain men. In this case, it is of the worst kind – pederasty…underage boys. Is that what you wanted to know? And," added Tollman bluntly, "excluding you from this part of the investigation is not to spare *your* blushes, it is to spare *ours*. I am sure," he continued in a softer tone, "that you consider yourself a woman of the world, Mrs E, but Billy and I don't want to have to consider your feelings when we start interviewing these boys. It's a brutal world they live in and they often don't have any sense of refinement or common decency. So you will oblige us by going to Lyons' Corner House and having a leisurely cup of tea, whilst we deal with this bit of unpleasantness."

Victoria nodded her head, shamed into obedience by Tollman's reasonable but firm protectiveness, and she stepped out towards Piccadilly Circus.

Tollman watched her walk slowly away and bowed his head in resignation before he stepped through the doorway in front of him.

As he entered, he noted that the hallway led straight through to the back door. To his left was a porter's cubbyhole, with a counter that could be raised for entrance and exit. Behind the porter's counter were pigeonholes for correspondence and a door, which was open, leading to a small parlour, where a small man was hunched in front of a fireplace.

The man glared at him as he flashed his warrant card.

Ahead of him, at the base of the stairs, Billy stood by a low wooden gate, looking upwards.

As Tollman approached him, he followed Billy's gaze and found himself staring at a sea of faces – some wearing make-up, some frightened, some defiant – all young men. Tollman estimated between the ages of fifteen and twenty, no more, it was hard to tell under the rouge and lipstick.

"Make sure they don't move," Tollman said to Billy, "I want to have a word with matey who runs the place. Any patrons in?" he asked, as an afterthought.

"What! At this hour of the morning, darling!" exclaimed

one of the older men on the stairs.

Tollman turned, grim-faced, to the crowd on the stairs. "When I want your opinion, son, I'll ask for it. Meanwhile, I would keep my mouth shut, if I were you, until I ask you for information, and then you'd better be bloody sure that you give me the right information, or I'll have you down the nick as fast as your stockinged legs will carry you. Do I make myself clear?"

There was a silence from the landing.

"While I am interviewing the porter," Tollman continued, "I want every bit of powder and paint off your faces. I want to see who has still got bum fluff on their top lips. Then I will decide how many criminal prosecutions we need to write up today."

One of the young boys started to cry and was comforted by an older one. Tollman's heart sank. "I hate this bloody job sometimes," he muttered to himself as he turned back to the front parlour.

"You heard the detective!" Billy barked up the stairs. "Go and get the muck off your faces!"

The short, fat man in the parlour looked sullenly at Tollman as he entered. "I don't know anything, so don't bother asking me," he said belligerently.

Tollman was in no mood to be messed about. "PC Rigsby!" he shouted, and Billy appeared. "This man is obstructing justice. Would you care to point out to him the error of his ways?"

Billy gave a small mirthless smile and said, "Pleasure, Mr Tollman," as he suddenly kicked the armchair backwards so the man found himself flat on his back, legs in the air and Billy's foot on his chest.

"I'm asthmatic!" the man yelled.

Billy cupped his ear in mock deafness. "Sorry, sir, you'll have to speak up. I'm a little hard of hearing." With that he put his full body weight on the man's chest by hopping on his other foot. As the man screamed, Tollman nodded appreciatively. "Very creative, son. Now let's see if he's decided to be more amenable, shall we?"

Billy dragged the man upright by his collar and perched him on the front of the tipped-over chair.

"Alright! Alright!" he was coughing and spluttering. "I'll tell you want you want to know. Get me some water!"

Tollman nodded to Billy, who went over to a small sink in the corner and drew some water from the tap into a nearby teacup with no handle. He grudgingly gave it to the man, who drank and coughed for a good two minutes before regaining some sort of composure.

"Ready?" asked Tollman, barely disguising his impatience.

The man nodded. "What d'you want to know?" he said hoarsely, sitting down in the armchair that Billy had now raised upright.

"Firstly, what's your name and, secondly, are you the owner of this establishment?" asked Tollman, getting out his notebook and pencil.

The man looked at him with barely disguised contempt. "Do you think I would be living in two poxy rooms in this dump if I was the owner?"

Billy cuffed him round the ear and barked, "Oi! Show some respect to the detective, or I'll have you flat on the floor under my boot again!"

The man glared at Billy and decided to co-operate more fully.

"The name's Fred Miller and I'm just the porter," he said sullenly. "I don't know who owns the place. All I know is that some woman comes every two weeks and collects the rents."

"Name of the woman?"

Miller shook his head. "She never gave one and I never asked."

"What does she look like…this woman who collects the rents?"

Miller reflected for a moment. "Powdered and painted… but that don't make her good-looking. Sort of medium height with fair hair. Hard face. If you'd have pointed her out to me in the street and told me she was a prossy, I'd have believed it."

"And was this woman here last night?"

Miller shook his head. "She never normally comes at night but, if she was here, I wouldn't have seen her."

Tollman was momentarily puzzled. "Why wouldn't you have seen her?"

Miller looked uneasy. "Because once it gets past seven o'clock in the evening, I shut that door and I don't come out – no matter what goes on upstairs." He lowered his voice and looked intently at Tollman. "There's some very important men come to this house to…conduct their business, if you get my drift. I don't want to see them and they don't want to see me. What a person doesn't know, or see, can't be sworn in court. The woman told me that. She said I was to mind my own business and stay in my room, no matter what I hear going on upstairs. So, if anyone came here last night, I wouldn't have seen them."

Tollman nodded. "I understand. Does the woman get involved with the…er…tenants upstairs?"

"Nah. She's like a ghost, she is. She comes early in the morning, about nine, when they're all sleeping. No one ever sees her except me."

Tollman filed this piece of information away and then said, "So now tell me what you *heard* last night."

Miller sighed. "The usual. Men coming in and going up the stairs. Some screaming…"

"Screaming?" Tollman was taken aback by the casualness of the remark.

"Two types," Miller continued unabashed. "On Tuesdays and Thursdays there is one of the youngsters upstairs who screams a bit. On Mondays and Wednesdays, there's an older man's voice, which sort of screams and moans."

"God help us!" muttered Billy.

"And you do nothing about this?" asked Tollman with a strong tone of distaste.

Miller was defensive. "I told you – I don't want to know what goes on in this house and who does it. Each to their own. It's not my cup of tea but let 'em get on with it. It's not my place to interfere. If they need a doctor, they've got one lined up."

"Name of the doctor?"

"No idea. You'll have to ask them."

"Did you hear anything else last night?"

Miller looked reluctant but said, "I heard someone come in the back door, run the full length of the hallway and go out the front."

"And you saw nothing?"

"I told you…I don't open that door after seven. Not for anything."

Tollman thought for a moment and then said, "Where's your accounts book?"

Miller reluctantly got up off his chair and went to a drawer and withdrew a battered leather-bound book. "There's nothing much in there," he said as he handed it to Tollman. "Just the rents and the fortnightly totals for when the woman picks them up."

"Mm." Tollman flicked through the pages. "When is the

woman due to collect again?

"Tomorrow."

Tollman thought for a moment and then handed back the book. "Here's the deal," he explained firmly. "You will say nothing of this to the woman. When she appears you will not have a conversation with her about our visit…"

"I don't anyway," interrupted Miller.

"Don't what?"

"Have a conversation with her. She comes in and says, 'Got the rents?', I give her the money, she goes. That's it. We don't exchange pleasantries. She's never shown any inclination ever since she employed me to be the porter here."

"*She* employed you?"

"Some two years ago now. I answered an advertisement in the paper. I came here, she asked me a few questions and gave me the job. I was lucky to get it on account of me being inside for three years for grievous. The rooms came with it. I was told what went on here. Told to keep my mouth and the door shut at night and that was it. She picks the rent up, gives me my money and goes. She ain't the owner though."

"Who is then?" Tollman was intrigued.

Miller shrugged. "Dunno. Some bloke, I suppose. I once asked for money to get stair carpet put down to muffle the noise of the patrons going up and down all night. She said, 'I'll ask my boss', and that was it. Next time she came, she said, 'He said yes', and gave me ten pounds to get it done. That's the only conversation we've had in two years."

"Right." Tollman scribbled furiously. "So, I will repeat what I just said. You do not mention that we have been here. This is part of a serious murder investigation…"

"Murder?!" Miller was alarmed.

"Oh, didn't I mention that?" Tollman feigned surprise.

"Yes. Someone murdered a witness that we were looking for, right outside your back door. So, if you mention to this woman who collects your rents that we were here, and she turns out to be the murderer, I will have you up in court as an accessory. Understood?"

"Understood," said Miller firmly. "But what about being had up for running a knocking shop? Am I facing that as well?"

Tollman looked at the man and said quietly, "Not necessarily. If you co-operate with us in this investigation, it will go well for you. If you do a runner, I will find you. So stay where you are…carry on with your job…and I will put in a good word for you when the time comes. Got that?"

Miller nodded.

"Good." Tollman turned to Billy, "Now, PC Rigsby, I'm afraid we have the unpleasant task of interviewing the lads upstairs."

✳

Beech had an idea and he turned to Caroline with a triumphant look on his face.

"Caro…you are going to pretend to be my secretary!"

Caroline looked at him in astonishment. "I beg your pardon?!"

"Look," he answered patiently, "we don't want this doctor to know that you are as highly trained as he is. If you go into his office and start asking him medical questions and displaying your credentials, he might get all defensive or, at worst, refuse to say anything. If he thinks that we are both ignorant laymen…women…you know what I mean…he may try to bluff and we can catch him out."

Caroline looked at Beech. "I can see the sense of that," she admitted, "but, Peter, why on earth would you take a secretary with you to conduct an interview?"

Beech grinned. "Ah! I've thought of that. I want you to bind my right hand up like Rigsby's. I'll pretend that it's one of my war wounds and that I can't write, so I need someone to take notes – which you will do for me – but it will also allow you to write down any questions you feel I should ask …couching them in layman's terms, of course. I will periodically ask you to give me the notes to check, so that I can read your prompts."

"You *have* worked this out, haven't you?" Caroline was impressed.

Beech smiled, her praise making him feel quite proud.

"I rather like the idea of dealing with this doctor by deception," she said cheerfully. "I'll go and get my bag and then I can tape up your hand. Perhaps you should limp a little as well?" she suggested as she left the room.

Caroline seemed to be gone for some time but, once she returned, she began to bandage his hand tightly, whilst chattering away about her planned role as his secretary.

"You should start off by asking him exactly what drugs he gave Lord Murcheson – although he probably won't tell you. He'll probably fall back on the old chestnut of patient confidentiality, which I personally think is ridiculous once a patient is dead."

"But we know what drugs he gave Murcheson," said Beech, puzzled by her statement. "We have them from the house."

"We know what drugs he *prescribed*, Peter. The ones he put his practice labels on. We don't know if he gave him other drugs – not obtained through a pharmacy."

Beech looked at her askance. "Would a Harley Street doctor do that?"

Caroline snorted derisively. "You think that because a doctor has a fancy practice and rich patients he is above making some extra money on the side? You heard Arthur Tollman's report about the aristocrats in the nightclub. They bring their own drugs – given to them by their doctors. I bet they're not written down in the practice books, just like the illegal abortions performed in Harley Street."

"Surely not? Eminent doctors? Why would they perform abortions?"

Caroline sighed, then smiled. "For a policeman, you are terribly naïve, Peter Beech," she scolded him gently. "They do it because their patients – Lady so and so and the Duchess of wherever – ask them to get rid of an unwanted or inconvenient pregnancy. Or they ask them to get rid of their unmarried daughter's proof of indiscretion. The trouble is that many of them might be top-notch physicians but they are not surgeons. I have patched up too many botched jobs amongst upper-class women to know only too well what goes on with so-called 'eminent' doctors." She patted his bandaged hand. "All done. Try and move it."

Beech found that the hand was completely rigid, although not uncomfortable. "Well done, old thing," he said. "Now go and get your coat and hat and let's be off."

"Actually, I've borrowed a coat and hat from Esme. I didn't want to be too expensively dressed. Not for a secretary. And my personal coat is from a private designer. Our man in Harley Street would spot its worth straight away. I also borrowed Mrs Beddowes best handbag and I have a notebook and fountain pen."

"Good Lord! I wondered why you were away for so long, just now. You have really thought of everything!" Beech shook his head in disbelief. "But I think the handbag was a touch too much."

"Not at all!" Caroline was adamant. "It's the first thing

they teach male medical students – 'base your fees on the price of a good lady's handbag' – so all the male doctors are very aware of what a good handbag looks like and what it is worth."

"Astonishing." Beech marvelled at Caroline's attention to detail.

The cab journey to the doctors was spent in companionable silence until the cab turned off Oxford Street.

"Remember, Caro," Beech murmured, "you are a secretary. That means you cannot venture any opinion or ask any questions. You will have no authority once we enter those rooms."

"Understood," Caroline replied. "It will probably kill me to keep quiet but I promise I won't give the game away."

Beech smiled fondly at her and they stepped on to the pavement to begin their little charade.

CHAPTER SEVENTEEN

A World of Pain

Tollman eyed the assembled young men in the bedroom. He was trying to estimate their ages and he was sure that no one would tell him the truth in that regard.

Before he had ascended the stairs with Billy, he had imparted some words of wisdom to the young constable.

"Whatever you see up there, lad, just let it wash over you. Don't react in any way. Don't show anger or disgust. We need information from these lads and we don't want to put them too much on the defensive."

Billy had merely raised an eyebrow and said sardonically, "What – you don't think I've had any exposure to nancy boys? I was in the Guards for four years. Plenty of them hire themselves out to old queers. I believe the going rate for a guardsman is a guinea. For some reason the Household Cavalry blokes are worth two guineas – don't ask me why – must be because they smell of horse liniment. And as for the boxing game – how many places do you know where blokes can go and gawp at young men in shorts being oiled up in the corner of a ring? I've been propositioned by my share of 'em. There ain't nothing that will surprise me about this lot upstairs. Don't you worry about me, Mr Tollman. I'm not one of your faint-hearted young coppers who hasn't seen the seamier side of life."

Tollman had given a weary smile and patted Billy on the shoulder. "You are a constant wonder to me, lad – and a constant reminder that I am getting old and ill-fitted for the way the world is changing."

But even Billy had been unprepared for the huddle of pale and frightened boys assembled in the room. Stripped of their make-up and bravado, they looked very young and some looked ill.

Tollman took a deep breath. "Are any of you here in this house against your will? If you are, we can help you."

All the young men shook their heads. Tollman singled out the one that looked youngest to him. "What's your name, lad?" he asked quietly.

"George Harris," the boy mumbled.

Tollman looked at the others. "Right. I want the rest of you to go into the room opposite and wait until I call you. I want to have a word with George here."

The tallest, and what looked to Tollman like the oldest, young man looked alarmed.

"No, I need to stay with him!" he said urgently.

"And you are?" Tollman enquired.

"Michael..." he seemed reluctant to give his surname.

Tollman looked at the pale youth, George, and detected a faint trembling. He nodded to the tall youth. "You can stay, as long as you don't interfere."

Billy shepherded out the rest of the youths into the facing room, closed the door on them and returned to stand behind Tollman. He removed his helmet and he saw George react at the sight of his facial scar.

"War wound," he said.

George nodded.

"Sit down, lad," said Tollman quietly. "I need to ask you some questions."

George sat on the edge of the bed and pulled his dressing gown further around his slight body. Michael came and sat next to George and put his arm around George's shoulders to reassure him. Tollman's sharp eyes noticed the small flicker of pain across the boy's face at his friend's touch.

"How old are you, George?" Tollman asked. "I want the truth now."

George looked at his friend, who nodded.

"Fifteen," he said quietly.

Out of the corner of his eye, Tollman saw Billy stir slightly and he put out a hand to warn Billy not to say or do anything.

"Now show me the injuries to your back, lad," Tollman said slowly.

George looked frightened again and his eyes began to fill with tears.

Tollman persisted. "I need to see your injuries, George."

Michael murmured quietly, "Do as he says…" and removed his arm from the boy's shoulders.

George stood up, a tear trickling down his cheek. He turned around and slipped his dressing gown down to his waist. His back was scarred with long whip marks – some livid, some old and some looked yellow with pus.

"Jesus Christ," Billy said under his breath.

"Who did this to you?" Tollman asked, his voice thick with pity.

George began quietly sobbing.

Tollman turned to Michael. "You know who did this. Tell me." He said it accusingly and Michael flushed.

"His patron," he said dully. "The man who visits him every week. The man who pays for his services, this room, his food, his clothes…"

"Name?"

Michael shook his head. "Don't know."

Tollman was beginning to get angry. "I want a name!"

224

George spoke quietly, his back still turned to the two policemen. "He calls himself David. That's all I know."

"Was he here last night?"

Michael nodded.

"What time?"

"Between eight and ten, I think."

Tollman looked at Billy. Their unspoken thought was that the time fitted in with the timing of Dodds' murder.

"Cover yourself up, lad," he said tersely to George.

Billy spoke suddenly. "The boy needs tending to. I can do it. I've patched up worse in the trenches."

Tollman nodded.

Billy looked at Michael. "I need a clean bowl of water with lots of salt in it. Has anybody got some iodine?"

Michael said he would find out.

"I need some clean handkerchiefs and an unused razor blade,' Billy continued. "Oh, and we need to give him something for the pain."

Michael fished in his dressing gown pocket and produced a packet. "Give him this," he said, before leaving to assemble Billy's first aid kit.

Billy opened his hand and showed Tollman the packet.

"One of those bloody packets of heroin again," muttered Tollman bitterly.

"The porter has them," said George quietly. "We buy them from him."

"Do you?" Tollman wasn't asking a question. He was making an angry observation. "Billy, you minister to this lad, while I speak to matey downstairs," and he walked out of the room briskly.

Billy held out the packet to George. "I don't want to give this to you but what I am about to do to your back is going to hurt like the blazes."

George gave Billy a very thin mirthless smile. "As you can see, I'm used to pain," he whispered as he took the packet. "And I'm also used to this stuff." Another small tear trickled down his cheek again as he began to sniff the powder.

✳

Tollman almost broke the door handle as he burst into the porter's room in a rage. Miller leapt up in concern and let out a roar of protest.

"Where are the drugs you sell to these boys?" Tollman hissed venomously.

The porter pointed to a cupboard in the corner and Tollman ripped open the doors. There were dozens of white packets in a box.

"Where do you get these?" he shouted.

"The woman brings them every month! When she collects the rents! I haven't done anything wrong!"

Tollman grabbed Miller's neck in a fury. "Wrong!?" He was apoplectic in his fury. "Wrong? There's a boy upstairs, a child, barely out of short trousers, who has been whipped within an inch of his life, and you've been selling him drugs! I suppose you would call it charity, would you!" He let the man drop from his grasp. "You disgust me! There's one thing turning a blind eye to a molly shop above your head. What's going on up there is beyond all that. It's child slavery and brutality."

"I didn't know!" Miller protested.

"You heard the screams every week. You saw the state of the boy. He looks like a walking ghost! You sold him drugs."

"These people live in their own cesspit!" Miller almost spat at Tollman in his righteousness. "You're right. I don't care if they live or die. They do what they want of their own choosing.

This is just a place to live and money in my pocket. If you don't like what's going on here – take it up with the owner!"

"I will, don't you worry," responded Tollman through gritted teeth. "And you – if you want to avoid a very long prison sentence – will do as I tell you until we put this miserable landlord and every one of the men who take advantage of these boys behind bars."

Miller stared at him for a moment and then burst out laughing. "The customers of this place are too high and mighty for you to touch…'Detective Sergeant'." He emphasised Tollman's rank as though to remind him of how lowly he was in the scheme of things. His voice dropped to a whisper. "Aristocracy…maybe even royalty…who knows. I may not see their faces but I've looked under that door and seen the finest handmade shoes go past. You try and prosecute any of them and you'll come a cropper…Detective Sergeant."

Tollman turned on his heel and left with Miller calling after him "the finest handmade shoes!" by way of emphasis.

By the time he had ascended the stairs again, his rage had turned into cold, hard resolve. Someone would pay. He would make sure of that.

George was lying face down on the bed, stripped to the waist while Billy worked on his wounds. He was softly moaning but had already descended into a drugged stupor, which dulled the pain. Michael was holding the bowl of salt water but turned his head away as Billy deftly sliced the razor blade into the infected stripes and they oozed pus. As he wiped away the infection with salt water, George cried out quietly but with no great anguish.

Tollman began to question the older boy. "There are how many of you in this house…eight?"

Michael nodded.

"How many of you have 'patrons'?"

"About four. The rest seek clients where they can."

"What clients? From where?"

Michael shrugged. "St James', the Turkish Baths, the Officers' Club, the barracks at Chelsea…"

Billy snorted and looked at Tollman. "Told you."

"…the Lily Pond…" Michael continued.

"The Lily Pond?" Tollman interrupted "Where's that?"

"It's what we call the far end of Lyons' Corner House in Old Compton Street. The waitresses reserve tables for us, where we can meet our clients."

Tollman realised, with a start, that that was where he had sent Mrs Ellingham. He had quite forgotten about her up until now.

"This boy's 'patron' – this David – how often does he come here?"

"Twice a week."

"When is he due again?"

"Tomorrow, I think. Yes, tomorrow."

"Tell me about this man. What does he look like? How old is he?"

Michael looked at the floor. "I've only seen him twice. We all try to keep to our rooms after seven in the evening, unless we have to go out to find clients. I don't have a patron so I go out. Once I passed him on the stairs. He was about fifty years old, I suppose, dark hair going silver at the temples. He was elegantly dressed. Expensive overcoat, shoes, carrying a hat and silver-topped cane. Wearing pinstriped trousers. I assumed he was some high-up Civil Servant or something. I smelt Bay Rum on his hair." There was a small pause whilst Michael struggled with his memories. "The…the second time I saw him was after…he had visited George. I sat and listened to George screaming…it was hard for me but he…George… had asked me not to interfere. But then I couldn't stand it anymore. I came out of my room because the screaming stopped and I thought, perhaps, the patron had gone. But he hadn't. He was still in the room – washing his hands in the basin and…smiling. George was lying on the bed…naked and bloody…the man told me to get out. I refused and said I needed to help George. He just said, "Please yourself", put his coat and hat on and walked out."

"What was his voice like?" Tollman urged him on. "Any accent or unusual speech defect?"

"No. Upper-class English through and through." Michael's face contorted into misery and he looked straight at Tollman. "I begged George to leave. I offered him the money to go somewhere else and get away from this man but he just said he had nowhere else to go and, anyway, he didn't care about being whipped. He felt it was just punishment for him being… the way that he is."

No one in the room said anything. Pity hung in the air like fumes from a gas lamp. Billy looked down at the drugged boy's back, now clean and free from blood and pus.

"How long has this been going on?" he asked quietly. "I see old white scars on his back."

"Not long. Those scars are from the beatings his father used to give him," Michael said matter-of-factly, then he laughed hollowly. "Trying to beat some manhood into him apparently. Most fathers can't cope with their sons being queer. Mine couldn't. He threw me out. Said I disgusted him. I was seventeen. But George was younger than that when he came here. His patron found him when he was fourteen."

Tollman wanted to vomit but he took a few deep breaths instead and it passed.

"Do you know how this patron found the boy?" he asked after a while.

Michael shrugged. "George never said. Through the network, I suppose. George was soliciting on the streets and word gets about. If someone is looking for a young boy, they only have to ask around and one of our own kind will tell them where they can be found. There's precious little brotherly love in this trade," he added bitterly.

"Iodine," said Billy, holding out his hand for the bottle. "And you can put down that bowl now and hold him down. When I put this stuff on it's going to hurt like the blazes. Not even heroin is going to spare him from it."

Michael nodded and obeyed, climbing up on the bed and pinning down the boy's shoulders. Billy poured the iodine in a livid orange stream over the wounds, deftly wiping the liquid over the entirety of the boy's back. George tried to arch upwards but Michael held him firmly down. Billy waited for the boy's screams and tears to subside.

"You got any bandages anywhere?" Billy asked.

Michael shook his head. "I don't think so."

"How about a clean sheet we can rip up?"

Michael released George's shoulders and stroked his hair. "In that drawer over there." He pointed at the dresser by the window.

Tollman rummaged through the drawers and produced a sheet. Then he produced a penknife from his pocket and began to slash two-inch slits along the edge and rip the sheet into passable strips for makeshift bandages.

"Right, let's sit him up," Billy instructed. "You hold him to your chest, so I can wrap these bandages round him."

Billy and Michael struggled with the dead weight of the boy, who was by now almost unconscious. Eventually, Michael was holding George to his chest and Billy began the process of winding the bandages around the boy's torso tightly until he was covered from armpits to waist and the iodine began seeping through the layers, making patterns on his back. Then they laid him gently down onto his front and left him to recover.

Tollman laid a hand on Billy's shoulder and said softly, "Well done, Billy, that was a grand job you've done there."

Billy smiled grimly. "It's a lot more difficult to patch someone up with shells exploding round your ears, Mr Tollman."

"Thank you," added Michael. "I never expected policemen to be so kind. It's rare in our world. Are you going to prosecute us?"

Tollman sighed. "I should, by rights, but I have bigger fish to fry here. I would like to lock up every one of your clients but I fear they may be too powerful and well connected for me to touch. Besides, locking up you and the other lads isn't going to make you change your natures, is it?"

Michael looked strangely at Tollman for a second, then said, "No. But I am tired of this place. So are the others. And maybe we'll leave soon...after we've... settled up."

Something rang a warning bell in Tollman's head when Michael looked at him but then he got distracted by Billy saying, "The lad should go to hospital. Those wounds need regular attention – proper nursing – or he'll die from an infection."

Tollman agreed. "You two get him dressed and I'll call an ambulance from the phone in the pub." Then he remembered what Michael had said about leaving and he turned back to him. "Michael, can you do me a favour? We need you and the other lads to conduct business as usual until after tomorrow. We want to keep a watch on the place and see if we can arrest this 'David' when he comes for his regular visit. None of you must breathe a word about the boy being taken to hospital. Just carry on as normal. We don't want word getting out amongst your clients that anything has changed. As far as they are concerned, we were never here. Understand?"

Michael nodded. "And whatever happens, you will let us go? We won't be dragged through the courts or imprisoned?" His eyes pleaded with Tollman.

Tollman hesitated and looked at Billy.

"We've got bigger fish to fry, you said," Billy reminded him.

Tollman was torn. "I shouldn't do this. The law's the law and I should uphold it at all times." He paused then nodded his head. "But sometimes you have to compromise. You help us with an arrest or two of your clients and we will turn a blind eye if you disappear. Miller downstairs will give us chapter and verse on the activities in this house, in return for a reduced sentence, I expect. Frankly, I don't know. I'm struggling between the King's laws and natural justice. I only know I want to make someone pay for the treatment of this boy."

Michael stood like a statue, displaying no emotion, and he simply said, "Then we are agreed."

Once the boy had been loaded into the ambulance, it was decided that Billy would go with him and report to the hospital that George had been beaten by his father. He would stay until George woke up and then tell him to say nothing about what had happened and to maintain the fiction that he was a victim of family violence.

Tollman went back into the house to impress upon the porter that he was to keep his mouth shut and go about his business until the end of the week, until everything was wrapped up. Tollman implied that the house would be watched day and night, so Miller had no hope of running without being immediately caught. In reality, Tollman was just crossing his fingers and hoping that everyone would co-operate as he did not want to draw on any extra manpower from the Yard. The fewer people who knew about it, the better – especially within the police force. There had been two occasions in his career where high-ranking police officers had been tipped off that there were to be raids on brothels and thus escaped the embarrassment of being caught patronising their regular haunts.

If Miller was correct about the 'quality' of the anonymous clients at the molly shop, Tollman was not about to sabotage an opportunity to arrest them, whatever their standing in society. He hoped that Beech would be persuaded of the justice of this, as he realised that he had deviated somewhat from the task of finding Dodds' killer. Yet, somehow, in the back of his mind, he was convinced that the events of today, and the characters he had encountered, were inextricably linked with the murder but there were no facts or concrete evidence to tie them all together. Tollman was a man who liked fact-based results and he was unsettled by his behaviour. He'd been moved by his emotions rather than his intellect today.

As he entered Lyons' Corner House, he braced himself for a ticking-off from Victoria Ellingham but, to his relief, he found her surrounded by empty cups of tea and engrossed in the newspaper.

"My apologies, Mrs E," he said, removing his hat, "events overtook us. I truly did not mean to be so long."

Victoria smiled. "No need for an apology, Mr Tollman! As you can see, I've been thoroughly reading the newspaper and drinking endless cups of tea." She leant forward conspiratorially, "And I've been secretly watching the comings and goings of a group of very effeminate young men over in the corner. It's been fascinating."

Tollman looked over to the far wall of the cafeteria. "Yes, Mrs E. I've just found out it's called The Lily Pond."

"The what?" Victoria was astonished.

"The Lily Pond. It's where male prostitutes meet and pick up their clients. Apparently, the staff of this establishment aid and abet them by reserving that area."

"Oh." Victoria looked concerned. "Shouldn't the police be doing something about that?"

Tollman looked resigned. "I expect they should but then they would just move on and gather somewhere else. They don't appear to be bothering anyone else and at least it's better than soliciting on the streets or in public conveniences."

Victoria looked nonplussed. "That's very…er…broad-minded of you, Mr Tollman. Somehow not the reaction I would expect from…"

"An old-school copper like me?" volunteered Tollman helpfully.

"Well, yes."

"It appears, Mrs E, that I am not too old to learn new philosophies, as the events of this day have proved."

"I'm intrigued. Are you going to tell me what has transpired during the last couple of hours? I feel that I have earned a detailed account of your activities," Victoria gently chided him.

Tollman smiled wearily. "I shall certainly tell you everything – perhaps leaving out a few of the more graphic details – but not here. Shall we return to Mayfair and await the return of PC Rigsby? Then we can make a full report."

"Of course. Where is PC Rigsby?"

"Gone to the hospital," Tollman replied but immediately leapt in with a reassurance that Billy was not in need of medical attention himself but merely escorting a witness.

"I do hope that PC Rigsby did not *cause* the witness to be in need of medical attention," Victoria said, in alarm.

Tollman shook his head and said, with satisfaction, "No, Mrs E. Quite the opposite, in fact. Billy Rigsby patched up a quite badly damaged boy in an efficient and impressive manner. Doctor Allardyce would have been proud of him. In fact *I'm* proud of him. Today I have acquired a new respect for young Rigsby that would normally take me about twenty years to acquire for another man."

Victoria was beside herself with frustration at not knowing about the momentous events that had caused such a transformation in both policemen.

"Well, we must get back to Mayfair post-haste. I'm not sure I can bear waiting any longer for a detailed account of what happened this morning but I sense that I shall have to. As a punishment for making me wait so long, Mr Tollman, you can pay for my many cups of tea. Here is the bill—" she presented a bemused Tollman with the slip of paper "—which you can settle whilst I avail myself of the ladies' facilities. Endless cups of tea do rather put a strain on the bladder!", and she swept grandly away in the direction of the 'facilities', leaving Tollman chuckling to himself.

CHAPTER EIGHTEEN

A World of Pain Relief

The consulting rooms of Dr McKinley at forty-two Harley Street were an oasis of privilege and calm. Tasteful flowers were arranged in the waiting room beside the deep chesterfield sofas and the latest editions of *London Illustrated News*, *The Lady* and the *Tatler* were available to read.

"I'm guessing that the good doctor's patients are mainly female," Beech murmured quietly to Caroline as they entered. The nurse at the desk looked up in surprise as they approached. Caroline noted that she was wearing a great deal of make-up.

Surely not suitable for the nursing profession, she thought to herself, but then she shrugged as she decided that she had no experience of the hallowed practices of the Three Streets – Wimpole, Wigmore and Harley.

There were almost four hundred physicians, surgeons and optometrists in the grand houses of those streets and they were all male. Such a world was closed to a female doctor, no matter how highly qualified. *Perhaps it's a requirement of these "eminent" men that their nurses should look like actresses.* The contempt she felt only reinforced her opinion of Dr McKinley. He was no better than a quack, she had decided – a peddler of drugs to keep the upper classes happy.

"May I help you?" the nurse asked, her brows knitted together in concern.

Beech smiled and flashed his warrant. The nurse's eyes showed alarm.

"Would you be so kind as to tell Doctor McKinley that

Chief Inspector Beech desires to speak with him." Beech was charm personified.

"Is he expecting you, Chief Inspector?" The nurse appeared immune to Beech's charm and she sounded rather cross.

Beech retaliated. "It is not a common habit for the Metropolitan Police to request an interview in advance," he answered briskly. "Kindly ask the doctor to receive us. At once," he added firmly.

That seemed to do the trick and it made the nurse flustered.

"I'm sorry, sir, but Dr McKinley has a patient with him at the moment, and I am not allowed to enter the consulting room unless summoned. If you would be so kind as to wait over there—" she indicated the waiting room "—he will be finished very soon and should be able to see you. He has no further appointments for an hour."

Beech inclined his head graciously and motioned Caroline ahead of him to the sofas.

"Would you care for a cup of tea while you are waiting?" The nurse had obviously decided to be amenable.

"No thank you," said Beech, "but perhaps you would care for some refreshment, Miss Allardyce?" He smiled at Caroline but she also politely declined and the nurse retreated back to her desk.

Beech began to take an artificial interest in the *Illustrated London News* whilst Caroline continued to surreptitiously watch the nurse. She seemed restless and kept glancing at, presumably, the door of McKinley's consulting room. After a few moments, it opened and the man himself appeared, dapper and effusive in his farewells to his female patient. Caroline suddenly grabbed the nearest magazine and placed it on her lap, hunching her shoulders, sinking her head almost on her chest and putting her hand up to rest on the side of her face, earning a quizzical look from Beech.

"I know that woman," she mouthed at him and he nodded. After the woman had passed through the reception and out into the street, he leant over and prodded Caroline's knee to indicate that she could sit upright again. The nurse, meanwhile, had disappeared in a flurry of starched white apron into the consulting room, whispering in McKinley's ear as they both retreated into the room and closed the door.

"Who was the patient?" whispered Beech.

"Lady Carson," Caroline whispered back. "The wife of Sir Edward."

Beech looked stunned. "The Attorney General?! How do you know her?"

"She's a patron of the Women's Hospital. I've met her on several occasions at hospital fundraisers. And she's one of those women who never forgets a face or name."

"Well," Beech muttered, "there's no denying that Doctor McKinley is very well connected."

"That doesn't make him beyond the reach of the law," Caroline murmured.

"No. But he may think that it does." Beech was rapidly losing confidence and Caroline patted his hand.

"It doesn't matter what he thinks," she whispered confidently. "No Attorney General is going to defend a bad doctor just because his wife is a patient."

The door opened again and Dr McKinley strode forward to extend his hand to Beech.

"Chief Inspector, I'm so sorry to keep you waiting. My nurse tells me you would like a word."

Beech stood up and raised his bandaged hand. "Forgive me for not shaking your hand, Doctor, but I'm afraid I caught some shrapnel in France and it's out of action for the moment."

McKinley looked concerned. "My dear chap! Are you being looked after – medically speaking?"

"Yes, yes, of course." Beech brushed it aside. "The army always looks after its own, you know." He indicated Caroline's presence and she stood up. "Miss Allardyce, my secretary. I'm afraid I need her to take notes, if you don't mind."

McKinley gave a small inclination of his head towards Caroline. She noted with satisfaction that his eyes ran up and down her coat, as if appraising her, and then he turned his head back towards Beech, obviously regarding Caroline as unworthy of any further attention.

"Please, come into my consulting room and we can talk in private." The affable doctor led the way. "Now, how can I help you?" he asked, once they were all seated and the door was closed.

"It's about the death of Lord Murcheson, Doctor McKinley," Beech began and the doctor's face clouded over.

"Ah yes. Most unfortunate. He was a very tragic young man."

"May I ask, Doctor, how you were informed of his death?"

"His butler rang me, after the death had occurred," McKinley said smoothly.

"At what time would that have been, Doctor?"

McKinley reflected. "It must have been mid-afternoon of that day. I know it was after Lady Harriet had been taken to hospital. Most unfortunate affair. I presume the poor young lady stabbed her husband in self-defence? I know that her husband was volatile and prone to fits of rage, alternating with depression. In my opinion, he was suffering from a brain disease. There was little I could do for him, other than provide pain relief. He should have been hospitalised but, of course, he would not agree to that."

Beech could see that Caroline was writing furiously and he said, "Thank you, Doctor, would you excuse me for a moment whilst I consult my secretary's notes? I find that when someone else is taking notes for me, I forget my train of thought."

McKinley nodded and smiled. Caroline handed over the notebook into Beech's left hand and he read "ASK HIM ABOUT THE DRUGS!!!" He gave her an impatient look as he handed the notebook back.

Beech resumed his questioning. "You mentioned giving Lord Murcheson pain relief. Could you possibly tell me exactly what you prescribed him?"

"Of course." McKinley got up from behind his desk and strode to the door. Caroline hastily covered over her notebook before he passed by.

"Nurse!" McKinley called as he opened the door.

"Yes, sir."

"Fetch Lord Murcheson's patient notes, if you please."

"At once, sir."

McKinley came back and resumed his seat. "I can tell you everything about the medicines, Chief Inspector, but please do not ask me for any further details about the patient. There are notes in the file that relate to intimate matters and I cannot divulge those to anyone. Not even his next of kin."

"Yes, of course, I understand."

There was a brief knock at the door and the nurse entered with a brown file of papers.

"Will that be all, Doctor?" she asked. McKinley nodded and she left.

Caroline determined to find a way to get closer to the nurse, to see if the make-up was hiding anything.

"Yes, here we are. I simply provided Luminal, which was for seizures...well, brain excitement generally...as I told you,

I suspected that Lord Murcheson had a brain disease, which was causing fits and blackouts. The second was for an opiate preparation to help him sleep. Both were in liquid form. Both to be taken orally. A teaspoon when required."

Caroline was scribbling again and this time Beech could quite clearly see she had written WHAT ABOUT THE OTHER DRUGS? He resisted the temptation to reach across and rip the page out and merely cleared his throat.

"Doctor McKinley, we found a great many other drugs in Lord Murcheson's bedroom when we conducted our search. I have a list here in my top pocket, if you would bear with me." He fumbled awkwardly in his left top pocket, with his 'good' left hand and managed, with some difficulty, to extricate a piece of paper. Caroline was impressed that Beech had thought to write down a list of the drugs.

"Forced March tablets, heroin cough mixture, opium pellets and some packets of powder which our police pharmacist has determined were heroin powder."

"Good God!" exclaimed McKinley.

"Did you supply your patient with any of these? Or would you have any idea where he might have obtained them?"

"My dear man, I most certainly did not supply any of those to Lord Murcheson." McKinley sounded impatient. "I would assume that the Forced March tablets were a supply he brought back from France, from when he was in action. The rest of the medicines you describe are freely bought from any pharmacy. If I had known he was taking so many other medicines, I should have refused to treat him any further. I suppose he had his butler purchase them for him, since, as far as I am aware, Lord Murcheson rarely left the house. He was in so much pain from his inoperable war wound that he could barely walk, unless fortified by pain medication. He never came to these consulting rooms. I always attended upon him at home. I suggest you question his butler. I'm afraid that I cannot help you."

Beech nodded. "Thank you, Doctor McKinley, You have been most helpful." He rose and motioned Caroline to do the same. "Please don't bother to show us out. Thank you so much for your time."

Once outside the room, Caroline whispered, "Wait a minute. I just need to check something," and she walked over to the nurse, leaving an anxious Beech wondering what she was about to do.

"Excuse me," Caroline said, affecting a timid tone of voice. "I have such a headache. Do you think I could have a glass of water?"

"Yes, of course, Miss, please follow me," and the nurse led the way into a small sluice room filled with medical equipment lined up by the sink awaiting a scrub. The other side of the room had wall-mounted cupboards filled with medicines and a long table in front, covered in trays of prepared packets of medicine. The nurse poured a glass of water and handed it to Caroline, who took a sip.

"Would you like an aspirin powder in that water?" she asked, walking over to the medicine table.

Caroline shook her head. "No thank you. I find water usually does the trick. Besides, aspirin powders taste so awful!"

The nurse smiled. "They do rather," she said sympathetically.

Caroline drained the glass, handed it back to the nurse, expressing her thanks and left to join Beech.

Once in the taxi, Beech said "What was all that about?"

Caroline smiled grimly. "I wanted to get closer to the nurse so that I could see if the excessive amount of makeup she was wearing was hiding anything. When I got up close to her, I could see that the glands in her neck looked slightly swollen above her starched collar. I would have to feel them to be sure. But, finally, when she gave me the water, I could see that the palms of her hands were red and blotchy."

"So? What does that mean?" Beech asked in a frustrated tone of voice.

"It means she is very likely in the secondary stages of syphilis."

"Again, I ask, what is the relevance of that? Apart from the fact that Doctor McKinley must be a very bad doctor if he employs a nurse displaying the signs of syphilis."

"Quite," Caroline agreed, "but perhaps you might be interested to know that, in the room where I was given my glass of water, there was a medicine table, upon which there were dozens of prepared packets of medicine that were the same size and folded in the same unique way as Lord Murcheson's packets of heroin and the packets of heroin on display in Maisie Perkins' brothel."

"Good Lord! Caro, that's a jolly useful piece of information! Perhaps Dodds was supplying the good doctor with the drugs."

"Or—" Caroline paused for emphasis "—the good doctor was supplying Dodds with the drugs. I'm willing to bet it was that way round. That McKinley is a nasty oily man and a terrible doctor! Did you notice that cologne he was wearing?"

"Not really," Beech confessed.

"Well, I did! And that's a terrible thing for a doctor to do."

"It is?" Beech sounded unsure.

"We were taught in medical school that we should never wear perfume or pomades or anything that would dull your sense of smell. Sometimes it's quite important for a doctor to be able to detect quite faint odours about a patient in order to come to a proper diagnosis. Like, for example, a fruity odour on the breath that can denote diabetes. That man is a terrible doctor."

"So it would seem." Beech marvelled at Caroline's deductive powers. "You've done a good morning's work, old thing! Once we find out what the rest of the team have dug up, we may be able to add more pieces to the puzzle. I have to say that after Dodds' death last night, I was beginning to think we had reached a dead end."

Caroline and Beech arrived home about five minutes before Tollman and Victoria.

"Where's Rigsby?" asked Beech.

"Taken a witness to the hospital," replied Tollman.

"Oh? Would you care to enlighten us as to how your morning has progressed, Tollman? It sounds a good deal more eventful than ours."

"Oh it was!" enthused Victoria, before Tollman could open his mouth, and she began relaying the tale of how they had performed an examination of the back alley behind the pub and how she had spotted that a door had been opened.

"Well done, Victoria!" Beech was effusive in his praise, something that Caroline noted with a small pang of jealousy. *I bet he doesn't call Victoria "old thing", like he does to me.* She decided to brush away her childishness by being equally admiring of her friend.

"So what did the door lead to, Victoria?" she asked brightly.

"I'm afraid I can't give you a description because, at that point, Mr Tollman banished me to the safety of Lyons' Corner House. Over to you, Mr Tollman."

Tollman sighed and divested himself of his overcoat. This

was going to be a tricky one. Beech looked expectant.

"Well, begging the ladies' pardon, but there is no other way of telling this, Billy and I discovered that the door led to a male brothel." Beech's eyebrows rose a little in concern. Tollman continued "…and not just your average male brothel but one filled with underage youths, the youngest of whom was fifteen."

Caroline and Beech made a collective noise of distaste.

"Quite." Tollman took another breath and proceeded to tell them the story of Billy patching up the boy and the information they gleaned from the older youth and the porter. He decided, for the moment, to leave out the arrangement he had come to with Michael about freedom from prosecution. He wasn't quite sure if he could keep that end of the bargain and he didn't want to debate ethics with Beech.

"Sounds like Billy did a first-rate medic's job," commented Caroline, full of admiration. "It's exactly what I would have done myself in the circumstances."

"Nasty, nasty business," muttered Beech. "But did you get any further with the murder of Dodds?"

"Well, sir," Tollman explained. "This piece of vermin who is the boy's 'patron', was there at the time of the murder and he obviously sounds like a man who is capable of anything. The porter, who is under instructions never to come out of his room after seven, no matter what he hears going on, reported to us that he heard someone running from the back door and out of the front door at the time of the murder. Then there is this mysterious woman who flits in and out on a regular basis to collect the rents on behalf of her 'boss'…" he paused, uncertain how to proceed, uncertain of what words to use, then he continued with some feeling, "You know me, sir. I like to lock villains up when I have a good body of solid facts to convict them with. This business in the molly shop has got my head spinning round. It's like London fog. Nothing you can grasp hold of. Yet I'm convinced it's all connected."

Beech nodded. "Go on."

"My feeling is that if we can apprehend both this woman and the sadistic 'patron', all the pieces will fit into place. It just so happens that the woman is due to collect rents tomorrow morning and the 'patron' is expected tomorrow night. If we were to lay in wait for the woman and then Billy and I could go back in the evening to catch this piece of filth...excuse my language ladies...we might find out something more useful."

Beech was about to speak when Caroline butted in. "I think Victoria and I should be involved in the morning caper." Beech began to protest when Tollman agreed.

"That would make sense, sir. Because we actually want to follow this woman to see if she will lead us to her boss and the two ladies could follow her at short distance, whilst you and I follow behind, in case of any trouble." To counter any of Beech's objections, Tollman added, "After all, they can go where we cannot – if the woman should go into a ladies' convenience or a ladies' garment shop."

Caroline turned to Beech with a triumphant smile and Beech reluctantly agreed.

Just then, there was a knock at the door and Lady Maud poked her head around.

"Victoria, my dear, there's a telephone call for you from Barnardo's."

Victoria looked startled. "Polly!" she said excitedly and sprinted out to the telephone.

"How is everything progressing, Peter?" Maud asked conspiratorially.

"I think we are just about to find out, Maud," he answered.

They waited in silent anticipation for a couple of minutes, and then Victoria burst into the room.

"We've found Polly. She's not at Barnardo's but they received a request for a reference from The Grove Fever Hospital, Tooting. Apparently, Polly is working there, on a trial basis as a cleaner!"

"Excellent!" Beech was overjoyed. "Now, finally, we may get some answers!"

"May I suggest that Mrs Ellingham and I go and fetch her, sir? We don't want to go mob-handed," Tollman advised.

"No, we don't want to frighten the girl. Yes, you do that Tollman. I have to put in an appearance at the Yard, anyway, and Doctor Allardyce starts her shift after lunch." Beech turned to Lady Maud. "Maud, is it alright if we bring the girl back here? Only I don't want her intimidated by being taken to Scotland Yard. We can question her here, whilst plying her with some of Mrs Beddowes excellent tea and scones or something."

"Not at all," Maud said graciously. "Only too pleased to be of assistance."

Just as Victoria and Tollman were putting their coats on, Billy came through the front door.

"Hello, lad, how's things?" Tollman asked.

"He'll be alright. They're looking after him at Charing Cross Hospital. They reckon he'll be in for about a week. I've spoken to him about keeping his mouth shut and everything. He's good at that, he says, and he won't be any bother. Where are you both going?"

"Polly's been found, safe and well," said Victoria brightly. "Mr Tollman and I are going to collect her and bring her back here."

"Oh, that's good news, Miss!" Billy seemed to brighten up.

Beech and Caroline appeared, at the sound of Billy's voice and they both congratulated him on his morning's work. Caroline even hugged him, which made him blush.

"Rigsby—" Beech patted Billy's back "—there's no more can be done until this afternoon. Why don't you go and visit your mother and aunt. We won't be questioning Polly until she's been fed and watered and feeling safe. I shall come back here at about three o'clock. Doctor Allardyce will be working, of course."

"Yes, sir. Thank you, sir." Billy grinned happily, then he noticed Beech's bandage. "What have you done to your hand, sir?"

Both Victoria and Tollman expressed concern and apologised for not noticing it earlier. Beech laughed and waved the bandaged hand in the air.

"There's nothing wrong with my hand! It was a subterfuge Caroline and I adopted for our trip to see Murcheson's doctor and we don't have time to tell you about it now."

And with that, everyone, except Caroline, left the house. She went back into the study and looked at her notes from the meeting with Dr McKinley and decided to go down to speak to Esme.

In the kitchen, everyone was quietly preparing lunch. Cook, Mary and Esme looked up as she opened the door.

"Hello, Doctor," said Mrs Beddowes breezily. "What can we do for you?"

"I'm afraid that it will be just myself and Lady Maud for lunch, Mrs Beddowes. Everyone else has had to go out."

"Oh dear...well, never mind." Mrs Beddowes seemed unconcerned.

"There is one piece of good news, however – of particular interest to Esme," Caroline continued and Esme looked up, intrigued. "Polly's been found."

There was a chorus of approving comments and Esme burst into tears. "Oh, thank the Lord! Is she alright, Miss?"

"Yes, she's perfectly fine and working in a hospital as a cleaner. Mrs Ellingham and Mr Tollman have gone to fetch her and bring her here. You will be able to talk to her later but I'm afraid Mr Beech has to question her first."

Esme nodded happily, dabbing away her tears with a handkerchief.

Caroline turned to Mrs Beddowes. "Cook, do you mind if I borrow Esme for five minutes? I just want to ask her a few questions."

"No problem, Miss," said the affable Cook. "I just need her back to serve lunch up, that's all."

Caroline assured her that it would only be a few minutes and signalled to Esme to follow her upstairs. Once they were in the study, she picked up her notebook and pen again.

"Sit down, Esme. I just wanted to ask you a few questions about Doctor McKinley. Mr Beech and I went to see him this morning."

Esme's face darkened. "Evil man he is. Sorry, miss, I shouldn't have said that!"

"It's quite alright Esme. To tell you the truth I'm not that fond of him myself. Now, when we saw the doctor, he said that Mr Dodds telephoned him to tell him the news that Lord Murcheson was dead. Do you know anything about that?"

"Well, I did hear him making a telephone call to someone, just after you had taken Lady Harriet off to hospital but I was in such a state – I fainted you know – that I didn't hear who he was talking to. I can't believe it was the doctor, though, because Mr Dodds didn't sound very respectful. I did hear him say, 'I'm not dealing with this on my own…' like he was very angry. I mean a butler wouldn't talk to a doctor like that, would he, Miss?"

"No, I suppose not. Do you remember anything else about the telephone conversation?"

Esme thought for a moment and then said, "I didn't hear much of the conversation after that but he did raise his voice at the end and he almost shouted to whoever it was 'sort it out or I'll take measures'. He did sound very angry, Miss."

Caroline noted this down in her book. "So, Esme, the doctor said that Lord Murcheson never, or rarely, left the house and that the doctor always visited him. Is that true?"

Emily made a disapproving face. "I only ever saw the doctor come to the house once in the whole three months His Lordship was back from the war. I suppose he could have come when I was out on errands for Her Ladyship but that was only once a week. No one ever mentioned to me that he had visited whilst I was out and Cook would have told me. She loved to gossip. I did see a nurse once, though…"

"Oh?" Caroline's interest was piqued. "When was this?"

"Late at night. Must have been about ten o'clock. I had a cold and my throat was so sore. I snuck down to the kitchen to make myself some hot lemon and honey. We weren't supposed to come downstairs after nine at night – Mr Dodds' orders. He said His Lordship would be on the prowl and it would be safer if we stayed in our beds…"

"What about Polly?" Caroline interrupted her. "How did Polly manage to overcome Mr Dodds' orders?"

Esme smiled. "She could be really stubborn, could Polly. When he found her, the first time, and told her off, she said 'My Lady asked me to be near her at night, Mr Dodds. Are you going to go against the wishes of Lady Harriet?' He just sort of growled at her and left her alone after that. She said to me that if he complained again, she would ask him why *he* wasn't the one protecting Her Ladyship. I'd like to have seen him answer that one."

Caroline went back to Esme's previous narrative. "You said you saw a nurse one night? I'm sorry I interrupted you. Can you tell me more? You said you came down to get some hot lemon and honey…"

"Oh, yes. So I'm creeping down the back stairs to the kitchen when I hear a taxi drawing up, so I looked up from the stairwell window and I see this nurse get out of the taxi, carrying a bag and Mr Dodds must have been waiting for her, because he came down the front steps to meet her. He probably didn't want her to ring the bell and wake everyone up."

"I see. And where was Lord Murcheson at that moment?"

"Probably sleeping in the downstairs drawing room, Miss. He didn't sleep upstairs much, unless he was very drugged. He was in a lot of pain with his back and he didn't like to go up and down the stairs. But, sometimes, he would be so fired up, Polly used to say, that he would take those stairs without any bother and come looking for Her Ladyship. Polly said that he was very drugged when he had those episodes."

"Did he ever attack Polly, in order to gain access to the room?"

"Not that she ever said, Miss. She would just tell him that Her Ladyship was ill and he would go away. Without a murmur, she said. Although, sometimes Mr Dodds would come and get him and take him back downstairs. Mind you, Polly had only been guarding the mistress for the last month. Lady Harriet had started being sick in the mornings and not feeling quite right and that's when Polly decided to guard her."

The pregnancy, Caroline thought. Polly started guarding her when Lady Harriet found out she was pregnant.

She asked Esme one last question. "So, you don't know how often this nurse visited?"

Esme shook her head. "No, Miss. The doctor should have come more often in my opinion. Towards the end, Lord Murcheson was having one of his violent rampages practically every two days, according to Polly. She was worn out with it all."

"Thank you, Esme. You can return to the kitchen now."

Esme stood and curtsied. "Thank you, Miss."

Caroline sat and mulled over her notes. To her analytical medical mind, it seemed to her that Lord Murcheson's night-time rages becoming more frequent were perhaps a sign that someone had been giving him stronger and stronger drugs. Dodds? The nurse? Or the doctor? Or perhaps all three. Then there was the question of Lord Murcheson being infected with syphilis. He could have contracted it in some French brothel but the pathologist said that he was in the *primary* stage, which meant he had most likely contracted it after returning to England. As the man barely left the house, the disease must have been brought to him. Caroline smiled to herself with satisfaction. She was pretty sure that the nurse at McKinley's practice had displayed the signs of syphilis in the *secondary* stage. It seemed to Caroline that the nurse had been offering services to Lord Murcheson above and beyond the medical. Frustratingly, she would have to wait until tonight to tell Peter.

CHAPTER NINETEEN

Children Lost and Found Again

Billy was unusually quiet when he turned up at the Murcheson House.

"What's up, son?" Elsie asked. "You look as though you've lost a shilling and found sixpence."

"Nah," Billy answered, pecking his mother on the cheek. "Just had a tough morning, that's all."

"I've just boiled the kettle. Sit down and have a cuppa." Elsie always felt that tea could solve the problems of the world.

Sissy entered from the garden, accompanied by Timmy, who threw himself at Billy with frenzy of tail-wagging.

"Hello Billy. You look as though you've lost a shilling and found sixpence."

"There's a hell of an echo in here," said Billy sardonically, as he picked up the small terrier and made a fuss of him.

Elsie chuckled. "I just said exactly the same thing to Billy afore you come in, Sissy."

"Oh well. Great minds and all that."

A mug of tea was placed on the table and Billy sat down, undoing his jacket and removing his helmet. He gave a sigh of relief.

Elsie and Sissy sat down at opposite ends of the table and looked at him.

"What?" Billy said with a touch of annoyance. "Have I grown another head or something? Stop looking at me like a pair of vultures!"

"We're waiting for you to tell us what's wrong, Billy," said

Sissy patiently. "We know you. You've got something on your chest and you need to get it off. Come on. Stop messing about."

Billy sighed in exasperation. "All right. But it's not pleasant and I'm not sure it's fit for women's ears."

Elsie laughed. "He thinks 'cos we're living in a mansion we must be refined ladies, Sis! Don't be daft, son! There ain't nothing you can't tell Sis and me. We're grown-ups."

Sissy nodded. "We've seen and heard things that would make your hair curl, lad. Don't be shy. Unburden yourself."

Reluctantly, Billy began to tell them about the events of the morning, accompanied by much tutting and head-shaking from his mother and her sister.

After he had finished telling them the story of the boy that he had taken to hospital, Elsie said, "Well, I can see that you would be down in the dumps after a morning like that. But you did a good job, Billy! Your boss thought so and the lad's in a safe place where he's being looked after now."

"Yeah, but that's the problem, Ma. The hospital's only going to keep him for a week and what happens to him then? I hate to think of him going back to his previous life."

"But he won't be going back to that house, will he?" reasoned Sissy. "'Cos you're going to catch the evil swine who did this to him and you're going to close that place down."

Billy was frustrated. "Yes, so what's this lad going to do then? Go back to soliciting on the streets? He's got nobody. He told me in hospital that he tried to get a job as a wood-turner, 'cos he likes making things, but his father told the factory boss that he was queer and so they wouldn't give him a job. Now he thinks that he's only good enough for prostitution." Billy shook his head. "I don't know why I'm in a lather about it. I thought I was harder than that."

"Just like your dad, Billy," said Elsie, patting his hand. "He was a big, tough guardsman but, deep inside he was a right soft 'un. Wasn't he, Sissy?"

Sissy seemed distracted. "Wait a minute…did you say he liked making things? This lad…wood-turning?" Billy nodded and Sissy started getting excited.

"Elsie! Do you know who I'm thinking of?" She nodded and smiled, encouraging a response from her sister.

Elsie thought for a minute…a light came on in her eyes… and she shrieked, "Tolly!"

Sissy laughed. "Yes! Tolly! Match made in heaven, don't you think?"

Billy looked puzzled. "Who?"

Elsie and Sissy tried to explain to Billy, their words tumbling over each other in their excitement.

"We know this elderly chap…Tolly…"

"Confirmed bachelor, if you get my drift…"

"Cabinet-maker…"

"Such a lovely man…"

"Lives on his own…"

Billy interrupted. "Hold up! Hold up! I'm not giving this boy over to another old geezer who takes advantage of him!"

Elsie and Sissy expressed outrage.

"Tolly's not like that…"

"Lovely, gentle man…"

"Old enough to be the boy's grandfather…"

"Wouldn't lay a finger on him…"

"Teach him a trade and all…"

"We wouldn't be party to that sort of thing, Billy!"

Billy held his hands up to silence them.

"So," he said firmly, by way of clarification, "this old man, this 'confirmed bachelor' who is a cabinet-maker, would take in this boy, treat him like a grandson and teach him a trade?

No funny business. I won't be made to feel like a pimp?"

"The idea!" Elsie said. "What d'you take us for?"

"The thing is," explained Sissy, slowly, "Tolly would *understand* what it's like for the boy, being as he is of the same persuasion, as it were. The boy could learn from him…you know…acceptance of his…nature…and some self-respect."

"Sissy's hit the nail on the head, Billy," Elsie emphasised. "It seems to us that these two could *help* each other. The boy would have a proper father…well, grandfather…and a proper home. Tolly would have what he always wanted…a boy to pass his cabinet-making skills on to and, if truth be told, some company. He's always been very lonely, has Tolly."

"Course, we'd have to *ask* Tolly if he was agreeable," added Sissy. "He could be too set in his ways to want the responsibility. But it's worth a try."

Billy began to feel hopeful. But there was another problem.

"I don't have the time to sort this out," he said. "I've got too much on my plate for the moment."

Elsie took his hand again. "Bless you, son. *You* don't have to do anything! Me and Sissy'll sort this out. It'll be a nice little project for us, won't it, Sissy?"

Sissy looked like the cat that got the cream. "It certainly will. We'll go and see Tolly this afternoon and see what he says. Then, if he's agreeable, we'll go and see the boy in hospital. Did you say he was in Charing Cross?"

Billy nodded. "Prince Edward ward. Where does this Tolly live?"

"Lambeth," said Elsie, "There's a bus down the road that goes straight there."

"Lambeth's good," said Billy. "It would get the boy away from his old haunts up West."

"I'll whip up a batch of teacakes before we go. Tolly's

favourite." Sissy was up and bustling about. "Now, while I'm up, how about a couple of sandwiches, Billy? Cheese and pickle alright?"

Billy suddenly felt hungry and a lot more like his old self.

"Cheese and pickle would just hit the spot, Aunty."

Tollman and Victoria arrived at the formidable Grove Hospital after a very long walk from Tooting Railway Station.

"It's a fever hospital, Mrs E, very contagious diseases," Tollman warned. "I doubt that they'll let us past the front gate. In which case, I don't think I should flash my warrant card, because young Polly might leg it. Perhaps you should present yourself as a friend of Lady Harriet's, come to take Polly home, in order for them to go and fetch her without a fuss."

"Good idea, Mr Tollman," agreed Victoria. "But do you think you could arrange for a cab to take us back home? I don't fancy our chances of keeping Polly in our grasp if we have to walk all the way back to the station."

"Oof. I don't know where we would find a cab round here." Tollman looked stumped, then he added, "Tell you what, you take Polly to one side and I'll flash my warrant card at someone and see if I can get one of their vehicles to drop us down to the station."

Their plan of action agreed, they stepped inside the huge iron gates and went to the porter's lodge. The porter came out and Victoria explained to him her task. The man then pointed out the way to the administration block at the beginning of the large, sprawling complex of buildings and they set off once more.

"I have a feeling this is going to be a long job," muttered Tollman. "We may get passed from pillar to post before they let us see the girl."

"Chin up, Mr Tollman," said Victoria brightly. "We've made it through the gates quite easily and these places are rather efficient. I'm sure it won't be as bad as you think."

Tollman, therefore, was pleasantly surprised when, in the administration block, a woman scanned a huge blackboard and immediately located Polly. "Oh yes, she's a probationer on the scarlet fever wards. Block number two. Shame you're taking her away. She's got two ticks for punctuality and hard work. I'll get her wages ready. She's got two shillings to come. Mildred?" she called over to another woman, "Go and get Polly Sutton from Block Two, please."

Mildred nodded and left. Victoria gazed out of the window and exclaimed, "Good Lord! There are children in beds outside the building!"

"Yes ma'am," the woman confirmed, unlocking a cash box and counting out Polly's wages.

"It's not very warm today," Victoria observed.

"No, ma'am, but it is sunny and they're well wrapped up. It's good for them. Doctor's orders."

Victoria shuddered at the thought of the children being outside in the elements but assumed that the doctors knew what they were doing.

Just then Mildred arrived back with Polly, instantly recognisable to Tollman and Victoria from her photograph. She was carrying her coat and hat and looked very nervous. Victoria smiled to reassure her.

"Polly, I've come to take you home," she said simply.

Polly curtsied. "Is Lady Harriet dead?" she quietly asked.

"No, Polly," Victoria assured her. "She is very ill but appears to be on the mend."

Polly smiled and tears began to appear in her eyes. "Thank

the Lord," she murmured. "I have prayed for her every day, Ma'am. Truly I have."

"I'm sure that helped," said Victoria kindly. "This is Mr Tollman. He's here to help us."

Tollman tipped his hat towards the girl and she nodded.

"Polly, could you sign for your wages please?" said the woman and Polly duly signed and received her two shillings.

"I liked it here," she said simply to the woman, who looked sympathetic.

"You're a good worker, Polly. Look." She pointed to the blackboard. "Matron gave you two ticks."

Polly smiled and turned to Victoria. "Can I see Lady Harriet now?"

Victoria took her hand and held it firmly. "Very soon, Polly. I promise."

When they reached the porter's lodge, Victoria and Polly stood apart, whilst Tollman went into the lodge to have a quiet word about transport. As luck would have it, there was a freshly scrubbed ambulance about to travel all the way to the centre of London to pick up two children with tuberculosis. Tollman, Polly and Victoria clambered in the back and the ambulance set off. Soon, the rhythm of the ambulance movement made Polly's eyes close and Victoria gently suggested that the girl lay down on the trolley and get some sleep.

"She looks exhausted," Victoria whispered to Tollman as the girl soon succumbed to a deep sleep.

"Well, she's been on the run for six days," he whispered back, "not knowing what had happened to Lady Harriet and all. Her nerves must be worn to shreds. The sooner we can get this case wrapped up, the sooner that girl can sleep soundly without worrying what's going to happen when she wakes up."

✳

Beech had dealt with a mountain of paperwork by the time he was summoned to the Chief Commissioner's room. Sir Edward looked up as he entered and smiled briefly.

"How is the Murcheson case going, Beech? Any developments yet?"

"Rather a lot, sir. We're hoping to wrap it up very soon."

"Are you, by God!" Sir Edward motioned Beech to take a seat. "Fill me in."

Beech went through the detail of their investigations so far, and Sir Edward made various noises of astonishment along the way.

"So this seemingly cut-and-dried case of a titled lady stabbing her husband in self-defence has now developed into two murder hunts, gangland involvement, two brothels and a distasteful underage prostitution ring! Does that about sum it up?"

Beech gave a wry smile. "Pretty much, sir."

"So, how is your team shaping up?"

"Pretty damn good, sir, if I might say so. Better than I'd ever hoped. Tollman and Rigsby are first-class policemen and the ladies…well, I have to say I've been astonished at how much they have contributed to our work so far."

"Mm. Sounds like it. Just thought I'd let you know that the word is that a regional police force have been given permission to sign up their first woman police officer this summer. She's to be given full powers of arrest too."

"Well, that's good news, isn't it? What police force?"

"Lincolnshire. However, please don't mention this to your ladies and get their hopes up. The Home Secretary refuses to countenance women police officers in the Metropolitan area – says the work is too dangerous in London – and, besides, even if he changed his mind, it will be a very long time indeed before a woman would be allowed to be a detective."

"Pity," Beech felt deflated.

"But," Sir Edward added, with a suspicion of a twinkle in his eye, "if your team were to produce solid evidence of a body of work, say, over a two-year period, that might be enough to convince senior members of the police force and the Home Secretary to change their minds – don't you think?"

Beech realised that he had just been given the go-ahead to carry on with his team for a considerable length of time and he beamed. "Yes, sir, I do."

"Good man. As long as you keep your head down and no one gets wind of our arrangement, you should be able to produce some good ammunition in the future to argue the case for women in the force."

"Yes, sir."

"Good luck with your arrests tomorrow."

"Thank you, sir."

As Beech got up to leave, Sir Edward added, "By the way, Beech, don't be surprised if a D-notice gets slapped on the Murcheson affair, once it's cleared up. The Government takes a dim view of news that may affect the nation's morale during wartime and the stabbing of a drug-addled Lord of the Realm, crazed with pain because of his war wounds, would probably fall into that category. It will most definitely be D-listed if the Lord is connected to brothels – male or female, London gangsters and a quack doctor who has the Attorney General's wife as a patient! I'm sorry but it all sounds like very sensitive material to me."

"I understand, sir. So what shall I do with my final report?"

Sir Edward looked at him steadily before answering. "You will give it to me. I shall lock it away to be resurrected at a suitable time."

"What about any arrests we may make, sir? How will they be treated?"

"Closed court, probably. Did you know that Lord Murcheson was in Military Intelligence?"

Beech was surprised. "No, sir, I didn't."

"Bloody useless at it, apparently. Do you know how he received his 'war wounds', for want of a better term?"

"No, sir, I do not."

"He was shot in the back by a Frenchman whilst escaping from a farmhouse where he had been caught in flagrante with the man's wife."

"Good God!"

"Mm. Quite. Hardly the stuff that VCs are made of. Nevertheless, however terrible he was as a soldier, he was a Lord and he was in Military Intelligence. That is enough to warrant a closed court in the Government's eyes. So, I'm afraid there will be no public glory for you in any arrests, Beech."

Beech felt stung that Sir Edward would think that public approbation was his desired goal. "That is fine and dandy, sir, since I have no desire for publicity whatsoever." He spoke as calmly as he could, given that he felt annoyed.

Sir Edward smiled. "I believe you, Beech. Don't take it to heart, man. I wouldn't have agreed to go along with this scheme of yours if I didn't believe that you would be happy working constantly in the shadows. The policemen who look for personal glory are always the ones who make mistakes or become corrupted by their ambition. Good luck tomorrow."

The interview was over and Beech left feeling that he had acquitted himself well.

✳

All had gone well for Elsie and Sissy when they visited their friend Tolly in Lambeth. Being such a kind man, he had wept when they told him of the boy's ordeal, smiled at the fact that the boy liked to work with wood, and wept again – this time for joy – at the thought of having a companion in his last years.

He ate his teacakes with pleasure and fretted about the state of his little house and workshop.

"I've lived alone for too long! Everywhere is a mess."

Elsie reassured him that before they brought George round, she and Sissy would clean his whole house from top to bottom.

"I'm a demon with a bucket and mop, Tolly!" Sissy said, laughing.

"Why are you doing this for me?" Tolly asked in wonderment.

"We're doing it for the *two* of you…and our Billy…he's been worrying about this lad ever since he took him to hospital. He won't stop fretting until the boy has a decent place to stay."

Elsie felt she had to insert a note of warning. "Now, don't get your hopes up too much, Tolly. We still have to talk to the boy. He may not agree. But if he's as gentle and nice as Billy says, then I'm sure he will."

"He's not a bad boy, Tolly, despite his past. Billy says he's been very badly treated by his father and this…this animal…"

"I don't care about his past," whispered Tolly. "We've all done things we're ashamed of. Perhaps I can teach him to have hope for his future."

"That's what we thought," answered Sissy, brushing away an annoying tear that had suddenly and wilfully threatened to roll down her cheek.

"Now," said Elsie briskly, as if to ward off this sudden affliction of crying that was affecting everyone. "We're going to see the boy today and have a chat with him. Then we'll come round tomorrow and start cleaning. Mind you, we'll have to bring Timmy. We can't leave him alone all day."

"Ah, Timmy! How is the little rascal?" Tolly asked.

"*More* of a little rascal!" announced Sissy and they all laughed.

Elsie gave Tolly a kiss on the cheek and started packing up her bag. "Now don't you fret overnight. Even if the boy is reluctant, we'll win him round. You know how persuasive me and Sissy can be!"

Tolly nodded happily and shuffled slowly to the door to wave them off.

Sissy looked at her sister and wiped her eyes again. "Elsie," she said, "You and I are going to have to be put through the wringer tonight, we're going to be that wet from crying!"

"I didn't cry!" protested Elsie.

"You ain't seen the boy yet," was Sissy's grim rejoinder.

✻

Polly and Esme clung to each other, silently, on the steps of Lady Maud's house. Esme had been hovering on the basement steps all morning, waiting for Victoria and Tollman's return and, as soon as she saw them step out of the ambulance with Polly, she flung herself at the girl with gibbering apologies for having 'let her down' and 'not helped her look after Lady Harriet'.

Polly said nothing; she just enveloped Esme in her arms and put her head on her shoulder. It seemed to Victoria that the two girls clung to each other for ages. Two young friends reunited. Finally they separated and Polly said, "What is this place?"

"It's where I live," said Victoria. "There is no one at Lady Harriet's house now. So you are going to stay here for a little while. Shall we go in?"

Polly nodded and immediately went to follow Esme down the basement stairs but Victoria stopped her.

"No, Polly. The front door. Esme, you can come too."

The two girls held hands as they walked up the stairs into the house. Tollman thanked the ambulance driver and gave him some money. "For a drink when you're off-duty," he said and then he followed everyone up the stairs.

Victoria took Polly into the study and sat her down.

"Now, Polly, Esme is going to go downstairs and get you something to eat and drink." She turned to the maid. "Esme, could you please get Polly some sandwiches and some tea, and some of those little cakes Mrs Beddowes makes for me?" Esme nodded and disappeared.

"Once you have eaten, Polly," Victoria continued gently, "Mr Tollman here, and, perhaps, another very nice man called Mr Beech, are going to ask you some questions about the night of Lord Murcheson's murder." A look of fear came into Polly's eyes and Victoria took her hand. "It's alright, my dear. I shall be here all the time. No one will hurt you. Everyone here just wants to understand what happened."

Polly looked straight at Victoria and said, "I killed him, you know. It was nothing to do with Lady Harriet. He was trying to kill her and I had to stop him…" then she started crying.

"Calm down, Polly. Wait until you have eaten and Mr Beech gets here. No more confessions now."

Polly nodded and once Esme appeared with a tray of food and drink, the girl realised how hungry she was and began to take tentative bites of a sandwich. Victoria allowed Esme to stay, under her supervision but she made it very clear that they were not to discuss anything to do with the murder or that night or subsequent events. She didn't want Esme to frighten

Polly any more than necessary.

Fortunately, Beech arrived within five minutes and Billy, a few minutes after that. When Polly saw Billy's uniform she began to cry, and poor Billy was sent out of the room, Esme too, and they both went down to the kitchen to have a chat to Mrs Beddowes.

"Now," said Beech gently. "I'm Mr Beech, this is Mr Tollman and this is Mrs Ellingham. We're very pleased to meet you."

"Pleased to meet you, sir," Polly mumbled.

"Polly, I need to ask you questions, Mr Tollman is going to write some notes and Mrs Ellingham…well…she's just here to look after you. Alright?"

Polly nodded.

"Good." Beech sat down opposite the girl and tried to look relaxed. "So what can you tell me about the terrible night when Lord Murcheson got stabbed?"

Polly's face suddenly became stubborn. "I did it, sir. I killed His Lordship because he was trying to kill Her Ladyship. It wasn't anything to do with Lady Harriet!"

Beech, Tollman and Victoria all exchanged looks.

"Well, now. We're not sure about that, Polly. You see it takes an awful lot of strength to plunge a pair of scissors into a man – especially one as deranged as Lord Murcheson must have been – and you are such a small girl."

"I'm strong!" Polly objected. "You ask the Matron at the Grove Hospital! I can scrub floors all day long! I'm good and strong!"

"There is also the problem that Lady Harriet has signed a sworn statement confessing to the murder herself…"

"No!" Polly almost screamed in distress. "She didn't do it! She couldn't have done it! She was in a dead faint when I ran out to get Mr Dodds…" She suddenly realised that she was deviating from her story and stopped. "I did it. I told you. Lady Harriet is—" she couldn't bring herself to say that her beloved employer was lying "—confused. She fainted. Maybe she thought she'd done it. But she didn't. I did."

Beech leant forward. "We know that Lady Harriet didn't kill her husband. We have a doctor who will swear that Lady Harriet's injuries were so severe that she could not have raised herself from the floor to stab her husband."

"She couldn't?" Polly was confused. "Then why did she sign a confession?"

"We think she did so to protect *you.*" Victoria said, "because she thought that *you* had killed her husband."

"I…I don't know what to say." Polly looked distraught. "I thought *she* had done it, while I was downstairs. And she…"

"…thought *you* had done it whilst she was unconscious. You have both been trying to protect each other." Beech was satisfied that they had made a breakthrough with the girl and would now learn the truth. "Alright, Polly. No more of this nonsense now. Tell us everything that happened that night and you will be helping us and Lady Harriet find out who the real killer was."

Polly looked helplessly at Beech and then she nodded and began.

"I was sitting on a chair outside Lady Harriet's room, as usual. I usually went up there about nine o'clock when everyone else went to bed. Everything was fine but then I must have fallen asleep…I was that tired, I couldn't help myself. Next thing I know, I woke up with a start, 'cos His Lordship had come roaring up the stairs, like a madman he was, shouting, 'It's not mine! I know it's not mine!' I stood up to bar his way but he just knocked me over and went straight into Lady Harriet's room. She was asleep in bed and he…he just dragged her out of the bed…like she was a rag doll." Polly paused, obviously distressed.

"Have a sip of tea, Polly," Victoria helpfully suggested.

"I'm OK, thank you, Ma'am. It's just horrible remembering it all. I'll be alright." She resumed her narrative. "Lady Harriet was screaming and I couldn't understand why no one was coming to help her…I mean he was yelling, and she was screaming and I was yelling at him to stop. I grabbed hold of him but he just threw me to one side again. Lady Harriet was on the floor and he kicked her, she fell backwards and he…he…just stamped on her, really hard. She gave a terrible scream and then fainted. I ran, ran as hard as I could downstairs to the kitchen to get help. I banged on Mr Dodds' door for ages, screaming for him to come and help and then he appeared behind me. He must have been on the ground floor all the time and I couldn't understand why he hadn't come up after His Lordship when it all started. I couldn't understand that," she repeated.

Beech sensed the girl had temporarily become distracted, so he urged her on. "What happened then? Once Mr Dodds had appeared?

"He told me to calm down and I got frantic. I screamed at him that Lord Murcheson had killed Lady Harriet. Hadn't he heard the screams? I asked. He told me to stay there and he would go upstairs and sort it out. He said on no account was I to leave the basement until he said so. I said yes and started crying and he left. Then he came back, about five or so minutes later, looking really shaken, and he said that Lady Harriet had stabbed His Lordship. Then he took me upstairs to help Lady Harriet. I couldn't understand why no one else in the house had come to help us. There had been such a racket…"

"Polly," Beech explained, "no one else came to your aid because Dodds had drugged them. They didn't know they were being drugged. One of our constables found out, to his cost."

Polly looked shocked and then angry. "How could anyone be so evil? Why did he do it?"

"We don't know that, as yet. Possibly so that no one would notice him coming and going. It appears he had other… business interests to deal with. Now, Polly, when you were downstairs…when Dodds asked you to stay there…did you hear anything?"

Polly thought hard for a moment. "I was crying quite hard and, in any case, you don't hear anything in the basement. The door is padded and when it's shut, you can't hear anything. But you can hear people walking about above you and you know when the front door is closed. I did hear someone running from the stairs to the door and I heard the door close. I thought it was Mr Dodds. I dunno. I don't know what I thought, I was so scared."

"Polly, what happened…what did you see when Mr Dodds took you back upstairs?"

"Well, when he came and got me, he said, 'you and me are going to be in trouble now', and he dragged me upstairs. When I saw His Lordship with the scissors in his chest, I thought Lady Harriet had done it. She was moaning a bit and not quite awake but I thought perhaps she'd done it and then fainted again. Dodds told me we should get Lady Harriet dressed and downstairs before the police came. So we did. It took us a while, because she was a dead weight…although there was nothing of her, really. I could see that she was beginning to bleed…down there…" Polly looked embarrassed "…and I said to Mr Dodds that we should call a doctor. He said he would, as soon as we got her downstairs. We managed to lift her up and she sort of came round a bit but I could see she was in pain and we struggled down the stairs with her…"

"What time was this, Polly?" Beech interrupted.

"I don't know, sir. I wasn't taking much notice. Probably about two in the morning."

"What happened then?"

"Lady Harriet came round and the first thing she asked was, 'Where is my husband?' Dodds said, 'He's upstairs, madam, and he's dead.' I thought she was going to faint again and I said again to Mr Dodds that we should get a doctor. Then she grabbed my hand and said, 'Polly, you have been very courageous tonight.' Then she said to Dodds that she didn't want me to be questioned by the police and that he was to take me to her old convent immediately. I protested and said I wanted to stay with her but she said no. She wanted me safe and she wouldn't see a doctor until she knew I was safe. Dodds told me to go and get my hat and coat and be quick about it. So I did."

Beech thought for a moment and then he asked, 'Polly, did you see any blood on Mr Dodds at all?"

"No, sir."

Beech looked at Tollman. "Whoever stabbed Lord Murcheson would have had blood on their clothes from the arterial spurt." Tollman nodded in agreement. Beech turned back to Polly. "When Mr Dodds came for you, in the basement, and took you up to the bedroom, did you see any blood on Her Ladyship's nightdress."

Polly shook her head. "No sir. It was only when we sat her up to dress her that the blood started coming between her legs."

Beech continued. "So when you went to get your coat and hat, what happened then?"

"I came down the stairs and Mr Dodds was coming back in

the front door…"

"Where had he been?" Beech interrupted.

"I don't know, sir. I didn't think about it. He just told me to say my goodbyes to the mistress and to be quick. I went into the library and she kissed me and told me to be brave and not to tell anyone what had happened. Mr Dodds would take me to the convent and then come and get me when everything was settled. Then Dodds dragged me away and he hailed a taxi cab on Park Lane and took me to the convent."

"What about when he came to fetch you from there. What did he say then?"

Polly tried to hold back her tears at that point. "Well he told one of the sisters that Lady Harriet was better and I felt that everything was going to be alright. But when we got in the taxi cab he had waiting, he told me that was a lie. Lady Harriet had been taken to hospital, near to death and he was taking me somewhere else for my own sake. He said that the police thought that I had murdered His Lordship and he had promised Lady Harriet that he would hide me. I said I thought I should go to the police and tell them the truth, and he said that Lady Harriet would be upset if I did that. So I asked why I couldn't stay at the convent and he said that I had to keep moving around. Then we got to Mrs Perkins' place and he told her that she had to keep me there until he came back. I don't think Mrs Perkins liked Mr Dodds. He took her in another room and I heard him shout at her…I couldn't make out what he said. She looked upset after he had gone. She said I couldn't stay there…no matter what Mr Dodds said…and she asked me if I had any family I could go to. I told her I was a Barnardo's orphan and she said I should go back there and gave me some money."

"So how on earth did you end up at the Grove Hospital,

Polly?" Victoria enquired gently.

"I got on the bus to go to Liverpool Street. I didn't want to go back to Barnardo's. I didn't want them to think I'd done something bad. Someone had left a newspaper on the seat in the bus and on the back there was an advertisement. It said, 'Have you had scarlet fever? If so, you could come and work at the Grove Fever Hospital.' Well, I had scarlet fever when I was a child at Barnardo's, and the advertisement said they were paying good money for cleaners and ward orderlies, so I got off the bus and got on another one that was going to Tooting. I didn't mean to be so much trouble!" she wailed. "I didn't do anything bad, ma'am! Mr Dodds will tell you. I was only looking out for my mistress!"

Victoria put her arm round the girl to comfort her.

Beech sighed. "Unfortunately, Mr Dodds is dead, Polly."

Polly's eyes widened. "What happened?"

"He was stabbed in the chest, like Lord Murcheson, and, from what you have said today, it seems very likely that he was stabbed by the same person."

Sissy and Elsie sat outside Prince Edward Ward in nervous anticipation. They had arrived about half past five, only to be told by a formidable Ward Sister that visiting hour was not until six and they would have to wait.

"Who are you visiting?" she had asked. "Visiting is restricted to relatives only, you know."

"We're visiting George Harris. I *am* a relative, on his mother's side," Elsie had said, off the cuff. "Mrs Rigsby, and this is my sister," indicating Sissy at her side.

Sissy had decided to elaborate. "He probably won't remember us. We haven't seen him since he was a baby. There was a bit of a disagreement with his father. Nasty man," she'd said, grimacing.

The Ward Sister had looked entirely disinterested and had said, "You may wait there. A bell will ring when the visiting hour starts."

"She's a bit of an old tartar, isn't she?" Elsie had murmured as they'd duly taken their places on the bench in the corridor.

"Well, they have to be stern, don't they? Especially on the men's ward. Can't stand any nonsense from the male patients, can they?" Elsie had nodded in agreement.

Now, the bell rang, and everyone on the benches stood up and began to make their way through the doors. Elsie took a deep breath.

"My heart's going like a hammer and tongs," she said.

"Mine too," replied Sissy. "Come on, Else. We've come this far. Brave it out!"

They went through the doors nervously. "How will we know him?" whispered Elsie.

"Simple," said her sister, pointing, "he's the young lad over there. The only one with no visitors."

George looked up quizzically as two plump cheerful ladies appeared at the end of his bed.

"Hello George. I'm Elsie. I'm Constable Rigsby's mum," said one.

"And I'm Sissy, Constable Rigsby's Aunty," said the other, then she added, "We've got a proposition for you."

Matron appeared and asked for the Ward Sister's daily report. As she flicked through it, she noted that various patients appeared to be improving, especially the boy who had been beaten by his father. "George Harris?" she asked Sister. "Appears to have eaten something?"

"Yes, Matron. His back has been very well dressed by the

police and he will soon have any drugs out of his system. We had a bad time this morning, when he was admitted. He was trembling and vomiting but he appears to have turned the corner this afternoon. He had some tea and toast. I expect he will improve even more now that his long-lost relatives have come to visit."

Matron looked over to where two middle-aged ladies were sitting on the bed stroking the boy's hair and holding his hand whilst he appeared to be alternating between weeping and smiling.

"Those visitors are sitting on the bed, Sister." She frowned. "Give them one more minute then tell them that sitting on the bed is forbidden. One minute, Sister; otherwise the other visitors may follow suit," and she left.

"Yes, Matron," the Ward Sister muttered, and she began to look at her apron watch.

CHAPTER TWENTY

Plans Unravel

The day did not start well. Caroline rang to say that there had been an explosion in a munitions factory overnight and she was wanted in surgery.

"Fifteen dead and thirty-five wounded. All women except for one male supervisor. Half of them have gone to the London and the other half have come here," she explained breathlessly to Victoria on the telephone. "I'm so sorry to let everyone down."

"Don't be silly," Victoria replied with concern. "Even if you had been here, you would have been too tired to do anything. We can manage."

"Victoria, I need you to tell Peter something for me."

"Yes, of course. Do I need to write it down?" She searched frantically around for a pad and pencil.

"No, no," Caroline said, "Just tell him that I was talking to Esme and she let slip that she saw a nurse come to visit Lord Murcheson, one night – not the fateful night, I should add, but on an earlier occasion. Apparently, Dodds used to insist that no one came downstairs after nine o'clock at night but she had a cold and came down to make a hot drink and she saw the nurse arriving. Now it could have been Dr McKinley's nurse…well, I would think so…and the nurse that Peter and I saw yesterday, I think, was in the second stages of syphilis. She could have been providing…er…extra services to Lord Murcheson, which is how he contracted the disease. That's all. How is Polly Sutton?"

"She's fine. We put her up in a room with Esme and I should think she's still asleep. She didn't do it, Caroline. She gave us a detailed account of that night. She thought Lady Harriet had done it but her statement pretty much proved that Lady Harriet couldn't have done it. Also…here's the thing…it doesn't seem like Dodds did it either…" Victoria stopped speaking because she could hear Caroline speaking to someone else.

"I've got to go now, Victoria. I'm needed. Good luck for this morning." Then the line went dead.

Beech and Tollman arrived early. Billy was up and about before they arrived and appeared in his civilian clothes. Lady Maud commented, at the breakfast table, on how smart he looked.

"Although I do rather like a man in uniform, I must confess," she said, winking at Billy, who grinned.

Victoria could see that Beech was fretting over the news that Caroline would not be available for the surveillance operation this morning.

"I'm not happy with you following this woman on your own," he said in a worried tone of voice.

Victoria was exasperated. "Really! I do wish everyone would stop treating me like cut glass!" She glared at Beech, which caused Tollman and Billy to take an unusual interest in their toast in embarrassment.

"I could take Caroline's place," announced Lady Maud in a firm voice, that brooked no argument.

"What!?" Beech was taken aback. "No. That's preposterous!"

"Do tell me why," said Lady Maud acidly. "I am perfectly capable of accompanying my daughter on a brisk walk around the West End. If this woman suspect should turn violent, I can always cosh her with my umbrella or my handbag. In fact I shall borrow one of Mrs Beddowes' flat irons and put it in my handbag after breakfast."

This made Victoria giggle and Billy grinned again. Tollman allowed a small smile to play around his lips and Beech just looked outmanoeuvred. He sighed in defeat.

"Very well. But…Maud…no theatricals please. The purpose of the exercise is to be as inconspicuous as possible."

"Well, I was hardly going to burst into song in the middle of Piccadilly," she murmured sarcastically, making Billy choke on his toast and start a coughing fit.

"Cough it up, lad," said Tollman cheerfully, banging Billy hard on the back. "Take a swig of tea."

Billy nodded and obeyed, both laughing and coughing at the same time.

"So," said Beech loudly, trying to assert his authority, "the plan is this – Maud and Victoria will casually walk along opposite the house; Rigsby, you will lounge around in a doorway opposite the house; Tollman…you and I will be on the same side, up towards St James'. When this woman enters, we will wait until she comes out and then we will all follow her at a respectable distance from her and each other. Rigsby, you must never lose sight of the two ladies and Tollman and I will never lose sight of you. And Rigsby, if you see any trouble, you must sprint ahead to aid the ladies. Understood?"

Everyone nodded. Just then there was a knock at the door and Mary entered.

"Beg pardon, Chief Inspector, but there is a telephone call for you."

"Oh?" Beech looked puzzled and followed Mary out to the hall.

"The trick is, ladies," counselled Tollman, "that when you are following a suspect – undercover like – you must act completely natural. Never get too close to them. Stop occasionally to look in a shop window. Don't draw attention to yourself."

"What do we do if she gets on a bus, or goes down the Underground or hails a cab?" asked Victoria.

"Good question, Mrs E.," said Tollman approvingly. "That would be the point at which Billy and I would take over. We need a pre-arranged signal if she looks like she's boarding transport. Then Billy here can sprint after her and, hopefully, get on the same bus or train. I doubt that she'll get a cab but, if she does, we'll have to get one to follow it."

"I could open my umbrella," volunteered Lady Maud, helpfully.

"That'll do it," said Tollman. "That'll do nicely."

Beech returned looking flustered. "I've been summoned to the Yard," he announced. "Apparently this wretched munitions factory explosion may have been deliberate sabotage and I have to interview the factory manager. Matter of National Security."

Everyone looked anxious until Beech said, "Well, there's nothing for it. Tollman, you'll have to be in charge of this one. We can't abandon things now. I know it's a great deal of responsibility but I'm sure you can cope. It goes without saying that you will be responsible for the care and safety of the ladies."

"Yes, sir. Don't worry, sir. Billy and I know what we're doing."

"I'm sure you do." Beech turned to the women. "Ladies, please do exactly as Mr Tollman bids you. Nothing rash. No heroics."

Mother and daughter assured Beech that they would take great care and be sensible, and he reluctantly left for

Scotland Yard.

"Right," said Lady Maud, "I'm going to get that flat iron and then I will get my hat, coat and umbrella."

Everyone was in position in Piccadilly by eight o'clock. Billy was, ostensibly, reading a newspaper in a doorway. Lady Maud and Victoria were taking an unusual interest in the billboard of the Criterion Theatre and Tollman was loitering on the corner of St James'. Despite it being only eight thirty in the morning, there was a considerable amount of traffic. Buses were disgorging shop girls at Piccadilly Circus, delivery vans were weaving their way around the pedestrians and bleary-eyed soldiers were sitting on the steps around Eros, recovering from a heavy night "up West". Tollman's only concern was that Victoria and Lady Maud looked a little out of place at this hour of the morning. It was too early for such obvious well-bred ladies to be shopping and he hoped that they wouldn't be spotted by the suspect.

After about half an hour their patient wait was rewarded. A woman carrying a canvas bag approached the door of the house and knocked. The door was opened and she stepped inside. Billy was just about able to make out the face of the porter as he hustled the woman in. He looked across to Victoria to make sure that she had seen the woman enter and they nodded at each other. He smiled as he noted the determination with which Lady Maud was gripping both her handbag and umbrella. After no more than two minutes, the woman appeared again, this time clutching the canvas bag to her chest. Billy folded his newspaper up and prepared to move. To his dismay, she walked across the road, almost towards him, and stood at the bus stop. He waited for another two or three people to join the queue and then he sauntered over to stand behind them. He looked around and noted with some amusement that Lady Maud was frantically trying to open her umbrella as per the arranged signal.

Bless her, he thought, she's doing her best.

Tollman casually joined the queue behind Billy.

"Keep your eyes ahead, lad," he muttered. "And sit well apart from me."

Billy duly obeyed and when the bus arrived, he sat to the right, two seats behind the woman and Tollman sat to the left, even further back. Billy briefly looked out of the window to where Victoria appeared to be consoling a disappointed Lady Maud and he smiled. *Never mind, Your Ladyship…you'll have better luck next time.* The bus drew away. It proceeded up Regent Street, stopping once or twice for passengers, and then turned into Oxford Street. At the first stop, the woman got up. So did Tollman, but Billy waited until the bus was almost about to pull away before he dashed off, which allowed him to be a comfortable thirty yards behind Tollman, who was a similar distance behind the woman. They followed her as she walked up a street off to the right and they stayed in the same positions until she crossed the junction of Wigmore Street and Harley Street. Tollman walked up the steps of the first house and waited for Billy to pass. He indicated that Billy should take the lead now. Billy nodded and quickened his pace and he heard Tollman come back down the steps behind him and begin to match his footsteps. Then the woman crossed the road, stopped outside a house, took out a key and let herself in. Tollman shouted, "Now, lad! We need to catch her with that money still on her!"

Billy sprinted across to the house and began hammering on the door. The astonished woman opened it, canvas bag in her hand, and before she could speak, Billy stuck his foot in the door, flashed his warrant card and said, "You're nicked, madam."

A breathless Tollman arrived and panted, "We are arresting you under The Offences Against the Person Act 1875. And, madam, you are under suspicion of committing so *many* offences under that Act that I do not have time to list them all now."

The woman looked shocked and she backed into the house, helpless and unable to speak. Billy and Tollman pushed their way inside and Tollman produced handcuffs from his pocket.

Tollman noted the plush surroundings and, in particular, a telephone mounted on the wall.

"PC Rigsby, kindly telephone West End Central and request a Black Maria. Madam, I must ask you to give me that bag you're holding and submit to handcuffs, otherwise I shall add 'resisting arrest' to your long litany of crimes."

The woman handed over the bag and Tollman attached the cuffs. He looked in the bag and produced a brown paper bag containing plenty of paper money.

"Constable Rigsby, I am asking you to attest that I am in possession of—" he rapidly counted the large notes "—fifty five pounds."

"Noted, sir," replied Billy, as he agitated the cradle of the telephone and raised the earpiece to his ear. "West End Central Police Station," he ordered in response to the operator's query. "And make it quick, love."

Tollman turned back to the woman, who was, by now, sullen and defeated.

"What's your name, madam?" Tollman enquired briskly.

"Ada Yardley," her reply was brief.

Tollman looked around. "What sort of place is this, then?"

he asked, noting the plush sofas and flowers and magazines. "It wouldn't be another knocking shop by any chance would it?"

Ada laughed drily. "In Harley Street?" she said sarcastically. "Don't you know a doctor's office when you see one?"

"Can't say that I do, madam. Not having ever had the money to visit a Harley Street doctor. So, why, may I ask, are *you* here?"

Ada looked sullen again. "I work here…as a nurse."

"Ah," Tollman looked interested. "But you don't get paid enough, I suppose. So you decided to run a few businesses on the side."

Ada looked at him with contempt. "I'm saying no more. Not to the likes of you. I want to speak to your Chief Inspector. I *know* things that he's going to be very interested in."

"Oh well, it's your lucky day then, Ada. Because my Chief Inspector is back at the Yard just dying to meet you."

"Mr Tollman," Billy interrupted, "the West End boys want to know what the house number is? I didn't look as we came in."

Ada answered. "Number forty-two, dear. Forty-two Harley Street. The office of the very well-connected Doctor McKinley." She gave Tollman a sneering smile of triumph.

✳

Beech was just coming out of a meeting when a constable informed him that Detective Sergeant Tollman had a suspect down in the holding cell and would he please come and interview her. She was asking for him specifically, the constable relayed.

Ada Yardley had been moved to an interview room and was seated at a table, flanked by Billy and Tollman. She looked defiant.

"So, Miss…" Beech looked at Tollman for information.

"Ada Yardley," Tollman volunteered.

"Miss Yardley," said Beech, "we have recently met, in Doctor McKinley's office, as I'm sure you remember."

"I'm not responsible for anything," she said belligerently, as Beech sat down opposite her. "I didn't know there was money in that bag. I was just asked to pick something up. I didn't know what it was."

Tollman tutted. "Try again, love" he said. "We have the porter's testimony that you came regularly every fortnight and asked for the rents."

Ada glared at him, unsure of how to proceed. "I was made to do it," she said flatly. "I didn't want to, I was threatened."

"By whom?" asked Beech.

Ada looked at him in disbelief. "By McKinley, of course! Who do you think owns all the brothels? Do you think I'd be working for that man every day if *I* owned such places? I'd be living at the Ritz, drinking champagne, wouldn't I?" She snorted derisively. "Well, I'm not going to prison for this. I'll tell you chapter and verse about the good doctor, but I want a deal."

Just as Beech was about to consider making some concession, a constable knocked and came in with a message. Beech opened the note and it read,

Didn't get a chance to tell you this morning. Caro rang and said Esme saw a nurse, one night, at M's house.

Beech passed the note over to Tollman, who read it and, in turn, passed it to Billy. They looked at each other.

"Unfortunately," Beech said in his firmest voice, "the Metropolitan Police does not do 'deals' with murderers."

"What?!" Ada looked terrified. "I haven't murdered anybody!"

"You were seen," Beech added, "by a maid, at Lord Murcheson's house." He carefully didn't mention *when*.

Ada's expression showed that she was trapped. "No! No! It was self-defence," she admitted in a whisper, "the man was crazed. He was trying to kill me. Look!" and she clumsily, with her hands cuffed together, pulled off the scarf she was wearing to reveal livid marks around the base of her neck, that were turning into ugly bruises. Beech realised that when he saw her, at the doctor's office, her high starched collar would have covered them up. "Murcheson was trying to strangle me. He'd already done something to his wife. She was lying on the floor in a dead faint. I…I had to do something! I grabbed the scissors and stabbed him – in the chest. I didn't know what else to do! As God is my witness, I never meant to kill him!" She was beside herself with fear and anger now, although there were no tears forthcoming. Ada Yardley was a very tough woman and not given easily to tears.

"Tell us exactly what happened that night," said Beech, "and everything you know about the doctor's little businesses and we will ensure that you do not hang. I can't offer you more than that."

Ada nodded, defeated and began to explain, whilst Tollman took copious notes.

"McKinley used to send me to Murcheson's house with drugs – sometimes powdered heroin – sometimes, if Murcheson had had a bad week, he would send me round to give him an injection."

"Of what?"

"A cocaine solution, into the vein."

"How many times did you go round to Lord Murcheson's house?"

"Twice a week, no more."

"Did Dodds know about this arrangement?"

"Who?" she seemed genuinely confused.

"Er…" Beech tried to remember Dodds' aliases.

"George Sumpter," offered Billy helpfully.

"Oh, *him!*" Ada was bitterly scornful. "*He* set it all up! Him and the doctor are thick as thieves…well, that's what they are, aren't they? Thieves and criminals, the pair of them."

Beech noted Yardley's use of the present tense when discussing Dodds/Sumpter but he let it pass for the moment.

"So Sumpter arranged for you to call on Lord Murcheson?"

"Yes, he told the doctor that I should never come before nine o'clock, to make sure that the household staff were in bed. I never got paid any extra for these out-of-hours visits!" she said, in an aggrieved tone.

"So that's why you decided to offer Lord Murcheson some extra 'personal services', was it?" Beech was guessing here, based on Caroline's deductions about the syphilis, and realised he had hit the mark when the seemingly tough Ada flushed under all her make-up.

"So what if I did?" she said sullenly. "His Lordship was offering to pay handsomely for…certain things. I'd have been a fool not to take him up on it!"

Beech nodded. "Now tell us about the night you allege he attacked you. Tell us exactly how everything happened."

"I arrived about nine thirty. Sumpter was waiting, as usual, outside the front door. He told me never to ring the bell; he would always be waiting. Then he took me into Murcheson, who was in the ground-floor parlour. He was three sheets to the wind already. I don't know what Sumpter had been giving him but he'd been drinking as well. He told Sumpter to clear off and he would call for him when he wanted him. Anyway, Sumpter went and Murcheson asked if I had the syringe with me. I said yes and I gave him the injection. Then…he wanted personal favours from me but he was so boozed and drugged up that he couldn't…perform…if you get my drift. Well, that sent him into a rage…like I had never seen before…and he went crashing out of the room. I stayed where I was because I wasn't supposed to be seen by anyone, on Sumpter's orders. Then I heard all the screaming – two women it sounded like – and Murcheson yelling like a madman."

"And you still stayed in the parlour?"

"Yes. I thought the whole household would be awake because of the noise and I stayed where I was. I heard one of the women come running down the stairs, sobbing and screaming some man's name out – it sounded like 'Mr Hobbs'…"

"That would be Dodds – Sumpter's alias."

"Well, I didn't know. Murcheson was still yelling upstairs. Then Sumpter appeared in the parlour and said Murcheson had gone crazy and I should go upstairs and calm him down with something. He meant more drugs but I knew that would only make things worse, so I ran upstairs and tried to reason with him. His wife was in a dead faint on the floor – her hair was all a mess and her nightdress was up around her knees – I thought maybe he'd tried to force himself on her. Anyway, Murcheson had gone truly mad. He was almost foaming at the mouth and that's when he tried to strangle me. I struggled but he was very strong. I felt the scissors on the bedside table and I let him have it. He looked rather surprised for a moment and then dropped to the floor."

"And what state were you in?"

"I could hardly breathe, my throat hurt so much, and I had blood all over my apron. Anyway, I staggered out and met Sumpter on the stairs. I told him what happened and he told me to get out of the house as fast as possible, he would sort everything out. So, I grabbed my bag and ran out of the front door."

"What did you do with your bloodstained apron?"

Ada looked confused for a moment and then said, "I took it off and threw it down the basement steps and then I ran until I reached Park Lane, and then I got on a bus."

"Yes, we have that apron," confirmed Beech, "Dodds…er, Sumpter, had put it in one of dustbins."

"Bloody fool!" She almost spat the words. "Cared more about his own neck than mine."

"So, when did you next meet Sumpter?"

She looked surprised. "I didn't! I haven't seen him for a week or more. In fact, he should have come round to the doctor's office yesterday to get more drugs but he didn't turn up."

Beech and the others exchanged glances.

"Did you have any telephone communication with him?"

"No," she said flatly. "I never do. Sumpter only ever rings Doctor McKinley. I'm nothing to him. Just a go-between. McKinley's the man with the money and he and Sumpter work everything out between themselves."

Beech again noted the use of the present tense. Yardley was seemingly not aware that Dodds was dead.

"So who told Doctor McKinley that Lord Murcheson was dead?"

"Me. The next morning, when I went into work. I said he'd have to give me some money so I could go away and he said he needed to speak to Sumpter first. So he tried. He couldn't get hold of him by telephone in the morning but then Sumpter rang in the afternoon. Then McKinley came to me and said it was alright. The police thought either Lady Harriet or her maid had done it and I was to carry on as normal. No one knew I had been there. I was safe. But, obviously, he was wrong," she added bitterly.

"Right. Have you got all of that, Detective Sergeant?" Tollman nodded. Beech continued. "Now, Miss Yardley, I want you to give us 'chapter and verse', as you called it, about Doctor McKinley's business dealings but, first, I wonder if Constable Rigsby might not go and get us all some cups of tea. I sense that this may be a long business."

"Yes, sir," said Billy and he went off in search of refreshments. As he was organising the making of the tea, he saw two detectives come along the corridor, towards the holding cell, with a suspect in tow. One of the detectives was Carter, who gave Billy a quizzical look as he passed.

"Where's your uniform, son?" he growled.

Billy flashed him a smile and said cheekily, "In the wash, detective," which made Carter scowl at him. A moment later, seeing Billy carrying a tray of tea things into interview room one made him scowl even more.

When Billy set down the tray on the table, he took Tollman to one side, "Carter's on the prowl," he murmured in a warning tone of voice.

Tollman nodded and asked to be excused for a moment. Carter was loitering in the corridor and immediately buttonholed him.

"What are you up to, Tollman?" he asked menacingly, "and what's Rigsby doing out of uniform? Wouldn't fancy himself as a detective, would he?"

"What makes you think that anyone is 'up' to anything, Carter?" answered Tollman, assuming an innocent air.

"You're interviewing a suspect – some woman – in there. You and Rigsby were seen bringing her in. If you're treading on our toes, I might have to complain to the Chief Commissioner that Rigsby has been promoted to detective without any proper authorisation…"

Tollman smiled grimly and lowered his voice, "And I might have to tell the Chief Commissioner that I saw you in the Tango Club the other night."

Carter's face froze and there was a silence.

Ah, so he *is* bent, thought Tollman.

"I was undercover," said Carter but they both knew that the silence had been too long between statement and reply.

"So, here's the arrangement, Carter," Tollman continued, in a soft but determined tone of voice, all the while looking Carter straight in the eyes, "you keep your nose out of our business and we'll keep our nose out of yours – providing you don't break the law, of course. Understood?"

Carter didn't say or do anything; he just looked at Tollman, his face burning with resentment. Tollman cupped a hand over his ear, as though he were deaf and said, "Sorry, I didn't hear your reply!"

"Understood," muttered Carter and he walked swiftly away. Tollman gave a grim smile and thought, round one to me, I think…but he'll be watching us a lot more now.

Lady Maud was aggrieved that her very first piece of under-cover police work had been a damp squib and she was irritable all the way home. The umbrella was pronounced "useless" and given to Mary to dispose of. Once in the maid's hands, it immediately opened up of its own volition, thereby causing Lady Maud to say "Now we shall have bad luck, all day! As if we haven't had enough already!" as she stomped into the study and poured herself a consoling brandy.

Victoria decided to divert her mother's attention by delving into the case notes she had been keeping on the team's work and producing a sheet of headed notepaper. She held it under the nose of Lady Maud, who promptly said, "What am I looking at, dear?"

"This the list of the Board of Trustees at Doctor Barnardo's Homes, mother. I was wondering if you knew any of them?"

Maud peered intently at the document. "Mm. I think I know three of the gentlemen reasonably well and two of them I would regard as no more than passing acquaintances. Why do you ask, dear?"

Victoria then explained about her visit to the Girls' Village in Essex and her concern about the fact that all the girls were only being trained for a career in domestic service.

"But, Victoria, what on earth is wrong with that? I know several aristocratic households that positively seek out Barnardo's girls. They are very well trained. Particularly those that train as nursery nurses."

"Yes, but just think, mother. The world is changing. We have women undertaking all sorts of clerical and industrial jobs nowadays and I am genuinely concerned that some of these girls may be going into households where the husband comes back from the Front severely damaged, like Lord Murcheson. I'm concerned that these girls should be trained in something other than domestic service."

"Well, Victoria, I can see your point but you must remember two things. One is that domestic service provides a roof over a girl's head which otherwise they would have to pay for themselves. Not easy in the big cities. And secondly, all the young men are rapidly volunteering for the war and leaving households desperately short of domestic staff. I'm not sure that this is the time to suggest an alternative training for these young girls. However, I shall plan a dinner party in the coming months and invite the three gentlemen on that list, and their wives, and I shall ask their opinion on the matter. Would that help?"

"That would be wonderful," Victoria beamed and she could see that her mother had almost totally forgotten about this morning's debacle and her irritability had quite disappeared. All Lady Maud needed was to feel useful again.

Beech was concerned that Ada Yardley would be missed by Dr McKinley and this would raise an alarm but she told them that he did not work on Tuesdays and Thursdays and those were the days she was instructed to go and collect rents. Furthermore, Ada was refusing to co-operate any further until she had some food and a rest, it now being lunchtime, so she was taken back to the cells.

"In any event," said Beech, "we can't arrest McKinley until we have all the facts and I can obtain warrants to search his premises and seize records. So we shall just have to adjourn for an hour, whilst Miss Yardley has some food. By the way, I expect you have noticed that Ada Yardley seems to have no idea that Dodds is dead. So there is, in my view, no point in questioning her about his murder. I feel that we should try and get as much information out of her about the man this afternoon, however."

Billy and Tollman agreed and the three of them went about their various tasks. Tollman used the time to find a typewriter and formulate Ada's confession from his notes. Beech had not wished to give the work to a general clerk in the Yard. Billy went back to the police hostel to change into his spare uniform, ready for the arrests that he and Tollman were hoping to make back at the molly shop that night. Beech grabbed a bite to eat at his desk whilst dealing with yet more paperwork.

They all reconvened after an hour and Ada was summoned

back from the cells. Tollman handed the typed confession to Beech, and Ada was given a pen to sign her name.

"You guarantee that you won't be charging me with murder?" she said, pen poised above the confession.

"No," said Beech firmly. "I'm afraid the law is such that we will *have* to charge you with murder…"

She protested but he continued, "The way it works is that you sign your confession alleging self-defence, all of us here will attest in court that you gave us detailed evidence that the act was self-defence. We have various other documents, like Lady Harriet's confession to his murder and her maid's initial confession to the murder, which all muddies the waters. We have statements from the household staff that Lord Murcheson was mentally unstable and we will supply your solicitor with all the material necessary for your plea of self-defence. The likelihood is that you will be convicted on the lesser charge of manslaughter and we will ask the judge for reduced sentencing in the light of your co-operation on other matters. But I cannot, I'm sorry, guarantee anything. However, we shall endeavour to get you the best legal representation that we can and co-operate fully with all enquiries. You have my word."

Ada knew she had to be satisfied with that and she signed the paper. Then began several long hours of extracting as much information as they could from Ada Yardley.

It transpired that Dr McKinley owned and operated four brothels – three female and one male. To Tollman's surprise, Ada told them that Maisie Perkins' establishment was owned by McKinley. She also gave them the addresses of two others in the Paddington area of London. Every Tuesday and Thursday she collected rents from these establishments and sometimes delivered drugs. She would return to Harley Street after each collection, "I don't want to be carrying that sort of money around on the streets," she said firmly, and she would lock the money away in Dr McKinley's desk. She said that she knew that several of his male patients had been referred by the doctor to these brothels for "therapeutic" reasons. Billy snorted and Tollman raised his eyebrows.

McKinley owned a house in Chislehurst in Kent, where he sometimes spent the weekends. He also had a small flat above his consulting rooms. Ada gave them his bank account details – he banked at Coutts in the Strand.

"Does he, by God!" exclaimed Beech, knowing full well that Coutts only accepted customers who had very substantial amounts of money. Ada said she sometimes put money in the night safe of the bank, when asked to do so.

They discovered that Dodds/Sumpter obtained large quantities of drugs via his criminal connections that he then sold to the doctor. McKinley then required Ada to adulterate the heroin with other substances and to package them up into single doses. These were given to patients for a variety of ailments and they were charged ten times the actual cost of the drugs. Ada could not verify how much Dodds/Sumpter was involved in the day-to-day operation of the brothels but she suspected that he had, on occasion supplied new girls. She said he was "a slippery customer". She knew he had a record for petty crimes and she said that it was McKinley that recommended him for the job as Lord Murcheson's butler. How the doctor and the petty criminal originally formed a relationship was a mystery to her. Beech asked her if she knew of any particular places that Dodds/Sumpter frequented – he was wondering if she might slip up and mention the pub in Piccadilly – but she said no. "I have never associated with him outside of the doctor's surgery or Lord Murcheson's house. Nor do I wish to." Again, to Beech it was plain that she did not know that the man was dead.

It took at least an hour for Ada to write down the names of all of McKinley's patients that she could remember. With dismay, Beech noted that the list contained a great number of eminent politicians and their wives and families.

This will never get to trial, he thought despairingly.

Finally, Ada could give no more information and, as it was nearly five o'clock and Beech had warrants to obtain, they wrapped everything up and Ada was sent back to her cell.

"We will arrest the good doctor first thing in the morning, Tollman," ordered Beech, "Meanwhile, I know you have this business in Piccadilly to wrap up tonight so you'd better go and get something to eat."

"Yes sir," said Billy with feeling. "I'm looking forward to nabbing old Bay Rum."

Beech looked quizzical. "Who?"

"Sorry, sir," replied Billy, "Just my little nickname for the bloke, on account of one of the lads we interviewed said the man smelt strongly of the Bay Rum he put on his hair."

"Ah." Beech smiled faintly. "Well, good luck then and keep me informed."

CHAPTER TWENTY ONE

The Rats in the Trap

At around six thirty, Billy and Tollman arrived at the Piccadilly house, to find Michael sitting in the fading light in, what had been, George's room. Michael informed them that he and the others would be leaving the place tonight, but that he would stay, just to identify George's patron.

"You said to carry on as normal," he said, "so those of us with patrons will conduct business as usual. The rest, except me, have already gone. They won't be coming back."

"That's a pity," Tollman replied. "We were hoping for some statements."

Michael shook his head. "They don't want to be involved and I told them you had promised to leave them alone." Then he had said an odd thing to Tollman. "Look in our rooms afterwards. We'll leave you some useful information." Then Michael asked about George.

"He's alright," Billy said. "He's going to stay with a kind elderly gentleman, a cabinet-maker. George is going to look after him and the old man is going to teach George a trade."

Michael gave Billy a sad smile and said he was glad. Then he instructed Tollman to pay no attention to sounds on the stairs. To wait until the door handle was turned by George's patron before they sprang into action.

Tollman assured him that they would wait until the man stepped into the room before they arrested him and Michael left to return to his own room.

Tollman turned to Billy and enquired whether the

information about the lad, George, was the truth or a lie.

"God's honest truth, Mr Tollman," Billy replied. "Sorry, I haven't really had time to tell you."

Tollman expressed his admiration but Billy shrugged and said, "Nah! It wasn't my doing. It was my busybody mum and her sister who sorted it all out." But Tollman knew that it had been at Billy's instigation and he patted his shoulder in appreciation.

So, there they were, sitting and waiting for the sadist who nearly killed George. It was almost dark now and they began to hear the front door open and close beneath their feet. Men were arriving. First, one, who went past the room in which they were sitting and up the stairs above their head. Then, about twenty minutes later, another arrived, but he too went past their room and on to the end of the corridor. Tollman and Billy sat in the gloom with mounting frustration. "Come on! Come on!" Billy muttered under his breath. Tollman put his hand out to silence him. Soon…very soon…they hoped to make their arrest.

Beech arrived back at the Mayfair house to find Victoria, Lady Maud and Caroline eating dinner and he quickly joined them. He was feeling enthusiastic about the day's events because, at last, he could tell the Chief Commissioner that they had solved the murder of Lord Murcheson.

The ladies looked at him expectantly for news of the day and he waited until Mary had served him and left the room before he launched into a detailed explanation of Ada Yardley's confession and the revelations about Dr McKinley.

"I knew he was a terrible man!" cried Caroline, feeling vindicated.

"Of course, you were absolutely right, Caro," replied Beech, "and also about the nurse passing a venereal disease on to Lord Murcheson. Once Ada Yardley is on remand at the women's prison at Holloway, I shall need you to examine her thoroughly and produce a report for the court, if you wouldn't mind."

"My pleasure…" Caroline responded and was about to continue the conversation when Lady Maud interrupted.

"Peter! Caroline!" she said abruptly. "I am as broad-minded as the next person, my dears, but I draw the line on discussions about venereal diseases at the dining table!"

Suitably chastened, Peter and Caroline mumbled apologies whilst Victoria grinned. "So," she said brightly, "the Murcheson case is all but wrapped up and we can tell Lady Harriet that she and Polly are in the clear."

"Yes, absolutely," Peter agreed.

"Caroline! You and I shall take Polly to see her mistress tomorrow, and break the good news," Victoria decided.

"Where are Mr Tollman and PC Rigsby?" enquired Lady Maud, going off at a tangent.

"Er…they are making an arrest in the house in Piccadilly tonight. Hopefully they will be apprehending the terrible man who abused the fifteen-year-old youth." He laughed as he recalled Billy's nickname for the perpetrator. "Or rather, they will be arresting Old Bay Rum, as Rigsby calls him."

"What?" The ladies all looked amused and quizzical.

"Apparently, one of the witnesses said that the man in question smelt of the inordinate amount of Bay Rum he put on his hair. Hence Rigsby's nickname."

Suddenly Caroline dropped her knife and fork on her plate with a resounding clatter. "Oh my God!" She looked stricken.

"Caroline?" asked Lady Maud anxiously.

"Peter!" Caroline was visibly agitated now. "That's what I smelt!"

"What?"

"When we went to McKinley's surgery. It wasn't cologne; it was Bay Rum...McKinley must be the man they're going to arrest!"

"Good Lord! I'd better get over there!" And Beech rushed out of the room, leaving the three ladies looking flustered and concerned.

✳

There had been one other man come up the stairs in the molly shop and then everything had gone silent.

"Perhaps he's not coming tonight," whispered Billy in frustration.

"Patience, lad. Patience," murmured Tollman under his breath.

Finally, they were rewarded by the sound of more footsteps and, yet, there had been no sound of the front door opening and closing. They both realised that the man must have come in the back door. The only customer that night to do so.

The footsteps ascended the stairs, almost to the top, when the door opposite opened, and they heard Michael say quietly, "I have a message from George."

"No!" said Billy urgently, knowing what was about to happen...but before they could move, they heard a man scream, a thud and footsteps running down the stairs.

They rushed out into the corridor to find a man slumped on the stairs with a knife through the base of his neck. Blood was everywhere. Michael had delivered his message with devastating efficiency and they saw the back door swing shut as he left.

"Shall I run after him?" Billy asked.

Tollman shook his head grimly. "Natural justice, we said, didn't we? Besides, he'll be long gone now."

Suddenly, the front door opened and Beech appeared at the foot of the stairs. "Good God!" he said as the blood trickled down towards him. "What happened?"

"We were tricked by one of the lads," said Tollman. "He said he would stay to identify the suspect but, instead, he was lying in wait to kill him, in revenge for his friend being abused by this man. The lad was too quick for us, sir. He did the deed and ran out before we could apprehend him, I'm sorry. We'll have to get an artist at the Yard to do a drawing and see if we can do a manhunt."

Beech digested all this information and then said, "Right, I see. Unfortunate business all round. Could you turn the dead man over, Rigsby? I want to see his face."

Billy duly obliged, even though the body was slippery with blood and he found it hard to get a grip.

Beech clasped his hands together on top of his head and stared at the body with an expression of total frustration. "Gentlemen, meet the eminent Doctor McKinley," he said simply and with an air of finality.

All, however, was not lost. Tollman remembered that Michael had said that once the arrest was over, they would find some information in the rooms. They moved the body, after making some notes and noting the time of death, and began to search the rooms.

"Well!" exclaimed Tollman, when they opened the first door on the second floor and found a man in his underwear, gagged and bound to a chair. "It appears they've left us *plenty* of information!"

Upon continuing to search, they found two more men

– one had been drugged into a comatose state and the other had been plied with drink until he was insensible. All the other rooms were empty. Cleared out and clean as a whistle. Except for Michael's room. There was a simple note on the bed, which said, "I DID IT FOR GEORGE" – and that was it.

"Right!" said Beech, cheering up a little. "Let's phone the Yard and get a body wagon and a Black Maria down here and clear this place out. We'd better formally arrest them first – well, the one who is compos mentis – and the porter downstairs."

"Yes, sir," said Tollman. "Er…what shall we charge them with, sir? Offences Against the Person or Sodomy?"

Beech felt reckless. "Why not both? And possibly a few more charges, depending upon what we discover when we get down to the Yard? Let's see if we can get the most out of this situation." Privately, he had the distinct impression that the three clients, gifted to them by the prostitutes, looked like 'men of substance' and would never see a trial. But he was going to enjoy making them squirm.

The next day, Caroline, who was off-duty, and Victoria took Polly to see Lady Harriet who was, by now, sitting up in bed and improving daily. When they opened the door, both Victoria and Caroline watched in silence as the mistress and her maid clung to each other in a tearful embrace, which displayed their obvious devotion to each other.

"Lady Harriet," said Caroline after a while, "the police have caught the woman who killed your husband. Neither you nor Polly had anything to do with it. This woman has confessed and you will both be absolved of all charges."

Lady Harriet expressed her gratitude and gently asked Polly

to leave the room for a moment. Once the girl was outside, she motioned Victoria and Caroline to be seated.

"Tell me truthfully," she asked, "was this woman a prostitute? Was she, as I suspected, visiting my husband regularly?"

"Yes," answered Victoria quietly. "She worked for your husband's doctor – Doctor McKinley."

Lady Harriet's eyes widened in surprise and then her face assumed an expression of distaste.

"So…McKinley was giving my husband copious drugs and supplying him with a woman as well. How despicable! Have you arrested Doctor McKinley?"

Victoria and Caroline then took it in turns to explain the labyrinthine twists and turns of the case, sparing no detail, even though Victoria kept profusely apologising for the sordidness of the world they had been investigating.

"It is almost certain," Victoria finished the account, "that Doctor McKinley murdered your butler, Dodds, although the police have no way of proving it, now that McKinley is dead."

Her recent experiences had given Lady Harriet a hardness that she had not known before and she did not demur at any of the tale that unfolded.

She sighed. "How sad that two men, my husband and McKinley, who had such high positions in life, chose to take a path of unbelievable degeneracy. Such a waste! As for Dodds… well, he obviously chose his path in life some time ago and I've no doubt, if he was involved in all the things you say, he would have died brutally in some way or another."

Caroline took a deep breath and said, "Lady Harriet, forgive me, there is something of a medical nature I have to tell you."

"Go ahead, doctor."

"I'm afraid that your injuries were so severe that you will

never again be able to have children."

Lady Harriet nodded and was silent for a moment. Then she said, with a small smile, "Thank you, doctor, I half suspected as much but, you see, it doesn't really matter…as I have Polly. I have decided that I am unsuited for marriage anyway. I will adopt Polly and educate her – not as a titled lady – which is a useless function in life but, hopefully, as a well-educated woman, rather like you, doctor, who will find her own place in the world. I shall retire to my hus…" she stopped herself and then continued "…to *my* country estate, where I shall recuperate and Polly will take care of me. I cannot bring myself to set foot in the London house again but I shall not sell it. Polly may find it useful when she is older." She sighed. "I suppose I must tell the staff in Belgravia that they are no longer needed."

"Um…no, Lady Harriet," volunteered Victoria and she proceeded to tell her about the staff resignations and Constable Rigsby's female relatives taking refuge from the Zeppelin bombing.

"What a splendid solution." Lady Harriet seemed rather pleased. "I shall send the two ladies a monthly stipend so that they may continue to look after the place!"

All matters being settled, Polly was retrieved from the corridor and, as they left, Caroline looked back to see Lady Harriet animatedly talking to the girl and holding her hand.

Epilogue

Epilogue

Beech was proved right. The Attorney General intervened, once the facts of Dr McKinley's 'businesses' were presented to him. The fact that a senior Civil Servant, a minor politician and an eminent bank manager suddenly 'retired' and disappeared from public life, went unnoticed by almost everyone.

Ada Yardley was swiftly brought to trial in a closed court and was acquitted of murder but found guilty of the lesser charge of 'manslaughter with mitigating circumstances' and a secondary charge of prostitution. Lady Harriet had not been required to appear in person to give evidence – the court accepted her written evidence – but Polly was brought, trembling, into the courtroom and relayed the details of the night of the murder. Beech gave evidence of Ada's co-operation and the final sentence was ten years. Ada was grateful for that.

The porter of the molly shop was similarly sentenced to ten years for 'knowingly aiding and abetting the operation of an illegal establishment under the Offences Against the Person Act' and whilst he grumbled at Tollman throughout his court hearing, he also knew that he had got off lightly.

None of the prostitutes from the molly shop could be found and Beech graciously omitted to mention in his report the fact that George Harris was now rehomed in Lambeth and was happily learning the trade of cabinet-making.

Dr McKinley was mourned by all his grieving patients who were told that he had died from a sudden heart attack. As he died intestate and had no family, his considerable wealth was drained from his bank account by the Government, as was its right, and added to the public purse. His house in Chislehurst and his premises in Harley Street were searched and provided accounts books and other evidence that showed just how extensive an empire he had operated. Maisie Perkins was visited by Detective Sergeant Tollman and 'advised' to retire, as her premises would be closed down, as were the two brothels in Paddington and the house in Piccadilly.

Beech's final report was submitted to the Chief Commissioner, who pronounced it 'fascinating reading', and then it was locked away until it could be used at a suitable time, when the 'powers-that-be' decided to consider the merits of women police officers in London.

Caroline busied herself with lobbying various charitable ladies, who in turn would persuade their husbands in the Government and Industry, that it would be a good idea to allow regular weekly medical inspections of women who worked in the munitions industry.

Meanwhile, Victoria turned her attention to drafting proposed amendments to the safety legislation for workers in factories, in the vain hope that she might use Lady Maud's influence to put the amendments discreetly in front of certain Members of Parliament.

Everyone tried to busy themselves, anxiously awaiting the next case that would galvanise them into action, which was why, three weeks after the fateful night that Lord Murcheson was stabbed, Billy Rigsby had volunteered to accompany the maid, Mary, to collect the regular hamper of food sent down to Waterloo Station from Lady Maud's country house. He didn't usually do this job but he was so restless and just wanted to get out of the house. Mary, of course, was delighted and she chattered aimlessly about this and that. Billy was barely listening but he was wise enough in the ways of women to occasionally smile and nod and interject with "get away!", as though he was hanging on every word.

As Billy presented the note to the railway porter and took delivery of the basket, he idly looked at a line of fresh army recruits lining up for the next train bound for the South Coast. He felt a small stab of pity.

Poor buggers, he thought, they don't know what they're facing.

"Oh look, Billy!" exclaimed Mary. "Soldiers!"

Billy rolled his eyes upwards. "You don't say, Mary," he said with a touch of sarcasm in his voice. "Anyone would think there was a war on!"

He picked up the hamper and allowed Mary to take his other arm.

As long as she doesn't get any ideas, he thought to himself. I like my women with a bit more between the ears than this one.

Suddenly he stopped dead and stared straight ahead at the line of young soldiers.

"What we stopping for, Billy?" asked Mary.

"I've seen someone I know," said Billy, quietly.

"A friend?" asked Mary.

"Not really," Billy replied in a distracted voice, staring straight at the face of Michael, who was returning the stare with a look of alarm in his eyes.

Suddenly, Billy put down the hamper, stood up straight, stamped his feet to attention and saluted. The youth flushed with relief and he nodded an acknowledgement.

"Whatever did you do that for, Billy?" asked the vacuous Mary.

"Honouring a man who's probably going to be dead in a month's time," he replied curtly, which he instantly regretted, as Mary looked as though she was about to cry. "Come on, girl!" he said in a cheerful voice. "How about I buy you a nice cup of tea and a cake? Eh?" Mary's face brightened and she nodded. Billy looked back at the line of soldiers but they had suddenly moved forward onto the platform and he couldn't see Michael anymore.

"Right, young Mary," Billy stepped forward smartly, "Let's get that cup of tea and you can tell me all about Mrs Beddowes' bunions, or whatever is the topic of the day."

Next in the Mayfair 100 series…

A DEATH IN CHELSEA
By Lynn Brittney

Beech looked at his assembled team and watched their faces change from bored resignation to excited anticipation as he uttered the words…

"We have another case."

It had been almost a month since the team had successfully brought their first crime to a speedy conclusion and the lack of a second case had made time weigh heavily with all of them. Now, their relief was palpable and an air of expectation filled the room as they waited for Beech to explain further.

"Last night, Adeline Treborne was found hanged in her bedroom."

"The Society gossip monger?" Caroline interrupted in astonishment.

"Yes," Beech continued, "She was…"

"That woman was disgusting!" This time it was Victoria interrupting, with some feeling.

Beech stared at the floor in resignation, as the two women vied with each other to remember the worst anecdotes they could about the unfortunate Adeline Treborne.

Victoria was first. "I've never forgotten the time when Caroline Cheshire – she was eighteen at the time – fainted at her own coming-out party – and the Treborne woman intimated in the newspaper that Caroline was pregnant…"

Caroline was outraged. "What about the time she wrote a piece about the orchestral conductor, Sir Emory Peters? She practically named every single one of his male lovers!"

"If I might continue…" Beech said, raising his voice, which made Arthur Tollman hide a smile behind his hand and Billy Rigsby flush slightly. Caroline raised her eyebrows and Victoria pursed her lips. "Miss Treborne's mother, the Duchess of Penhere, is of the opinion that her daughter was murdered."

"God knows there must be enough people who wanted to perform the deed…"muttered Caroline, refusing to keep her opinion to herself.

"Peter," asked Victoria, in a concerned tone of voice, "Are we only to be given crimes involving the aristocracy?"

Beech looked irritable and sounded even more irritable. This was not how he had imagined his announcement being received.

"Do you want to work on this case or not?" he asked bluntly.

"Yes!" came the unanimous response from the team.

"Then kindly allow me to explain the details – without interruption." He glared at Victoria and Caroline and a silence fell across the room.

Also by Mirror Books

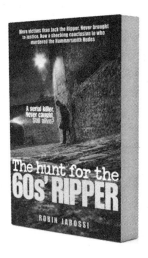

The Hunt for the 60s Ripper
Robin Jarossi

While 60s London was being hailed as the world's most fashionably vibrant capital, a darker, more terrifying reality was unfolding on the streets. During the early hours a serial killer was stalking prostitutes then dumping their naked bodies. When London was famed for its music, groundbreaking movies and Carnaby Street vibe, the reality included a huge street prostitution scene, a violent world that filled the magistrate's courts.

Seven, possibly eight, women fell victim – making this killer more prolific than Jack the Ripper, 77 years previously. His grim spree sparked the biggest police manhunt in history. But why did such a massive hunt fail? And why has such a traumatic case been largely forgotten today?

With shocking conclusions, one detective makes an astonishing new claim. Including secret police papers, crime reconstructions, links to figures from the vicious world of the Kray twins and the Profumo Affair, this case exposes the depraved underbelly of British society in the Swinging Sixties. An evocative and thought-provoking reinvestigation into perhaps the most shocking unsolved mass murder in modern British history.

Also by Mirror Books

1963 - A Slice of Bread and Jam
Tommy Rhattigan

Tommy lives at the heart of a large Irish family in derelict Hulme in Manchester, ruled by an abusive, alcoholic father and a negligent mother. Alongside his siblings he begs (or steals) a few pennies to bring home to avoid a beating, while looking for a little adventure of his own along the way.

His foul-mouthed and chaotic family may be deeply flawed, but amongst the violence, grinding poverty and distinct lack of hygiene and morality lies a strong sense of loyalty and, above all, survival.

During this single year – before his family implodes and his world changes for ever – Tommy almost falls foul of the welfare officers, nuns, police – and Myra Hindley and Ian Brady.

An adventurous, fun, dark and moving true story of the only life young Tommy knew.

Also by Mirror Books

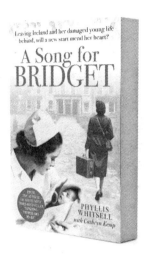

A Song for Bridget
Phyllis Whitsell

THE UNFORGETTABLE TRUE STORY BEHIND SUNDAY TIMES
BESTSELLING MEMOIR, FINDING TIPPERARY MARY.

A brutal and touching account of the life of Bridget 'Tipperary Mary' Larkin.

She faced poverty, bereavement, cruelty and abandonment many times
over yet never lost the heart to pursue true love.

Returning to rural Ireland in 1938 and a young girl full of hope and
expectation, A Song for Bridget recounts a series of tragic events that
eventually bring her to Manchester and Birmingham and a desperate daily
struggle to survive.

Bridget's haunting story, told for her by her daughter, is a perfect example of
both the fragility and resilience of the human spirit.